EXHALATION

A novel in the NANDRIA Series

by

MaryJane Nordgren

Published in the United States by
TAWK Press

Trade Paperback Edition

ISBN-13: 978-1-956892-54-3

Cover Art by Maryjane Nordgren and Michaela Thorn

This book is dedicated to so many writing friends in Writers in the Grove and around the world and to my patient and supportive family.

But foremost, EXHALATION is dedicated to my friend, humorist and graphic artist, William Arthur "Bill" Helwig, who was the practical facet of TAWK Press. Bill was lost to cancer in September 2023. Many people struggle with the enormous loss of a gifted, generous friend, as do I.

The NANDRIA Series has been my attempt to capture
characters from the 1940s who created my world and my
assumptions about what was valuable and who was not. As
a child, i heard, and perhaps repeated, words like colored,
pickaninny and darky, if not niglet and bootlip. So many
use charged language to assert superiority over Blacks and
other peoples. While i was too young to know they were
slurs, they influenced my assumptions i now know were
invalid, but which i understood as the way the world was.
Being family, i love both sides. It is my hope that these
stories may give insight into the foibles and fears of each of
us. Perhaps we may see each other as humanly vulnerable
rather than evil.

The NANDRIA Series

NANDRIA'S WAR

FLOAT

CAGED

EXHALATION

Other books written by MaryJane Nordgren:

EARLY: Logging Tales to Human to be Fiction
IVAN: Biography of Ivan U. Marble
QUIET COURAGE
SEEDS OF… (anthology editor)
SEEDS OF…II (anthology editor)
Kin to Earth – Chapbook
FRAIL the BRIDGE – A Poetry Collection

Please visit: maryjanenordgren.com

Exhalation

Chapter 1

Boonetown, Missouri, Tuesday, August 13, 1940

Even before the Great Depression, it was a quiet town, and quieter countryside, in southwest Missouri. Ripe with rolling hills; painfully watered crop and garden rows; paint-peeling houses, barns and wood slatted sheds; a single-track railroad right-of-way through the center of town and rutted asphalt main street granting access to its few commercial concerns—all now uniformly baked to a dry beige-gray in the August heat. Beneath that coated surface, roiled a decade and more of discontent, frustration, fear, and hatred for what the past had dealt and the future had barely promised, and now threatened.

Garum, a six-year-old with his father's burrhead hair but straight nose—thanks to, his pa had told him, a long-ago 'master' just outside of New Orleans—studied the soup can. He'd used it for worms but hadn't had any luck catching anything for dinner for his pa or himself. But as he trudged back up the rutted dirt road from the streambank, the label itself caught his interest. He could sound out the letters, thanks to Miz Nandria and her story telling and alphabet teaching.

'T-o-m' (Tom was one of the white boys who came to hear about Peter Pan), he recognized right away. And the 'a' said its name. That left the 't-o' which should have sounded like 'goin' to the store' or pa's 'I need you to...,' but he'd eaten the contents at noon, and he knew the 'o' sometimes said its name, too. So, he read the label as 'tomato' proudly to himself.

What he couldn't read was the funny writing instead of printing near the top. 'Cuh-ah-mm-puh...." came okay. But what about a 'p' and then the next letter a 'buh'? The 'ell' made 'bell' but what to do with that 'puh' just before it? And what if, with the scrawly letters, he wasn't reading them right at all?

He concentrated so hard trying to do what Miz Nandria had taught them that he didn't hear the car motor until he leaped into the ditch, still holding the can. It happened so fast that he stood weak-kneed looking at the can rather than trying to see what had nearly hit him until it was all but lost in the dust it kicked up. The only thing he could make out was that the back-end seemed odd. And he thought he heard a cackling laugh.

"Sorry, Pa," he whispered, knowing his father, Dolph Tacker, would have no sympathy for him.

"Ya gotta keep your eyes open, boy. There's a lot'a things—and people—in this life, willin' and ready to smash yer face," he'd warned again and again. But Garum had let himself get engrossed in his new reading skills and near got himself run over. As angry with himself as with the driver who hadn't even honked to warn him, Garum hurled the can up on the road, then climbed up to kick it. And kick it again, and again. The few worms left in the can scattered in the dust. Now what was he gonna feed his pa?

The Minnicks' Negro daughter-in-law put her hand down to steady herself, but too near the burner on the wood stove. Nandria lifted it quickly and sucked her fingertips. Clamping her mouth, she willed herself not to cry out. But her ten-month-old Rose had heard her gasp and was whimpering in the highchair at the far end of the oaken table in the Minnick kitchen. Before Nandria could steady herself to go to her beloved, biracial daughter, she heard her young math pupil hurrying in from the living room.

"Miz Nandria, are you alright?" Ronda cried. "Here, let me get the baby for you. Why don't you and wee Rose go sit on the porch for a bit? You look exhausted. I can finish stirring that stew and set it to one side. The men aren't even finished in the barn yet." With her huge mother's nursing ways already a part of her outlook on life, Ronda Bean was filling out in promise of becoming a tall, buxom woman. Only fifteen now, Nandria believed, the nurse's only child had not yet mastered grace over her growing proportions. But she was already aware of people's needs and had Sadie and Ron Bean's heart for caring.

"Thank you. Have you completed your math assignment, then?" Nandria asked as she worked her way to her little one by leaning against the table with her undamaged hand. "I understood your summer school final would be soon."

"Oh, didn't I tell you?" Ronda asked, raising the wooden spoon she'd be stirring with and allowing the stew broth to drip back into the pan. "Teacher said I was doin' so well, he'd give me a quick oral test so I wouldn't need to take the final. Isn't that the greatest? You've done me so much good, Miz Nandria. I don't know how to thank you."

Nandria smiled despite the green tint at her lips. But she couldn't turn to allow the young woman to see it. The room was spinning, and baby Rose was about to let out a wail. Rose reached up and Nandria lifted her, finding comfort in those strong little arms that clung to her. Humming 'Oh, freedom, oh, freedom,' Nandria carried her precious child to the enclosed porch and sat with her on the rocking chair beside the brass bed. Rose had grown less interested in nursing. But now her momma was upset; Rose knew it through her skin. Anxious, the baby cuddled close and demanded that comfort and reassurance. Rose had only nursed for a few moments before both were asleep in each other's arms.

Ronda hushed the men at the door to the porch when they came in, tired, for their evening meal. Grover Minnick frowned but sat on the bench to take off his heavy boots with little more than a grunt of protest. Bodie, the aging handyman, waited for his turn to sit, but Greg Paisler tried to draw the girl outside to talk with her. Instead, she indicated he was to come into the kitchen where she went immediately back to stirring Nandria's stew.

"You've seen how little she's able to eat. She's exhausted, Greg. I'm worried," Ronda explained low.

Glaring at Paisler's boots still on in the kitchen, Minnick harrumphed as he continued on into the living room to check on his wife. "Doris. Little Mother," he whispered as stood over her, half-smiling at her snoring over her crochet work in her corner of the couch. He bent to brush a silvering strand of silken hair from her pert little mouth before lowering himself into his easy chair to await the call to supper. "Where did your mind go, sweet little Mother?"

Bodie tiptoed into the kitchen in his worn slippers. "I set Miz Nandria's pillows around them 'case she lets go of the princess in her sleep," he said as he closed the door between porch and kitchen. "Here, lemme stir that there for ya, gal. So's you 'n' Greg can get the rest on the table before the mister'll wanna be fed."

"Thanks, Bodie. It's all mostly done and ready, but the last minutes before we sit down there's always a thousand things to get done at the same time."

"You're staying, then, Ronda? After supper, I mean," Greg asked.

"Well..." The girl looked too frustrated with the immediate demands to be able to think how to answer him.

"I mean, I was gonna take you home on the way to the KKK meeting, but I can come back for you." He shrugged. "Anyway, you've got enough to worry about right now. We can see how it goes after the meal, I guess. How can I help?"

"Oh," she giggled, throwing up her hands. But together, at times bumping into each other—perhaps not always of necessity—they served the meal. Minnick seated his Doris, who asked him to say grace. While Ronda poured coffee, Greg set the stew pot onto the table in front of Mr. Minnick for him to ladle out servings. He drew out Ronda's seat beside Mrs. Minnick then sat in Nandria's usual place at the lower end of the table. He needed to bounce up to let Bodie slide behind him to his place against the wall after again checking on the sleeping mother and child. Doris cocked her head to one side, sure there was something different at the table this evening. But, in her confused state, she could not figure out what it might be. She brightened when, supper nearly finished, Nandria carried Rose into the kitchen. Greg hopped up to settle them and offer food. Rose laughed at picking up wedges of potatoes and carrots with her fingers and slurping up the broth

Bodie spooned for her. Her momma stirred at the bits in her bowl but ate almost nothing.

Talk around the table centered mostly on whether the crops would survive the dry spell. That somehow twisted itself into whether or not 'that Roosey-velt' would have the gall to announce he was running for a third term as president. Minnick tilted back his chair with a sharp thud against the wall, face reddening. But Doris distracted him with her plans for the evening.

"Well, now, young mister Paisler, if you'll fetch fresh milk from Glory, we women will now turn to making my favorite dessert from when I was a little girl."

"Oh, and what might that have been?" Minnick wanted to know. "Pie, I hope? A cream pie, maybe?"

Smirking, Doris shook her head. "Nope. Not a pie. But I bet it'll be that little one's favorite, too," she said, pointing at giggling Rose bouncing on Bodie's bony knees.

"I don't know what her favorite dessert's gonna be," Bodie laughed, "but it's clear Little Miss Popularity likes me best of all her make-believe uncles."

"Just what is it you're set on making as this special treat, Mother?" Minnick demanded. "Something our boys liked?"

"Junket."

"Junket?" Ronda giggled. "That sounds like those rusting cars in the lot beyond the railroad tracks in town."

"Now don't you go pooh-poohing until you've tried it," Doris counseled. "You don't know how much I loved it when my auntie came to visit us up in the north country. She'd get raw milk from the dairyman between us and town and make up batches and batches. Flavored some of them with cinnamon, some with fresh fruit. Mama liked hers after it'd set in the ice box a while, but I loved it just like it was new made up—room temperature or a bit on the warm side. I got the recipe here. Copied it out just like my mama wrote it down for me when Mr. Minnick and I was first wedded. You want to help me get it together, Ronda Bean? I bet your own mama will love junket if she don't know about it already. And with your pa a milkman, she'll have plenty of fresh to make her own for you, won't she?"

"I bet Eleanor Roosey-velt don't make her husband eat junket of a night," Minnick grumbled. "That much I'll say for him at least. Anyhoo, you womenfolk have fun junketing. It's time your men took off for town. Second Tuesday, and Sheriff Yakes thinks he's gonna be up for leading our meeting in person."

"Oh, yes. I near forgot. Your Ku Klux Klan meeting. You go. I'll be sure to save you plenty of junket," Doris promised, and Minnick's frown of distaste did nothing to deter her. "Now, Mr. Minnick, you know you'll love it. Funny how I ain't thought of it in years until just yesterday when the girl said something about the baby's favorite foods."

"Yeah, well, if that youngster loves it, you can give her my share," Minnick declared. "You coming, Paisler?"

Knowing from her mother just how hard the gut surgery to stop his bleeding ulcer had been on the sheriff, Ronda Bean frowned. "The sheriff..."

Greg Paisler stepped up close beside her. "Now, don't you worry, Miss Bean. I'll keep a close eye on Sheriff Yakes to see he don't overdo nothin'," Greg assured her. "You want a ride into town, Mr. Minnick? I can bring you back here to see that Miss Bean gets home safe after."

Minnick almost nodded. Lately, his pickup had been as ornery as his tractor. A ride sounded good, but he never knew when his Doris might need him. He'd need his once-blue truck in case. "You comin' along, Bodie?" he asked his handyman, shaking his head to young Paisler.

"I think I'll stay and watch out for the womenfolk this time," the frail, elderly man said and grinned at his boss's nod of approval.

"Eat hearty. Don't put off on my account," Minnick told him. "Come on, then, Paisler. Time we're on the road."
They sat on the bench near the outer door to pull on their boots quietly when Nandria crept out to the enclosed porch with little Rose nearly asleep against her mother's shoulder.

Chapter 2

"That steeple's gonna need painting, Reverend Kylie," Frank Paisler remarked as he stood at the bottom of the stairs leading up to the sanctuary door. "Looks like the wood might be rotting out underneath, in which case it'll need replacing."

Sighing over his double chins, Dean Kylie slid a blunt finger beneath his starched collar to ease the rubbing at his neck. "When will you be able to do that, Francis Paisler?"

The second of the eight sons of farmer Zeb and Cynthia Paisler, Frank realized that, despite many warnings, he had walked into a trap. He'd come when the minister of the Boonetown congregation had beckoned to him as he parked his truck at the side of the church. They'd walked together to the front of the church before the Klan meeting began. Ducking his chin to hide the smile that came to his lips at being caught, Frank cleared his throat and looked up to give the answer that his mother would approve. "It will be my pleasure, sir. Just let me check with my father to know when he can handily let me go from field work on our farm."

Kylie's harumph seemed to shake his rounded form. He gestured again, this time to invite Frank to follow him around the corner of the church toward the storm cellar steps into the basement. "I'll be starting the meeting."

"Yes, sir. I'll just stop a moment to see if I can clear a time with my brother Eli."

"Your father won't be coming?"

"Not this time," Frank stammered, for the first time embarrassed. Zeb Paisler had not forbidden his older sons to attend the KKK meeting, but he had said that the organization might not be merely a chance for weary farmers to learn from each other and enjoy each other's company. Perhaps it was more sinister than that. He had no proof, but rumors he'd heard gave him pause. Characteristically, he would not pass on the rumors he'd heard. Their next younger brother Greg had all but stopped attending, also, after talking long and hard with Will Minnick before the Army captain had been ordered back to Europe and who knew what fate in that growing war. Frank had come to this meeting reluctantly with his oldest brother, Eli.

"I'm going. How else am I gonna find out what's real?" Eli had said, and Frank had tagged along.

Personally, Frank had always enjoyed watching and listening to his father's friends gripe about weather and financial conditions. Perhaps the most gregarious of the eight Paisler sons, Frank admired their neighbors' courage in carrying on despite so much stacked against them. He wished his soon-to-be father-in-law Mr. Freshstalk, the banker, could find even more ways to help the men weather this decade-long tempest of the Great Depression.

"Well, so it hasn't started as yet?" Mr. Freshstalk asked as he hurried past Eli and Frank Paisler toward the cellar stairs.

"The meeting? No, sir," Frank explained. "With the sheriff still laid up despite not wanting to be, Reverend Kylie'll be starting the meeting any moment now."

"Good," the distinguished banker exclaimed. "I so hate for a meeting to start late. Disrespectful of the time of those who have come on time."

Newly arriving, Minnick told Frank and Eli that Greg would be right behind him. Then he hurried down the concrete, storm cellar stairs.

"After you, sir," Eli told Mr. Minnick. Both young men were still chuckling at Frank's falling into the minister's trap. Frank grinned as his only older brother laid a heavy hand on his shoulder and shook his head. "Pa's gonna get a kick out'a you getting caught like that."

Frank and Eli had stepped aside to allow Mr. Minnick to precede them down the concrete steps, but they butted in front of their younger brother as he tried to follow. Greg laughed and let them.

The ceremonial part of opening the meeting was, as always, a display of the minister's theatrical talents. Kylie was in his glory. Closing his eyes, Frank recited the oath with the others as undertone for the reverend's sonorous baritone. As usual, he let his mind wander during the ceremonial and business parts of the meeting. He liked to watch the men and think of how they lived their lives. The work. The drudgery and disappointment. How they had changed over the past decade from what he remembered of them as a boy.

It was when they began wrangling and swearing that he truly tuned in. His focus came back to sharpen on the minister. Only then did Frank realize how much weight the man had lost. How much trimmer he seemed. Not bloated, either with fat or self, if looks could be believed. Something had changed for or in the man, Frank decided. Finally liking him more than he ever had, Frank wondered if the Paislers might want to get to know the Rev. Kylie better. And then the voices grew louder and more rancorous as the discussion dissolved into growing argument.

"Wendell Willkie should be our man. We all know that!"

"How can we decide if we don't know yet who they'll run if F.D.R. declines to run for a third term?"

"What right's the man got to make him wanna run again?" "We've already put up with him for eight years." "Nobody in this country wants no king, that's for sure!"

Frank couldn't suppress the smile lifting the corners of his mouth as he watched their faces grow redder as their tempers rose, each with the conviction of being right and everyone else being wrong.

When the group broke up, Frank hurried to catch up with Doc Ricartsen in the parking field. He wanted to ask him how the sheriff was recovering and what might have happened to make the minister slim down the way he had, but Eli was in a hurry to get started to the home place. The two oldest Paisler brothers left with the others as Pastor Kylie declined a half dozen offers of a lift the short way to the manse. The minister took off walking, whistling as though he enjoyed what he had always hated until now. Something, indeed, was different about the community's pastor.

"Will you see that Miss Bean gets home, sir?" Greg asked Minnick as they were nearly the last to leave the basement hall of the church. "Or may I?" he blurted as Mr. Minnick looked about to agree that he would.

"Yeah, yeah, boy. You take care of it. I'll be along." The weary man waved vaguely.

Greg frowned, unsure. This was unlike what he'd seen from the stubborn farmer, since he'd been working Will's part of the Minnick land in his absence. "Well, okay, thank you, sir," he muttered, but Minnick was already climbing up to the parking field. Still, it meant Greg was in charge of seeing Ronda Bean home safely. He grinned as he climbed the steps out into the half-moon lit night.

Only a few men lingered in the parking field around the church after the KKK meeting. Mostly farmers who rose with the sun, the overalled men had slouched into their pickups or jalopy sedans and driven home to crawl into bed, exhausted.

For reasons he could not have named, Grover Minnick remained beside his once-proud blue pickup, his left, thickening love-handle pressing into the door handle. He'd been eating a lot more these months, since Will's dark woman was cooking. It tasted good. And it was a comfort, somehow, though he would not admit that.

Wishing not to drive out into the country to the generations-added-onto farmhouse Minnick had for decades called his, he stood with one foot up on the running board. He knew Doris would be tossing and turning in her sleep without him to curl next to in the night. She would be restless, but at least her pathetic neediness would not be demanding his strained, yet patient, continual reassurance.

What's happened to you, girl? Where is your head? I know your heart is still with me, but what's the matter that you can't seem to hang onto reality anymore? Oh, my darlin' gal, what in the Lord's sweet name can I do to make you well again?

Minnick leaned hard into his truck's door and slid, hanging onto the wing window brace, letting himself down to sit on the running board. He looked up as he felt someone approach. It was his egg and poultry farmer neighbor, Heinz Nickleberg. The hollow-cheeked farmer sidled close and stood, long, narrow feet wide apart, to offer Minnick a glass-lined thermos. He hiccoughed and grinned, slurring his words. "Thirssy, Minnick?"

"A bit," Minnick heard himself answer. He reached for the thermos, unscrewed the cap and tilted it to his mouth. He coughed, sputtering. "What the devil you got in here, Nickle?" he managed when breath returned.

Laughing, Nickleberg reached to take the thermos from Minnick's shaking hand as gangly Doc Ricartsen and store owner Isaac Owens looked over from where they had been talking at the bottom of the church's front stairs. "What've you got there, Minnick?" Owens called.

"Somethin' the reverend wouldn' approve us partakin' of in his church lot," Nickleberg giggled. He swiped at a downy chick feather puff clinging to the side of his thermos as he lifted it again to his lips and then waved it toward the other two men in invitation.

"How about we shift this part of the meeting to the back room of my store?" Owens suggested. "Can't stomach the idea of what Pastor Kylie is likely to go on and on about on Sunday if he hears tell of us drinking near his sanctuary."

Murmuring, Doc and Owens took off sauntering to the center of town. Nickleberg stared a moment at his sedan with its back sawed off to mimic a pickup to carry chicken cages, crates, and farm necessaries. Minnick hauled himself upright and stepped forward to follow the others to Owens' store. He halted when Nickleberg muttered, "We gonna be in any condition to walk back here for our trucks? I sure hope not," the older man chuckled. Minnick sighed as he watched the egg man dance to his sedan-turned-truck to drive into the center of town.

Minnick climbed up behind his own steering wheel and sat a moment undecided.

I ain't one for drinkin' much. You know that, Doris. So don't blame me for this once lettin' loose and getting full bear drunk—not that you'll ever know, I hope.

Swallowing his conviction that this was not a good idea, Minnick turned the key, listened to the engine cough to life, and shifted into first to crawl over the railroad track and park beside the boardwalk in front of Owens' general store. He parked heading west so he could simply pull forward when he was ready to leave the proposed party.

Owens' store was the center of Boonetown, both literally and socially. Not that there was much else in the way of business. Freshstalk's bank. Doc's old house-turned-medical-clinic with his living quarters on the upper floor, which he'd never gotten around to painting. Mrs. Drangler's low-ceiled hut that she used for her seamstress shop. She'd gotten a bargain on that. The close ceilings made it so uncomfortable for people of regular height, that old Doc Marburger had been glad to sell it for any price. But for Mrs. Drangler, being as short as most ten-year-olds, the low roof was no problem. There were a few other storefronts, but most were open only by appointment or by stopping by the house and asking the owner to meet at the store. Tonight, Boonetown was so dark, it invited no one.

Isaac Owens lit a low kerosine lamp at the back of his store. It was enough. Minnick shoved open his car door, relieved to be anywhere other than at home where his failures to protect his wife and sons haunted his dreams into nightmares. Nightmares he could share with no one, now that Doris was losing her mind to only God knew what. Even Doc Ricartsen— with all his years of schooling—didn't know.

Best to just go in, get staggering drunk, and forget it all. Only it won't be clear sailing. You'll have to stagger past Will's woman and that little pickaninny of hers. Your own fault that she sleeps on the back porch. You're the one who wouldn't let her use your son's old room upstairs. So even that trial is your own fault, you dumb ox. Why in all that Missouri holds sacred in this 1940 would Willard hook up with her, even if she is smart as a whip and close to being beautiful? She's a darky. That boy knew better'n to do that. And then to send her here, of all places. Let her stay in England where she's from if they have a place for her. Not here. Lord, Minnick, you need to get stinkin' drunk this night or you're like to go out of what little mind you've been able to hang onto 'til now.

Minnick climbed up the board walk stairs, pushed open the door, strode between the tables of tools and gear and clothes and what-alls to join the men in Owens' butcher area beyond the counter. They looked up but continued complaining about Nickleberg's stinginess with his thermos.

"Hey!" Minnick groused, reaching to grab a pull at whatever it was the egg man had in there. The pull was hard, and once again Minnick was reduced to red-faced coughing and heaves for breath.

The others laughed. Doc pounded on his back. Owens took the thermos from his hands, but after a quick drink, passed it back to Nickleberg, who sneered, "Ain't much for drinkin', are ya, Minnick? But I guess you're tryin' to get over that sergeant fella tellin' ya your Will was being tortured in Bermuda."

"Bermuda?" Minnick sputtered.

"That's just off Florida, ain't it?" Owens questioned.

"If the boy was there, I'd go see him if I had to walk. But he ain't there. It's someplace else, deep in Europe." Minnick looked at Doc, pleading to be told where his Willard was.

"Not so deep in Europe. Belgium, I think. Not long ago overrun by the Nazis."

"Ain't that what that Sarge said? That Will was supposed to have been sent there to spy?" Minnick rolled his eyes toward Nickleberg, then quickly closed them as the world spun. "Say, whad'ya put inta this here thermos, Nickle? Feels like I swallowed straight m... m...mmmsh."

"Mash?" the egg man chuckled, wiping his mouth with his forearm. "Yeah, somethin' like that. Good, huh? You'll sleep good tonight, Minnick. Even with that colored huzzy under your roof."

"Especially since he ain't as used to it as you are, Nickleberg?" Owens sniped.

Nickleberg glared, realizing now that the storeowner had caught him more than once being under the weather when he delivered the plucked chickens and eggs of a morning.

Knowing Nickleberg's quick temper and long memory for an insult, Owens twisted away to snatch up a towel to wipe his face. Only he grabbed a towel that he'd used earlier after a butchering session. Growling at the sticky residue over his eyes and chin and the coppery taste of blood in his mouth, he swore half-aloud. "Sheet!"

"Better lamb's blood than the stuff in that thermos," Doc laughed, handing him a large, somewhat cleaner handkerchief from his hip pocket. "And I've tasted both now, thank you, Mr. Nickleberg."

The others felt for Owens. They'd tasted some dirt and waste, too, in their lives. But the storekeeper's gyrations and expression drew wanna-be intoxicated guffaws from his friends. They seldom indulged in anything beyond bathtub beer and this stuff was far stronger than what they were used to.

Owens rose and stomped out, returning in a bit with a clean towel dripping clean water, until he applied it to his face. He stared at them as he wiped, until each in turn sheepishly looked away. Minnick turned toward Nickleberg and was surprised to see tears welling in the man's bloodshot eyes. "You can't blame me. I don' sleep," Nickleberg whined through his sagging, gray-white mustache. "I gotta have the strong stuff, or I can't even close my eyes."

Minnick watched Doc rise to square up over the egg man, frowning as though he were about to bawl him out, probably for not telling his physician that vital symptom. But then the colt-like, gangly general practitioner sighed and set down the tin cup Owens had given him. He looked at Nickleberg with an expression between exasperation and pity. "Gennelmen," Ricartsen announced as he gathered himself to leave.

"How come?" Minnick demanded of his strange friend with the thermos, but it was the doctor who responded.

"How come am I goin' home to fall into the nearest flat surface to sleep the sleep of the dead? Do you know where I was at two this mornin'?" Ricartsen shook his head as though trying to remember the answer to his own question.

"No, Doc, how come Heinz here can't sleep?" Minnick clarified. "How come he has'ta get drunk to be able to close his eyes?"

Owens twisted to gape at them. "Wha'? Who can't close his eyes? I could climb onto this table and snore by the time you could snap your finners." He tried to demonstrate, but his fingers refused to cooperate.

"Heinz Niggleberg here," Minnick muttered, barely able to articulate the name.

The men gaped at the egg farmer; Minnick leaned forward to listen.

"I see that wee tyke," Heinz whimpered, rocking forward and back, hugging himself with his arms tight around his shoulders. "H-head s-smashed." He burst into guttural sounds that made the others shudder.

"Sometimes," Minnick managed, "ya gotta do that to save the cow…"

But Nickleberg rocked harder, weeping and shaking his head. "Weren't no cow," he wailed. "It was a woman. A spook woman trying to stop 'em from hurtin' her man… Set the house on fire and grabbed her an'…"

The others gaped, stupefied by the images called up to their minds.

"Wha'? Whadchu talkin' 'bout?" Owens stammered. "Who?"

"Nothin' like that's been done 'round here," Minnick protested. "Not since me and missus's been here. Fire?"

"Him, the postmaster. Post office burned so he moved it to their house. Only then it wen' up in flames so high like it was made of tinder," Nickleberg muttered, his eyes closed against a memory. "She was runnin' out with her pickaninny at her shoulder…"

"A spade was postmaster?" Owens cried. "Not in Missouri, he wasn't."

Nickleberg reacted as though he'd been slapped. "Wha'? No. Not in Missery. Must'a been in the sweet Carolinas." He broke into a sloppy baritone crooning that made Doc rise again with his hands over his ears.

"Enough! I don't need a lullaby—just a bed." Stumbling to the front door, Ricartsen pushed it back until its window rattled as its wood frame thudded against a box of secondhand and handmade boot socks for sale, cheap. "G'night', all," he called back over his bony shoulder and disappeared. The others waited to hear him tumble down the steps from the boardwalk, but when they heard nothing of the kind, they passed the thermos around a final time. Nickleberg stopped caterwauling long enough for the long drink it took to empty the dented container completely.

Owens raised a hand in response to Minnick's thanks for hosting. He could barely raise his head to see Minnick stagger with Nickleberg to the door. He listened, but there were no tell-tale thuds or screams or curses, so the storeowner rose, unsteady but determined. He wiped down and straightened up and followed his friends to the door and made his own way home, drunker than he'd been since his boy had cursed him for wanting father and son to manage this store.

Garum chomped on corn from the back yard and blueberries along with a few scattered gooseberries, though it was late for them. He was ready to scamper outside for more of the same when his father came home, but Dolph shook his head. "Beulah had pulled pork. She tried to save some for me to bring to you, but Ephraim come over, so I said you'd prob'ly already et so go ahead and give it to him. You catch some fish, did ya?"

"Sorry, Pa, not a one was bitin' today, but when I come home, I had corn. And a couple gooseberries. Never did expect to find any this far inta August. I bet your garden's the only one anywhere 'round here's got any at all, this late."

Dolph was watching him, his tall forehead wrinkling. "But somethin' ain't right, boy. What?"

Garum squirmed. He'd been hoping he wouldn't have to tell, but somehow his pa always knew when something was up. And Dolph didn't like to hear what it was from nobody else.

"Nothing much," Garum started, but went straight to it when he saw his father's expression. "Just a car—or somethin'—on the crooked road. Only I didn't hear him until he was right on me. But I jumped quick 'nuff so he never touched me."

"Car? Whose? Nobody down that road's got a car. Only a couple pickups that you couldn't miss hearin' even if you was deaf."

"Well, I thought it was a car, but when I looked up after, seemed real odd."

"Didn't ya hear nothin'?"

"Well," Garum tempered. He hadn't wanted to tell this part at all. His father glared, and Garum came out with it fast. "Well, I thought mebbe there was a laugh. Cackle-like."

"And?" Dolph leaned toward him to demand.

"And somethin' like, 'almost got me one this time'."

"White man," Dolph spat, plopping into the wooden chair at their table. "I just come through town and seen all of 'em at their white church for their KKK meetin'." Shaking his head, Dolph pushed away the tackle box he'd only then pulled toward him. He looked up, surprised to see his son settling in for the evening. "Ain't you goin' over to Minnicks' place to hear that lady read about the pirates?"

Garum shook his head. "Miz Nandria ain't feelin' real good, the kids say. Mebbe tomorrow night. Think I'll practice writing my letters some." He knew his father liked to watch. He'd even found some scrap papers with Dolph's attempts to copy what his son was doing. Garum made sure to say each letter out loud as he practiced forming it, so his father would know what it was and what it 'said.' So Dolph, too, could learn to read.

Chapter 3

Wednesday, August 14, 1940

Sheriff Yakes turned on Ella Mae Drangler's bed and immediately regretted his movement. His grunt of belly pain brought Ella Mae hustling to his side. Her short stature and expression of wonderment made her look like a cherub. An angel child in cream-white robe. But he'd never had a girl child, only the boys. Twins. They come together. Went together. He frowned.

"Piermont, what...?"

"What time is it?" he asked, seeing only darkness at her bedroom window.

"The Grandfather just chimed four, but you was groanin' too loud to hear."

"Ju-ust a twinge," he managed, seeing the concern on her wrinkled face.

"Now, Piermont, you just lie back there," she scolded, covering him with the hunter green quilt she'd made for him.

"I'll fetch you a cup of coffee and a scone so you can get some strength up before you try standin'."

"Who can stand up under your ceilings?" he complained, laughing. He reached to take the hand that was fussing with the gray-blue-green squares around his shoulder. "You're too good to me, woman. If you don't let me push myself, I may give up on ever trying to do anything on my own again and lie here beholdin' to you for the rest of my days."

She straightened, though that did not add much to her height. He watched expressions play across her pleasant, round face. Expressions that told him, as she never would have, that she was willing to do that if he should come to need her to.

He sighed. He had never meant to burden her at all, let alone for the rest of their lives. He stared at this tiny, feisty female who had taken him in after Doc had opened up his belly on July the fourth to stop the exsanguinating ulcer that would have bled out his life. "Ah, Ella Mae," he murmured. "Elm. It's shorter. But sturdy and trustworthy, like you. You gotta let me up. Let me get back my strength so I can do somethin' for you, for a change."

She rolled her eyes in mock surrender. "All right then, get up and bump your head and see if it's any never mind to me," she scolded, but with twinkling, navy-blue eyes.

"All right, then, I will." He shifted, straining to sit up at the edge of her bed. It hurt, but he wasn't about to let her see how much.

"You was better at that a week ago," Ella Mae observed. "What happened when you went out last night?"

"Just to check," he muttered. "Sheriffin's mostly about knowing what's goin' on. There," he huffed when he'd made it to sitting upright. He pressed his midsection and lifted his chin in triumph, but he was swaying, and she could see that he was. "So, where's that coffee you promised?" he asked, hoping she would go to the kitchen and let him get up and move on his own. But she wasn't ready yet to leave the subject.

"You said you heard something. Last night. What was it? Is that how you got hurt again? Somebody punch you in the gut?" she demanded, rapid-fire. "Who?" She stood now, hands on ample hips. "Who hit you, Piermont?"

"Some drunk," he muttered, trying to rise.

"'Some drunk?' You know everybody in town and for miles around."

"Got to. Sometimes it saves a lot of fussin' if you know 'em and what's like to've set 'em off."

"But this time? Town folk? Or from out in the boonies?"

He faced her without answering.

"So, did you get him straightened out? Why'd he hit you?"

"Too drunk. Could barely hear me, let alone do like I said."

Who? she mouthed, but he'd made it clear he didn't want to give her a name. "You got him in jail?"

"For what?"

"Hittin' an officer of the law, to say nothin' about disturbing the peace. And he must'a been loud for you to hear him from in here."

"You didn't hear him? You're a lot closer, sleepin' out there on your sofa."

She touched her ears and shook her head. She drooped then, mindful of how much less she was than she'd always been. He wasn't getting any bargain, and she was lucky to even think he might care.

"Fallin' apart are you, old lady?" Leaning hard with his left hand on the poster at the foot of her bed, Yakes clucked his tongue as though scolding her for decrepitude. His grin built slowly as he realized again how fond he'd grown of her.

"Oh, Piermont," she whispered stepping closer. His smile had told her that no matter how much she would worry about his interactions as sheriff, he wanted it that way. She'd better not fuss—ever. Ella Mae straightened her shoulders, setting the pins and needles even in the collar of her robe glistening in the light from the living room. She turned to gather his robe from the hook on the door. She tried to drape it over his shoulders, but he grimaced and took it from her.

"I ain't no invalid."

"If you're gonna insist on being up at this ungodly hour, I wish we'd brought over your slippers. But never mind. I'll help put your shoes on those long feet of yours when you're ready. Nobody who's gone through what you have should need to bend over to put on his own socks and shoes. And I'll put an extra sugar lump in your coffee this morning. So there," she snuffed, hurrying away.

He could hear her bustling in the kitchen, knowing she'd give him privacy until he groaned again. And then she'd come to help, whether he wanted it or not.

"Elm," he called when he could control his breathing after struggling to stand enough to fight his way into his robe, "any word yet about Will Minnick?"

"No, not yet." She entered with his shoes and clean socks tucked under her arm and carrying a breakfast tray. "I guess it's not for certain Will was even captured by them Nazis like that maybe-sergeant told Miz Nandria. The boy'd been in Missouri State Prison of late, so he really didn't know. Just had to say something when the whole community had him pinned down."

Yakes waved the tray aside and sat as straight as he could while she crouched to put his shoes on him. Bent like that, she could not see his face, and he was glad. He'd found himself remembering the anguish and the agony of that Fourth of July. It had been a month, and he'd been getting so much better until... "Let's move on into the front room for that coffee and bacon'n'eggs and scones, do you think?"

She wanted to help him up but held off when it was clear he wanted to do it himself. They shuffled into the living room. She found quiet ways, anticipating his needs, and giggling when he tried to thank her for her help and for her delicious efforts in the kitchen. He could almost hear the 'pshaw' she mouthed. When he went quiet after eating, she turned back to her hand sewing, humming under her breath. He fell asleep with his left hand around the coffee mug on the table beside the easy chair.

In the Minnick kitchen, Greg Paisler took little Rose's lifted, porridgy hand in his despite the sticky mess. "Hi, wee princess," he chuckled as he squeezed behind her to seat himself beside Bodie against the wall. He inclined his head as a bow of greeting across the table, and then sat to wipe his hand. "Good morning, Mrs. Minnick, and how are you today, ma'am?"

"Ah, young... uh," Doris Minnick began, then stopped, her mouth puckering as though she would cry. "Oh," she moaned and clutched at the scarf at her throat. "I...I don't rememb...all them boys—I...I don't remember which..."

Looking nearly as sad as Doris did, Minnick rocked his chair forward from its tilt against the wall at the head of the table. He reached to pat her hand to calm her.

"Shall I serve you two eggs or three, Greg Paisler?" Nandria asked from the stove.

"Ah, yes, Paisler," Doris exclaimed. "Now I remember. You're our neighbors' son. One of many," she giggled, delighted to have remembered so much when she'd been so confused only moments before. It felt good to be on top of her world again. Proudly, she beamed at her husband.

Glad, too, that his wife and partner of so many years was pleased with herself, Minnick was careful not to question her for the youth's first name. Nor did he ask her to explain why Greg was here on their farm as a worker rather than pitching in with his brothers on their family spread. That would truly task his Doris's ever more tenuous hold on reality. He could not ask her. He'd asked again and again why his Doris seemed senile although she was barely into her fifties, but no one had been able to answer. None of the doctors they'd seen had known, even Doc Ricartsen. Sighing, Minnick tapped his mug with his spoon to signal that that he wanted a refill of her delicious coffee to wash down the last of the enormous breakfast she had prepared.

Nandria, thin and quiet, set a full plate of biscuits and eggs over just easy in front of Greg, who smiled thanks. She poured coffee from the glass globe. At last, she sat in her place at the far end of the table to nibble on toast with a light smear of jam but no butter.

That seemed to be all she would eat again this morning, Minnick thought. It must be true what his Doris kept telling him that the gal was in a family way again. *What in purple blazes was Willard thinking? He's not even here to take care of either little one, to say nothing of that gal herself. She's educated, cultured. Been to them big-wig parties and confabs over the world with her parents. She don't fit here. Wouldn't even if she wasn't a coon.*

Minnick jerked as Doris touched his forearm to get his attention.

"Oh!" she cried, withdrawing her hand and, again, looking as though she were about to cry. He'd frightened her, which was the last thing he wanted to do.

His Doris had come as such a young bride from far north country on the strength of a love for him that had grown in so short a time, it was a whirlwind. *Just new married, buying this here farm so far from her folks, and then our two little boys as different as night and day. The Great War only barely over. The few years of seeming prosperity, at least for city folk. But debt was all we knew. Working eighteen and twenty hours a day every summer to get the farm up and running. Only then the depression hit, and that swallowed our hopes of a share in prosperity no matter how hard we worked. And then to lose both our boys. Fred to a stupid accident. And Willard —* *somehow a part of that accident though he escaped without a scratch — stayin' only long enough to finish high school and then enlistin'. An officer in the U.S. Army now. He keeps using that as an excuse not to come home to help make this farm prosper. Even sends that darky female he said he'd married in*

England, knowin' Minnicks has always been white. No explanation. No apology. Just parks her here. With her — their—kid, only ten months old. Standin' alone now, sometimes for close to a minute. Be takin' that first step in no time. I got to see my Freddy's first wobbling step. Missed out on Will's first—out in the field. Little do kids know what they're steppin' into, but...

"Huh?" Minnick started as Doris again touched his arm. Again, she looked frightened. He had to smile. Assure her everything was okay, even when it wasn't. Even when he didn't know any more than she did whether, let alone how, they were going get out of whatever the crisis was at the moment.

Minnick smiled and nodded. *Don't know how we're gonna feed this family, what with the trouble with the tractor. I was letting it go, figurin' on sellin' the place and settin' you up in town, little mother. Where you can be with friends and neighbors, like you never really been out here. But we got more mouths to feed and another on the way, thanks to your firstborn. Hell, I don't even know who would buy the place, let alone if what they paid'll be enough to keep us...*

She clutched his arm, looking confused. "Did ya hear him, Mr. Minnick? Bodie wantin' to know if you want him to rev up the tractor."

"If it'll go this morning," Bodie half chuckled. Their handyman since their boys were in cloth diapers, Bodie raised skinny arms and calloused hands as though letting it be up to heaven.

"Recalcitrant," Minnick murmured, drawing out the syllables as he remembered them.

"Hopin' that's a Willard word," Bodie muttered, shaking his head to show he didn't know just what it meant, but it would fit the tractor if it signified that the old warhorse sometimes worked and sometimes did not.

"Sounds like Willard's, all right," agreed Greg. "Or Miz Nandria's," he added. He glanced at Will's wife at the bottom of the table leaning over to wipe her little one's face. He knew she'd been up since before dawn cooking and would clean up the mess they'd made without a word of thanks. "I had to slather on the jam to keep your biscuits from floatin' away, Miz Nandria, they were so light." He rubbed his front to let her know he'd found them delicious.

"Nothin' unusual 'bout that, young scamp," Bodie chimed in, also to thank Nandria.

She nodded. Her attempt at a smile appeared to be weighed down by a tinge of green. She seemed to be having lots of trouble with this second pregnancy so close on the first one. But there was little either the old man or the young neighbor could do to make things easier for her.

Minnick patted his wife's hand and rose, scraping his chair legs on the linoleum. Doris smiled up at him. Bodie stood up as well to follow the boss out to the barn and on to the fields. Nandria picked up Rose from the highchair and carried her to the sink to give her porridge face a more thorough cleaning.

Greg started to gather the dirty dishes but left them in stacks at Minnick's frown.

Chapter 4

The sheriff awoke gently much later, his hand in his lap and the mug safe on the table beside him. Without speaking, he looked around in wonder. At the bluish-white, low, sloped ceiling glowing in the light from the front window. At the over-decorated walls crowded with framed sepia photos and needlework. At the female figure sculpted of what looked to be chicken wire and draped with a cloth Ella Mae had called taffeta that shimmered orange-red-brown. Like the burning bush. He stared a long time at the color and found tears easing the burning of his eyes.

"Patsy Lynn," he whispered, stroking the quilt on his knees as he had his wife's auburn hair.

"That you, Piermont Yakes?" a thin voice called from the kitchen. "Finally had enough nap, did you?" In a moment the round, child-like figure of Ella Mae filled the lower half of the doorway. The little woman held more of the auburn taffeta cloth across her arm with a wet spot. "Got a soil spot on this and just trying to clean it out with cold water, mild soap and a mite of borax so's not to waste the whole piece." Sighing, she stepped up to look him over.

"Stain's not coming out the way you'd like, I take it, Elm?"

"Elm?" Her navy-blue eyes widened. "I thought that's what you'd called me earlier, but with my hearing going the way of all things, I wasn't sure."

Head down, he sneaked peeks to watch her expression change from wonderment, to tasting the sound of it and finally to smiles of delight. She giggled, and he felt his lungs again fill with air. This time there was less pain with the deep breath than he'd been afraid would be back again. Yakes closed his eyes, sorry for losing part of the morning, but glad he was hurting no more than he was. Nickleberg had belted him a good one.

"Would you rather sleep? Lunch can wait, dear man," she smiled. "It's still early, what with your starting the day long before sunup."

He opened his eyes and peered at her with undisguised fondness.

She blushed; he chuckled aloud. "What, you fool man?"

"I'd been sitting here awake wondering if that chicken wire was you." It was an excuse, but he couldn't yet tell her how grateful he was. Let alone that her care had brought back feelings he never believed he could sustain again. Flat on his back and in pain, he'd been too vulnerable to talk about feelings. He studied her eyes before she glanced away at the sewing dummy. He knew she'd understood, and he took in a gasping breath.

Her head twisted as she turned to check him carefully with those incredibly dark blue eyes. And then she smiled, again knowing without words.

"No, silly, that ain't me. I'm twice that size around, and it still wouldn't quite close enough for buttoning. I'm a butterball. You can see that for yourself."

Yakes swallowed. Reaching to set his hand over hers, he swallowed again before saying, "Buttercup, that's what I called my missus."

"Patsy Lynn?"

He nodded. "Yeah, before...before she couldn't eat nothin'."

"Ah, Piermont," she whispered. She knew his wife had died horribly of gut cancer, and that many Boonetown folks believed he had killed her to stop her agony. Sighing, Ella Mae stepped away to bring the short-legged chair close to his easy chair. Before sitting, she arranged the taffeta material over her worktable and smoothed it to dry.

"That auburn stuff for the banker's gal?"

"Ain't everything?" She threaded a needle while shaking her head, and the sheriff watched her, open-mouthed.

"Can a whole girl fit inside that skinny frame?" he laughed, pointing at the impossibly slender sewing dummy.

"Hard to believe, ain't it? Like she's all feathers and no substance. And yet, you know, Piermont, for all the fluff, I think there is something there."

"I can't see her as a farmer's wife."

"Nobody but Francis Paisler himself can see her as that."

"Frank? Second of the Paisler sons, ain't he? Think the boy will change? The farm is Zeb and Cynthia Paisler's whole being. All their boys was raised like there never was a question but farming is their lives."

"Maybe there's more in Francis than even Zeb and Cynthia see."

"I just hope you're right about more in the gal." Yakes stirred to sit up a little. He shook his head when she reached to help him. "Gotta do for myself one of these days soon, if I'm gonna ever be a man again."

He heard her tiny huff. When he'd gotten himself as upright as his gut would allow without groaning, he looked at her. She sat chin down, as though concentrating on her sewing. He reached to touch her wrist. "Elm, I never meant to slight you. I couldn't ever mean that. Woman, you saved my sanity, my dignity, my life—and I know it. You mean... I mean, I can't..." Head lowered, he let her go and sat breathing deeply in and out.

"Tell me about your Patsy Lynn?" she whispered.

He sat with his eyes closed for long minutes. "She was all of everything to me," he stammered finally. "Especially after... after the boys..." He rolled his head on the top of the chair back. His eyes closed again.

"Do you want to tell me about the boys, Piermont? I've heard all sorts of stories, but the only thing them stories had in common was that you lost 'em both on the same day. I don't know how you survived a day like that." Her voice held sympathy rather than pity.

"Drowned. In... in the mill pond. Twins. One fell in and the other jumped in to save... You've known days like that your own self," he panted, opening his eyes to peer at her.

For once, she set her handwork aside. Tears welled in the dark blue eyes. "Yes," she whispered.

"Tell me."

"How? The words don't say it." She rose to fetch the taffeta.

"I know." He reached to take her tiny, calloused hands in his when she returned. "But it's too heavy to carry alone. I'm here, Elm. And that's your doing, more'n once. I wanna be here for you, woman."

They eased into themselves until they were quiet. Ella Mae Drangler shifted in the short-legged chair, laid her head on his thigh and fell asleep curled around the taffeta. Piermont Yakes watched her, still holding her near hand, until his own breathing gentled. When he closed his eyes again, he felt at peace as he had not since he'd lost his sons and wife.

Gertrude Nickleberg listened to the sedan-truck roar and squeal as it stopped near the kitchen door. Heinz had his feet on both the gas and the brake. With the clutch out, their modified egg truck hopped to a halt. Heinz only did that when he was drunk, and he'd been drinking far more lately than he had since the boys had left to start their own families. Something was very wrong. But nothing she did or said could get her husband to talk about it so she could straighten it out.

She grimaced. *So frustrating being a woman. I'm supposed to know without being given a clue. I'm supposed to fix things and keep them on keel without even knowing what's the matter. The man's right, whatever he does. The woman's wrong even when she does exactly what he tells her to because she didn't do what he didn't tell her, and she had no way of knowing about.*

She grimaced. *Other than that, Mrs. Lincoln, how did you enjoy the play?*

When Heinz did not come right in, Gertrude rose from the table and wiped her hands on an apron with few areas still clean. She peered out to watch her husband stumble back across the yard carrying seven beheaded pullets and scattering live ones. A wave of pity for the man swept across her like a gust of debris-carrying wind. Heinz had not been sleeping, and when he did, he tossed and moaned with nightmares. "You're drunk again! Why in the green earth do I have to have you in my life?" she whispered while he could not hear. He was coming in. Gert hurried back to her chair at the worktable. She did not want him to think she'd been spying on him. Drunk and irritated, her husband would not be in his best form.

Heinz Nickleberg stopped at the doorway to the kitchen where the woman had made his breakfasts for forty-seven years and ten, no, eleven months. Every one of them early morning meals had tasted about as good as the cardboard of the rolled oats box, notwithstanding that Quaker man's smile. Heinz tossed the pullets onto the table in front of her and lifted a huge hand to continue their argument of long before.

"All I said was that that loaf of bread was stale. Look," Heinz sawed off a slice from the loaf on the counter. Using its edge, he marked a white crumb line across the end of the butcher block worktable.

Taking up a pullet to pluck out its feathers, Gertrude bristled, the hairs at her chin glistening with sweat as she twisted her lower face in anger. "Of course, I know it's stale, you fool. But if I cut your toast from the new loaf, what do you say then? You yell at me that it's bad luck. That I'm courting having no bread at all. 'Always eat everything of the old loaf before cutting into the new loaf.' Ain't that what you've preached at me all the forty and then some years we been hitched?"

"Forty and then some," he muttered. *But marriage is until death do us part. It's been a while since I've thought of death ending the long years. Yours, of course.* Heinz leaned against the door jamb. His lips turned up in what looked like as much as he ever smiled. *Evidently, she'd thought of us parting, too. Well, that's the first time in ages that we've agreed on just about anything.* He hitched himself erect and stepped into the dreary kitchen. *How many thousand dozens of eggs have we candled here? How many beheaded chickens we plucked?* Another thought struck him, and he smiled again. *At least she hasn't thought of killing me, unless it's with her cooking. If that's what's she's doing, she's drawing it out mighty slow.*

Grinning outright, he bent to pin her in a rare embrace with his knife sharp against her forearm. Gertrude gasped, but, chuckling, he did not release her until she shoved him away.

There was blood oozing on her forearm. Only a smear. Her lips pressed to a single thin line, she knocked the offending knife to the floor and lifted her arm to show him. "Now see what you done, you old fool."

Shaking his head and grinning, Heinz shrugged his shoulders to deny any part in the bloodletting. "We've seen each other's hands chopped up good more'n a time or two. You want me to faint now?"

Gert stared, still thin-lipped. And then she laughed and reached for another pullet to pluck. "You old fool," she repeated, softer this time. "But, like I told you at breakfast, I'd still like you out of my life."

"Agreed."

"Only that ain't gonna happen, is it?"

He took up the next pullet and sank into his chair at the far end of the table where he'd sat for years, plucking, gutting, cutting, plucking, chopping, plucking, cutting, plucking for decades. His smile expired with the weight of memories. "No, old lady, I don't believe it will." He looked at her as she shifted in the chair, grimacing. She grunted, but he said nothing about her pain. She'd been living with arthritis for years, as he had with her grumblings and short temper when she hurt the most. But, he realized, even with all that, she'd been there beside him feeding the chickens, gathering the eggs, sorting out the best layers and setting them where the roosters could play, and then helping the hens raise those chicks to enlarge their brood. She'd been key to making their farm into a business. And raising their own two sons. "Ungrateful lunks," he muttered, stretching out his legs to ease his throbbing knees.

"Herman and Hiram?" she sighed. "Ain't you never gonna forgive them?"

"They're the ones that left, ain't they? I told them it would all be theirs. We had a good thing goin' here with the four of us working it."

She nodded, her sharp nose appearing to dip closer over her faint mustache toward her sharper chin.

"And don't go defendin' 'em," Heinz snapped.

Gertrude lifted her hands in denial.

"You always do. Just try again to tell me our payin' for their months at that agricultural school was a good investment for this farm. But what did it ever do besides give 'em ideas bigger'n they was? Married and took off, both of 'em."

"Good gals, the two of them."

"Vivian. Now there is a prize. Taller'n Herman. He looks like a boy beside her. And the way she bosses him around; it turns my stomach to see and listen to them two together."

"You made that clear," Gert sniped, but Heinz was full into his grousing mode and gave her no mind.

"And that Vertigo!"

"Veronica," she hissed correction.

"I thought with a name like Vert to go with your Gert, that them two at least would come back and take over with our help."

"Help? When did we ever help? 'Do this. Do that.' Of course, there wasn't ever any extra money for them to have stuff of their own. Whatever gave ya a fool notion like us helpin' them?'"

"When'd you ever talk to them that-a-way, woman?"

"Wasn't me. I let 'em keep their egg money for themselves. Only right. They'd done all the work and then some. And they ain't the only ones you drove out with your fussin' and carryin' on. But I don't know why I'm tryin' to talk to you, when you're so hung-over again this mornin'.'"

"Me? I never drove them boys out'a here!"

"Is that so? Don'tcha remember the card game that time when we all sat down together for little Brod's birthday?"

His eyes squinted; his face reddened. Clearly, he remembered, but he merely grunted his displeasure.

"We was laughing the way families do, Veronica and me setting back from your table. She was showin' me a new embroidery stitch that was so purdy I just had to learn how to make it. And you four playin' like the farm had been bet and Vi and Herman taking the lead again and then little Broderick yanked his mama's arm 'cause she hadn't been payin' attention to him."

"It fell on the floor," Heinz gasped.

"It was just her cards."

"She had the black ace. The ace of spades."

"It's just a card."

"No, woman," Heinz insisted. "When the dark ace falls to the floor, you stop the game. Right then and there. I tried to tell 'em, but they wanted to keep playing."

"Of course, they did. They was ahead."

"No, I was. It'd just turned again. But that was no never mind. It had to stop right then so the devil couldn't get in. Only that one knows what would'a happened to all of us if I'd'a let 'em keep playin'."

Gertrude stared. Even this many years later, her husband was frightened enough to be heaving to catch his breath.

"You all set for the egg run to Owens', are you, Heinz? I'll rinse and wrap these chickens and bring 'em out to you." *I still don't want you in my life, you old fool, but how can I leave you, afraid as you are of witches and the devil?*

"Dogfights over the English Channel," Doc told Mrs. Drangler over his shoulder as he bent to enter her bedroom where the sheriff was taking a nap after early lunch. She'd gone to his office to let Mrs. Bean know the sheriff had suffered a set-back.

"Huh?" From deep in Ella Mae's low bed, the sheriff looked up at Dr. Ricartsen. Straightening his shoulders, Yakes tried to look alert and in charge, but he couldn't hide the dark circles under his eyes or the bruises on his cheek. He cringed under his physician's scrutiny. "Dogfights? What's that?" he asked to put off the inevitable interrogation about what he had been doing and why he had not been following the doctor's orders.

"Dogfight?" the tiny seamstress echoed as she carried a tray of scones and a pot of coffee to set on the bedside table. Yakes had to twist quickly to snatch away his week-old newspaper. Ricartsen lifted the half-empty glass of water and put it out of the way on her bureau.

Ricartsen caught the sheriff's wince of pain even as he looked between them and blinked. *So, these two are teaming up against me. I should have suspected where Mrs. D.'s loyalties would lie, given a month of caring for this guy.* Grinning, Ricartsen sat down on the edge of the bed. "You both know what a dogfight is," he chuckled.

"Yeah, but not over a body of water," Mrs. Drangler laughed, reaching for a mug and the coffee pot. "Though I got to admit, I've seen our mongrel Ladysman carry a young bobcat into our pond to drown him or at least let him know for sure and certain he wasn't wanted near our few goats ever again."

Beaming up from over the scone he'd already stolen, Yakes winked at his short hostess. "But, Doc, you was goin' on about the fights over the English Channel. That means it's between war planes, then?"

Sighing with the two against him, Ricartsen slid his stethoscope under the sheriff's shirt and signaled for quiet while he listened.

Ella Mae filled the sheriff's coffee mug and set it beside him. "War planes. Ain't the English Channel right there alongside England? Does that mean them Nazis are trying to shoot and bomb directly over England's countryside? They might hit people's farms. That'd be dreadful."

"What kind'a air force do the Brits have? I know they got a navy like no other, but I don't remember hearin' much about them rulin' the sky the way they've always ruled the waves."

Ricartsen nodded again and lifted his stethoscope away from his ears. Thoughtfully, he reached for a scone, bit into it, and, eyes rolling with appreciation, reached for another. "Navy, yes, about the best," he managed between bites. "Planes and pilots, not so much. And it takes time to build airships and train boys to fly them. I sure hope they have that time they need."

"Amen," Ella Mae breathed.

"There'll be a lot of young, reckless fools give it a valiant try, though, won't there?" Yakes paused over the rim of his mug.

Tears sprang to Mrs. Drangler's eyes. She turned away to lift her handkerchief to wipe them away and blow her nose. "So brave. Such a loss to them as love 'em."

"How long's the dogfightin' been goin' on, Doc?"

"Off and on since about the middle of last month. But it's getting more and more intense. The Brits're trying to work out a warning system so their fighters can get off the ground and fight them over the Channel before they can get in to drop their bombs over land."

"Then, I'd bet London'll be on fire one of these weeks," the sheriff murmured.

Doc nodded, solemn. "As soon as Hitler can send enough planes to overwhelm what little the Brits can send up to beat them off. The radio commentators are pretty careful not to discourage folks with talk like that. But, if you listen between the lines and think it through, it's gotta be rough."

"And gonna be rougher. Them bombs'll be fallin' on civilians as well as military targets."

"Oh, Piermont, do you think...?" Mrs. Drangler gulped.

"It's been Hilter's way on the ground so far," the sheriff muttered. "Gotta think he won't stop at the same kind'a tactics once he's got the English people in his bombsights." He sat up and looked over at Ella Mae's distress. "But don't you worry yourself, woman. He ain't gonna get here."

She rocked, holding the handkerchief to her face.

"That isn't what worries her, Yakes," Ricartsen murmured.

"I know. She's the tenderheartedest..."

"And you've got a tender gut again, don't you, sheriff? What did you do?"

"Is that why you're here?" Yakes demanded. "Somebody must'a told ya." Frowning, he glanced over at Mrs. Drangler.

"Somebody with more horse sense than you seem to have."

"Ah, it's nothin'," Yakes muttered, but Ricartsen was already crushing the last of his scone into his mouth and leaning forward with his hands exploring the sheriff's midsection.

"Doc, don't...Agh!" he cried at the doctor's probing.

"I thought you were nearly healed."

"I did, too," Yakes grunted.

"Then, what?"

"Well, a bit of a tussle."

"You were in a fight with somebody? Who? Why, man? Didn't you know..."

"A drunk," Ella Mae said. "A mean drunk, by the way the sheriff here has been pussy footing around."

"Nickleberg?" Doc lifted his shoulder to mouth the name for only Yakes to see.

Yakes closed his eyes and nodded.

"The egg man hisself, is my guess," Ella Mae said aloud. "Folks are saying he was loud last night, and they were glad the sheriff went out to quiet him."

"Huh," Ricartsen breathed, shaking his head. He opened his mouth to tell them of last night's get-together after KKK but closed it without saying anything.

"I reckon Mrs. Bean didn't tell you when she got you up after I run over there. She don't like to pass on gossip, though I swear she knows what everybody in this county is up to at any given minute of the day."

"Mean damn drunk," Yakes swore as he lay. His breath was raspy after the doctor's palpation of his abdomen. He looked over at Ella Mae, ashamed.

"Mean damn drunk," she echoed to show him his use of profanity in her home was, in this case, justified. "He must've punched the sheriff right in the gut, deliberate. He knew."

"Right in...the bread...basket," Yakes panted as the doctor probed once more.

Ricartsen's eyes closed, then opened. Concern was written in his expression. "You doin' any bleeding, man? Above, or below?"

Ella Mae Drangler blushed, but the doctor paid her no mind. He wasn't going to let fastidiousness keep him from getting the information he needed.

Chapter 5

Little Rose was wide awake and feisty. She lurched forward in Nandria's arms, trying to touch any and everything in Owens' general store. Doris lingered in the corner near the bolts of material, chatting amiably with neighboring farm ladies. Nandria rested her hip against a corner of one of the Owens' display tables and tried to quiet her just ten-month-old so her morning sickness—it was well past noon—would settle into mere discomfort. She was swallowing again and again when Mrs. Owens approached with a sympathetic smile.

Nandria blushed. "Caught me," she murmured.

"Oh, yes," Mrs. Owens chuckled. "Many of us would. It must've been a man who first named it 'morning sickness.' It was what he saw before he escaped to work. Would you like to sit down in the corner there behind the counter? Shaking her head with as little motion as possible, Nandria declined. "From here I can watch Mother Minnick. She seems content. I hate to bother her."

"Oh, I'll keep an eye on Doris. Been doing it for months. No, for years now. I do wish one of those doctors Mr. Minnick takes her to see in Kansas City would come up with the answer about what is ailing her. She used to be such a vibrant lady." Mrs. Owens sighed. "But I guess if our Doc Ricartsen can't figure it out, nobody else can either. Why don't you mosey over there and sit down with your little one?" Bernice's soft voice rose as it occurred to her to ask to help her ailing customer. "Unless you'd like me or one of the ladies to take Rose?"

Nandria's dark eyes widened in fear. Bernice at once lifted her hands, palm up, and backed away. Since Nandria and the child had been threatened by the Bratton brothers, the young mother had seldom allowed anyone, except perhaps Cynthia Paisler, to even touch her little one.

"I guess she'd be a happier tyke in her mother's arms, wouldn't she?" Bernice gestured for Nandria to follow her to the counter. "Would you like a glass of water? Did you have the morning sickness this long into your time carrying little Rose there?" With a gentle hand at Nandria's back, Bernice escorted Will Minnick's woman and child behind the counter and saw them settle heavily in the corner. With a quick nod to her curious husband's lifted eyebrows, Bernice poured tepid water from the pitcher near the cash register and took the glass to Nandria.

"I'll be keeping an eye on Doris Minnick. Never you mind that your mother-in-law wasn't being seen to."

Isaac Owens frowned. He didn't like to encourage his wife's catering to everybody; it wore her out. But he most certainly didn't want to let a sick customer drive away the other customers. He was about to step near his wife to protest when Heinz Nickleberg clamored in through the back room hollering, "I brung the dead ones." Isaac hurried over to intercept the drunken man.

"So, you brought the chickens, did you?" he called so his customers would understand what the 'dead ones' were. "Got them all plucked?"

"Don' I aw-ways? Ain' that wha' we sai' we'do? Nickleberg looked about to take offense. "Whaddaya ya think' I am, a danged Demicrat? Promisin' a fish and givin' ya a snake?"

"Yeah, chickens are what you promised," Isaac countered, steering him toward the back room. But Nickleberg grabbed the end of the counter and lurched behind it. Nandria gasped and clutched Rose to herself. He snarled.

"If you ain't a Demicrat, man, then don't act like one," Isaac demanded low, hauling the egg man out from behind the cash register and toward the back room. "Drunk ain't no excuse for making this much of a fool of yourself."

Bernice was about to hurry to help her husband but spun at a piercing howl. Doris Minnick had dropped her shopping bag and was cowering near the display of secondhand jewelry. Her eyes screwed tight shut, she swayed and looked about to fall.

"Doris!" Bernice cried, rushing to her. Nandria, with Rose at her hip, was close behind but stepped to one side to avoid Isaac Owens looming behind her.

Behind the store where Isaac had left him, Heinz Nickleberg stumbled at the threshold to the loading area.

"You all right, mister?" a small voice asked.

Nickleberg grasped the doorframe and looked down at a ragtag, thin-armed Negro child. "M'boys won' help me. M'wife don' like me. Got no money and'll prob'ly lose my farm, but yeah, I'm fine and dandy. Whad's it to you, boy? Whose are you, anyhoo?"

The boy blinked at the flood of information and pair of questions, trying to decide what to answer.

"Garum," he said, finally, which answered none.

"Huh?" the man questioned. His stinking breath made it clear why he had stumbled.

Garum knew about heavy drinking. Uncles on his father's side got loud and funny every Saturday night. Until they weren't funny anymore. Garum knew when to disappear. He was about to wiggle out to the far end of the raised deck of the general store when the man seized his shoulder. He went limp, unresisting.

"You, boy. Whose are you? You a goo' workah, huh?" The man's tremble was shaking the child's whole being.

"I do good work, Mr. Bossman."

"I have a farm, jus' out tha' way," Nickleberg indicated by a vague wave of his free hand. "Raise chickens, turkeys. You know how to candle eggs? Clean the shells? Chop off heads?"

The boy's decision was made in another blink of those soft brown eyes. This might be a chance for Garum to earn some money. His pa would be so glad. It might even make him smile with joy. Garum had been able to get him to do that a time or two, and it had made his heart so glad he wanted to do it again if he could.

"Oh, yessir," he bragged. Only 'chop off heads' had caused him to swallow. The rest he could learn to do even to this man's satisfaction. He was sure of it. Hadn't Miz Nandria said he was smart, learning his letters and all?

"You can?" Nickleberg raised his eyebrows in surprise. He grinned. He'd found a treasure; someone to help with the stinky little jobs his boys had done for him. But they were grown up now. Herman and Hiram. Both had grown up and moved away when he needed them most. But here was a kid he didn't even have to teach with hard-remembered patience. The kid was a monkey. He could kick him around if he didn't measure up. The man grinned again, drooling into the stubble on his chin. "Well, you jus' show up tomorrow mornin'—early, mind ya—at my place just at sunrise tomorrow morning. We'll see if you do goo' work, boy. Sunrise, sharp. And you be ready to show me jus' how goo' you are."

"Yessir, Mr. Bossman. I'll be there," Garum promised, wondering where 'there' might be. The indistinct wave of the man's hand had told him almost nothing. But if it promised work and pay that might make his pa happy, he'd sure enough find a way to find out. Stepping clear of the man's hand, Garum held his breath, watching. The man stumbled the few steps down to his odd, sawed-off car. The roof over the back seat had been cut away and a piece welded behind the driver's seat to keep driver and passenger out of the weather. The old car was now effectively a pickup. That it was used to carry poultry and eggs was obvious from the smears of yellow, thick drippings of white now turned gray and brown, and old blood red. And feathers, mostly white, and mostly small, tucked into every conceivable crevasse of the car-turned-truck. And stuck to the smears. Long-ago broken eggs, no doubt. "I'll find ya," Garum vowed.

He watched until the man had stuffed himself behind the steering wheel and pulled out without looking. Luckily in Boonetown, that wasn't usually a problem. There was little traffic, especially on this back road. But it was still a stupid move. Like the white man didn't care one way or another if he lived to the end of the day.

Garum shook his head and scratched behind his left ear where the chiggers had bitten him. Frowning over how to get the information he needed, he wiped the bottoms of his feet the best he could on the rough wood of the deck and sidled to the back door of Owens' store to peek in. The service area obviously doubled as a slaughtering place, but it was cleaner than most Garum knew. He crossed to the door into the store itself. Standing back from blocking anyone, he twisted to peer inside.

Piles of folded material were being undone and left in scattered disarray by a sharp-faced white woman and a tall girl with golden, curly hair. They were seeking but apparently not finding a special color or feel or size. The sharp woman wore white gloves even in the summer heat, but the girl was holding her soft, right glove in her left hand as she rummaged. With each scrutiny, she left an untidy heap behind her. These had to be banker Freshstalk's wife and daughter. They'd been pointed out before, of course, but Garum had never dared get this close until now that it had happened accidentally. They weren't—especially the lady—they weren't as pretty as he'd thought from always seeing them at a distance as he worked in the fields.

"Oh, twizzles, I've snagged a fingernail," the girl complained. "And after I've spent most of the morning filing them with those emery boards you had the bank courier bring for us from Kansas City."

"Oh, dear," her mother commiserated, gliding over to examine the damaged nail. "'Oh, dear' sounds somewhat more elegant than 'oh, twizzles,'" she remarked as she gestured to the glove in her daughter's left hand. "That might have prevented this entire scene," she suggested, dropping the piece of cloth she had been inspecting. It slid off the edge of the rumpled pile and slithered to the floor.

Garum could see Mrs. Owens inching toward the Freshstalks, but she appeared to hesitate to confront them. Her usually welcoming smile looked sickly. Her right fist was cradled in her left hand as though to keep it from doing what it wanted to. The boy ducked his head to hide the smile he couldn't keep from curling his lips. When he could summon a blank expression, he slipped inside the store to pick up the cloth from the floor and fold it carefully. He watched Mrs. Owens' stiff anger ease to mere annoyance as the Freshstalks left without even glancing at the mess they had made. Grinning his 'I'll help clean this up' smile, Garum flipped the piles, folding, restacking, and straightening.

"You don't have to do that, boy."

"I know, ma'am, but I hates to see you work over again what you already done. I ain't busy right this minute." His hands worked efficiently and, with her help deciding particular piles, soon the material was again in proper display.

"Garum, isn't it?" Mrs. Owens smoothed the top of each stack and looked at him with a tired smile. "You're Dolph Tacker's boy."

"Yes'm. Best handyman ever."

"My, you are as quick with your hands as Dolph is," she chuckled. "And a thousand times quicker with your tongue. Your father doesn't say three words in a whole day when he does chores for us. I want to thank you for your help. Would you like to choose a stick of hard candy in the jar over there? What color do you like?"

"Oh, I like 'em all, missus, but what I'd really like would be to know something, if you'd help me." He tore his eyes away from the bright reds, yellows, and greens of the striped candy and faced her. He lowered his chin so she wouldn't see how he longed for the sweet treat.

"You want information rather than candy? Now that's a choice I don't see very often. What do you want to know, Garum?" Her voice was kind. Her expression held a degree of respect the boy had not been given by many. He felt suddenly warm.

"Well, I was just wondering, ma'am, who belonged to that odd see-dan with the back scalped off."

"And all the feathers? That's the egg man, Mr. Nickleberg's car. Or truck, maybe you could call it."

"Yes'm, I figured it must be. He's got a farm 'round here. Raises hens and turkeys and such."

"He does. He slaughters them. Saves my mister a heap of time and hassle, bringing them in all cut up. The beef people do that, too, but the lamb people hereabouts let Mr. Owens do most of the butchering himself. But you wanted directions to his place, didn't you? Your pa would know."

"Yes'm, but I thought I would surprise him. Mr. Nickleberg said maybe I could work for him if I showed up there with the sun tomorrow. But I don't want Pa to get his hopes up too high."

Mrs. Owens chuckled again, nodding. She'd seen how drunk the egg man was and understood he might or might not remember in the morning that he'd hired the boy the day before. "You know the lane that goes to the Minnick place? How far out that is on the rural delivery road off the main road? Well, about halfway to that, where the old Petersen's barn used to be—but you wouldn't know where that was. It burned before you could walk, probably. Anyway, about halfway to Minnicks' there's a crumpled chicken coop, mostly just sticks of wood now and the Nickleberg's mailbox with their name on it, I think."

"Nnn," the boy sounded. "The name'd start with a 'n', wouldn't it?"

"An 'n', yes," Bernice agreed, silently giving credit to Nandria Minnick for her teaching. "Nicklebergs are up that lane. Chickens everywhere but mind you don't hit one. You kill it, you bought it. I swear the man counts all those fowls eighty times a day. He'd know."

Garum highly doubted he'd kill a bird with his bike, but he nodded in appreciation of the warning. "Thankee, ma'am, er, thank you kindly, Mrs. Owens," he corrected himself with a touch of British accent that assured Bernice Owens that Miz Nandria must have been coaching the boy.

"Garum, I've got some broken pieces of those candy sticks under my counter I can't sell anyway. Would you like one?"

His grin told her that he surely would. He chose a long piece swirled with green and red and ran from the store with a wide smile.

Isaac Owens came up close behind his wife and pecked her on the left cheek when no one was watching. "How come?" he whispered.

"How come what, you sly devil?" She pretended annoyance, but her smile gave her away.

"How come you're so kind to the odd ones around here? A trash girl…"

"You mean, Zelma Bratton?

"And that boy?"

"Garum Tacker? Dolph's son. Why not? They can't help who they were born to. Why not be gentle with them? They are just children, after all. They've got to have a chance at being thought well of once in their lives. How is Miz Minnick, Isaac? Any word?"

Isaac bussed her on the cheek again. "Doc didn't seem too surprised when he saw Doris. Several of the women went with me when I carried Doris to Doc's. They can probably tell you better than... uh, oh, Ida Jane Freshstalk just came back in."

"I'll talk with her, Isaac dear." Mrs. Owens touched his arm to halt him. "She'll want to order material in a new color. Her mama will have a conniption when she sees our bill for what we allowed the girl to order, but her father will pay the bill after all the fuss dies down." She sighed as she hurried forward to greet the young lady with the long, golden curls and no sense of reality or what it would mean to be married to a working farmer.

Chapter 6

"Mrs. Minnick will be as right as she has been for the last few years," Dr. Ricartsen assured Nandria as he plopped down in his office chair. "Something she saw or smelled or just thought of set off memories that distracted her. Sent her into complete disorientation, so she cried out and crumpled to the floor." Shaking his head, the doctor sighed. "Let's give her a bit of time to rest, and then I think it will be well for you to take her on home. I would like to see her again tomorrow, if you could bring her in for me to check."

"Of course, Dr. Ricartsen. I will bring her tomorrow morning."

"Good. I only wish I knew what's been taking her downhill so far when by rights it shouldn't be so. We've tried consulting with some of the best in Kansas City and St. Louis. Even thought about Chicago..." He lifted his hands in surrender.

"I am assured you have done your best, Doctor."

"My best, oh, yeah." He grimaced, looking more horse-faced than ever. "No matter how much I try, I know that my own failings are going to hurt or kill a patient one day."

"Our best is the epitome of what any of us can accomplish."

"I know that here," he tapped his forehead. "But here," Ricartsen rested his hand over his heart and shook his head. "Well, that's a different story."

"Would that you always remain humble, sir. It contributes to our remaining willing to learn and to take responsibility."

"I'm not one of those docs with a fancy East Coast education. I'm a product of East St. Louis, I'm afraid." Ricartsen laughed, as he lifted long legs to prop them on his desk, then thought better of doing that in front of Will Minnick's cultured lady. "Sorry," he mumbled, grinning, but his voice struggled to remain baritone. "East St. Louis." He glanced across at Nandria, hoping the reference to the city of his upbringing would be sufficient explanation and excuse.

Nandria cocked her head to the right to peer at him. "I am sorry?"

Cracking the knuckles of his right hand, the gawky, country doctor dropped his eyes, embarrassed. "When I was a boy—I was born in 1910—my folks worked in St. Louis, but there was no way we could afford to live there. So, I grew up in a wild sort of place." He paused to look up at the woman's serene expression, again hoping not to need to go into details. But Nandria Brown Minnick was from London, England, and points international on visits with her father in the British Diplomatic Corps.

"Forgive me, Doctor, but I am not acquainted with your East St. Louis. St. Louis itself is an unknown to me. I arrived through Kansas City, you see."

He shifted his long legs and stretched them out under his desk until his long, narrow feet showed beside her chair. A slight smile crossed her face, mostly in her eyes. It gave him the courage to continue.

"I want you to understand," he exclaimed. "I want to help you understand us Americans so you won't judge us the way we probably deserve, but with a bit of forgiveness if you can find it in you."

Nandria lifted her shoulders and drew Rose, sleeping in her sling, closer against her chest. "I am not here to judge you, sir. Who would I be to judge you or anyone else?"

"But you are dark," he countered. "Around here, you are a sheboon. A golliwog, a..."

"A bambula? I was called that in France. Or, here in your United States..." Her voice dropped very low. "... a 'nigger'?"

Ricartsen stared at her. "Yeah. Yes. In this neck of the woods, that is exactly what you are, and enough of our good citizens have made that clear to you that you know it as well as I do." He drew up his legs and hunched forward, reaching to lay his hand on the desktop near her. "That's what I want you to understand. Why they do that. Why they see only the color of your skin and not you."

"Understand?" The question was barely audible. Nandria had visibly drawn into herself.

"Okay, okay, so maybe no one can understand. It's so layered and twisted and stinking. But I want you—if no one else in my whole life—to... to... get a glimpse at least of why you get treated the way that you do."

She inhaled so deeply that Rose stirred and whined before settling again into snuggled sleep at Nandria's hummed bits of "This little light of mine..."

"Is it like this everywhere in the world?" Doc asked, clearly wishing to know.

"No, not everywhere. Many places are so dense with all colors of human existence that I—we—are accepted simply as persons."

"Even you and Will? A mixed-race couple?"

Nandria stared to her right as though counting the towels neatly folded and stacked on one shelf of the built-in that lined the inner wall of his office.

"Sorry," he murmured when her silence came to be the only answer to his question. "So, prejudice isn't just the attitude of the U.S. of A. In a sad way, that makes us a little more in line with the rest of the world, though not a whit less guilty."

"Guilty," she echoed his word and turned so their eyes met. "I seldom allow myself to dwell on that concept. But I do try to understand. Have you read many of the writings of a W.E.B. Du Bois? His <u>Souls of Black Folk</u>, for instance?"

"I've heard of it. I ain't...haven't had much time to read, what with medical school and being the only doc for a long way around here." Ricartsen stopped. "No, that's not the whole of it. I haven't found a way to get hold of his books anywhere around here that wouldn't be instant news among the folk."

"You would lose many of your patients if they were to know you were reading Dr. Du Bois?"

He hung his head. "Guilty," he whispered but looked up as she chuckled at his re-echo of the offending word.

"There are degrees of guilt," she said. "Perhaps, none of us is free from condemnation." She looked away again, somber and deeply saddened.

"I...we in East St. Louis..." Ricartsen reared back in his chair, slamming it into the wall. "Hell, Nandria," he blurted, "we went after each other like ravenous animals after a carcass. And most of the time, that carcass..."

"...was a Negro," she finished for him when he could not.

"We were all at the bottom. And we snapped at and did dirt to anybody we thought might just be inferior in some way. Any way."

"The color of the skin was most easily identifiable."

He shrugged, lifting his hands up and out, palms forward. His helpless expression was so comical, Nandria could not help but smile. It broke the tension.

"Forgiven?" he whispered.

"For your upbringing?"

"For what my up-bringers did to your people."

"Mine, although I did not know them. Mine, although I could not have located the state, let alone the city in which they endeavored to live?"

"Yours, because you share with them a visible trait that in my world is dangerous. Deadly, at times. And I watched." He dropped his hands in a flood of horror and guilt as memory washed over him.

Nandria bent forward but stopped herself from touching or comforting him. When he could conquer his breathing and look up, she was peering at him.

Feeling the question in her eyes, he protested. "I didn't touch him. I didn't poke afterwards or take a souvenir toe or finger or laugh as he writhed. I..." Ricartsen's shoulders sagged; he stared at his desktop.

"A lynching. Individuals laughed?"

"Oh, yeah. And jeered. Cursed. Cheered. It was quite a show, and over that week, there were a lot of them."

"You were a child, were you not? Did you go to watch on your own?"

"A lot of kids watched. A lot of real little ones were brought by their parents or uncles or neighbors."

"So, your father was not the only man who believed this spectacle of humiliation and torture was fair viewing by their offspring?"

"Not just men. Lots of mothers were there with toddlers. Babes in arms."

"Your mother?"

He couldn't answer, but she knew.

Quietly, she gathered her biracial child closer against herself and rose. In silence, she left his office, closing his door with a nearly inaudible click.

In the kitchen-turned-sterilizing and prep room, Sadie Bean opened her mouth to greet her friend, but closed it and stood quietly, letting Nandria pass on out to the back porch where she sat on the steps, rocking and keening low.

Shaking her head, Sadie hustled up the corridor and entered the doctor's office without knocking. She found him weeping in his chair.

Chapter 7

Not wanting to be lost and not show up on time the next morning, late that afternoon Garum rode his bike west out the country road Mrs. Owens had told him about. The dust made him stop to cough now and again. He had to run alongside his bike to get it going again. Dust devils spun and danced deep in the fields. Hawks drifted, then plunged after mice scurrying among browning stalks. He could see why uncles and neighbors with a bit of land were complaining they might not get much of a harvest this year.

"Rain'd sure be a blessin' about now, Lord," he whispered. "Not that I'm tryin' to tell you how to run the weather or nothin'," he quickly explained. "You know best, but it sure would feel good to lift my face and have it splattered good with them big drops you sometimes send. Ah, thank You. See, there's the broke down coop Miz Owens was tellin' me about. And there's the big 'N' on the mailbox."

The rest of the letters were weathered and hard to read. Besides, the name was a long word and daylight lingered until late in August and then seemed to die quickly of exhaustion, so

Garum didn't bother to try to sound it out. He turned the bike up the rutted lane and hopped off. Pushing it up the rutted hill was hard, but it wasn't so steep that he couldn't manage. As he panted, it occurred to him that he didn't know what he'd say to Mr. Nickleberg if the man would catch sight of him. "Just hope the mister ain't home or there's somewhere I can take a looksee without him seein' me." It was as much prayer as statement to himself. Garum hoped the Lord might hear it that way. And then he heard a motor behind him. Garum flung down the bike and dropped to hide himself among the weeds just as the sawed-off sedan rumbled past.

"Well, I guess that makes sure of that," he whispered. "I'm givin' thanks, Lord. So, I'll be comin' in the mornin'—early." Gathering up the bike, he stood while surveying what he could see of the farm. Pa would love this land. He'd take a whole lot better care of it, too, if it was his. The boy was about to hop on to ride down the driveway when he heard what sounded like an angry yell and then a scream. A woman's scream. Stifling a cry of his own, Garum froze, listening. He knew even though he did not want to know that the scream had been a woman in pain. A white woman.

"Ain't nothin' you can do, boy," his father would tell him. "Whatever you try is only gonna get you into deep trouble, so you hustle yourself right out'a there, ya hear?"

Garum found the driveway easier going down than it had been struggling up. With any luck, he'd be able to get Pa's supper and still bike over to the Minnick farmstead before Miz Nandria had done with her reading. She'd just finished Peter Pan. He was as anxious as the other kids to hear what she'd chosen to read to them next. But that scream rang in his ears long after he'd turned into the dust of the county road.

In the yard in front of the henhouse, Gertrude watched the chickens scatter as the car/truck skidded to a stop in the yard. There was no point in hiding. He'd seen her and was shuffling toward her, slurring the words of a bawdy song he knew she disliked hearing.

"What's wrong, Mr. Nickleberg?" she whispered. "These many years I've stood beside you, sweated and wept with and for you. Why can't you talk to me? Please, Heinz, tell me what's wrong." But when he reached her, his foul breath made her frown in disgust. The song died in a bellow of rage as he raised his fist to punch her and then staggered toward their house.

She wiped the blood from her nose and, trembling, waited there with the hens to give him time to lurch inside. Give him time to settle from his anger before following him in. *Worst is, he probably won't even remember hitting me. Says he don't, anyway. And I swear he believes it when he says that. Oh, Lordy, Lordy, what am I goin' to do?*

From the kitchen, Heinz bellowed for her, and then stood, feet wide apart, at the sink, pumping the handle for water. He turned when she slunk in carrying the wire basket of eggs. "More eggs."

"Yes, thank heavens. Where would we be without them?" She sat at the worktable to wipe and sort them.

"Where are we with 'em?" Nickleberg rolled his eyes, knowing she was as sick as he was of this poultry farm and all the work that went with it. "Woman," he muttered as though he would take pleasure in going on to describe her in unpleasant terms. But he turned back instead, and pumped water to splash on his face and head.

Frowning, Gertrude studied him. "You fevering, old man?"

"Nah," he denied, but he wiped his forehead with the back of his hand and then used his palms to swipe down his dripping face. He wiped his hands on his overalls and staggered to the table.

"But you ain't been sleepin' worth sucked eggs." When he glared at her, she hurried on. "Now don't you go thinkin' I been spyin' on you, Heinz Nickleberg. How is a woman supposed to sleep through her man rollin' and tossin' on the bed beside her and then getting' up to roam the house like a wounded bear?"

He looked so stricken, that she reached to wipe the same egg she had just set into the carton.

"Heinz, sit down. Talk to me, please," she pleaded. "Something's been tearin' into you. Is there a problem about the farm?"

He sat, shaking his head; that frightened her more than if he had roared at her.

"Something you're not telling me. Is something wrong with our boys? Not the grandsons?"

"No," he exhaled and went quiet with his chin at his chest.

Her fingers drummed on the edge of the table. He stared at them, and she drew one hand within the other and laid them in her lap. But she had to go on. She had to know. "Heinz, it ain't somethin' wrong in you, is it? You seein' Doc Ricartsen for somethin' I don't know about? Tell me, please," she begged.

"I ain't seen Doc," he groused, then thought better of it. "Except..." he faltered.

"After that KKK meetin'? You come home drunk again in the wee hours this morning. What's eatin' into you, husband? Not knowin' is drivin' me into the ground."

"We men was just in a mood. We'd been talking about how that robber in the White House was thinkin' about runnin' yet again."

"Mr. Willkie deserves to be president. He's such a nice man. Stands so tall."

"Yeah, that's what we was sayin'."

"Who?"

"Just a couple of us. Owens. Ricartsen. Minnick. Somebody had a bottle."

"You drink in the church?" Her eyes went wide.

"No, no. After. At Owens' place."

"Doc, too? I thought he swore off after the Fourth of July and the sheriff needin' him and him half drunk. That resolution didn't last long. Hardly more'n a month."

"He just sipped. No more'n a taste. In fact, none of us really had much. It was just sorta like it loosened our tongues, and we griped. Lord knows, we've got enough to gripe about. But men ain't supposed to let loose like that 'less they're in their cups."

"Whether or not they truly are in their cups," she said, wondering. Her fingers picked up the rag. She began wiping and sorting again without being conscious that she'd started, stopped or started again. It was simply a task she'd done forever and would until the Good Lord gave her rest. But she frowned. "I guess," she mused, looking at this man who had shared her bed and her life these many years, "I guess maybe that's like a woman havin' a good cry. It makes things come so you can deal with them again. Is that so, Heinz? Does griping like that among you fellas make it so you can try to pick up and go on again? Huh?" The thought that men needed to get stuff off their hairy chests had never occurred to her before. *So, men are human, after all?*

He studied her without answering.

Tilting her head to one side, she looked at him, her fingers quiet. "Heinz, is there anything I can do to help?"

"Help?"

"I mean, if you want to tell me anything..."

"What would I tell you? What's ailin' you, woman?"

"Nothin'. Nothing. Never you mind." Gertrude withdrew the hand she had been reaching toward him and concentrated on the eggs.

Nickleberg sat staring at his hands for some time until, suddenly restless, he rose and shuffled to the wood stove to fill his mug with the coffee always warming at the back corner. Holding the hot mug by the body rather than the handle in his calloused hand, he brought it to his end of the table and reached to light the taper to candle the eggs. After a minute, he began hum-muttering a vague tune to himself.

"What's that song?" she asked gently, just wanting to know. "Seems familiar but I can't quite place it."

"Huh? What song?"

Rather than seem to accuse him, she lilted the melody in a sweet soprano. "...before I'd be a slave..."

"That's funny," he said, looking up, bleary eyes wide. "That tune's been runnin' through my own head. What is it?"

Without mentioning his hum-singing, she knitted her forehead trying to remember where she'd learned it. "A camp song? A lullaby, maybe?"

"Yeah, a lullaby. You used to sing it to our boys, didn'tcha?"

"Umm," she pondered, her fingers working automatically. "Not sure I did. But didn't your ma?"

"Sing that to our boys?"

"Seems to me…" Gertrude shook her head, unsure.

"Yeah, Ma. She used to sing it." He closed his eyes. "I do remember. I'd be half-awake in the night and whimper. Didn't dare cry or call out. Pa would'a beat me with his belt if I'd'a woke him. But Ma always heard, and she'd come up quiet-like and set on the edge of my bed. Draw the quilt up under my chin and stroke my hair up out'a my eyes. And when I'd quiet some, she'd sing that. Low. So low, I had to listen real close to hear her. And pretty soon, I was asleep again. Never heard her climb out'a the attic. But pretty soon it'd be morning and Pa at the bottom of the ladder, hollerin' it was time for us kids to get up and get to work. Chores to be done before breakfast."

Gertrude's eyes never left his face. It had been years since he'd spoken of his childhood, and never this tenderly. "It's a sweet melody, ain't it? Gets right inside a body," she whispered, humming it under her breath. The gentleness in his eyes as he glanced at her caused a stirring within her chest. "She loved you."

He looked at her with forehead creases easing and the corners of his mouth turning up. "Ma was gentle."

"He beat you a lot, didn't he, Heinz?"

His eyes closed.

Her question had been quiet and almost a statement. She knew the man had. That much information had come up again and again in their years together. Her right hand found its way to a dry area of her apron and wiped itself. It then stroked the scraggly hairs on his stubbled chin as she considered. "I'm sorry, love," she whispered. It had never been her intention to say that. It just came out, and, for a long minute he remained head lowered.

"All of us kids. Her, too," he muttered finally, fists tight. "Especially if she coddled us. Pa'd say, 'Life is tough and a boy's gotta be tough and strong if he's gonna make it.' She never answered back, but she never agreed with him, neither. Just mostly did what he told her and kept still."

Gert nodded. It was what women did because they couldn't do anything else.

But he didn't see her gesture. Something was heaving up from deep within him. "She never said a word for days after he took me to see that nigger lynched. Just held me night after night when I woke up scared."

"Took you to see...? How old were you?"

"Not so big. I don't remember exactly. I know he'd been trying to teach me to milk the cow, but my hands were too little to reach all the way 'round the teat, so I wasn't no good at it. Or maybe that was Elmer, next younger'n me. But we had to go 'n' see. Pa said so right to our faces," Nickleberg continued with force. "A man's gotta learn from the beginning that niggers can't be let get away with what they do. If you give 'em half a yard, they're all over our women. Gotta protect white women. A man's duty-bound to protect his females from such-like."

She frowned but looked down quickly when she saw the anger grow within him. "Yes," she said, to keep him from turning on her. "I'll get these finished. Why don't you go lie down for a bit until supper's ready? We've got a good start on tomorrow's order."

He rose, towering over her, startling when she cowered. For a moment, she was afraid, but this time he reacted with what seemed to be sorrow. "Lie down, yeah," he mumbled. He turned back to look at her quizzically before he shuffled to the bedroom door. "Don't hurry supper none," he added as he closed the door behind him.

"It's kept all this time; it'll keep 'til whenever you're ready," she promised, holding her breath until she heard him crawling into their bed. He was snoring before she could exhale. "Lordy, lordy, something's got him bad. He ain't himself," she muttered as she laid her head on her arms on the table. *But I wish it was. Himself. He ain't been this tender for how long.*

Chapter 8

"It's funny," Garum whispered to Todd Paisler that evening as neighborhood children gathered at Minnicks' in hope that Miz Nandria would bring her baby daughter out to read aloud to her. But he wasn't smiling, Todd saw.

"Funny?"

"I mean," the small ebony black boy lowered his voice and his chin even more, "I mean I never could look at Frog without tears comin' to my eyes, he was so crippled up. But now that he's gone with them carnival men, I..." His squeaky words trailed off.

"But now you wish he was here—to talk to him," the fifth of the Paislers' eight sons prompted. "What about, Garum? Something one of the rest of us could help with? Or mebbe Miz Nandria? Frog used to talk with her a lot."

"Oh, no!" Garum shied as though kicked.

The Paisler family training stifled the laugh that came to Todd's throat. This small boy was frightened. He didn't deserve to be humiliated by being laughed at. Swallowing, Todd inhaled to compose himself before speaking. He looked around at the passel of area kids gathering in scattered clumps near the Minnick barn and chicken coop, hoping to see Mr. Minnick's daughter-in-law soon. They'd loved the adventures of Peter Pan and the pirates. Even the boys had secretly liked Tinker Bell, although they had teased each other and laughed at the little kids about her. Still, when asked to clap to save her life, many had closed their hands together. Todd hadn't been watching Garum, but, somehow, he knew without question that this wide-eyed son of a fieldhand had clapped aloud.

Todd looked at each neighbor child, white and dark, and couldn't think of who would be a safe one little Garum could speak to. He squirmed. Whatever it was, Garum was afraid. Todd really didn't want to be the one to know. Sometimes being among the tallest if not the oldest in the group was a real pain. But he couldn't just walk away. He was opening his mouth to invite Garum's confidence when a murmur went up throughout the yard. Miz Nandria and her baby Rose were at the porch door. Todd was as anxious as the others to find out what adventure was going to be read to them next.

Miz Nandria handed what had looked like a thick slab of wood to Zelma Bratton in order to seat herself on the elm swing with little Rose on her lap.

"That ain't no book," Garum muttered, disappointed. "Ain't she gonna read to us?"

"Looks like the slate Ma uses to teach us Bible verses when we can't get to church come big snows in the winter," Todd answered low. He shook his head.

When Nandria was settled comfortably, Zelma handed back the slate. Nandria nodded thanks and smiled out at the half-hidden children. "Good evening, neighbors. Would you mind coming in a bit closer as my throat is somewhat dry this evening for me to try to sing loud enough for you all to hear?"

"You gonna sing, Miz Nandria?"

"My ma sings to us some nights when she ain't too tired."

"My ma only knows hymns."

"My sister went to a revival meetin' and tried to learn me some of the camp songs she learnt, but she says I can't carry a tune in an oaken bucket." As the other kids laughed and poked each other, they gathered in a rough semi-circle in front of the swing. Grinning up at their teacher, they joined Zelma singing their A B C song. Small chests puffed up with pride at Miz Nandria's growing smile of warm approval. They looked up as Greg Paisler came to the door of the back porch, but Nandria did not seem to have heard him behind her.

"Now that so many of you are doing well with your letters, I thought you might be interested in learning to read music." Nandria stopped at the total lack of comprehension on the faces staring up at her. Even Todd Paisler appeared baffled. She gazed at him, and he blushed and looked down.

"Master Paisler, forgive me for singling you out, but could you explain to me why you appear so puzzled?"

Exhaling, Todd lifted his chin, blinked at his brother in the doorway and shook his head. "I – I'm sorry, Miz Nandria, but I don't have any idea what you mean about 'reading' music. You listen to music. But, well, 'reading' makes it sound like it's got an alphabet, too, or somethin'."

"And so it does, Master Paisler. Music does have an alphabet, or something very like an alphabet and letters, only we call it staff and notes."

The children stared as she lifted the slate and turned it to draw lines. But her movements were awkward around little Rose, who was growing annoyed with her mother reaching around and against her.

"Let me, Miz Minnick," Greg murmured, reaching for the lovely ten-month-old.

Startled, Nandria cried, "Oh!" But seeing who was reaching for her little one, she smiled and allowed him to take Rose into his arms.

"Hope you don't mind, but I think I'd like to learn to read music, too," Greg grinned and looked out at the gathered children to encourage them to tell their teacher 'Yes.'

The muttered approval of such a plan intensified as the kids scrambled even closer around Nandria's swing. Todd grinned at Garum, who had crept forward until he was almost on top of his teacher's narrow left foot. Todd looked up at his older brother. Here was the answer to Garum's problem of someone to talk to. Greg would listen to that little colored boy as intently as he'd always listened to Todd.

But it was Miz Nandria who invited Garum to wait after the others had gone. "Master Tacker, forgive me if I am speaking out of turn, but this evening you have seemed troubled. May I inquire if there is anything Rose and I might help you to work through?"

The dark boy looked away, but then, clenching his fists in decision, gazed up at his teacher. "I gots me a job," he said.

"A job? Is it a good job? Are you happy with the work and the pay?"

"Well, no pay yet, but could be. And the work is fine. We got chickens, too, so most of what I'll do I already know how. Except for the head-chopping." He shuddered but quickly gathered himself to talk about the real point. "Only, it's what Pa's told me over and over." He stopped again, his face radiating his guilt that he was disobeying his father's word.

"Your father is...?"

"Oh, I forgot. You never knowed him, have you? Dolph. Dolph Tacker. Best worker around these parts. Even Mrs. Owens at the store says so. Pa does stuff for them lots of times."

"So, your father works for people in the community as well as I assume you are working for someone in Boonetown?"

"Oh, it's okay to work for them. But it's the missus. She don't..." Garum stopped again. How could he say what he'd heard and what he was pretty sure was happening to her? Miz Nandria frowned, puzzled, but her eyes showed such concern that the boy exclaimed, "I ain't supposed to get mixed up in what's happening to white folks, no how. Do the work and walk away, that's what Pa tells me."

Nandria started to ask what was happening and to whom, but the child's concern was about disobeying his father. Any other question she might ask would feel to him like a demand that he betray someone. Instead, she shifted irritable Rose against her aching shoulder to stroke her back. "I have not as yet met your father, Garum. But I have heard Mrs. Owens mention his name with respect. He has the reputation of being a man of integrity. Every fine man must work within the truth of what he believes."

"I ought'a do like he says, huh?"

She nodded and turned her attention to try to soothe her tired and fussy little daughter. The boy stepped away to let her take the baby into the house. Sliding his hands deep into his pockets, he turned to shuffle down the Minnicks' long lane toward where he'd left his bike.

"Miz Nandria's right," he told himself as he kicked a large clod of dirt into a scattering of dust, "and Pa's right. But that scream. How can I just do nothin'?"

Heinz woke cursing aloud through his hangover.

Gertrude rose from her chair, set her crochet work carefully in the far drawer where it would be safe and, eyes down, shuffled to the outside door. In the darkness she stretched her arms high, shaking an accusing finger up at the cloudless sky. "I can't do nothin'. But You could!" she whispered, then crouched and drew her shawl tight around her. Trembling, she moaned apology. "I know. I know it ain't up to me. Thy will. Only..." A single tear slid down her cheek. "Sorry. I'm so tired, Lord. I'll go sleep in the barn. Won't be the first time."

Inside the house, Heinz roared her name, growing angrier each time she did not answer. He staggered to the kitchen. "Well, all right then, you she-ass Molly!" he yelled as he clung to the doorframe to stay upright. "Gert! Gertie gal, where are you?" he whined, but that ended in a cough that doubled him. Heinz staggered to the nearest chair and plopped down. Rolling to splay his legs to ease their ache, he shifted his rump so he could lay his neck on the chair back edge and closed his eyes from seeing, again, the water mark on the ceiling.

"Gertie gal," he whispered with such longing that she would have run to his side if she had heard. "Ah, Gert, don't let me fall asleep unless I can truly sleep. I can't face that mewlin' pickaninny again. I can't. I didn't do nothin'. God, I swear it! Pa said it hadda be done. Pertec' our women. Keep Ma' an'all arwhitewomensaf safe fr..."

Head lolling on his neck rolling back and forth on the edge of the back of the chair, Heinz fell into nightmares. His thrashing pitched him to the floor.

His screams brought her where his whispers had not. Startling upright from the straw cot, she gathered her shawl around her and ran to the house.

"Heinz!"

She dropped to the kitchen floor and gathered his shoulders and head onto her lap, holding him and rocking, rocking and crooning, until he awoke. "Oh, my darling, what...?"

But he woke up frightened and angry. As was so often the case lately, Gertrude was the nearest target.

Chapter 9

Thursday, August 15, 1940

Early enough that the sun was only barely peeking through to the blue-peeling doghouse, Grover Minnick tapped his spoon to his mug without looking up. Nandria lifted tired eyes to glance over.

"I'll get it," Greg Paisler called as he rose and reached for the coffee carafe to refill his boss's mug. "Good flapjacks, Miz Nandria. So fluffy I had to fork them up quick before they floated away."

Giggling, Doris lifted her half-eaten pancake on her fork and twirled it in the air. "Float away," she called in a little girl's voice.

Minnick looked at his beloved, bewildered wife, swore under his breath and concentrated on spooning sugar into his coffee. Bodie twisted to help Nandria.

"Let me finish feeding the princess for ya, Miz Nandria. She's done pretty good with her pancakes, but mebbe I can get her to finish off her oatmeal, too. Them peach and apple bits sure make it go down happy for me. Rose, too, I reckon. You just take your time and see if you don't like the porridge that way yourself." She looked so tired. And gaunt. She hadn't been eating, or at least she hadn't been able to keep down what she did nibble on. The handyman was worried.

"Thank you, Bodie," Nandria said low. Instead of lifting her fork to eat, however, Nandria rose heavily to begin gathering dirty dishes to carry them to the sink crowded with skillets and pans.

Blinking, Bodie continued lifting the spoon to the little one's mouth as she sat in her highchair. He said nothing. Will's wife had to know for herself what would settle in her stomach. Many times, she had said nothing about what he was up to out of respect for him as an adult. It was his turn to give her that kind of respect now.

"Your family had much of anything to do with the Nicklebergs lately, Paisler?" Minnick asked.

"Nicklebergs?" Greg questioned. He stopped stacking dirty platters in front of him and turned to look at Mr. Minnick. "Well, no, I don't think so. Nothin' more than usual, anyway. Is there something wrong, sir? Somethin' Ma'll want to know about to see if she can help?"

Doris looked at her husband curiously. Turning to shield his gesture from his wife, Minnick mimicked someone lifting a glass to his mouth to drink.

"Booze," Doris exclaimed in a disgusted tone. "That Heinz Nickleberg can't hold his liquor worth a bean and a half. You know he used to beat her, Gertrude, I mean. Whenever he got drunk it was her fault."

The men at the table stared. Minnick, Bodie, nor Greg Paisler had known.

"How was it her fault?" Greg wondered.

"She'd hold him down and pour the stuff down his throat," Bodie scoffed.

"Not more'n once," Minnick sneered. "He'd put a stop to that."

"Like she done after the first few times when they was young," Doris chirped. "When she hadn't learned yet a woman ain't got to put up with that stuff."

"Mrs. Nickleberg put a stop to that, Mrs. Minnick?" Greg asked. "How could she do that?"

"Gertrude had the poultry knife in her hand when he come after her, that's how."

"She cut him?" Minnick bellowed.

"Told me she reached out without thinking," Doris explained. "She done sliced off half his beard and left an oozy little red line across his throat. Surprised her as much as him, but he never come at her again, even staggerin' drunk he never."

Even in the gray light of early morning, the paint on the door to Dr. Ricartsen's old house-turned-clinic showed that it had been rubbed raw around and below the knob. Nickleberg frowned as he reached around his wife's shoulder to open it. It made him mad when people in Boonetown with everything going for them and nothing to do couldn't even keep up with their places.

"Come on, woman," he growled at Gertrude as she limped up the step to the landing. "Don' know how ya goddus here, but I guess you mus'a wandded to see Rissers'n. So, go on in, will ya?"

"Knock first," she snarled through swollen lips. Her half-closed eyes glinted at him with hate.

Shaken, Nickleberg reacted with sarcastic anger. "Knock? N'body knocks at Doc's door. Sadie Bean says she's busy a'times and can' take the time t'le' folks in. You know tha'."

"Knock," she demanded. "I want Miz Bean and the doc and anybody else that's in there to see me first while I'm still outside."

"Why?" Heinz's eyes narrowed in suspicion.

"Because," she hissed, "it's in you to say later that I just come with a cold and that Doc and his nurse done this to me."

He raised his fist, but Gertrude slid the butcher knife out of her sling and met him fiery eye to blurry eye. It was then that the door opened from the inside. Huge Sadie Bean stood peering at their confrontation.

"What...?"

Gertrude slid her knife out of sight. "Who's inside? Have Doc Ricartsen come here."

Without the questions Heinz expected, Sadie twisted to call over her shoulder for Doc to come. At the command in her tone, Ricartsen hurried to his front door wiping his arms and hands of gore that made Nickleberg retch as fresh, red blood would not have.

"What? Great galoshes, woman, what happened to you?" He flung his towel at Sadie and, ignoring the man's growls, brushed past Nickleberg to examine what he could see of Gertrude's injuries.

Sadie caught the towel and twisted again to call to Mr. House, who was already stepping gingerly to the side of the entryway to see what was going on. Usually at this point, Mr. House would be complaining that this emergency would mean another delay in the doctor seeing to his boils. But he, too, was fascinated with witnessing for himself what would become, no doubt, the gossip of the day.

"I tried ta fix'r up," Nickleberg slurred as Sadie and Doc's ministrations forced him off the porch stoop.

Satisfied that Mr. House was seeing everything, as she'd surmised Mrs. Nickleberg had wished, Sadie started easing the woman inside the clinic. "What happened?" the nurse demanded.

Nickleberg responded with a whine. "She lef' shoes on th' table. I seen 'em. That's wha' happened. It's sheer evil luck ta leave a pair shooos on a taboon."

Even Doc looked up from his scrutiny of the swelling around Gertrude's eyes.

"A pair of shoes left on a table led you to do this?" Sadie exclaimed, turning on him. "What in the world possesses you, man?"

Ron Bean was far stronger than his jockey-sized body would lead someone to expect. When he'd showered under the backyard hose after his morning milk delivery, he carried his half of the sheriff's weight with his wife to Doc's house. Both Ron and Sadie pretended that Yakes was doing well on his own, but Yakes knew better. Cussing himself for still being so weak, the sheriff could blame at least part of his pique on the gut blows the egg man had given him. And here the drunken fool was at it again, punching and hurting, this time his wife, evidently.

Ella Mae Drangler hurried ahead of them to lean in to open the clinic's front door. Doc stepped from his office and took Sadie's place hustling Yakes in to sit at his desk. He nodded to his nurse and the others to step out to give the sheriff a few minutes breather. Sadie went quickly to check on Gertrude. Ron strode to the kitchen at the back of the house to pour himself the cup of coffee he'd skipped to help her bring Yakes. Ella Mae left to wait in the lobby only when Ricartsen shooed her out his door. He turned then on the sheriff.

"You gonna tell me outright now why you took a turn for the worse yesterday? Why did Nickleberg slug you, Yakes?" Doc demanded. Stethoscope out, he loomed over him. "What did he hit you with?"

Straightening as he could, the sheriff looked up. "His fists. Because he was drunk and loud in the middle of the night, and this is my town. I wouldn't stand for it."

Setting the cold stethoscope on warm skin beneath the man's shirt, Ricartsen nodded before listening. "He's a mean drunk."

Yakes knew better than to answer until Doc had risen to full, gangly height again. "He's a mean drunk and don't tolerate being told 'no' even when he's sober. Which hasn't been a lot lately. What's with him, do you know?"

Ricartsen pocketed the stethoscope and reached to palpate the sheriff's middle. It hurt, but not as bad as it had yesterday even without someone pressing on it. "Any blood? Black, tarry..."

"No!" Yakes snapped, not liking to be questioned about such things. "So, tell me about the woman."

Teeth gritted, Ricartsen nearly spoke in anger, but closed his eyes, weary. "Sorry, Sheriff. This whole thing grates me. And being up all night with somebody else and then, just as I was getting into sleep at near dawn, first House with his butt boils and then..."

"Yeah." He knew. Nothing more needed to be said about that. "So, he brought her in like this a day or so ago, too."

"Well, that's funny. Something maybe you better ask Mrs. Nickle about because I couldn't make much sense of it the way they were going on."

"Huh?" Yakes looked at him, confused.

Ricartsen wiped his hand over weary eyes. "I mean, I couldn't see how Nickleberg was with us enough to bring her anywhere. And Mrs. Nickle was barely conscious. She couldn't'a driven that crazy car of theirs."

"Meaning, you think somebody else brought them into town? Who?"

"I didn't see anybody. Come to think of it, I don't remember even seeing that odd car." Doc shrugged. "Anyway, it wasn't what mattered to me at the time. Her injuries—Lordy, but he beat her like I'd like to take care of that guy across the pond with the little mustache and even less humanity." He leaned back so hard into his chair that he shoved it with a bang into the wall.

Yakes suppressed a smile. He'd seen that happen before, and he'd even listened through the closed door when Mrs. Bean had found fresh damage to that long-suffering wall. But it wasn't funny. None of it. "So, about Gertrude. Will she live?"

"Most any other woman, maybe 50 – 50 chance. With Mrs. Nickle, feisty as she is, I'd say, yeah, probably. Though why she'd want to and go back to him, I don't understand. Don't she have family somewhere she could go live with?"

"Sons. Two. Both married, and I'd bet either one would be glad to take her in." Yakes sighed. "She ready to press charges so I can put our friend in jail and keep him there a while? Say, where is he? I didn't think to ask Ron Bean." Such a total lapse in procedural thinking scared him. It proved he was nowhere near competent yet. That was hard to admit.

"Sleeping it off in a cell. Ron and Sadie Bean are, shall we say, 'persuasive'?" Ricartsen looked up at a quiet knock at his office door. "Yeah?"

Sadie Bean leaned in. "Mrs. N. is awake if you want the sheriff to talk to her."

"Yeah!" the two men chorused in unison.

Gertrude would not admit her husband had beaten her, would not press charges against him and had no idea how she'd ended up on the doctor's doorstep.

Chapter 10

Later that morning, the tiny seamstress reached to open her low front door for Nandria. "Got Doris Minnick settled at Doc's, did you? How's she doin' this morning?"

Nandria, with a wan, greenish part-smile, bent with Rose to enter. "Dr. Ricartsen had requested that I bring Mother Minnick back this morning for reexamination. Oh, your home smells good. You have been baking."

"Sheriff Yakes so likes your recipe for scones, and I wanted to feed him good before he went on back to his office. I hope you'll let me feed you and little Rose, too. You can give me tips you might have to make 'em more like yours." Ella Mae rose full short height as she saw Nandria's nauseated reaction to the thought of tasting anything. "Oh, not that I'd want you to try them now. I'll wrap them in a tea towel – you won't need to bring it back. I make a lot of them all the time with leftover scraps. But then again, you are welcome to bring it back if you want to. My door is always open for you to bend down and enter." She laughed as Nandria was slowly lifting herself erect.

Nandria's lips curled up at their green corners. Her dark brows lifted as she looked to the chair where the sheriff had spent many waking, healing hours.

"Mrs. Bean sent me here while they check over Mother Minnick. They do not seem to wish to have others gathered there for now. Someone appears to have been hurt in the night. I hope you do not mind..."

"Of course, I don't. It's a pleasure, especially when you've got the little one here," Ella Mae assured her as she bustled to clear the sheriff's Kansas City News from the arm of the low divan for Nandria to sit with Rose. "I tried to tell him it was too soon to go to work, but you know how men are."

The beginning of a real smile broadened a little on Nandria's face. "Yes," she whispered, "I know."

Ella Mae peered into her visitor's expression. "Your Will is a very special person. But you've known other men. Oh, not like that. I mean, you've travelled with your father to countries I ain't even heard the names of. You know things, Nandria Minnick. You're a woman to be admired."

Sighing, Nandria repositioned her little girl on her lap and smiled at her with sadness.

"Not likely you'll get the admiration you deserve here in our county," Ella Mae said. "Nor this little Rose, neither. We was too beaten down by that horrible depression. Still ain't many with two dimes to rub together. Men out of work, couldn't support their families. Babies weepin' for lack of milk and poor young mommas so starved for nourishment, their own bodies give up on being able to breast feed their young'uns. It was awful here. And we seem to need somebody to blame. Was it that bad where you've been?"

"It was devastating for so many," Nandria whispered, remembering.

"And them it weren't so bad for, they closed their eyes and didn't care to see, did they?"

"The way of the world, Mrs. Drangler." Tears glistening, Nandria again focused on her child. "The Great Depression, it is being called, and it made so many suffer all over the globe."

"Well, praise the Lord, it's easin' some here in our cities, thanks to Mr. Roosevelt, though most around here won't give him any credit. But that easin' ain't really hit in the countryside much yet," Mrs. Drangler gossiped non-stop as she folded, smoothed and re-folded bolts of textured cloth and stored them on the cedar chest in the corner of her low front room. She clucked her tongue, making Rose stare. "Hope, if you dare to. But don't go buying stuff you really want. Only what you can't no longer do without. That's what banker Freshstalk advises. He ain't givin' out many loans yet. Tried his level best to carry folks through. Even helping as much as he could about our taxes. I guess that's why he's still with us here in Boonetown instead of being transferred to Kansas City or St. Louis. Them big banker folk must not like his branch not being real profitable yet. Greed sure don't care about hurtin' people, does it?" Setting an ornate, white silk blouse over her arm, Ella Mae seated herself on her short-legged chair to work at finishing touches.

"It is the Freshstalk daughter for whom you are creating the trousseau, is it not?" Nandria asked. "I have had little to do with their family, I am afraid. So day-to-day busy at my husband's family's farm."

"Workin' you like a mule, ain't they?"

Nandria's eyes widened. "A mule," she sighed. "Perhaps so, but is that not what is required? Both Mr. and Mrs. Minnick have and continue to labor to that extent."

"They're good, hard-working folks, all right. But it's their farm, not yours. I ain't sure Doris even knows that you're her daughter-in-law. She uses you like a maid and cook and laundry gal. And you don't seem to do nothin' about that."

"What, exactly, might I 'do about it'? I am a woman in a male-dominated society. What her husband decides I am worth, Mrs. Minnick is bound to agree, especially as she is so ill."

"You could leave."

"Ah," Nandria sighed and looked down at her calloused hands. "Leave."

"And you'd find a good place to go. You with your college degree and your connections with some of the best people in your England and probably a lot of other countries. But," Ella Mae tilted her head, realizing finally why Nandria stayed despite the hard work and humiliation, "your mother-in-law—the woman your husband loves—is ill. How can you leave her uncared for? Ah, so that's it." She closed those navy-blue eyes and shook her head, realizing only Willard could set his wife free from the burden she had taken on in love.

Ella Mae folded the final bolt of material but looked up at Nandria's intake of breath. Smiling, she carried the emerald-green cloth nearer for Nandria to examine. "You like this?"

"It is such a rich color," Nandria exclaimed. Her dark eyes shone with her longing for the renewing of such beauty as she stroked the texture of the cloth. She sighed, then peered over at her hostess, smiling bleakly. "Perhaps, when Mrs. Minnick is well..."

"If she ever gets well. But even what she used to be, so I'm told, you think she'll ever see past that dark skin of yours and accept you as Will's wife?"

"Mother Minnick is a product of her upbringing. As are we all until we have experienced enough of the world to grow beyond those limitations."

"So, you don't resent her?"

"She is my husband's beloved mother. If she sees me as a mule, I..."

"No, no, not that you look like one," Ella Mae protested. "Far, far from it. I ain't never seen a more beautiful darky."

Nandria went still.

"Now, don't you go getting' stiff and hurt on me. I meant what I said. You are. A darky. And you are an igmouse—ain't that the word you said to us once? An igmouse?"

Cocking her head in concentration, Nandria finally broke into a smile. "An enigma? A mystery? Something which is difficult to analyze and understand?"

"Yeah," Ella Mae laughed with her. "That mouse. But you are, don't you see? All you people are supposed to know your place, lower than any white man, woman or child. But here you are far above all of us. Educated, sophristicated, courageous, world-travelled, smart as a whip, used to the best."

Nandria's dark brows scrunched. "Hardly all that."

"Oh, yes, all of it. Every bit and probably a lot more you don't let us know about for fear it'd sound like you was braggin'." The tiny seamstress leaned forward, setting her collar pins ablaze in the reflected light from the narrow windows beside the front door. "Listen, Miz Nandria – and I ain't never called a colored woman 'Miz' unless it was with her last name as a matter of courtesy, at church, say – you are a 'nigma for us. But that's too close to the 'N' word we call darkies here to humiliate 'em."

"Nor is it a favorite word of mine," Nandria murmured.

"We do a lot of that. Humiliating." Ella Mae sat back deep into her chair. "Even Piermont Yakes, and he's one of the fairest men I've ever met. Ornery, stubborn, but fair."

"It is a primary reason for your devotion to him, is it not?" Smiling, though her upset stomach gurgled at the movement, Nandria cuddled little Rose against her as the baby lunged to grab up a pincushion on the sofa arm.

Jumping up to hand the child a sock puppet from her sewing basket, Ella Mae laughed. "Me? Devoted to Piermont? Hmmm, I guess it must seem like that, what with his being here to recover himself after that surgery. You are skilled there, too. Doc said so hisself."

"Experience gained of necessity."

"Huh?"

"I voyaged to Canada from my England via a Canadian hospital ship."

"On your way here to Missouri?"

"My husband was to head the defense team assigned to the ship as we journeyed to show his parents their grandchild. I suppose that was as a favor to him for something he had done to aid the Canadians. I truly do not know what Willard does or for whom. His missions are always secret; he gives me no clue and does not wish to talk about them. Europe is in a chaotic turmoil of killing such that Americans seem to know nothing about. I suppose it is due to the fact that you have not had wars on your continent such as we have had in Europe. We know the devastating results of wars that use our cities and towns as battle ground."

"Oh, we've had wars burn down our homes, too. Indians, when we first settled. And the war between our states. That was a nasty one. Tore families apart, killing each other. Don't seem to've got over it still, if you ask me. Somebody sticks a little Rebel flag in their hat, and you should see the darkies go pale, or mad. I watch. A lot of people don't, but I watch. Some—the young men in particular—some of them look like they could tear that guy limb from limb. But, of course, they don't."

"Can you blame them for their reaction?"

Ella Mae Drangler scooted forward until her feet nearly touched the floor. "I try, hard, not to blame nobody for nothing. Learned there's so many things go into whatever brought that particular reaction at the particular time to that particular person. Nothing's simple enough for me to know enough to blame. Oh, but we're gettin' deep, ain't we? I didn't mean to. Sorry. I just wanted you to taste test my new batch of scones, but I can wrap 'em up for you to take home. See if they tickle dear Doris's fancy. And, speaking of Miz Minnick, I think I see Sadie Bean leading her over here now."

"Oh," Nandria groaned.

"Why, girl, you're worn plumb out." Mrs. Drangler rose to her small feet. "Doris is more'n a handful and, with you being sickly with a new babe growing and taking care of little Rose here and them at the farm, you're plain tuckered out. Why don't I see if I can find someone to take charge of the missus for a bit and let you lie down?"

Nandria's pleading dark eyes were confirmation that Will's wife would be highly appreciative of such respite.

"Now, who?" Ella Mae's thin lips puckered, and her high forehead furrowed as she thought and walked to her door. "Me, of course," she whispered, laughing, as she opened it to invite Sadie and Doris in. "Who else?"

Declining to bend far enough to enter, Sadie crouched far enough to talk into Ella Mae's ear. "Things're gettin' real busy..."

"Mrs. Nickleberg? Doin' okay? And Piermont? You can tell your doc I was plumb put out that he wouldn't let me stay."

"Well, I...," Sadie started to explain but really had nothing she could say. She changed the subject. "I phoned the Paislers to have Greg sent in to help the sheriff. Meantime, my Ron is minding you-know-who." Sadie sighed, her eyes weary and unsure.

"Oh, yeah, of course. Just let me invite my friend in here for a bit," Ella Mae said aloud. "And we thank you, Mrs. Bean. Wish you could stop here a while and taste my new trial of scones, but we understand. Why don't you take a few back with you for you and the doc?"

But, with a relieved touch on Doris Minnick's arm as a farewell, the huge nurse turned to hurry back to Ricartsen's clinic.

Ron Bean leaned over the disgruntled egg farmer sitting on the cell cot peering at the food on the tray Ron had handed him.

"Soup's cold," Nickleberg groused. "And how'm I supposed to get that there butter to melt into it when the biscuit's even colder? And eggs is s'posed to be hard boiled through but this one's got a runny spot deep inside. Prb'ly one o' mine so that

Isaac Owens won' hafta pay me for it. And there ain't no sugar in that slop you called coffee."

"Sorry," Ron muttered, but he wasn't. "Isaac Owens meant to bring it right over, but he got busy with a customer's order. I'll look and see if the sheriff's got some sugar stashed in a drawer somewhere."

"Yeah, yeah. So, how long you gonna keep me in this here jail cell? You got no business..."

"We're waitin' to see how your missus is comin' along."

"Wha's tha' got to do with me bein' locked up? Wha's wrong with her?"

"You don't remember?"

"Remember wha'?"

Shaking his head, Ron reached to take back the tray, but Nickleberg growled and held on.

"Okay, okay. Listen, why don't you just finish this and relax for a while until the sheriff can come so you can talk it all over? It's been a beautiful hot, clear day. Good for just setting a spell while you have time, for a change."

"No sign of rain again, I bet." Nickleberg grimaced as he took another bite of the biscuit he'd disparaged, cold as it was.

Ron pursed his lips and counted to ten before answering. "I didn't see any."

"This here biscuit weighs a ton."

"Mrs. Owens offered to make up something for you to eat. She's one nice lady, always doin' something more'n she needs to for someone."

"Busybody. Meddlin' busybody. Tha's what she is," Nickleberg grumbled. "Jus' like my woman."

Ron walked away to keep from socking the man in his big nose. Closing the cell door, he reached to turn the key and then remembered that the sheriff had told him only to pretend to. "I guess some women are pretty remarkable. The condition your woman was in, all Boonetown's wondering how she got you into town in the first place. You didn't seem to be in any condition to drive." He turned and walked out before Nickleberg, mouth stuffed, could comment.

Chapter 11

Nandria heard them giggling—Mother Minnick and Mrs. Drangler. It was a pleasant way to awaken after a nap of who knew how long on Ella Mae's sofa. Reaching for little Rose, Nandria gasped until she realized she could hear the baby laughing with the women in the kitchen. Sighing, Nandria closed her eyes in a quick prayer for Will. Carefully, she rose to join them at the round kitchen table. Doris had been having such a good time, that it took some persuasion for Nandria to get her mother-in-law to come out to the Minnick truck to ride back to the farm.

Even jockey-sized Ron Bean bent a little at the threshold of Mrs. Drangler's low-ceilinged home.

"Hello, Mr. Bean," the diminutive seamstress smiled. "Come on in. Welcome."

Behind her husband, Sadie Bean ducked nearly in two to enter and, risking as upright as she could manage, nearly filled the confined space.

"Mrs. Bean, you are most welcome. Please, come in and have a seat," Mrs. Drangler murmured to her huge friend with an apologetic smile for the necessary discomfort. "But our sheriff's asked you two to get him up and going after his lunch and nap, hasn't he? I understand. Here, Piermont, let me take that knee cover out of your way."

Sheriff Yakes frowned at her fussing as Ron Bean maneuvered to be near him in a position of leverage to help him rise.

"There we go. Feels good to stretch a bit, don't it, Sheriff?"

"It does, Bean. That it does," Yakes answered. "And a bit of sunshine and fresh air'll make it even better." With Ron close to support him, he stood nearly upright and shuffled from the easy chair toward the front door. How Sadie managed to stay out of his way was an unexpected bit of dexterity, but the sheriff was soon leaning against the outside wall. His face was red; he panted a bit, then visibly settled himself from shoulders to knees.

Mrs. Drangler bustled out after him. Seeing his determination to do this on his own, she chose to shut her mouth and say nothing. Smiling in the doorway that surrounded her like a picture frame, she radiated her pride in the man.

"Ready to go back in and sit down?" Ron asked, arm extended to support the sheriff when he turned.

"Ain't goin' back in. I've got work to catch up on. With a little help, I'm goin' back to my office. I can sit there. Lord knows I've set there enough hours till now, I guess a few more today won't hurt me none."

Ella Mae Drangler gasped, and Yakes turned to look at her. "Wh—whatever you think," she managed, but clearly, she was not in favor of the reinjured surgical patient pushing so hard. Still, knowing he was determined, she managed a smile. "You go ahead. I'll bring over a scone and fresh squeezed orange juice in a bit."

"More'n three minutes, I hope," the sheriff grumbled, but there was a gentleness to it that deepened her smile. "Or, better still, ten."

"Four, anyway," she laughed and watched Ron Bean walk beside this ornery man she'd grown so fond of across and down the street to the sheriff's office. "Or three and a half," she mumbled, stepping back into Sadie Bean looming behind her. "Oh! Sorry, Mrs. Bean."

"Would you mind if we step outside for a bit?" Sadie suggested as she hurried to duck past the tiny seamstress.

"I plumb forgot you were in there. Sorry. I know you're busy and need to get back to Doc Ricartsen's, so I won't keep you unless you'd like one of my fresh-made scones. That Nandria Minnick gave me her recipe and…"

"I'd like nothing better, but…" Sadie patted her broad hips as she stepped outside and straightened with a sigh of relief. "You've been kind and generous to take care of the sheriff. Got him on his feet much earlier than any of us expected. Gut surgery is hard on a man."

"It was you and your Ron who were generous to come to help him move. He's a proud being and would have cussed himself as an invalid if he'd had to depend on me. Though I wasn't expecting him to go to work twice this day. Men!"

Sadie laughed. "A-men to that!"

Nickleberg snuffed at the aroma of the covered tray Mrs. Drangler was bringing into the sheriff's office. It was closer to seven than the four minutes she had joked about. She'd tried to wait but couldn't make it to the ten Yakes had asked for.

"Whatcha got there, little seamstress? You good in the kitchen as you are with a needle?" the egg man called from his cell.

"Scones, Mr. Nickleberg," she laughed, setting the tray on her Piermont's desk. "For Mr. Yakes, but don't worry, I've got some for you, too. May I take them back to him?" she asked, turning to look at the sheriff. She frowned in growing concern as she gathered two scones from the cloth bag and set them on a small plate. "And some coffee?"

Yakes' nod was the best he could do, and she knew it. His returning to his office this afternoon had been a mistake. She had been sure it would be, but he had to decide for himself. Without comment, she stepped through the open door to carry the treat back to the cells.

"Sober now, are you, Mr. Nickleberg?"

He snarled, but she stood facing him—eyes alert and knowing—unafraid. He looked down to concentrate on the warm scones. "Sugar in the coffee," he muttered after a taste. "Thanks. That Ron Bean didn't remember this morning."

"And your wife was in no condition to remind him," she pointed out.

He looked down again, this time ashamed. "How is she?"

"Your wife? Bruised. Battered. Hurting. As expected from the way you treated her. When are you gonna stop your drinking, Heinz? Gert deserves better from you."

"She does," he slobbered into his coffee. He peered at the little woman with a pleading expression that would have moved her if she hadn't seen it before. Without another word, she turned to walk away, shutting behind her the door between the cell block and the office. Taking a moment to straighten her skirt and swallow her anger, Ella Mae stepped over to drag up the chair from across the desk to sit close beside the sheriff.

"I stopped to talk with Mrs. Bean. The doctor woke up a while ago and looked over Mrs. Nickleberg, who is demanding to be let go so she could tend to her chickens."

"Doc's gonna let her go home? How can I send her with that man of hers?"

"You don't want to."

"No, I sure don't, but unless she presses charges, I've got no right to hold him. He's pretty well slept off his drunk."

"But he'll do it again—drink and take out whatever's ailin' him on her."

The sheriff picked up a scone, bit into it, and set it on the desk where it surrounded itself with a scattering of light flakes.

"I know it. You know it. And I'd be willing to bet even Gertrude Nickleberg knows it," Ella Mae cried. "But she won't be the cause of him staying in jail, will she?"

Only the sheriff's jaw moved as he thoroughly chewed his scone a moment before answering. "I've talked and talked to her these last couple of months, but..." He lifted his hands palm up, and she saw the pain that caused him and the sweat glistened along his hairline. Leaning toward him, Ella Mae patted his arm.

"It's her choice. Nothin' you nor me nor Doc nor anybody else can do. I'm gonna ask Ron Bean to help you back home to my place and then set here with the man. For once, Piermont Yakes, don't ask me not to line up what's right to do. You know it is."

When he didn't answer, she rose to walk up and around the block to the house Ron Bean had built for his enormous bride.

Greg Paisler leaned over the steering wheel of his truck as he kicked up dust behind him on the way into town. His brother Sam had been sent to the Minnicks' field to tell them that the sheriff needed Greg in town. Sam had said that Pa had muttered something about it might be cheaper to rent a phone for Grover than to keep sending working young sons to fetch the wayward Greg. The brothers had laughed. Minnick had listened and nodded, but he hadn't laughed. *I wonder about those pack set, walkie-talkie things I've been reading about. It'd save having to send somebody to get me. But, even with a walkie-talkie, Mr. Minnick would still be unhappy losing me working when he needs me the most.*

Greg parked his truck and hustled into the sheriff's office, surprised to see it was Mrs. Drangler waiting for him.

"Good on you for comin', Greg Paisler," the tiny woman praised. "We got the sheriff to go on to my place for much-needed rest. I guess we're to let Mr. Nickleberg take his missus on home to the poultry farm, though none of us wants it that way. But we can't hold him when she won't say he's the one who beat her."

Eyes wide, Greg took in the story without comment.

"The big trouble is, Nickleberg don't remember where he parked his sawed-off pickup when he brought her in. So, several folks are out looking for... wait, here comes Ron Bean now. That was quick."

Bean entered, dusty with fatigue. When he caught Mrs. Drangler's eye scrutinizing him, he grinned and plopped into the chair near the door. "It's just that it's been a long day, Mrs. D., from when I start in the morning. Now don't you worry. My Sadie will feed me, plump my pillows, and I'll be right as rain after some sleep. Anyhow, we found that feathermobile. Right out in the open."

"Where?" Greg asked, confused. "How come Mr. Nickleberg didn't know where?"

"If you'd seen how drunk..." Ron shook his head. "Anyhow, there it was among the rusted junkers off from the railroad shed. But why he'd park it there... anyhow, it's ready for somebody to take him..."

Mrs. Drangler opened the passageway to the cells. She had the key in hand to unlock Nickleberg's cell but startled back when the man lunged at the bars, hollering. "So, you finally found my truck, did you? Find the thief that stole it?"

Seeing Mrs. Drangler cower away from the man, Greg stepped close to take the key from her hand. Gently, he pushed her toward Ron Bean who was striding toward them.

"Nobody stole your vehicle, Nickleberg," Ron said. "It was right where you, or maybe your missus, left it when you came to Doc's. With the junkers by the railroad shed."

"Oh, yeah? Why'd either of us wanna leave it anywhere but in front of Doc's? You say we was both staggerin'. Why'd we wanna park where we had ta walk so far, huh?"

"Well, why would a thief leave it in town? If he wanted it, how come he'd bring you all the way to Doc's and then leave the thing in town when he could've just kept going with it south or west to the state lines and be gone?"

"Why are you so angry with the world, Heinz Nickleberg?" Ella Mae whispered.

Furious, Nickleberg plodded between Greg and Ron to Doc's house-turned-clinic. Dr. Ricartsen's shake of the head when he led Nickleberg to the small examination room made him angrier. But when Gertrude turned her bruised and swollen face to him as she struggled to sit at the edge of the bed, the egg man grunted in pained surprise.

"I never!"

"Ye..." she started, then bit her lip and went quiet. "Come on, let's go home."

"Better to stay here where we can keep an eye on you, at least for the night," Sadie Bean coaxed.

"Much better, Mrs. Nickleberg," Doc agreed. "Stay here for a while."

"Work to do at home," she declared. When she'd shuffled through the lobby, Nickleberg reached to help his wife down the steps to the walkway, but she shied away. Furious, he stood apart while Ricartsen and Ron Bean helped her to the car as Greg climbed into the driver's seat. Doc opened the back door for the egg man, but Nickleberg stomped around to the driver's door and gestured for Greg to get out. "My truck. I drive."

"But I..."

"Out!" Nickleberg raged.

"Go on, young Paisler," Gertrude sighed. "He'll get us home, don't you worry."

Reluctant, but with no valid argument or authority to use against Nickleberg's demand, Greg unfolded from behind the steering wheel. He stood aside with the others, frowning in protest as Heinz spun the wheels taking off west.

Gertrude moaned at the accelerated movement. Heinz glanced over. Was she trying to shame him? But her eyes were closed. She was biting her lips again, trying to suppress the sounds of her pain.

"I never..." he began again, but she ignored his denial. I never, he told himself. *I wouldn't. I didn't...they're lyin'!* But he said nothing aloud until she moaned again on the long lane up to their farm. "Almost home, Gertie Birdie," he murmured, but she never opened her eyes until they were gliding to a stop beyond their main chicken coop.

She twisted to see him yank on the emergency brake, his feet full to the floor over both clutch and brake. Shifting to sit up closer to the door, Gertrude swayed, eyes closed. "Arrg," she groaned as she pawed at the door. "Heinz, we've gotta get them brakes fixed. One of these days we ain't gonna be able to..."

"I've worked on 'em, dammit, woman," he snapped as he staggered out and slammed his door shut.

Hauling herself to her feet, she opened her one good eye, moaning, in fear this time.

Nickleberg was instantly contrite. "Ah, Gert, don't ride me. Just don't. I'm at my wits' end. No sleep. No money to fix right even the needfuls around here." Burying his face in his hands, he plopped onto the running board and growled. It ended in a howl, yelling at the sky. "What's the use? Why work ourselves like darkies in a field when it don't get us nowhere?"

For just that moment, Gertrude wondered how the darkies did it: how did they, whose lives were just as bleak and maybe even more so, how did they not end up screaming and stomping and beating their women? Or maybe they do only we just don't see them do it. But Heinz had jerked to his feet. She shrank against the doorframe. She screamed.

Chapter 12

Friday, August 16, 1940

Garum's pa was gone when the boy awoke the next morning before dawn. Must'a got a day's work somewheres. Good. And it would be good. Pa was always better off coming in from a day's work. Even thirsty and tired to the point of near-dropping and gleaming all over with sweat, he was easier to live with when he had a few coins in his pocket than when he'd lounged and fretted and cussed out the day. There was no promise of being hired from one day to the next. Nothing the man could count on. Nothing to build his dreams on and it ate at him. Pa hadn't said so, but Frog had told Garum that was probably the reason his own mother had wandered away.

"It's easier for a man to take," Frog had explained. "I guess a woman's gotta believe her dreams are gonna come true even if it's someday. And around here, there ain't no someday for coloreds like us who got nothin' to build on. And get that taken away if we do start to gather in a bit of somethin'. Glad my pa's had his own tools right with him and could work on any truck or car and not hafta worry about gettin' hired into nobody's field."

"I miss you, Frog," Garum murmured as he rolled out of his cot. He'd need to hurry to get to the Nickleberg's chicken farm if he wanted to arrive before the man came out of the house in the pre-dawn dark to slouch to the low, long coop. He'd heard the Nicklebergs had gone back home after being at Doc's for most of the day. But the boy took a moment to bow his head for a quick plea that his and his pa's might be steady jobs. He grabbed a fistful of Pa's cornbread and hurried down the already dusty road.

Mrs. Nickleberg was bruised, somber and taciturn, but Garum understood her grunted directions and began by gathering the eggs in the deep, wire baskets. He handled them carefully and stacked them precisely so none would break. When he brought them back into the house, Mrs. Nickleberg, pale and swollen, sat stoop-shouldered at the table in the kitchen. She grunted when she saw him but exhaled as they took turns reaching into the basket. She did not smile but came close when they'd sorted and wiped and candled each egg and set them small side down in containers, ready for market.

"Not bad," she breathed. "Not a single egg damaged. Maybe you'll do." She lifted her chin to peer at him as though remembering. "It was you, wasn't it?"

He froze, unsure how to answer.

"It was you and some tall fella. Your brother? Your pa?"

His round eyes widened. He knew the mister had rattled her brain with his blows. Garum had even begun to hope that she'd forgotten about his pa. So, bringing Pa into any discussion of that way-early morning when the Tackers had loaded them into their car-truck and taken the missus to Doc's was the last thing he wanted. His lips pursed as he tried to keep them from begging that that be forgotten.

"Does my husband know?"

His head twisted side to side once of its own.

Sighing, she surveyed the eggs in their regimented rows. "Best to let it be that way, then," she whispered. His nod was volitional.

"Yes'm." And then the clear relief of his feelings came through with a blurted, "Thank you, ma'am."

Frowning, she stared as though seeing him as a vulnerable child for the first time. "Why, boy, he wouldn't hurt you," she exclaimed, then shook her head. "If he was sober. But that you know what he done, he wouldn't like that. He surely wouldn't." Still shaking her head, she rose painfully to shuffle to the kitchen sink. "The mister'll be wantin' the manure gathered and spread, boy. Best hurry on out and get it done for him."

"Yes'm," he muttered and scampered outside.

Leaning on the counter, she watched him go, so much like her two sons when they were little, but of no account because of the color of his skin. The thought startled her. She'd never even considered the possibility of a colored boy being like, let alone equal to her own sons. "And yet..." Sighing again, Mrs. Nickleberg started preparing the hearty breakfast she had made for her husband every morning for decades. A long time before he'd again taken up drinking himself into troubled sleep. She startled at a roar outside. "Heinz? Heinz!"

Garum was darting away from the man clumsy in his drunkenness. "You hired me, mister," he kept calling reasonably. "Don'tcha remember? At Miz Owens store? You said to come early, so I done it. See, the sun's only just..." he panted, scampering toward the house. He stopped abruptly, seeing Mrs. Nickleberg at the door. Raising his hands, Garum motioned as though shooing her back inside.

Nickleberg loomed behind him. Huge hands grabbed his shoulders and flung him aside as though he were a grain sack less than half full.

Gertrude started out toward them, and then backed away, hurrying into the kitchen for her knife. Heinz caught her before she reached the table. She jerked away and ran back outside.

Garum scrambled to his feet and ran to yank at the man's arm. "Mister, please! Please, don't! She's your missus, please!" He grabbed onto Nickleberg's arm and held on.

Roaring, the man twisted at the interference. "Wha...? Get off me!"

But Garum held on even when the man lifted his arm against the child's weight and swung him into the side of the egg truck. At the whack of boy against metal, Gertrude hurried, reeling, to the car-truck. She leaned in to press and hold the horn. That obnoxious noisemaker was the one part that still worked, with a vengeance.

Nickleberg's hands lifted to cover his ears. "Quit! Lay off that horn, woman! Oh, my head," he moaned.

Scrambling to back out of reach, Garum cautiously got to his feet ready to run. But, seeing the man wrapped in his own misery, the boy eased closer to the lady. "You all right, missus?" he hissed. "What can I do?"

She stared at him with her one good eye, then went limp. The blaring noise quit. He eased her to the ground.

"Oh, missus, don't die. Please, don't die. Ain't nobody gonna believe Pa'n me ain't the ones kilt ya." He looked up, hoping against hope that Mr. Nickleberg had come to his senses enough to know his lady needed help. But the man was stumbling away toward their lean-to of a storage shed. "Whaddle I do, Pa?" the boy whimpered, knowing there was no one to hear or help him. Crouching beside the lady, tears blurring his vision of this should-be-prosperous farm, Garum found himself humming the tune Miz Nandria had taught them last night. "Twinkle, twinkle little star. How I wonder..." It was like the music to the A-B-C song, too, but it was its own self, as well, somehow. How he wondered about those notes Miz Nandria was showing them.

The woman inhaled deeply beside him and tried to turn onto her side. Garum scooted to his feet to help her. He watched her eyes, holding his breath, while she struggled to make sense of where she was and what had happened.

"You're here, Miz Nickleberg. In your driveway, by your house," he whispered and scooted again to help her sit upright.

She swayed. "Boy?"

"Garum, Miz Nickleberg. I come to help you gather the eggs. Remember now? They're all in their places on your table. Sheriff done said he'd send somebody out to fetch 'em to Mr. Owens' for ya. They all been worried about ya out here so soon…" He stopped his chatter when he saw the confusion and growing fear on her face.

"So soon?" Gertrude Nickleberg stared. The vertical creases on her forehead deepened as she tried to think. "So soon? After what? Why'd you say, 'so soon'?"

"Uh, well, you kinda hurt your head, Miz Nickleberg. Doc didn't really want ya to come on home yet. He wanted ya to stay with him at his horsespittal…"

She laughed. It sounded more like a cry of fear than a laugh to Garum, but it hurt him somehow. White folks laughed at him over the oddest things, sometimes. He worked hard to do like Miz Nandria taught them: to speak careful and say each letter clear.

"Horsespittal?" she kept repeating, laughing each time until her swaying threatened to topple her.

"You know, that old house in Boonetown where he fixed up the main floor to take care of folks."

"Hospital. Nothin' to do with horses."

"Oh." *So, I'm wrong again, even when I try so hard to do it careful.* In his shame, Garum had sat up away from her, so he needed to lunge to help her lie down gently on her side as she collapsed. "Twinkle, twinkle, little star," he sang low in clear soprano, like a lullaby he almost remembered his mother murmuring to him long ago.

"They waited as long as they could, hoping you would return to inform them of your call to act for the sheriff," Nandria smiled as she beckoned for Greg Paisler to enter the Minnick back door. Her eyes narrowed as he entered. There were fresh scrapes and bruising on his cheeks and darkening along his jawline.

"Sorry, it took longer than I expected to gather the eggs—and Mr. Nickleberg. Did they go back to the east field, do you know, Miz Nandria?" he apologized, his voice a bit muffled with his injuries.

"They did, but before you go, I must ask if you have partaken of a noon meal?"

"Well, both Mrs. Drangler and Mrs. Bean invited me, but I was afraid to let Mr. Minnick down by not coming right back." He hesitated. His stomach had been growling the entire drive from Boonetown to the Minnick farm.

Nandria gestured for him to enter the kitchen. "Your share of the noon meal has been warming, awaiting your arrival. Please be seated at the table." When he began to protest, she added, "Those orders were from Mr. Minnick himself."

"With your prompting, I bet," he snickered, but sat in the nearest seat, while pointing at the wooden spoon lying across the rim of the large pan with an inquisitive look.

"It prevents the contents from boiling over," Nandria explained.

"Oh," Greg chuckled, knowing he'd need to tell his mother about that. "Thank you, Miz Nandria," Greg said gratefully as she set his plate and bowl in front of him. "You are a thoughtful one." Sighing with anticipation, he hauled Rose's highchair closer and tickled her under the chin to hear the little girl giggle.

Rose laughed, despite his interrupting her delicately fingering up bits of her mother's biscuit she'd crumbled. Then she lunged to reach for Greg's bowl.

"Burny, little Rose," Nandria cried. "No! Burny!"

The baby drew back chubby little hands.

"She knows what that means. The hard way, I'm guessing."

"Unfortunately so," Nandra responded. "I was neglectful."

"Kids are so quick. Good thing they learn quick, too. At least mostly," he chuckled and Nandria, smiling, sat beside him rather than continue to work in the kitchen. "The missus taking a nap?"

"She tires so easily," Nandria said, her voice betraying her own longing to lie down to rest. He glanced up at her with sympathy that made her turn away to hide her weariness. "Is the sheriff healing properly?" she asked to change the subject. "I hope nothing was far amiss that he needed you to act for him once more." She touched his chin to turn his face so she could see the coloring bruise on his jawline.

"Well," Greg said between mouthfuls, then set down his knife and fork until he'd finished chewing. "May I ask you something, Miz Nandria? Something that don't make a lick of sense to me." He explained with few details how Mrs. Nickleberg had been even more battered when he went out to the poultry farm to get the eggs and butchered chickens to deliver in town. "She wouldn't let me touch her and downright refused to let me take her to see Doc again. She said she and the boy..."

"Boy?"

"Oh, yeah, she had little Garum Tacker with her. Said he'd come to help her with the eggs and chores. She said he'd been doing a good job taking care of her. But when I asked her how she'd come to be hurt even more than yesterday, she wouldn't say a word. I went to talk with Mr. Nickleberg, despite her tellin' me to leave him be. I found him in their shed, dead to the world, but I'm afraid I woke him none too easy." Greg rubbed his jaw but continued before Nandria could comment. "He kept yellin' about the shoes on the table and that it was all her fault. When I got him settled some and into my truck, he kept mumbling, 'I don' remember; I don' wanna remember.' Does that make any sense to you?"

"Then Mr. Nickleberg caused your injuries?"

"Just a bruise. No real harm, and only 'cause he was startled awake, Miz Nandria. He didn't mean anything by it."

Nandria hummed.

"You don't think it was an accident that he fought me?"

"I merely surmise that Mr. Nickleberg awoke in anger."

"Or fear, maybe?"

Offering Rose the last spoonfuls of her stew broth, Nandria nodded. "Perhaps."

"What about the shoes on the table? What was that all about?"

"I can only rely on my reading about superstitions in your United States. As I recall, there are several gestures or actions that may lead to bad luck or even to evil entering one's life."

"Kind'a like letting the devil loose to come at a person?" Greg asked, laughing.

Rose looked up into his face. She cocked her head to one side, both to avoid the last spoonful of broth and the better to stare at her big friend.

"Sorry, little princess." Greg scooched down to peer at her eye to eye. "You're even younger than Levitt. I keep forgetting how my booming laugh can startle a wee one. But your mama's saying that anybody could believe that leaving shoes on a table could be the cause of her getting battered like that, well, it's just hard for me to do much else but laugh out loud."

"And yet, many people around the world truly believe and restrict their lives with such beliefs. Tell me, please. You have known the Nicklebergs for some time. Are they inclined to superstition?"

"Huh? You mean, have I seen them do things like toss salt over their left shoulder if it spills?"

"That would be to throw it in the eye of the devil, so he is temporarily blinded and slower to hurt one, I gather."

"Really? Huh. What else? I mean, I have seen him go way out to get around a ladder even when the rest of us just slip underneath it when the way is blocked."

"Have you played cards with the man, perhaps? Might you have observed any unusual behavior?" Nandria reached with the corner of her apron to wipe her daughter's face.

"May I?" Greg asked before lifting the baby out of the highchair to carry her to the sink to wash her up after her meal. "I do the after-dinner clean-up for most of my little brothers.

Ain't done it for a little girl very often, but I bet it's pretty much the same."

Smiling as Rose lifted her arms to Greg, Nandria consented with a happy sigh. Rather than rise, she simply sat doing nothing. It felt delicious to rest, even if only momentarily. Laying her arm on the table, she let her head sink onto it and closed her eyes. "Will," she whispered.

It surprised her from a brief nap when Rose squealed above her. "Darling?" she cried, confused.

"Brand spankin' fresh and clean, Mama," Greg laughed, handing the little girl with wide-spread arms to Nandria as she sat up. "No, you just sit there. Won't take me a minute to finish off these dishes. You two need to just hug for a bit. And, no, Mr. Minnick ain't gonna know this was done for ya. And even if he did, it's the least we can do to help you with all you do for us around here."

Grateful for the young man's thoughtfulness, Nandria remained in her seat with her daughter on her lap playing with those chubby, curious little hands and drinking in those huge, dark eyes. "Da-da-da," Nandria coaxed and was delighted at Rose's grin as she worked to mimic the sounds. "Your daddy will be so glad to hear you, precious one. So glad." Overwhelmed, Nandria brought the child up close against her shoulder and kissed her spiraled black curls. "Oh, darling."

Greg glanced over from the sink and then turned back to setting the last of the pots on the rack to dry.

Chapter 13

Unable to move without disturbing the woman, Garum waited as patiently as any child could until his legs threatened to jerk out from under her weight if they could not be moved soon. At last, she stirred.

"Wha'? Who…?"

"It's only me, Garum, missus. You was cryin' an' I tried to dry your tears an' you fell asleep. Feel better now?" he asked, squirming carefully to release his numb, pin-and-needle aching legs. He had a time getting them to hold him and work at his will when Mrs. Nickleberg rose awkwardly.

She held her head, then shuffled toward the hen house. "Heinz!" she called. "Heinz Nickleberg, where are you?"

"Ah, missus," he sighed. Not daring to contradict whatever the white woman had in mind to do, he followed her.

"You don't have the radio Willard bought?" Doc asked. He frowned and settled his long legs under his desk in his office. "Minnick took it for himself, didn't he?"

"Mother Minnick settles to some of the music programming, especially Mrs. Kate Smith."

"Kate Smith does have a pleasant voice," Sadie Bean commented as she stepped into the doctor's office to add to the piles of clean linen on the far shelf. "I saw a picture of her," she started and then clamped her mouth, red-faced.

Ricartsen chuckled. "'Neither half of her is thin,' that's what your Ron said when you two saw the picture, isn't it? I've heard him, but you're right, he does like her singing."

"Well, I'm hardly the one to comment on how dainty any woman looks."

"There are no God-given definitions of what a woman should or should not appear to be, only what she should be within herself," Nandria murmured. "You might be surprised by what different cultures see as beautiful in a woman—or in a man."

With a gesture, Ricartsen invited his nurse to sit and join them for the moment. It was quiet. Even Mr. House had not been back to complain about his boils.

"Would you like coffee?"

"Oh, sit a minute, Sadie Bean," Ricartsen barked. "You make me feel guilty to even think about relaxing."

With a wry grin, Sadie pulled up the heavy upright chair from the corner and sat beside Nandria. "So, this time it isn't me urging you up to your bed when there's a lull. But there you are, shaking your head while you twirl the dials on that radio of yours to listen to all the news that tears you up inside until you're ornerier than a sat-on bee."

"You have heard of new developments in the war in Europe, Doctor?" Nandria's voice was high with anxious concern.

Both Ricartsen and Mrs. Bean sobered as they realized they would need to break terrible news to their friend. "I – I thought you probably already knew and was taking the news well. Already settled inside yourself," Sadie murmured. "Sorry, or we wouldn't have been joking between us."

Nandria glanced over with forgiveness, then turned to the doctor. "News, Dr. Ricartsen?"

He squirmed, withdrawing his legs from under his desk. "I...I..."

Sadie sat up to turn to face her friend. "Dogfights. Over the Channel." At Nandria's slow blink of acceptance. "And more, dear one. Some Nazi bombers are getting through."

"London?" Nandria breathed.

Both nurse and doctor sighed.

Gertrude searched all the outbuildings, her voice growing more and more hoarse as she cried her man's name. Garum, tagging behind, pleading low, watched without being able to help her. Finally, she slumped at the door to the shed. The boy ran to her.

"Gee, missus, I tried and tried to tell ya'. Your mister ain't here. Don'tcha remember?"

"Wha'?"

"This here mornin'. We was sortin' and candlin' the eggs I brung in, and Greg Paisler come to fetch 'em into town for ya. Don'tcha remember?"

She sat up enough that he was able to help her rest her back against the shed doorway. "I...I seem like I know somethin'...and then it slips away. Like I dreamt it or somethin'. Tell me, that young Paisler son was here at the farm, you say?"

"Yeah, he was." The boy settled on the scratched and pecked-at ground beside her. "The sheriff told him to come. We pretty near had the eggs ready for him, but the mister hadn't said even started with his axe on them chickens for meat, and..."

"Of course, the mister hadn't chopped heads yet. You he wasn't here," she snapped, and Garum stopped explaining. At the boy's confusion, she peered at him, suspicious. "Paisler took my man?"

"W-well," Garum stuttered, knowing that what he had to tell her, she wasn't going to like. "Well, you see, Greg Paisler seen that you was even bloodier than you was yesterday."

She shoved her back up against the doorframe to lift herself erect. Garum worried about her getting splinters from the neglected wood, but there was nothing he could say. "Ah, missus, why don't you come in for coffee? Pa says I make good coffee. I gotta let him be the decider 'cause I don't like the taste of it, no how."

Having reached full height leaning against the rough wood, Gertrude stared at him.

Seeing her bewilderment, Garum hoped it meant she had forgotten again about her husband and his fight with Greg Paisler. He rambled on until, finally, he took her hand to lead her toward her house. He reached beyond her to open the back door. "Pa says—he's got chickens, too, you know," the small, dark boy rattled on as he gently helped her up the stoop and into the kitchen.

"No." The wife of the Boonetown community egg man stiffened. "How would I know?"

"Oh, yeah," Garum blinked, trying to figure out what he'd just said so he'd know what she was objecting to. Chickens. We've got chickens, too. As he seated her at the table, he continued with more enthusiasm than he felt. "Oh, yeah, only we keep them up in a wire cage above the ground. They can come right out into it from the hen house. We've got seventeen layers now. Up from two a lady in Fox Haven gave us when I was just a little mite. Pa said we wasn't gonna eat 'em, then. But I remember I was plenty hungry then and could'a et 'em both, feathers 'n' all." He looked up; he cringed.

The lady was staring at him, mouth pressed tight.

"Uh, s-sorry, ma'am," he stammered.

Except for the dark face, he reminded her of her own two sons as little boys when they'd offended their father. Even then, it wasn't hard to make Heinz furious. His wife for all these decades, she had seldom seen Heinz carefree, let alone joyous.

Her sons had given her joy, and here was this tyke bubbling over with news and pride about a father who had so much less. How could she be angry with his innocent bragging? A child is a child. Black or white.

The insight startled her. That a Negro could bring up his own in love and pride, she'd never considered before, lost as she was in her own daily world of disappointment. "Well," she exhaled, "I guess I'll need to meet this paragon of virtue." Looking at the boy, she laughed aloud at the child's confusion. He had no clue what she was talking about. A 'paragon' was beyond him, but he'd probably heard of virtue in Sunday school. Gertrude softened toward Garum, dark face and all. She smiled.

Garum's expression remained cautious, but at least he was no longer quite as frightened as he had been a few minutes ago.

"Garum, I'd like to meet your father." And then it dawned on her that she had already met the man. It was he who had helped her when she was first hurt and helpless. He was most probably the one who had stuffed Heinz into the vehicle and taken him along to town. The boy couldn't have done that alone. Neither of the Nicklebergs remembered how they had gotten to Doc's. The colored man had helped this boy, even knowing as he was doing it that her husband would beat him to a pulp if Heinz had awakened from his drunken stupor. And she had never thanked him. Clearing her throat, she addressed the child. "If your pa can come sometime today or tomorrow, would you kindly ask him to drop by? Some time when my husband is likely to be somewhere else."

She had seldom seen, except in horses, eyes go so wide that there was white all around the dark pupil. It made her chuckle and reach to pat the boy's arm.

He stood in utter amazement.

Something nagged at her: Heinz wasn't there now. Something about the Paisler son. Something... "Where's my husband, boy?" she growled.

Her tone brought Garum to attention. He was wary again, not simply amazed.

"Where'd that Paisler take him?"

"T-to town. With the eggs. You – you refused to go to Doc's," Garum stammered.

"To town? To the sheriff, you mean? Paisler took my Heinz to the sheriff. I never said he hurt me. I never said that."

"No, missus, you wouldn't tell him, but he knowed. And he went out to the shed. Your mister... well, Greg Paisler's a mite bigger and a lot younger..."

"We gotta go," she cried, standing up. She swayed. He caught her, but he couldn't dissuade her.

"You can't drive, missus. You can't."

"So, you drive."

He stood blinking. "But..."

A rat snake slithered for cover. Garum leaped toward the sawed-off car-turned-truck.

Rose lunged forward in her mother's arms, reaching deep into the mailbox. "Mmmmm," she giggled. She straightened, lifting out three envelopes. She tore into one.

"Yes, darling, mail," Nandria praised. "What... oh, sweet Lord!" Nandria stumbled, clutching her little girl. It was Rose who clung to the letter. "Good girl," Nandria mumbled as she regained her balance. "I like your priorities. That letter must be about your daddy." It had the oddest address: to the wife of Cap'n Willard Minnick.

"D-d-da-da."

"Yes, my darling, yes." Nandria studied the front of the envelope, frowning. She set little Rose in the stubby grass at the foot of the mailbox and braced herself to open the letter. *My love, my sweet love, how I wish this is word that you are on your way home to us.*

Rose was hauling herself to stand beside the post for the mailbox when she spotted a grub. She plunged to catch it and bring it to her mouth. With the motherly squeal that sounds the same in any language, Nandria reached to scoop up her child before she could eat it.

"Well, my little adventurer, I suppose we must walk back up to the house before I can trust you long enough to be able to sit down and read this." She smiled as she wiped her daughter's hands with her apron. "I just hope your grandmother is still napping. She would want to read it as well. However, just this once, I want a letter about your daddy for my very own."

Still fighting the stubborn shift of gears, Garum stretched out his leg for his foot to be able to depress the clutch, but he couldn't do that fully without losing control of the steering wheel. The country lane was just too narrow for him to shift up and still keep the odd car from scraping the rough-leaved dogwood, wild grapes, and Virginia creepers that encroached from either side. Nickleberg might not forgive new scrapes. *And that'd be yet one more charge against me. So, mebbe I better just creep along in this here low gear. At least we're goin' forward.*

At another pothole, the modified sedan jounced. The woman groaned. Garum looked over at her and nearly sideswiped a bur oak.

"Sweet sassafras," Garum mumbled, "that would'a made a pretty gouge."

"Wha'?"

Startled, Garum again yanked on the steering wheel and swerved them close to another car-tree collision. Instead, his foot slipped off the clutch. The motor sputtered, and they jerked to a stop. Clinging to the wheel, the boy glanced over his extended right arm at Mrs. Nickleberg. "You awake, ma'am?"

"Y-yes, I think so. Who are...? Oh, the boy..." Her good eye closed and then opened again as she seemed slowly to register present reality. "Did I ever thank you? And the man who helped?"

"Pa."

"Yes, he had to be your pa. You're the spittin' image. You two took me to Doc's in town, didn't you? But you didn't stay to tell them nothing."

"Pa said we'd better go."

"Yeah, I suppose the less you seem to be part of whatever happened, being darkies like you are. But that was a day or so ago, wasn't it?"

"Yes'm." the boy admitted, squirming.

"And now here we are in my husband's car going, it looks like, down our farm drive. Why? Where's my husband?"

"Greg. Paisler. He's been doing stuff for the sheriff 'til he can work again. Don'tcha remember?"

"Oh, yeah," she whispered, considering. "Greg Paisler, you say? He's son number four, ain't he?"

"Three, I think, ma'am," Garum corrected quietly before he thought to shut his mouth as his father would have cautioned. When the woman took no offense, the boy let out his breath.

"So, what are you doing now? Stealing this car? But everybody from here to Omaha is gonna know whose it was."

The steering wheel seemed to glow hot. Garum hid his hands under him as he shrank lower and lower under the wheel. "Oh, no, I wasn't stealing no car! I never!"

"Then what?"

The boy squirmed. "I – I was takin' you..."

"Taking me? Where? Why?" But the last question was nearly swallowed in her distress as she remembered why. "The mister. Drunk again, ain't he? Where is he?"

"Well, I did see him crawl into a corner in your shed, behind some grain sacks." It wasn't quite a true answer. He'd seen Greg haul the man out and stuff him into his truck, but Garum wasn't sure Mrs. Nickleberg was ready for that part of the story.

"Is he alright?"

"Well," Garum tempered. He would have been glad to slide right out of this car and leave it to the missus to drive wherever she'd decide to go. Pa was right. Best not to get mixed up with white folks' problems. She's awake enough now. I gotta get out'a here. But she was so hurt. He couldn't just leave her with her man's fist speaking for him. He looked over and almost reached to touch her arm, she looked so sad.

"Was he crying?" she asked. "Crying in his sleep?"

Garum's head nodded though Mr. Nickleberg hadn't been sleeping. Not then.

"Oh, sweet goodness, we gotta go back to him. Turn this thing around and go back, boy."

Garum blinked. It had taken all he could do to drive this far forward.

Chapter 14

Sighing, Nickleberg dropped his clenched hands between his knees to the braided rug at his feet. The others waited until the man heaved another sigh. "Lord take me, I don't remember," he whispered. "Thought it was another bad dream."

The sheriff peered at him from Mrs. Drangler's easy chair. He'd wanted to go to the jail to interview him but had had to admit to himself he wasn't up for it.

Banker Freshstalk had loaned one of his two bank security men to go with Ron Bean to bring the man to the seamstress's low door.

"Up to you, sheriff, I guess, but..." the guard protested, reluctant to leave the prisoner with only Ron Bean and the ailing sheriff.

"Now don't you worry about us, Mr. Clayton," Mrs. D. assured him as she handed him a tray. "Just hurry on back to the bank while those scones are still warm if you would. I put a jar of fresh butter in under the tea towel, so they'll slather up real good if you get 'em back fast. And be sure to tell Mr.

Freshstalk how much we appreciate his letting us borrow you. Thank you kindly."

Clayton nearly stood up too soon after ducking through the doorway, but, at the last moment, Mrs. Drangler gave him a quick shove in the back and got him out without banging his head or dropping the tray. She snatched up her piece of taffeta as she hustled back in to sit to listen.

Ron Bean helped himself to a second scone and sat in the chair nearest the front door. He, too, was listening.

"What happened this morning?" Yakes asked again with that low, authoritative voice he could command.

Nickleberg shook his head and moaned. "N-nothin'. I swear."

"I've tipped a jug with you enough times over the years. I know you can be a mean drunk, Nickleberg."

"I swear, Yakes. I don't know. Lord help me, I just don't remember."

"My deputy says your Gertrude is swollen and bloodier even than she was when you brought her in to Doc's—when was that? Seems longer than a day or so, but I'd guess it was even longer for your wife, Nickleberg."

"I wouldn't hurt Gert! I'd kill anybody who'd try!"

Ron set his mug on the floor and crouched forward, ready to intervene, but the sheriff lifted a palm to halt him.

"I think you would, Heinz. I honestly think you'd beat to a pulp anybody who'd threaten your wife—if you was sober. But how often you been sober this past month?"

Nickleberg's head drooped between his knees; his rough fists dug into his eyes.

Mrs. Drangler set her sewing to one side and rose quietly to go to him. The sheriff frowned but she was already bent over him, her small hand on his shoulder. She gave Yakes a nod as though asking to try it her way, at least for a few minutes. "Heinz Nickleberg, this is Ella Mae Drangler. I know about feeling bad, guilty even. Believe me, I know. But it doesn't do any good to weep and wail. What we need to do is find out what's happening so we can make it right. Come now, isn't that the real way of it? Can you tell us about those dreams? The ones that keep you from sleeping?"

He tried. Shuddering with the effort, Nickleberg finally lifted his head and took the scrap of cloth she gave him to wipe his nose and eyes. With a grateful glance at Ella Mae, he tried to square his shoulders. He could not look the sheriff in the face. Instead, he again studied the braided rug.

Yakes waited until he was quiet. "The dreams, Heinz?" he prompted. "Something that comes up in the dark? Or something you remember?"

"Nah shore," Nickleberg croaked, then shook his head and swallowed. "Not sure. I'm rememberin', I think. Long time ago." He did look up. "I must'a been a kid." When no one spoke, he went on. " It sure comes on like a newsreel. Black and white," he snorted. "Black versus white. Now, that's funny." But it wasn't. It made him close his eyes even to think about it.

"Where are you?" Ella Mae asked gently as she picked up her taffeta and sat down.

"Where?" Nickleberg shook his head without opening his eyes. "My folks come from South Carolina. Lake City. Big black bugger got made the postmaster. Every time my pa even thought about that, a huge red rash'd climb up out'a his shirt and up his neck 'til it took over his face. Even his scalp and his ears. We kids, my brothers 'n' me, we loved to watch, but we knew better'n to be anywhere in reach of his hand when it happened. He'd be so mad..." Nickleberg chuckled and went still.

"So, your town had a spook postmaster. How long did that last?" the sheriff wanted to know.

"Only a while. The Post Office got itself burnt down. I guess the men thought they'd bake Baker, but he wasn't inside. And he didn't quit. He took all the stuff he could still use to his own house and run it from there."

"Where his wife and young'uns lived?" Mrs. Drangler gasped.

"I guess." Nickleberg shrugged. "Anyhoo, they was inside when a crowd—hundreds, I heard tell—came at it one night and set that house afire." Shuddering, he went still.

"What did the mob do, Nickle?" Yakes demanded.

"I...I reckon mebbe it's that night I keep seein' in my dream." But his face showed his confusion. He shook his head again, slowly. "Them jigaboos come runnin' out. The woman was carryin' somethin'. I remember that. Folks said later it was her baby." He looked up without focusing as Mrs. Drangler cried out and stuffed her fist into her mouth.

"Oh, no! No!" she whimpered and rose to sidle off into the kitchen.

"All I remember as a kid was the gunshots. More'n one. Folks rumored later that bundle she was carryin' got hit in the head. Killed dead enough even for Pa." His laugh brought Ron Bean to his feet, but the sheriff gestured for him to go on outside. He did.

"Was it your pa who taught you about the shoes on the table, too?"

"No," Nickleberg looked thoughtful as he tried to remember. "No, don't think that was Pa. My mother, I guess. Her and her brother, Uncle Rankleson. Art Rankleson. There was a whole lot of things you should never do. Ma would correct us if we forgot as we went along. But Uncle Art'd cuff us one—a good one—so's we'd be sure to remember next time. Didn't your folks teach you about them shoes, sheriff? All sorts of ways the devil can sneak in when you ain't lookin'. No wonder your boys..."

Yakes did stir then. "Never mind about my boys," he snapped. "I'm tryin' to understand why you're goin' after your wife with your two fists. That's the devil I'm tryin' to deal with right here, right now."

Abashed, Nickleberg slouched forward again, staring between his knees at the multicolored braided rags of the circular rug. "I never," he whispered, then looked up. "What're you trying to do to me, Yakes? I never touched my woman. I wouldn't. Why're you accusing me of such a godawful thing like that? I thought you and me was friends."

Later that afternoon, Mrs. Drangler bustled across the street to scurry up the walkway through Doc Ricartsen's long, patchy front lawn. She knocked once to alert Sadie Bean and entered. "Miz Bean, you here?"

"Where else would I be?" the large nurse grumbled as she strode up the corridor to the empty lobby. "Oh, Miz Drangler, it's you. Sorry, we just sent Mr. House on his way..." she stated as though that would explain her grouchiness. It did.

"Another...?"

"Another boil on his nether parts. I wish some civic-minded group of men would take it upon themselves to throw that man into the creek twice a month to get him somewhat clean and let his behind heal itself for once and good." Sadie sighed and motioned for Ella Mae to come to the back of the house and sit with her over a cup of coffee, then went suddenly alert. "Unless you got problems with the sheriff, Mrs. D.?"

"No, no. Piermont is getting ornery and that's the best sign. In fact, it's why I come. Greg Paisler brought in that feather farmer," she stopped to giggle at the name. When she could speak again, she continued, "I mean Mr. Nickleberg, to let the sheriff hear his story and decide if he wanted to put him in jail."

"So, Greg found him all right?"

"Dead drunk at home."

"Piermont insisted on sitting in the front room to see him. He's pretty tired but wants Doc to come if he can, to talk with him. Nickleberg kept sayin' he don't remember but it was Gertrude's fault whatever happened because she left the shoes on the table." Her dark blue eyes widened questioning how that could be a cause of being beaten.

Sadie paused for a moment, then strode to the doctor's office door and knocked. "You in there?"

A tired voice answered. "Yeah."

Sadie opened the door to lean in. "Mrs. D. says the sheriff's settin' up in her front room. Wants you to go over there to tell him about the Nicklebergs."

The lean, young physician lifted his head from his desk where he'd been listening to war news on his radio. With colt-like awkwardness he rose from his chair, sending it back against the wall with a thud.

Sadie shook her head but said nothing about yet another scar on the wall.

"I'll go right now," he said, but he was swaying on his feet with fatigue.

"And then you come right back here and totter upstairs to bed, you hear? Nobody can do a soul a lick of good after being up two nights in a row. Got to sleep sometime."

Smiling, Doc made a slight bow to his nurse, picked up his doctor's bag and walked on fairly steady feet past the women and out his front door. Mrs. Drangler hurried after him.

Sadie stood a moment in the doorway looking after them, wishing she could go, too. But the clinic might have a patient come wanting or needing. And there was plenty of clean-up work to be done in the kitchen-turned-utility room. Sighing, she turned to work knowing that Mrs. D. would tell her soon what was said between them and that the little seamstress wouldn't then gossip with anyone else. She was like that. Telling news only to those who needed to know.

Barely navigating in his fatigue, Ricartsen banged his forehead against the top of Mrs. Drangler's door even as she— he'd let her enter first—turned back to remind him to stoop down.

"Oh, Dr. Ricartsen, oh, I'm so sorry."

"No, no. My own fault. Been here before," he muttered. Holding his head, he ducked down until he was all but crawling inside.

She made him stretch out on the sofa.

"Good thing you got a hard head, Doc," the sheriff chirped with less sympathy than Ella Mae thought was called for. "Ah, give him a glass of water and stop fussing over him, Elm. The man needs sleep, so the sooner we get this talking done with, the better. You okay to answer a couple of my questions, Doc?"

"About Nickleberg?"

"I don't know what to do with the man. His wife is black and blue, eyes puffed near closed, even worse'n yesterday, so Greg Paisler tells it. She won't tell on him doin' it to her, and he denies ever touching her, but there was nobody else within miles. Can he truly not know what he's done?"

"Um, thanks, Mrs. D.," Ricartsen murmured to Ella Mae as he took the water she handed to him. "Yeah, that's better. Ummm. Now, are you asking for a medical opinion, Yakes? That would come under psychiatry, and I've got no training there. It would just be my own guess from what little experience I've had. I imagine you've seen even more of what happens to people's minds after a real ordeal than I have."

Nodding, the sheriff went quiet. "Some, I guess. Over the years. Strange things happen. Even stranger things happen within folks." Yakes went so still that Mrs. Drangler looked up from her hemming, ready to go to him, but Ricartsen gestured for her to let him be.

"You know what we're talking about, Mrs. D.?"

Her lips pressed tight, she nodded.

"But what's the damage that's blowing Nickleberg's mind?" The sheriff sat up, scowling. "All right, so he's not sleeping. Says it from bad dreams. Even mentioned something about a baby. At Owens' and then again, today. He was telling Elm and me about that lynching of the postmaster. White mob burned the man and his family out when he wouldn't give it up. Didn't want no colored to have a job like that."

"Infant. Shot in the head," she murmured.

The doctor winced.

"And that was enough to send you into weeping for them, woman. But it don't seem like enough to set the egg man off like he is. He could talk about it clear enough."

"Anything happen to Nickleberg's own family that you know of?"

Both Yakes and Ella Mae shook their heads. "He and Gert have two fine boys with young families of their own," Yakes said.

"Either boy would take in Gert if she'd go." Mrs. Drangler added.

"And neither would take in the mister, I'm thinkin'," the sheriff sputtered. "He was hard on them growing up, from what I hear. Something like my own pa makin' men of 'em."

"But I do believe both your pa and Heinz thought they was doin' best, Piermont. It was the way their folks had raised them, so it must be best for their sons as well, don't you think?"

It was the doctor who agreed with her. "My father made me go along to see the mobs at their ghoulish work."

Yakes nodded. "So, we've both seen more than I'd like anybody to see..."

"At a tender age," Ella Mae murmured, clutching the skirt she was hemming. "So young to be taught some people aren't human beings."

"But we both went through that, too. We ain't perfect, Elm, but we don't beat our women. So why?"

"Different people; different reactions." Ricartsen shook his head, then rested it in his hands. "Happens in medicine all the time. Just about the time I think I have the right dose for adult males, I give it to another man, and he turns red, white, and then blue, struggling just to breathe."

They sat quietly some minutes until Ella Mae's hosting duties crowded in on her. She rose to offer the doctor something more than water to drink, but the sheriff bade her never mind.

"What the man needs is sleep, Elm. Doc, go on home and crawl into bed no matter who thinks they need just one more thing from ya. Just stumble on by 'em. You'll do 'em more good a bit later after you've slept at least until you're a human being again. Go!"

Chapter 15

Doris Minnick, groggy, sat in her corner of the couch hunting for her crochet hook. "Well, drat them gremlins who keep moving things around on me. I can't find my hook anywhere. If I go to another size, it shows up in the finished doily. If it was a washcloth, it wouldn't matter that much I guess, but a doily's got to be done right if it's gonna be fit for company to see."

"Ummm?" Nandria looked up from her struggled reading of her letter about Will. It was written in cramped, small letters that tumbled over one another as though written in the dark. Or in a dreadful hurry. She wasn't even sure it was Will who had written it. "Oh? Oh, Mother Minnick. Yes, yes, I am coming. What is it you needed?"

"My hook," Doris complained. "That thing keeps finding places to hide. How can I finish this doily for Mrs. Nickleberg if I don't find it? She had a bad fall, that young man from G.E.M. told me. Or was it Mrs. Owens? Bernice isn't real pleased with that young man. He drives that truck of his way out to the country folk and then they don't have to come into the store so much, like they used to. Maybe it was Mrs. Owens who was telling me. Do you remember, girl? Oh, you found it. Well, I guess it hadn't gone as far as I thought it had." She smiled at the hook Nandria handed her but not at her daughter-in-law.

Nandria sighed.

"Why, girl, you've got dark circles under your eyes. I didn't know coons could get dark circles under their eyes."

Nandria sank into the straight chair across from Grover Minnick's easy chair. "Yes, I suppose the circles would show if they became dark enough. A sign of fatigue," she added low, but Doris had already taken up the doily thread and crochet hook and was busy at her handiwork.

"You remember Gertrude Nickleberg, don't you, girl? Remember the nice man who helped us park our truck at the Fourth of July carnival? His wife. They came afterwards with a pie to share with us. I think that was before Heinz had started his bad drinkin', but I'm not sure about that. He seemed okay at the picnic, but Gertie was a bit drawn, I thought. And now Gert has taken a fall, and I wanted to make something to take to her, so she'd know how much the neighbors think about her." Doris stopped to look at the half-created doily. "I don't guess this is gonna help her all that much, though, is it? Should've made dish cloths. With all the blood and guts on their kitchen worktable, dishcloths would've been more practical for cleanin' up. Oh, dear, I guess I ought to tear this out and start with something that'll do Gert more good." She set the hook on the cushion beside her; at once it slid down between the pillows and would be lost to her when she went to pick it up again.

"Perhaps, Mother Minnick," Nandria sat up to suggest, "perhaps you could set the thread and work you have accomplished thus far aside. That way, yes. The material you had been using is perhaps delicate for what you plan to make now."

"Well, of course. I can use cotton yarn. Save this for workin' at later for Christmas for somebody. Yes, of course. Come

December I'll be glad I thought of that." Patting the light scarf she always wore at her neck, Doris beamed at the dark young woman. "It won't take me but a bit to whip up a few dishcloths. Will you take me to the egg farm later this afternoon then, so I can give them to Mrs. Nickleberg? You know where their farm is, don'tcha?"

So tired that she did not want even to move, let alone drive, Nandria nevertheless nodded agreement. "Perhaps when Rose awakens from her nap."

"My middle name is Rose. Did you know that?"

"Yes, Mother Minnick, we knew," Nandria whispered, but her mother-in-law would not remember that she and Will had named their daughter after her. It was useless to try. Instead, she slid down to rest her neck against the chair back. Closing her eyes, Nandria slipped into light sleep clutching Will's letter in her apron pocket.

Gertrude Nickleberg awoke, frightened by her heart fluttering in her chest. "Oh!" she murmured. Blinking, she turned slowly in the passenger seat as though the home she'd known for decades was somehow new to her, and strange. "Nothing makes any sense." She stared with her one good eye at the shed and the long, low main chicken coop. "Where?"

Garum watched her try to open the other eye. "Where, missus? You mean where is the mister? Well, don'tcha remember..."

She whipped around to look at the boy. "Who? Who are you?" she demanded as though afraid.

"Oh, sweet savior Mr. Yea's Us," he rasped and huddled deeper under the steering wheel of the Nickleberg sedan-turned-pickup truck. "I – I'm just Garum. The boy your mister hired to help you."

"Oh, yeah. That boy..." she muttered and laid her head in her hands. "Where's Heinz? You know, don't you?"

Clinging to the wheel, the boy murmured, "Well..."

"Yes, I think you do. And this is my husband's car."

"Ah, missus, you know I didn't steal this. You said you wanted to come back here to your feather farm."

"My feather farm," she murmured, half remembering, "...ain't all feathers. So much to do. We can't go nowhere 'til we do chores. Come on, boy, work to do."

The lane from the country road up to the Nicklebergs' farm was rutted and dusty. Nandria bit her lip at each pothole; Doris muttered and groaned; Rose, standing on her grandmother's lap to see out the truck window, giggled.

"There's their sawed-off sedan. Never seen another like it. But at least we know they are home," Doris said as they pulled up beside the shed.

Nandria had not told her that Greg Paisler had taken Mr. Nickleberg into town for the sheriff. Nor had she corrected her mother-in-law's assumption that Mrs. Nickleberg had hurt herself in a fall. It was not her place to say, since Grover Minnick had not seen fit to give his wife the facts of the situation. Besides, Nandria thought, lifting Rose out with her as she climbed down from the once-blue pickup, I am far too worn to be able to do an adequate explanation that will not cause her panic. I only wish there had been time to consult Mr. Minnick before we left on this visit. I have no doubt he would have talked Mother Minnick into staying home today.

Doris had already gathered up her crocheted dishrags and was hurrying to the door to knock. She gasped when a small Black boy answered.

"Uh, hello. What are you doing here?"

"I'm Garum, Mrs. Minnick."

"You know me?"

"Oh, yes, Ma'am. My pa—Dolph Tacker, he's my pa—don't you remember him and me coming to help on your farm during harvest?"

"Well, I... But what are you doin' here, boy?"

"I work here. The mister said. And the missus, she needs help right now."

"So, she was hurt pretty bad from her fall, then."

The child looked up at her, frowning.

"Who is it? Who you talking to, boy?" The voice from the kitchen sounded exhausted and maybe even frightened.

"Mrs. Nickleberg?" Doris called. "Gertrude, that you? It's Doris Minnick from up the road a piece. I come to see how you're doing."

"Doris? Oh, I'm such a fright. You don't want to see me like this." The voice now sounded plaintive.

"Fiddlesticks. I've seen bumps and bruises before," Doris said, brushing by the boy and entering the hallway.

Nandria, carrying Rose, hurried after her. "If Mrs. Nickleberg would prefer..." Nandria started, but Doris had already entered the kitchen.

"Oh! Dear Lord, have mercy."

"The boy won't bring me a mirror. Do I look that awful, Doris?"

"Your face!" Doris swayed. Nandria came up behind her to guide her to sit in the chair across the worktable.

"I tried to tell you not to come in," Gertrude mumbled and then, head down, went quiet.

"You must have fallen off a roof to be so battered. You seen Dr. Ricartsen, have you?"

Nodding, but not looking up, Gertrude moaned quietly. "Off a roof? Yeah, I guess that would account for it. A roof."

"Oh, you poor dear. I could leave my girl here to take care of you."

"This here boy is all I need. He's doin' fine."

"You sure? All that's gonna take a long time healing. Your mister good with you, is he? Well, you're gonna need rest and quiet even more than talking with a friend. But here, I brought you some dishcloths I thought you might use. They're soft enough, maybe they'd do for patting down your bruises, too. Oh, I wish I'd brought more than the casserole of what we made for our menfolk's supper. I'll have more food sent over. The church ladies will..."

"No, no, please. Dear Doris, please. Don't let them fuss. Don't let them come. Tell them I'm doin' well but would rather not be seen at this time. Maybe later, when I'm not quite so colorful."

"Or swelled up. Dear me, Gert, I ain't seen ballooning like that since—well, since the time those young people hauled that darky behind their truck."

Nandria moaned and stepped back against the door frame.

Both women looked over at her and then, shrugging, at each other.

"Well, Gert, if you're sure I can't do nothing for you..."

"Uh, uh. Just time, I guess, Doris." She didn't thank Doris Minnick for coming.

"Time heals all wounds; that's what the preacher'd say. We could send for him to come to you. No? Well, send that boy if you do think of something me and Grover can help you with."

Gertrude's shoulders drooped with exhaustion. She shook her head and lowered it onto her arms folded on the table.

"Don't get up. I know our way out. Be sure you'll let us know..." Doris backed past Nandria and the baby and turned to hurry down the hall to the door.

"Mrs. Minnick does not know what truly happened, Mrs. Nickleberg. I am not certain how many people do."

"Ah," Gertrude breathed. She lifted her head in gratitude and watched Nandria leave.

Greg Paisler sat down at the supper table, mostly to be able to help Nandria with the clean-up afterwards. He knew neither Mr. nor Mrs. Minnick would give her a hand, and she looked so tired.

"So, what have you been up to this day, Mother?" Grover asked his Doris as she seemed to be bubbling over with news to tell him over their coffee and apple pan dowdy.

"Went to see how Gert Nickleberg was doing." She beamed. "Took her some little things I'd made and a casserole after her fall."

Greg's eyebrows lifted but he said nothing.

"That was nice," Grover murmured as he patted his wife's hand and then tilted his chair back against the wall.

"Well, I thought it would be. But she is so purple—near black—and swelled up, you wouldn't hardly recognize her if you bumped into her on the street. I swear, she must'a come off the roof to get banged up the way she was. I told her we'd help any way we could, but she said the little darky boy with her was doing what was needful."

"Darky boy?" Minnick questioned.

"Tacker's boy, she said. You had a coon named Tacker help with harvest last fall?"

"Dolph Tacker?"

"Yeah, I think that's what the boy said. Come to think of it, ain't he one of the little ones come here of an evening to hear the girl read to them? I thought he looked familiar, but they all look alike to me."

Grover stared down the length of the table as Nandria rose to begin stacking the dirty plates. "Is he?"

"Garum? Yes, he has learned the basics of reading. And he appears to be excited about learning how to read music."

"What's the boy doing over at Nicklebergs'?"

Nandria paused to wipe Rose's apples-and crust-smeared face. "As I understand it, Mr. Nickleberg hired him the other day while you and I were in town seeing Dr. Ricartsen, Mother Minnick. He helps gather and sort the eggs and ready them for the Owens' store."

"Huh. So, there was somebody there besides Heinz," Grover mused.

The others stared.

"You don't think a boy that size could..." Doris exclaimed.

"No, but he's got a pa big enough to do a whole lot of damage."

Chapter 16

"Where you been, boy?" Garum's father's voice was harsh. He rattled the burger turner sharply against the edge of the wrought iron skillet in successively louder waves of agitation. "I called and called you, but you never did answer. Been off again learnin' to read? Whad I warn you about that? We ain't nobody's favorite dumb as we is. We don't need to give 'em no more excuse to whup us for actin' uppity."

"N-no, sir. Miz Nandria only comes out some evenin's to read to her little one. We kids kind of sneak to be around her so we can hear."

"So, where you been this whole blessed day? You ain't been stealin' or nothin', have you?" Dolph stepped toward him, turner raised.

"Oh, no, Pa. Nothin' like that."

"Well, what, then?"

"I... I been working."

"Workin'? For money?" Dolph stared at his son, eyes flickering between incredulity and envy.

"Well, sir, not for money—yet. But he promised."

"Who?"

"Them N-Nicklebergs what got the ch-chicken farm," Garum stammered.

"Chicken farm." Dolph sat down heavily in the only other chair at their table. The sturdy one. He shook his head, sadly, Garum thought.

"I know we're buildin' up our chicken farm, Pa. We're workin' it good. Even better'n Mr. Nick, in some ways."

"That place's got..." Spreading his calloused hands, palms up, Dolph could only contrast what the Nicklebergs had with what he could never build, even in his dreams. Sighing, he closed his eyes.

"Oh, Pa, that Mr. Nickle, he ain't got near your smarts. He's got such a good place, but he's drinkin' and he ain't takin' care..."

"Drinkin'? Hard liquor?"

"Well, I ain't for sure, but he curls up in the corner of the shed and sleeps, snorin' somethin' awful. And his missus..."

"What about her?"

"I feel sorry..."

"Don't waste your time! The idea, feelin' sorry for no white man as got land and two hands to make it into somethin'."

"But his lady. She's hurtin' and..."

"You think your own ma ain't hurtin'?"

Garum stared, mouth open in an 'O' that was his face from nose tip to sharp chin.

"What ails you, boy? You look stupefied as a cracker white gived a fork to eat his peas with."

"I got a ma?"

"Got a ma? 'Course you got a ma."

"Where? I thought she was... You showed me her grave up in the Ozarks... I was little, but I remember..."

"Your ma hated the Ozarks. Too rugged and no people anywhere around. Lonely and scared, that's what she'd be up in them hills. She'd haunt us if we ever buried her there."

"But I remember... didn't you cry out, 'Mother'?"

"My mother. It was my mother," Dolph peered at his son as though seeing him for the first time. "Lordy Moses, boy, how could you remember that? You was toddlin' around in diapers. You had one soggy one draggin' near onto the ground. I didn't know you could even understand words, let alone remember 'em."

"But..." Garum stared at his father's head shaking in denial. "But, if that was your ma, where's mine?"

"In Pittsburgh," Dolph spat, flipped the over-cooked, greasy burger onto his son's plate, shoved the skillet off the fire hole of the stove, and stomped out of their cabin

Garum sat a long time, blinking.

Pittsburgh? What is a Pittsburgh? Wait, that's a city. Where? Somewheres up north. Ma is up north. Does she like it up north? Then she can't like me much. Did I make her run up north, like Frog's ma did when she seen him so busted up and ugly? Lord'a'gocean, that's even worse'n having her buried.

Nandria was later than usual getting out to the elm swing that Friday evening. A few of the kids were busy in their tin tubs for their weekend bath for the holiday of each weekend and had not come. Many of the others gave up and slipped away before Nandria and Rose came out from the enclosed porch. So, there were only a few children to gather around Nandria's feet. Garum stayed back near the peeling blue doghouse.

With little Rose grinning on her lap, Nandria set the slate she had carried outside down on the ground beside her. Though her face, her whole bearing showed her fatigue, she smiled and looked around at the children. When she met Garum's eyes, her smile deepened in invitation. He crept forward but not quite into the circle. Questioning him with her eyes, she nodded that where he chose to stay was acceptable to her, but he was welcome to come closer.

"I thought that since it has grown almost dark already, that we might just try to sing a bit this evening. Is that acceptable to you, Rose's friends and companions?"

The kids nodded and inched closer.

"'This Little Light of Mine' is such a sweet song. My mother taught it to me and my younger brother..." Wiping her eyes with the edge of the light blanket she had wrapped around Rose's shoulders, Nandria cleared her throat to continue. "It is a fun, light air to sing, if you would like to learn it now? Perhaps later we can try to write out the music for it. At least the first few lines so you can see that music does indeed have an alphabet and sentences that can be read by anyone who cares to learn."

The children's eyes grew large. Many looked skeptical but willing to take their teacher's word for it until they could see for themselves later.

Clearing her throat again to begin a husky line of "This little light of..." She stopped, grinning apologetically.

"You gotta cold, Miz Nandria?" Zelma Bratton stood up near the side of the wooden swing seat. "Or are ya just so very tired?"

Closing her eyes, Nandria nodded, although it was not clear which question she was answering.

The knob-kneed girl turned to the encircling children. "Anybody out there know that song Miz Nandria was trying to sing?" She was met by blank faces. "Well, it don't matter. It's a promise for later then, ain't, er, is it not, Miz Nandria? You'll learn it to us when you feel better."

Murmuring well wishes interspersed with sighs of disappointment, the kids got up and wandered away. All but Zelma. And Garum, who had retreated to the doghouse.

"You ain't gonna bother her now, Garum Tacker."

"Thank you kindly, Miss Bratton," Nandria told the girl. "Your graciousness was appreciated. As for Master Tacker, I believe we had a few words to discuss. He will leave then. I am sure I am well enough for those few words. But I thank you for your concern." She smiled.

Zelma looked a threat at Garum to keep his few words 'few' indeed, nodded to Nandria and hurried away.

Sighing, Nandria huddled in the swing. "Will you come forward, Master Tacker? Or shall Rose and I rise and come to you?"

With tears glistening, Garum stood up, swaying.

Gathering Rose close against herself, Nandria slipped from the swing and stepped toward him. "Won't you come and sit on the porch steps with us? My Rose would love to have the opportunity to know you better."

His chin quivering, Garum hung his head. "I gots a mama."

"Pardon me, son, I could not hear you. Did you say that you have a mother?" Nandria reached to rest her hand on the boy's shoulder. His shuddering told her she had heard correctly. "Oh, Garum, come." She led him to the porch and had him sit beside her on the wooden steps. She drew him to her. His head rested against little Rose's back, but the baby only twisted to stare at his face without protest.

The boy wept. She held him, rocking but saying nothing, until Rose squirmed and then arched her back to push him away. To soothe both the children, Nandria began singing, low and husky, 'This little light of mine. I'm gonna let it shine.'

Rose stared up at her smiling mother. Her gathered howl melted into a frown and gurgle. Garum lifted his head, embarrassed and ashamed. But his movement caught the baby's attention. She grinned at his face glistening with tears.

"Oh, missus, I'm so sorry."

"There is no reason to be sorry, Master Tacker. You have recently heard overwhelming news. Rose and I are proud to share your special moment with you. Would you like to tell us about it, or shall it merely be our secret?"

Garum opened his mouth, but he could not speak. Rose lunged to explore his face with chubby fingers.

In the front room-turned-bedroom of their rambling farmhouse, Grover Minnick lay staring at the deep shadow of the tall dresser beyond his bare feet. *Too dratted big for this room. Parlor, that's where it should be. Or back up in their bedroom. But when she wasn't safe to leave alone up there, we had to move down here to the first floor. She wouldn't leave any of these clunky big pieces up there. For storage for the seasons, I tried to tell her. If we left it and the tall dresser up there, it'd be great for winter undies and sweaters in the summer. Up there. Out of the way. But, no. She had to have it all down here. Thank goodness Heinz Nickleberg happened to be here. He durn near twisted his back outta shape helpin' me bring that monster down here.*

A low groan escaped his lips. Minnick muffled it and turned with his back to his wife. Sobs rose from his chest, threatening his throat. Doris stirred. Closing his eyes, he froze in place until her breathing calmed again behind him.

Why in the Savior's name did Nickleberg start in on the stuff about the baby? Wasn't it enough that he'd been part? Did we have to know that? Did he have to bring up those ugly times? He was laughing—oddest laugh—but swearing it was what all darkies deserved. Like we didn't know it's our sacred duty to protect our womenfolk. We grew up in the South. We know what we have to do. Been drilled into us since we wore short pants. Keep 'em in their place. You gotta, or they'll...Lord, who knows what they'd do!

He turned onto his back again, feeling Doris's warm body beside him as she had been all these godawful years. Warming him. Comforting him when drought or fire threatened to wipe out everything they had sweated, ached and toiled for until each was ready to collapse with hunger and fatigue. She'd given everything she had and was. Given him sons. Asked so little for herself. Looked at him with an adoration he didn't deserve. How could he not protect her and the other white women? Protect her even when they'd just met. He'd been young then. Just feeling the changes in his body that young manhood brings to take over who you thought you were.

Lord, that was scary and exciting all at the same time. Each degree of change. The shoulders widening, thickening with muscles that made the girls stare. Chest broader, growing fur you could see them wanting to touch. Voice lower, richer, like you could command an army, but you knew you couldn't. Not yet. Promise of power. Promise of action, excitement. Heroism. And down there, hair and changes, growth in places nobody was supposed to see but all the other changes announced. Promised. Everybody knew, but nobody spoke about in polite company and only in ribald raillery among the guys.

Promise, yeah. But what did it really foretell? Work. Labor that hurt and took your being with little or no reward. Never-ending pain, anguish, fear. A farm that demanded all of you, but at the end of the season only laughed and promised 'maybe next year, if you're lucky, you fool who keeps trying.'

And the boys. Fred, a fool kid with no thought he might die. And die, he did.

And Willard. Look at the wife he sends here.

Biggest fool of all, I took her in. Well, she is good for the missus. Works like a field hand. And Doris so young to be a tottering, feeble-minded old lady. Oh, God, what did I do wrong? Castor Pigeon. I was so young. All the men... Yes, I done it. But why visit punishment on my lady? God of mercy, help us!

Sobs then. Sobs he couldn't stop. For the promises unfulfilled and now unfulfillable and another war coming on. Depression and despair. More mouths to feed with only his bare hands and aching back to give them what they needed to have. But mostly for the ugliness of the past. Ugliness he'd kept locked inside himself year after year. Until now he couldn't.

"Mr. Minnick, what...?" Doris woke and turned to him. "My darling, what...?"

He twisted to rise and escape the room and her, but she hauled on his shoulder and drew him back. She held him, shushing and humming "Rockabye baby, on the treetop..."

Minnick melted into her arms, weeping quietly now, but allowing the aches and anguish and disappointment and fear to ease slowly from his body. He huddled in fetal position on their double bed and let her stroke his temples, his taut jawline, his tight shoulders and back, singing low until he slept. The first sleep without nightmares of battered toddlers since Heinz Nickleberg had reminded him of the worst moments of his youth.

Nandria sat at the edge of the brass bed, listening. She'd awakened believing it was Rose weeping but knew before she was fully conscious that it was an adult, not a child, crying. Visions of Willard weeping that way swept through her. She rose, whispering. "Will, it is your father weeping. Anguish..."

So much anguish. And so much more to come before these Nazi criminals are bested. As they will be, Willard. With you fighting them, they will be conquered.

Rose stirred, fussing the ten-month-old's protest at being awakened before her period of sleep was completed. Nandria hurried to lift her little one from her crib to cuddle and nurse her. She knew her father-in-law would not want anyone to be aware of his overwhelming emotion. "I shall wait this morning before I begin breakfast preparations," she told little Rose. "We can pretend we slept in until after Mr. Sun has fully emerged from behind Mother Earth's curvature. How would we like that?"

Rose unlatched to look up into her mother's eyes and giggle.

In their front bedroom, Doris clung to her man, awakening him. "What, Grover, darling? What?"

Minnick swiped under his nose and wiped his hand on the edge of the bottom sheet. Slowly he turned onto his back and lay for some time fighting the panic of his dream to be able to face her. When he could at last look at her, he saw the terror in his wife's pale eyes. "Ah, pretty little Doris, it's nothing," he murmured, caressing her hair.

"My husband's not one to fret over nothin'. You gotta tell me."

When he couldn't calm her, he finally realized only the truth would give her ease. For whatever reason, his Doris was with him, mentally and emotionally, at least for now. "Pretty little lady," he whispered.

She giggled, remembering their days of courtship. "Not so little now, Mr. Minnick," she whispered, snuggling at his side.

"But still the prettiest lady in the county—in the whole blamed state of Missouri," he whispered back, stroking her graying hair away from her cheek.

"Tell me, please, Grover. Tell me. Whatever it is, we can fight it together like we've always done." She raised onto one elbow to stare into his eyes.

He blew out a long, slow exhalation. "Remember that Pigeon creature?" he asked finally.

"The darky?" She frowned. "You ain't remembering that, are you? He had it coming to him. You had to. Uppity, he was. He had it comin'!"

Minnick closed his eyes.

She sat up beside him, pulling the top sheet up to cover her sagging breasts that had slipped from her tangled nightgown. "Now you listen to me. You was one of a bunch..."

"A mob," he corrected low.

"A group of young men doing what they had to do. However unpleasant," she insisted. "You were strong to protect white women, and you done your duty, like you should've. Dear knows what he would've ended up doing to some innocent white gal."

Minnick muttered softly through clenched teeth. He was sweating but chilled, not knowing how to explain.

Doris touched his cheek and followed his jawline with the tip of her finger. "Mr. Minnick, Castor Pigeon got what he deserved."

"No," Minnick heaved up away from her caresses. "No! Ain't nobody deserves what that man got. Nobody, don't you see? No human being deserves to be treated the way he was."

"Human?" She blinked. "But, Grover dear, he was a coon."

He twisted back to stare at her. In all innocence and acceptance, she believed what she said. Just as she had years before when a hired Negro caught his fingers in gears while trying to fix something in the field. Grover had been devastated as he told her about the fellow runnin' off, clutching his hand.

"Now, just don't you fret over nothin' like that," she'd told him. "So, he loses a finger or two. Wasn't your fault, even if you are his boss man. He was careless. Besides, those people've got a whole raft of medicine men to chant over them. Probably wrap it in some sort of disgusting goo and sing magic over it 'til it grows back. My pa grew up in the Deep South. Near the mouth of the Mississip. He knew all about that stuff. So don't you worry none. They got their own ways. Best you just stay clear of whatever they might do."

She'd been so certain her father was right. It was the way things were—the way things were supposed to be. Her father had said so, so it must be true.

She looked that same way now. Totally sure. If he disagreed, if he questioned her certainty, with the way her mind had been wandering... Lord, it would tear apart her world and rip out what little hold she had on sanity.

"Sweet savior," he whispered and reached to enfold her in his arms. "Yes, yes, pretty little lady," he crooned, knowing that she was wrong. "Of course, you're right."

Chapter 17

Saturday, August 17, 1940

Zeb Paisler stretched his shrapnel-damaged leg to ease its aching as he sat on the milking stool. The cows mooed, content with his gentle easing of the fullness of their udders. Sighing, he took in the heavy, warm scent of the animals, their hay and their excrement. Closing his eyes, he listened to the sharp squirt of the milk hitting the side of the pail and the comfortable grinding of bovine teeth as the cows fed.

Every morning. Each day begins with an hour among these creatures of God's handiwork. Trusting. Stubborn in their mild way, but gentle for the most part. Fond of their calves. So many grieve when their little ones are taken away. I never could be in the beef-selling business. Slaughter, sweet Savior, I've seen too much of that. And now another war brewing and no way I can shield my sons from it. They'll hear the drums and calls for glory. I won't be able to tell them war isn't quick over or glamorous. It'll test their bravery in ways they can't imagine: their courage to face the horrendous, painful and treacherous day after day after day with no respite or relief. Oh, Lord, if it be Thy will, keep the war over there. Keep my boys here with their mother and me...

"Pa?"

The young voice startled Zeb out of his reverie. Wiping his forehead with his forearm, he looked up at his third son Greg and nodded. He'd been aware without acknowledging it that Greg had been with him in the barn, cleaning and straining. It was Greg's way of telling his father that, even though he'd gone to help the Minnicks on their farm, he still wanted to be part of his own family. Early nearly every morning, Greg had come to help out with the milking, although that had not been among his assigned duties. For that, Zeb was grateful. The boy's brothers had overridden his objections to the assignment of field crops. They'd done it with little heed to his warnings. So, he'd struck out on his own to help Will Minnick as a way of protesting their refusal to listen. But he was still part of the family, and for that Zeb was even more grateful than for the extra help each morning.

"Got something on your mind, son?"

"Well, in a way, yeah, I do. Sir, you know Mr. Nickleberg pretty well from over the years."

Zeb nodded as his fingers told him Wilma's udder was drained for this morning. He wiped the teats and patted her side before rising to lift the pail of milk she'd given. He stretched tall, repositioning his bad leg to be sure it would hold him when he put his weight on it. Then he looked at his son. "What about Mr. Nickleberg, Greg?"

The third son was now taller than his father by at least the height of his thick hair combed high. Zeb smiled, realizing that Greg combed it that way on purpose. Perhaps not to outdo his sire but surely to compete with Eli, the eldest of the boys. *So many struggles fight on in silence inside a family,* Zeb realized again as he watched his son work out some difficulty within himself before speaking.

"Something you learned while doing for Sheriff Yakes, son? So, you're not sure how much you can break confidence by telling me?"

"Pa," Greg said, looking his father at eye level and reveling in the discovery of how close he was to reaching the height of the man who had been his hero all his life. There was a note, too, of relief that Zeb had understood without requiring Greg to put his dilemma into words.

They moved toward the filters Greg had already set up for the first processing of this morning's milk.

"Something our neighbor's done distresses you, son? You believe he's the one hurt his wife. Drunk again, wasn't he?"

Greg nodded. "Why won't she come out and say it was him who beat her?"

Lifting the pail to pour into the filter, Zeb's usually true aim was off. Milk and froth spilled over the filter and onto the floor.

Greg bent to wipe up the liquid, and then splashed clean water to take up the dregs of white. Zeb kept a clean dairy barn. Greg looked up from the floor at his father's next question.

"The man tell you he's been havin' bad dreams?"

"How'd you know, Pa?"

Setting the pails in a row for Greg to hose out, Zeb rubbed his bad leg and rested his haunches on the edge of the nearest bales of hay. The normal wry twinkle was gone from his eyes. "War does terrible things to a man's soul."

"War, Pa? Mr. Nickleberg was in the Great War?"

"There are not so great wars as well, son. Terrible wars that tear men apart mentally limb by limb." Zeb appeared to collapse within himself, slowly shaking his head.

Although he was bursting with questions, Greg knew to go quiet for his father's sake. Now was not the time to ask them.

Garum never told his father of Miz Nandria's comfort. Ashamed that he'd brought his troubles and his father's business to the house of white folks, he knew he would never tell... *Wait! Miz Nandria ain't white.*

The boy stopped pedaling his bike up to the rutted lane to the chicken farm. He stood on his left foot with his right leg draped over the bar as he shook his head. Miz Nandria wasn't white, yet she lived in that house with the man who never missed a chance to say something at Garum's father. Called him 'boy' when even white folks should be able to see he was a strong man. Only hired him at harvest times, but then, Pa said he always paid him what he'd said he would and right then when the work was done. You had to look out. Mr. Minnick was fair when it came to handin' out the money due. "Not every farmer does that. But you stay careful. He's white and any white can get you set on fire at the drop of his hat. And he will if you cross him, even without meaning to." How many times had Pa warned him just that way?

Garum shook his head again. Why would Miz Nandria live there? And her baby, even if little Rose was part white. It was her mother's part of her that made her less in Whites' eyes than the pretty little tyke she was. Bright and quick to learn. She'd be walkin' soon, and lots of kids didn't learn that fast, Garum knew.

With wonder, he pictured Miz Nandria's dark hand on his arm telling him that what he was feeling was natural and good. Comforting him, maybe the way a mama would. The way his own mama must have, if only he could remember.

Swiping at the dust that irritated his eyes, Garum swung his leg from over the bar. He'd need to walk his bike up the rest of this lane. There was no chance he could run alongside and leap on. Not uphill like this and with all the ruts and pebbles. Not when the sun hadn't yet peeked enough above the east hills to let him see what was likely to snare his front tire and pitch him off if he tried.

Shaking his head, he whispered a thank you to Miz Nandria for listening last night. But he still couldn't make sense of who she was, a Negro lady holding her own, it seemed, in a white world.

Miz Nickleberg was still asleep when he got to the house. He filled the kettle and set it on the hottest burner, but he knew better than to fuss with the fire in the stove. The egg farmer's lady would decide how much wood. He would fetch it for her, but only after she'd made up her mind. Gathering the wire baskets, he slipped outside to feed the hens and clean and refill their water troughs. With them busy making gluttons of themselves (he chuckled to himself at that expression Miz Nandria had read and then explained from one of the stories), Garum went about gathering the fresh eggs into the baskets. He'd take the eggs in and leave them on the worktable while he came back out to shovel the floor of the hen house. He'd started to make a compost pile like his dad's at home. Mr. Nickleberg hadn't seen it yet, so he wasn't sure the man would approve, but maybe if he explained what it was for. When the man was sober. Like Mrs. Nickleberg had said, he was kind enough, when he was sober.

She was up and stirring in the kitchen when he had finished in the hen house. He was glad he'd stopped to wash up before coming in.

"Well, boy," she managed through puffy lips. "I guess you've been with the hens. I see you brought in the eggs. We'll need to wipe and sort 'em. Not sure who—if anybody—is comin' to take them to Owens'. But we might as well get them ready, just in case somebody does. Unless you're up for drivin' us into town?"

Garum's eyes widened, but he stopped his head from shaking the vigorous 'no' his whole body was telling him. If he wanted to get paid for this job, he had to be able to do whatever they asked of him. He couldn't say 'no' or he'd be let go with nothing to show for all the work he'd already put in. Garum blinked and took a deep breath, hoping his lady would forget that one as a bad idea. She'd been in that sawed-off car with him. She knew.

"Well, come on then, let's get these eggs ready," Gertrude mumbled. She reached for the cloth, but it was dry.

"I got it," Garum chimed in, hurrying to moisten and wring four cloths. He handed her two, then sat near her with the others, ready to wipe, candle and sort. Already they worked well together, each quick with decision and blessed with agile hands. No need for talking. Except Gertrude Nickleberg's pain and confusion escaped in sighs that brought tears to the boy's eyes. "Oh, missus," he whimpered.

Gertrude stared at him. She had not realized she'd sighed. Wondered what could be distressing the youngster. "What, boy? You hurt yourself?"

"Oh, no, ma'am. I'm fine." He lowered his eyes to concentrate on the eggs in front of him.

"You sure sounded like something was digging at you."

"Well, missus," he stammered, thinking fast, "I guess I was wondering how to bring up some ideas me and my pa had with our chickens. Nothing fancy, like you folks's. Leghorns mostly. But Pa's been trying different ways. Like puttin' their hen house up a ways. And building a porch-like for 'em. With chicken wire for them to walk on when they wanna come outside. He thinks maybe they'll be healthier up like that. And it sure makes it harder for the foxes to get at 'em when we're gone away from the place all day."

"And?"

Shrugging, he breathed deep in gratitude that she seemed to have forgotten the idea of his driving her to Boonetown. "Well, missus, I didn't mean nothing. Except if you and the mister'd like to try and see if it'd work here for your feather farm?" His voice trailed off. He watched her face as she considered.

It was hard to tell with all the swelling, but it seemed as though she scoffed at first, just as he had expected her to. Then muttered, "Heinz'd... oh, sweet sugarbirds, he'd look. Might even see somethin' worth his while and build the like here if he wanted. But you, boy, he'd never take a suggestion from a spade. Never. You may as well tell your pa to keep his ideas to himself. My man wouldn't listen, even if was something that'd make this place better for itself and us, too."

"I'll tell him, missus. We won't bother you none. Promise."

Gertrude stared at the boy until he squirmed.

"It's just me, Garum, ma'am. The boy your husband hired to help you here on your feather farm."

Gertrude lifted her aching head to peer at the skinny arms, the sharp chin and the still rosebud mouth. If this boy kept that definition of even those thick lips, he'd find many'a gal thinking about kissing them. It was the worried eyes and furrowed brow that brought Mrs. Nickleberg back to the here and now. Her mind fumbled for something in what the boy had said that had chuckled somewhere deep within her. "Say that again, boy," she slurred, resting her head in her scabbing right hand.

Seeing her, the boy frowned with even more concern. "Say? What? Oh, missus..."

Lifting and dropping her idle left hand, Gertrude indicated what had just gone on before. "About this farm. Somethin' about what you called this farm."

Her voice was petulant but seemed about to be disturbed and angry. Garum wracked his brain to recall just what he'd said. "About this here beauteous farm, missus? Why, I..."

"You called it somethin' funny. Father farm? No, that wouldn't be funny, I guess. Not here." Her voice trailed away. A shroud of pain or depression enveloped her, making Garum desperate to remember what he'd said that she'd found funny.

"Not father...feather!" His dark-chocolate eyes lit up. "Feather farm? This here feather farm? That's what folks call it. Feather farm." He ended on a note of hope.

"F... feather farm," she rolled bits of air beneath her upper front teeth and lower lip to create a series of f's until finally finishing the feather word. The corners of her mouth turned up, ever so slightly and then drooped again as though she were very tired. She looked at the anxious child. *So like little Hiram. Curious. Always thinkin'. Shame it won't do this one any good.*

She set the last of her eggs in the containers to go into town. "Come on, boy. Let's get these out to the truck. I think I can drive this time. With them short legs of yours, dear knows them eggs'd probably rot in old age before you could get us to Owens' store. "Thank you, son," she whispered as she drew he helped her up.

It took all his strength to help her stay upright. Together they struggled toward her room just off the kitchen. He helped her stretch out on the bed smothered in handmade quilts.

Gertrude was surprisingly strong when she awoke. After a bit to eat, they toddled out to the sawed-off sedan-turned-truck. The walk wore her out.

"You drive, Hiram," she murmured.

Garum peered at her, opening his mouth to correct her. "I'm Garum, ma'am, not Hiram," he wanted to say. But he closed it again without saying anything. Reluctantly, he closed her door when she had gotten herself into the passenger seat. From the running board, he climbed over the driver's door, slid down behind the steering wheel, and took the keys from her outstretched hand. The drive down Nickleberg's lane went fairly well. This time the trees and even most bushes stayed on their own sides of the pathway. He'd learned to stay in the ruts. Even the country road to the highway into Boonetown had ruts to stay in, but it was hard to see them when he was situated to reach the pedals. And when he rose to be sure where he was on the road, his feet left the clutch and the gas. The engine sputtered and stalled. Finally, the woman told him to get out and help her around to trade places. Her driving was surer until she dozed. He needed to grab the wheel and steer them zigzagging along the middle of the road until her foot strayed from the clutch and the car jerked to a stop. He let her sleep. Gertrude's driving was somewhat steadier after her nap.

She was at the wheel and mostly awake when they pulled up in front of Owens' store. Luckily, the way was clear. Garum climbed around the gearshift to step hard on the brake pedal for them to park at an angle that most people could get around without too much hassle.

He whistled with relief.

"What'd you say, boy? You whistlin' at some white lady, are you? That could get you mussed up good."

"Oh, no, missus. I wouldn't do nothin' unrespectable like that. Never, I wouldn't." He was shaking.

"Of course not," she soothed. She'd meant it as a joke. *I can feel this boy's fear. It's so real I can feel it through the shakin' of this here car.* Again, Gertrude Nickleberg felt something in this boy she'd never really known. To talk about, surely. Laugh about with some of their friends. But here, in this child, she could feel it, and it disturbed her. "Everybody knows you wouldn't, boy," she said, but even while the words were in her mouth, she knew that some would jump on an opening like that. Jump on the boy and 'muss' him up real good. They'd be grinning. And their mates would be whooping it up in glee. Shuddering, she let go of the steering wheel to fuss with the door handle. But Garum had already bundled out and was scurrying around the vehicle to help her.

"Why don't you go on ahead to the doc's place, missus? I can take them eggs in to Miz Owens for you."

"Dr. Ricartsen? Why? Nothing's the matter with me that time won't heal."

"Uh, mebbe for them headaches that make you so sleepy?" Garum suggested. " It's kind'a scary to see you sitting there talkin' to me and just doze off. Sometimes I gotta catch you from fallin' off your chair."

"Oh, pshaw," Gertrude protested. "I never..." She stopped and looked at his face and knew it was true. As many times as Heinz had roughed her up, he'd never made things this bad for so many days. And he was always sorry, vowing never to do it again. How many times had she believed him? And it was getting worse. Something was so screwed up inside her man that she couldn't keep up with his turning on her anymore. *Maybe I better talk with the doc. Maybe he can give me some clue of what's wrong with Heinz. How to get him to stay sober so we can keep the farm going. The 'feather farm,'* she chuckled.

"Well, boy, maybe I will talk with Doc Ricartsen, being as we're already right here. But first I gotta talk with Miz Owens. We neither of us does this here egg truck much good with the way we drive. Miz Owens and me better figure out some other way to get these eggs into town for a day or two."

They climbed the stairs into Owens' store. The two women talked, but nothing came handily to mind that might solve their problem. Bernice finally just said to skip a day or two of trying to bring them in. If anyone really needed fresh eggs or chicken, she'd send them on out to the Nickleberg farm to get their own.

Frustrated but knowing no better way to handle things, Gertrude Nickleberg nodded and headed for the door with Garum scurrying along behind her. It took all his persuading to remind her that they had been heading over to Dr. Ricartsen's, and then to talk her into it again.

The Minnicks were there in the doctor's office, Grover and Doris on chairs across the desk from Doc. Nandria held her Rose in the far corner. Sadie Bean heard Gertrude enter, but she wasn't in time to keep Mrs. Nickleberg from hauling open the doctor's office door. She slipped in behind the woman, intending to escort her back out into the lobby. But Ricartsen motioned for his nurse to let Gertrude be. And the little dark boy who had scurried in behind her. Befuddled, Grover forgot what he had been saying. He stopped, glanced at the dark boy, and then stared at Gertrude.

"Mrs. Nickleberg?" Doc half-rose to address her. When she stared at him blankly, Garum hurried up to the edge of his desk.

"Uh, Dr. Ricartsen, we, er, that is, she—Miz Nickleberg here—she's still havin' trouble in the head. Rememberin' things. Like where she is and what she was gonna do. And stuff," he added low when no one responded. "Ain't ya, missus? I mean, we brung in the eggs but she don't..." He stopped and twirled his index finger above his right temple.

"Oh, you poor dear," Doris cried, turning to Nandria. "Girl, bring the lady a chair. She looks exhausted."

"I got it," Sadie interrupted, hurrying to slide the last upright chair from the corner up near the desk and motioning for Gertrude to sit. She did, looking bewildered.

"Wha...?"

"How are the headaches, Mrs. Nickleberg?" Doc asked kindly.

"Headaches? Yeah, I guess I do get headaches. This time." Gertrude patted and pressed most of her face. She bent forward, speaking into her hands in a voice that brought tears to Doris's eyes. "I can't seem to find nothin'. The boy, here, he finds stuff for me, but he won't bring me to my mister."

"To Heinz?" Doris exclaimed, indignant after Grover had told her about it maybe being Heinz who had beat her. "Why in the world would you want to be anywhere near that man?"

Gertrude lifted her hands and appeared to be about to rise. Sadie, clucking and cooing, settled her back into her chair and stood behind her.

"Now, now, Mrs. Nickleberg," Doc coaxed, "you know where your mister is."

"I do? Where?"

"In jail, where he belongs," Doris huffed. "After what he done to you."

Gertrude turned to stare. "After what he done? What'd he do?"

The Minnicks and Doc exchanged glances. The boy shut his mouth tight and covered his eyes with his hand.

Doris sat up, ready to say outright what she'd heard, but, at a gesture from Doc, Minnick pressed her arm and shook his head. "Now, Mother..."

Gertrude reached to draw down the boy's hand from his face. "You know about this?"

His eyes pleading, Garum gulped and nodded once, quickly, as though the answer had been jerked from him. "He was drinkin', missus," he murmured.

A series of protesting, searching, denying expressions flitted across her frown. She stood, swayed and stepped forward to lean on the doctor's desk. "Doc, what...?"

"Do you remember coming here with your mister a day or so ago? You had a knife," he prompted quietly.

"Oh," she exhaled, shaking her head. While the others watched her rock in her chair, Gertrude remembered. "I wouldn't've hurt him none. He...we've been...all these years." She shook with silent heaves, grieving as farm wives and peasants have over thousands of weary years.

It was the boy who stood close beside her. The adults could barely hear him whisper-humming, "...hide it under a bushel, no. I'm gonna let it shine."

Grover Minnick looked over from comforting his wife. *That boy couldn't've done her like that.* "What've you a been doin' lately, boy?" he demanded aloud.

Garum, eyes fully dilated, stared a moment at Mr. Minnick, then eased back toward the door.

Inhaling quickly, Sadie stepped toward him, but the boy was already gone.

Chapter 18

Beulah was the first to see the Tacker boy as he entered, breathless, the gospel tent by the river. She hurried to him where he stood searching. "Your father's not here, Garum. Is he working somewhere today?"

The boy's eyes were wide as he stared at her without seeming to understand her words. She reached to touch his arm, but he shuddered and spun. Big Beulah's massive shoulders drooped as she watched him run away.

"You're trembling, Miz Nandria." Greg Paisler shifted little Rose onto his left hip and touched Will's wife on the shoulder to confirm what his eyes told him.

She stood over the supper dishes suds in the Minnick kitchen sink, leaning hard on stiff arms. She was exhaling in slow, deliberate respirations, trying to regain control. She made no move to answer her daughter's reaching for her.

"What is it, ma'am? What?"

"I...please, forgive my display of emotion."

"There's nothin' to forgive, but if I knew what was... whoa, Nandria, here, sit down. I've got the baby. Let's just take care of you for the moment. Now, here. Good. Just rest your arms on the table and lay your head down on top. Ma did that a time or two with one of the boys. Fainted, like. No, come to think of it, it was when she was with the twins, Ned and Travis. There, now. Better? No, don't try to get up yet. You just stay still. This little girl and I know how to do dishes. And don't worry about Mr. Minnick. He yells, but that won't hurt me none. Anyhow, he and the missus are snoring in the living room, so just forget him and rest right there."

Shaken at the unexpected weakness in Will's self-contained wife, Greg tickled Rose under the chin to make her laugh. Those huge, dark-chocolate eyes had looked so frightened, he was afraid the baby would cry and get her mother trying to be up and tending her again. "We're gonna be just over there at the sink. Whewww," he breathed when Nandria laid her head on her arm across the table and went still. Lifting tangled eyebrows, he whispered and smiled to reassure the baby at his hip. "Your mama's gonna be fine, little lady. Just way too tired. Let's us get these dishes done for her. By then she'll probably be up and wanting you, so I better love you up while I got this chance. See these suds? We're gonna have us some fun."

Dishes done and set in stacks when Greg wasn't quite sure where all of them went, the two of them tiptoed into the living room to check on the senior Minnicks. They found Doris sound asleep on the sofa and Minnick in his easy chair. Making a face of conspiratory delight to little Rose, Greg tiptoed with her back through the kitchen. But they had not made it out the porch door when they heard Nandria call softly after them. Little Rose perked up at the sound of her mother's voice.

"Right here, Miz Nandria," Greg called back. "Just about to go on out to the barn, but we're fine."

She appeared at the doorway, paler than he'd ever seen her but reaching for her little one. Grinning an assurance he did not feel, Greg maneuvered her into the rocking chair and set

Rose on her lap. Once Nandria had settled modestly to nurse, Greg squatted beside them to be sure both were well.

"I've dismissed your class for tonight. Now, do you think you could down a little supper yourself? You haven't eaten what a bird would need these last days when I've been here. You fix big meals, but you don't eat any of them. Are you sleeping all right? Do you want Ma to come and be with you a while? She'd be glad to."

Nandria shook her head, and Rose looked up from nursing within her nest of flannel sheeting, afraid again. "No, no," Nandria cooed, both to forestall Greg's offer and to settle her baby.

"Well, something's got to be done for you."

She did not answer. He watched her huddle closer with her child.

"Miz Nandria, if Will was here, you know he'd do for you—whatever and hang any expense. I can't do what he'd do, but you know he'd want me to try. Please, please let me bring Ma."

Her head bowed. Greg took that as agreement, whether or not it had been intended.

When he realized the other children had already left, Garum searched the barn and chicken coop, hoping to find his teacher without needing to go near the farmhouse. With no sign of Miz Nandria outdoors, the boy crouched beside the peeling blue doghouse and wept.

A ghost hovered at his shoulder.

Garum started up, swallowing a scream and a cry. "Mamaaaa!"

The wraith-like figure touched him with boney fingers. "Master Tacker, what...?"

She bent down to hold the frightened boy and found herself sprawled on the grass. Panting, she sat up to gather him in her arms, rocking and humming.

At last, he could mumble, if not speak. But Nandria was able to make out enough of the words to understand his terror.

"People are beginning to believe your father may be guilty of beating Mrs. Nickleberg? Ah," she sighed, leaning back to look up at the unmoved expanse of Missouri sky. It shone with the same uncaring azure that it would at Dolph Tacker's lynching, if this child was correct. Nandria had no doubt that the boy's insight was accurate. Her slender shoulders sagged until she was draped over Garum more than cradling him.

He struggled to sit upright to peer at her. "You all right, Miz Nandria, ma'am?" Those huge dark eyes widened in concern. "I never seen you so peak-ed."

"Weakness is no excuse for lack of compassion," she murmured. "Please, forgive me."

"Forgive?" he asked, confused. When she didn't answer, he shook again, this time with concern. He had no idea how to take care of a baby, let alone a baby girl. Let alone one that was part white. What would he do if Miz Nandria fainted on him? "Where's little Rosebud, ma'am?"

"Asleep in her crib. On the porch."

"Lemme take you in there. So you're with her. When's your Mr. Will comin' home, ma'am?" he added as he helped her to her feet. *I sure wish he was here about now.*

Nandria gestured for him to help her to the rocking chair, but he got her to lie down on the brass bed. When she slept, he tiptoed into the house to see if anyone else was there to take care of them so he could slip away. He found no one but the master sleeping, mouth open in the big easy chair. And then the mistress; she was asleep, too, sprawled across the sofa, a hook thing in her hand and a lacy thing of fine yarn spilling over her knees. He didn't dare touch it even though it looked like it would fall to the floor.

Even white folks know how to stoop and pick somethin' up from the floor. We've got that much in common, anyways.

Backing into the kitchen, he peeked into the pantry. His jaw dropped to see so many jars and cans of food. He blinked, envious and aware suddenly of the always ache of his stomach. It took everything his father had taught him not to sneak a piece of the cake from inside its glass dome or at least a slice or two of the homemade bread he could feel within a cloth bag. Blowing out his frustration, he knew fear. What if he was caught? The white folks would blame his pa. Make things even worse for him that he'd fathered a thief. Garum made himself turn away from the stored food and shuffle to the enclosed back porch.

"Is Mrs. Minnick well, Master Tacker?" Miz Nandria whispered when he returned. "Should I be rising to go to her?"

"Sleeping, ma'am. Gots her chin on her chest and snoring a bit kind of sleepin'."

"She is well, then," Nandria sighed. "Thank you for checking. And thank you for my few moments lying here. I must have fallen asleep as well. It felt wonderful and, I must admit, I did not wish to arise quite yet. But, please, Master Tacker, draw the rocker nearer so we may talk quietly."

Garum shoved and pulled until the heavy rocking chair was close beside the bed. He sat forward so it tipped near her but found when he was settled that again he could not speak.

"Your fear may be justified, Garum. But you are a caring and courageous young man. And because you show such traits even though you are very young, I believe your father must also be a courageous gentleman of deep integrity."

"P-pa," he whispered, his eyes glistening with tears. She touched his hand.

They sat long minutes, until Garum felt her weariness and gently helped her to ease back into the pillows. Staring, mouth open, he whispered something.

Nandria shook her head, unable to hear, but, suddenly realizing what he must have said, gently shook her head again. "All mothers love, Master Tacker. Yes, yours as well. Know that in your heart. Your mother loves you, whether or not she is able to tell you so directly."

Shuddering, he swallowed and rose to stand up on his own. He shifted as though to run away.

"Your father," Nandria asked. "Does he know of his peril?"

He stared at her, confused. Smiling apology, she rephrased. "Does your father know the danger he is in?" Nandria swallowed at her own dangling participle, but the boy had understood.

"He knowed it could come to this when he first come to help me with Miz Nickleberg. But he helped her anyway. I shouldn't'a never aksed him."

"It was his decision, Master Tacker. And that decision demonstrated the measure of the man. 'Though time slay us...'" Her voice trailed away as she closed her eyes, thinking of Swinburne and so many others who had tried to put the mystery of death and life into words. When she opened them again, minutes had passed. The boy had slipped away. Quietly, she wept. For Garum, for Dolph Tacker. For Will Minnick. Tennyson's words came to her lips.

"But what am I?/ An infant crying in the night/ An infant crying for the light/ And with no language but a cry."

Cynthia Paisler set Todd to watch over the twins at the Minnick elm swing. She carried baby Levitt on her hip to knock at the porch door. Without waiting for an answer, she opened it wide and stepped up inside.

"Mrs. Minnick," she called low.

"Mother Minnick is in her room," Nandria said from her rocking chair in the dim shade of the far corner of the porch.

"I meant you, Nandria Brown Minnick," Cynthia declared. "You deserve to be called by your name, and I mean to do just that. Now, my son is plumb worried about you." She stopped to assess what she could discern of the pale Negro woman. "And, from what I can see with my own eyes, he is right to be concerned. What is it, my friend? Shall we take you to Dr. Ricartsen? Ah, child!" Cynthia slipped Levitt to the floor and bent to hug Rose and her mother. "What's wrong?" she asked gently. "Have you gotten word about Willard? I can't imagine anything else breaking you so completely."

Nandria sobbed.

"Here, let me take wee Rose and put her to play with Levitt," Cynthia suggested when Nandria's sobs finally diminished. "They'll be fine together. I'll fetch something for them to nibble on from the kitchen." Easing Rose from her mother's arms, she set the frightened baby on the floor beside her own one-year-old son, where the two were soon captivated by one another. Hurrying to the kitchen, she came back in a moment with crusts of bread and a chair from the kitchen table to seat herself close beside Nandria. She leaned near, saying nothing.

At last, Nandria twisted in her seat, lifting her apron up and out to reach into its pocket. She drew out a stained and rumpled envelope. Holding it in trembling hands for a long time, she finally offered it to Cynthia.

"Only if you want to share it with me," Cynthia murmured. "I don't have to know, only to understand that something is wrong for your dear husband."

The letter shook but was not withdrawn. Quietly, Cynthia reached for the envelope. The handwriting was sprawled, not at all what Cynthia remembered of Will's. It read: *To wife of Cap'n Willard Minnick, Boonetown, Missery, U.S. of A.* Cynthia's eyes widened. She glanced at Nandria, but that dark face could only nod at the oddity they'd both recognized. Blinking, Cynthia slid the rumpled pages from the envelope and read, with difficulty. "So jumbled," she exclaimed, referring to the handwritten words, and to the thoughts. Will seemed to have been tired, or frightened, or both. But his desire to reach out to his beloved wife was clear. Cynthia swallowed hard. *If my Zeb were to write this to me, I...* She could not finish the thought. Looking at Nandria with renewed empathy, she watched the younger woman again close down within herself.

"Have you...have you shown this to the Minnicks?"

A single shake of the head and pleading look were answer.

"I know, how could you? Grover would explode. And to even consider such a...such a desperate letter, let alone the odd envelope with no return address. No way to find out who sent this on for Will. Such a doubt would unhinge Doris for sure. Oh, Lord, dear Nandria, no wonder you are heartsick. What can I do?"

"Sss...," Nandria stopped to swallow, nearly smiling. "So like you, woman who works immediately for solution." Her eyes went sad again. They closed.

Cynthia played with the little ones until she could set Rose, sleeping soundly, into her crib. She gathered her Levitt and walked with him up into the north field to talk with Grover Minnick, who wiped his sweating face and stood, mouth open, to watch her stalking toward him.

"I've just come from visiting your daughter-in-law. I suggest you have Dr. Ricartsen come to see her, or perhaps you taking her and your granddaughter into town to see him. If she has something contagious, you'd best keep Doris far from either one of them. In fact, you'd better not let your daughter-in-law cook or even clean for you Minnicks until she is well. Can't be too careful, you know. Not with as fragile as Doris is. Well," she finished to the astonished man, with a look around at Bodie and her son Greg who'd come up near but were as mute as their boss. "Well, enough said. I left some scattering of a lunch in your ice box, but you'll know better'n to wake either Mrs. Minnick when you go down to the house."

With a wave that Levitt copied even as she turned with him, Cynthia marched back down toward the Paisler pickup and, presumably, off to her home.

The three men looked at each other, eyebrows tall. Greg turned away to hide a smile he wouldn't have been able to explain.

Chapter 19

Garum sat a long time in the dusk with his back against the upright for the chicken's wire platform extending outside of the Tacker's hen house. He'd considered building a small one onto the Nicklebergs' for the missus, but the mister was bound to come home to her one of these days. Garum knew in his bones that as soon as Mr. Nickleberg found out a colored boy had done it for him, he'd tear it down with a vengeance. In fact, the way Mr. Minnick had looked at him, Garum was sure somebody'd soon be blaming Pa for beating up Mrs. Nickleberg. He and his pa would have to leave. Leave all this that the two of them had skimped on food to forage materials to build. Leave it all behind and flee far from Boonetown for their lives.

He'd spoiled everything for his father. Once the suspicion took hold, folks in robes or maybe just hoods would come with fire brands. Garum twisted to retch at the thought of what would come next. He'd never seen anything like that, but he knew. His pa had, but he didn't talk about it. Just told his boy to never meddle in white folks' goings-on.

But Garum hadn't listened. He'd listened to a white woman's confusion and pain. Got himself—and Pa—involved. And now Pa would pay an awful price for his son's disobedience.

A glimmer: Maybe they could go to Pittsburgh...

Tears erupted. There wasn't any Pittsburgh. Anyway, Ma didn't want him. She'd left and never come back. And now Pa wouldn't want him, either.

Garum jumped at his father's gruff voice.

"Where you been, boy? What're ya doin' sittin' here moonin'? What's the matter with you?"

Scrambling to his feet, Garum ran to Dolph. Grabbing him around the waist, the boy buried his face against the rope tie of his father's britches and wept. The man shuddered but finally settled his hand on his son's head, caressing him. When the boy did not sniffle and stop his crying, the man squatted in front of him and drew him close.

"What, Gar? Whatever'd they do to ya, son?" He longed to tell the child everything would be all right, that he would protect him, avenge him, make it right—but he knew he could not. Breathing heavily, he held him closer, then hardened. Standing erect he held the boy away, commanding that he look up at him. "What you done, boy?"

Garum started to shake his head in protest, then crumpled in his father's hands. "I done it, Pa."

"So, what you done? They after you?"

"Kin...kin we go ta Pittsburgh?"

Bernice Owens stood upright at Mrs. Drangler's doorway, refusing to bend to enter. Her jaw was set tight as she shoved forward a tray covered with a cloth napkin.

Both Ella Mae and Sheriff Yakes stared at her clear fury.

"I brought this for you two. I hope you'll forgive the portions are only for one, and that man did fuss and muss it up some, but he didn't touch it except with a fork. He kept sayin' it wasn't just late. It wasn't fit to eat. I hope you won't feel the same way, but if you do, just toss it to the pigs." She thrust the tray at Ella Mae and turned to stomp away.

"Hold on, now, Mrs. Owens," the sheriff cajoled from his seat in the easy chair. Ella Mae stood with the tray in her hands between them, not quite knowing what to do. "Of course, if that's the supper you cooked up for our prisoner..."

"It is."

"Then, knowing how well you cook, I'm sure there is nothing wrong with it that Heinz Nickleberg would find if he wasn't fightin' through a hangover. He may even be in DTs by now."

"DTs or PDQs, he's got no right to speak to me that way. I'll be blasted if I ever make him another meal. Period."

"Nor should you," Ella Mae sputtered. "With you helping run that store of yours, you don't have time to cater to an ingrate, no matter who he is."

"Agreed," Yakes said with a gesture for the irate storekeeper to come in and sit down. "Sorry we had to ask you to take him on. But the sheriff's office wants to treat our few guests as well as we can. It's just that right now, Nickleberg is friends with nobody and nothing. Sorry."

"And we're glad for the vittles," Ella Mae grinned, sniffing at the lamb chop and potatoes basking in smooth gravy. "I'll bet this treat does the sheriff here more good than a month of Doc Ricartsen's pills."

Bernice's expression softened almost to a smile. "Well," she tempered. "Well, I hope you like it then, sheriff. I know my Isaac always does. I can't eat it myself as the day's last meal. Too tired to sit down and let it digest proper. Speaking of which, I better hurry back to the store. Do enjoy it, Sheriff Yakes. And I'll fix toast or something light for the man for breakfast, but I'm hoping you'll be sending him home soon. He's been a doodle to try to please, that's for sure." Bernice left in a far better mood than she'd come.

Ella Mae settled the tray on Yakes' knees. "I'll bring coffee to go with that, Piermont." As she scurried to the kitchen, she looked over her shoulder to see him lifting the napkin and smiling. "By the way, you decided yet when you're gonna send him back to poor Gertrude?" she called.

The lamb chop and gravy still smelled delicious, but the sheriff's smile had dissolved when Ella Mae carried in his mug of coffee. "What am I gonna do with that man, Elm?"

As the sheriff lingered over the errant meal, Ella Mae hurried to Dr. Ricartsen's office to consult with Doc and Mrs. Bean.

"How is Mrs. Nickleberg, really?" she wanted to know. "Piermont is gonna have to let her man go again soon. Can Gertrude survive having him back with her?"

"Anything here for now?" Doc turned to ask Mrs. Bean. "No? Well, then let's leave a note and you and me walk over and talk with the sheriff about this." He wanted help. He wanted input that would lessen the burden of the responsibility for the consequences of what he had to say. Even knowing that, Sadie scribbled the note and went with them to Mrs. Drangler's. Her need to bend nearly in half to enter left her hunched on the hard-backed chair she chose at the front corner of Mrs. Drangler's living room. Doc perched at the end of the sofa, elbows on his knees and face in his hands.

"How can I answer that, sheriff? We both know what he's gonna do to her sooner or later," Ricartsen anguished. "Yeah, Nickleberg's out of his mind when he thrashes her. But how much of that is the drink? Is the man sane otherwise?" Doc lifted his hands to spread them in pleading. "How do I know? Yeah, I've had medical training, but even people who study human behavior and sanity get it wrong."

"I know you don't want to be the one to seal the woman's fate any more'n I do, Doc, but we gotta do somethin'. And soon. Soon as he calls for a lawyer."

"Soon as he's got through the worst of the DTs." Doc sighed. "First time young Greg Paisler's seen much of that and it's shaking him."

"Better for him from this side than from Mrs. Nickleberg's," Sadie muttered. Doc looked over at her, nodded in agreement and went sad again.

"Maybe he wants to be punished," Ella Mae breathed as she sat down in her own hard-backed chair beside her handiwork.

"What, Elm? What're you saying?"

"I was just thinkin'...about somethin', er, someone, actually. Knowed he done real wrong..." She sighed, closed down within herself, and said nothing more.

"You mean, maybe somewhere inside, Nickleberg blames himself and wants to be punished?" Doc picked up on her thought. "So, that's why he isn't doing more to try to get out of jail? He believes he belongs there? Hmmm, that almost makes sense, in a twisted kind of way."

"Too twisted for me to follow," Sadie said, splaying her fingers on her thighs. "But it still leaves us with no idea what to do about the man and sending him home to beat on Gertrude again. She was near out of her mind the last time we saw her." She looked at her doctor to agree and pick up the discussion if he wanted to say more about Mrs. Nickleberg's condition.

Both the sheriff and Mrs. Drangler stared at the colt-awkward physician. "Well, she was confused. Couldn't seem to remember what had happened to her, or who had done it. Minnicks was there in my office, talking about something else entirely when she barged in. Doris Minnick evidently finally heard the stories and spilled the beans about her husband beating her, but Mrs. Nickleberg got upset that she'd say such a thing."

"Dolph tacker's boy was there," Sadie reminded him.

"Yeah, he was. He's Been working up at her place for her. Evidently drove the Nickleberg car-truck into town for her, much of the way, to bring the eggs to Owens' store."

"That boy?" Ella Mae protested. "He ain't any bigger'n a mite. How could he reach the pedals?"

Laughing finally, Doc explained. "He didn't much of the time or was standing up on the pedals and trying to see over the dashboard. It's why she was the one who got that machine of theirs into my place. But evidently, he couldn't trust her to stay awake." His face went sober once more. "Lord, I wish she'd let me keep her, at least overnight. Even if the man was free then, he couldn't get at her if she was with me. But when the boy ran away..." Doc seemed to be lost in thoughts that made him even sadder. Sadie Bean finished for him.

"Mrs. Nickleberg just huffed on out of the office and out of the clinic altogether. None of us could talk her into staying. But at least we made sure she didn't go to the jail. That would have settled the argument."

"Not settled it any way I think we would've liked," the sheriff exhaled.

Rolling her eyes, Sadie nodded.

"Well, if clever Mrs. Drangler here is even partly right, maybe we can just leave Heinz where he is, at least for a while." Yakes looked around at each of the others, hoping for their even tacit approval.

Since no one had a better suggestion, Doc rose and took a fistful of treats that Ella Mae had snatched up quickly to offer. Stuffing his face, Ricartsen ducked out the doorway toward his clinic. Shaking her head thanks but refusing the offer, Sadie nodded and crouched to follow him out.

"Take some for your Ron, Mrs. Bean. Looks like you won't have time this evening to do much special baking, and these are already made, ready to go. Or, never you mind right now. I'll wrap some and bring the bag over to you in a bit. Thanks for coming. You're a voice of reason, and we sure need reason until the Lord can show us the best answer." Ella Mae ushered the huge woman out the low door and stood to watch her cross the street with long strides. She startled at the sheriff's expression as she turned back. "What, Piermont? You look like you got somethin' mighty uncomfortable to say."

"Come and sit here on the couch near me, will you, Elm?"

Snatching up a skirt to hem and clutching it to her, Ella Mae sat down on the middle cushion of the sofa. "What is it, Piermont?"

"It struck me how you'd know about Heinz Nickleberg feeling guilty and wanting to be punished. You were thinking of someone. Someone in particular. Someone close to you. Someone who broke your heart." Yakes leaned to brush aside the handiwork she'd gathered to her. He took her hand in his. "What happened, Ella Mae? Was that your man you were thinking of?"

"Oh," she murmured and slid back into the sofa. But he did not release her hand. Instead, he struggled up out of the easy chair to lower himself beside her. She watched the beads of sweat come to his hairline and settled herself close, waiting for the question she dreaded. *Maybe it's time. Maybe, if this man is going to mean something in my life, maybe it's time. Maybe then he'll tell me about what tears apart his insides, too. Then I'll know. Maybe then we'll both know.* She set her free hand over his.

"Who did that make you think of, Elm? Your man? What was his name?" Yakes struggled to remember as she sat quiet. "Roy? No, Ray. I remember because you were my one ray of sunshine at that point. I would rather have died then. Did you know that? If it hadn't been for you..."

Without looking up, she squeezed his hand. He eased back into the cushions.

"You don't have to tell me nothing 'less you wanna, Elm. In my life, the women have always been the ones with the courage to be honest. But if it's too painful..."

She did sit up a little, patting his hand. "It's all right, dear man. It was a long time ago, and there have been good moments since. Warm times and beautiful sights and sounds that help the pain to heal enough to be able to go on. You're part of that, you know. I wasn't sure I'd ever feel about any man the way..."

"Ah," he cried and leaned to lift her hand to his lips.

Swallowing hard, Ella Mae began that story as though she were telling a once-upon-a-time tale. "We had a farm. In Iowa. Just twenty acres, but in a valley that the Raccoon River floods now and again. Near Des Moines, but back country then. Quiet. Good land. A good place to raise our family. Or so we thought, Raymond and me. Lydia, we brought with us as a wee babe. Sweet girl." Ella Mae stopped to shake her head and close her eyes. Yakes waited for her to go on.

"Little Randolph was born there on that farm. Almost before we got the house ready. I was afraid I'd have to birth him in the barn or chicken coop, but Raymond worked day and night and just got the farmhouse in shape for us to move in." She stopped again, her facial expressions slithering from joy to disbelief, fear, terror, grief, relief, despair, acceptance, grief again. At last, she whispered, "It was tornado country." And looked at him with the most painful smile the sheriff had ever seen.

He knew. He knew that smile, and the man felt it tearing his gut the way the ulcer never had.

Gasping, he reached to draw her to himself.

Chapter 20

"Why, Pa?"

They'd eaten a late Saturday supper. Corn and beans and the lettuce and greens Garum had gathered from the drying garden out back. Dolph Tacker, in a rare mood with a half dozen Walking Liberty half dollars in his pocket, had made rhubarb-dandelion pie. The rhubarb was tough. Probably should have been left alone to ready itself for the winter. But Garum relished the pie, since his father had not seemed this happy for such a long time. Not enough to bake a pie. They sat with their backs against the only blank wall of their chicken coop and licked their fingers. Dolph hauled a huge red cotton cloth from his hip pocket to wipe away the last of the sticky remains. But Garum shook his head when offered. Still sucking his fingers, the boy was too warmly satisfied not to want the experience to the very dregs.

"Why what?" Dolph asked at last.

Hesitating for fear of spoiling the joy between them, Garum almost did not continue. But he so wanted to know. "Pittsburgh," he mumbled.

Dolph's expression sobered; he looked away. But he didn't seem angry. That was a good sign. Evidently, he'd enjoyed the closeness, too, between father and son. Garum held his breath.

"It's where her folks went."

"My grandma and grandpa?"

Shaking his head, Dolph twisted to hawk and spit. "Not hardly. Your ma worked for 'em. White folks. Cooked, cleaned, did their dirty clothes. Washed and dressed their kids. Sat with them kids when they went out on the town at night. They done that a lot. Dress up fancy and go out with the high falutin' buddies that don't know you and me are alive on this earth, let alone invite us along." He turned back, flinging out his hand toward the boy. "Hell, they wouldn't even let me stay with her when they was away. And the two of us married and all. 'Not fittin', so they said. So, she was in one place and you and me, we was in another. So, when the mister got transferred out of the south to Pittsburgh..." Dolph spat again. "...she had to go, too. 'How could they get along without her? Their kids loved her so.' Like there was no love between a man and his wife. And what about her own son lovin' her and wantin' and needin' her?"

Wiggling down so he was flat on his back, Garum screwed up his eyes and clenched his fists to keep his father from seeing his tears.

"And when I aksed just them questions right to that white man's face, he told his woman to call the police to come fer me," Dolph hissed. "And she...your ma. She made her choice." It wasn't what he'd meant to say. But Garum knew what he was trying to tell him. His father would walk away from anyone not behind him when he made a stand like that...Put himself out there to be beaten rather than back down... So, Ma went with them. North. Deeper into white country, and farther from him or any chance he'd ever find her, let alone mean anything to her.

"Oh," he whispered. His hand went to his belly where the pie now sat heavy.

Sunday, August 18, 1940

Dawn was already cracking the egg of the sun on the eastern horizon when Garum hauled his bike up the Nickleberg lane. He found Mrs. Nickleberg sound asleep in her bed and tiptoed out to start the work with the hens. On a Sunday, he thought she might want to take the car-truck into town to go to church. He might be able to hide upstairs in the choir loft, or he could wait outside for her if she wanted to go. But first, he'd better hurry to get everything gathered and fed and swept and watered. And when she wasn't awake when he took in the eggs, he decided to work a little on the chicken wire 'porch' for the hens. He'd figured out how to extend it from the far end of their coop. It would keep the hens off the ground and protect them from the fox he'd seen. That tawny ginger-gray, sleek animal he'd watched stalking closer and closer, and then running off when he stamped toward her. She must have kits somewhere, though they might be run off on their own by now in the summer. Anyway, she was getting braver and bolder, and she'd snatch one or two of the hens if he couldn't get the porch built pretty soon. No telling how Mr. Nickleberg would react when he saw it, but by then that fox would be the man's responsibility. He could scare her off any way he saw fit. Probably shoot her, but Garum couldn't do that. How could anybody shoot such a beautiful animal? Weren't they God's children, too? Beulah said all critters were children of the Lord God.

"Even us coons," he whispered and shook his head. Realizing the joke he'd unwittingly made, Garum laughed like his pa. But the bitter sound only brought back into focus the terrible predicament he'd caused for his father. Garum bit back a sob and forced himself to get to work.

Immediate chores done and everything laid out for the 'porch' and only needing the missus's approval, Garum headed for the farmhouse to wipe and sort the eggs he'd taken in earlier. He listened at the doorway. No snoring, but no stirring sounds either. He rinsed a couple cloths and sat down at the worktable.

Chilled, he turned, suddenly scared. The woman held a shotgun, and it was aimed, wavering, all over him.

"G'mornin', missus," he stammered. "You was asleep when I first come. It's me, Garum, your egg gatherer, remember?" he added when she continued to stare at him and aim. "We set together at this table here and wipe them eggs I bring in. Candle 'em, set on their little ends..."

The shotgun lowered so it would take off only his legs, but Garum swallowed, grateful for any improvement.

"We drove us into Boonetown yesterday. Remember?" he squeaked, fighting for breath to keep going. "I could get us down the lane but how hard it was for me to see over the dash when I had to stand on the clutch to shift gears? Remember how you laughed? You got us into town."

"My man's in jail," she moaned as she collapsed into her chair at the worktable.

Sweating, now that the shotgun lay steady on the table pointed at his head and upper chest, Garum worked to swallow the whimper that was overtaking his best efforts. "Ah, missus..."

"You knew."

The boy's face confessed his panic.

Gertrude leaned forward, revising the aim of the long barrel. "What did that coon do to get my man in jail?"

"Pa? You mean my pa? Pa helped take you to Doc's, that's what Pa did," Garum declared. He was angry that his father was being accused of something bad when what he had done was something good. "Pa didn't wanna, 'cause he says we ain't never to meddle with white folks' problems. But he seen how battered and cut up you was, so he broke his own rule and got you to the doc's to get fixed up."

Staring at the defiant child, Gertrude leaned back to wipe her eyes. She let the shotgun roll a bit so it no longer pointed at him. He breathed long and deep but stayed where he was. Surprised when she looked again that the boy was still there, Gertrude had a fleeting moment of truth. She raised her arms to protect her face. From what? Not Heinz, surely. But in those flashes, she did remember what she didn't want to be true. She swept the shotgun off the table onto the floor. Garum startled, afraid it would go off on its own. But it merely fell with a terrible crash and thud.

"Ah, child," she moaned, reaching out her arms for him to come to her.

He hesitated, but the woman's expression was of such anguish, that he hurried to her to be enveloped in her arms. "Mama," he murmured but the sound was swallowed as she pressed him to her bosom.

It was after church and Sadie's hearty Sunday dinner when Ron Bean came to help the sheriff shuffle across the street to his jail. Heinz Nickleberg lay back on the cot with his arm crooked over his face. He wouldn't talk.

"What do we do to help your woman, Nickleberg?" Yakes persisted. "She's out there all alone."

Heinz didn't move.

"Mrs. Owens is setting up a list of farmers out your way who regularly come into town. She's asking them to stop to pick up the eggs and poultry when they go near, but there are days when she'd have to drive in on her own. She's in bad shape, Heinz, but she won't let nobody stay out there with her. Several women have offered. She says 'no' in such a way that even they don't try to argue with her. And she won't go and stay with nobody, neither."

"I'm sick."

"Not near as hurting as your wife," Yakes murmured, but then blinked and shook his head. "Yeah, you were that. DTs, Doc called it. Too much liquor over too long. But you're pretty much over that now. And Doc says you'll stay okay as long as you quit drinkin'. So maybe that's a good idea."

"What?" Nickleberg growled.

"To stop drinking."

"You with the Temperance League or something, Yakes? Seems to me I remember you taking some deep swallows of what I passed around without saying much against it then."

"Yeah," Yakes agreed. "I've been known to down a swallow or two from your jug a few times, Heinz, and that's why I'm talking to you as a neighbor. A friend."

"Friend?" the egg farmer roared. "You're talkin' to me from the other side of iron bars! What kind'a friend locks a man up?"

Reaching forward from the chair Ron Bean had set for him, Yakes yanked at the cell door. It screeched open.

As Nickleberg's jaw dropped, his eyes widened. Slowly, he rose to stand leaning one hand on the bars next to the open door. "What the hell? This your idea of a joke, Yakes? How long...?"

"Your wife won't press charges, so..."

With swift motion, Nickleberg was into the doorway. His vicious kick at the leg of the chair sent the sheriff sprawling on the concrete floor. Nickleberg stared at Yakes crumpled and moaning. He hesitated, bending back as though to help him up. But his anger was kindled. Anger at himself and everyone involved that he'd sat how long behind bars when there was no lock holding him there, but no one had told him. Anger enough that he left the sheriff clutching his belly and struggling to sit up. Anger enough that he stalked up the only paved street in Boonetown, heading west.

He was well into the dusty lane of the country road when he met a young Negro boy leading a mule. Nickleberg was still angry. Angry enough to make the boy unload the mule and set that cargo beside the road. "I'm taking this here mule, boy. You can come for it at Nickleberg farm. But right now, I'm ridin' it home."

Saying nothing, the boy looked between the goods he had been taking to town and the man riding away, whipping up the mule that had not hurried that fast in a month of new moons.

Near the bottom of the farm road leading up to his egg spread, Nickleberg found the car-turned-pickup. The vehicle tilted half into the ditch; the driver's door hung ajar. Feathers drifted in the dust of the lane. At least one egg was splatted against a rough stone. Too angry to think to tether the mule, Nickleberg man-handled the driver's side as he pushed the frame to the right to get three of the four tires on the roadbed. He got in and fought to start the motor.

The mule wandered, munching, toward taller weeds and grass.

At the farmhouse, Gertrude sat erect, listening. Garum, stock still, stared and then listened intently, as well.

"It's the egg truck," she rasped. Gertrude listened to the sedan-truck door slam but not latch. Heinz only did that when he was drunk. Surely, he hadn't been drinking, not again. Thrusting the child from her, she staggered to her feet. "Sweet Lord, please... Boys, hide! Run! Get out of here!"

Garum scampered but turned at the door to look back. The woman who had held him was swaying.

Chapter 21

"When are you going to show me the letter?" Doc asked quietly as he leaned back in his office chair. "Or have you decided not to?"

Little Rose fussed in her mother's lap. Nandria leaned to set her on her feet where she clung to the straight-backed chair seat. Grinning, Rose looked up, drooled and, startled, promptly sat on her bottom. She pouted once, but immediately found strange and wonderful things she hadn't explored before and scoot-crawled toward them.

"Let her go," Doc commanded. "Sadie Bean keeps this place clean enough to eat lunch off of. I know. I've been so tired a time or two that I've dropped what she gave me. I just picked it up and ate it anyway. And I'm still here, ornery as ever." He looked tired. He caught Nandria thinking just that and shook his head. "Not as worn out as you look, woman. Will would have my head if I didn't find a way to keep you with the Paislers. Grover's been workin' you like a mule."

"He works himself just as hard. As did Mother Minnick as well, I suspect, when she was able."

"But that's up to the two of them. You are my responsibility. Given to me by your husband. I intend to do my best to protect you until he can come and take that cloak off my shoulders. So, tell me again what the letter said. Why are you so concerned about him this time?"

With a glance at Rose pulling herself to a stand against the chair in the far corner, Nandria closed her eyes and exhaled slowly, deciding. Then she reached into her carryall and handed the doctor the envelope with the strange address of 'Missery, U.S. of A.'

"That don't look like Will's writing, to me."

"Nor did it seem so to me, doctor. I assume someone found Will's letter and thought to do him a favor by posting it for him."

Ricartsen cocked the envelope toward her.

"Okay if I open it?"

She nodded and looked around at Rose, who had found a crumpled wad of paper and was gurgling as she batted it and crawled after it to hit it again. As her little girl was safe and occupied, Nandria returned her attention to the physician reading Will's scribbled note.

"Hummm," Ricartsen grumbled, rereading the letter, "he doesn't sound happy, does he?"

"As I read between the lines, I fear he was tense. In longing to be safe, perhaps, and longing for home. Frightened," she added low.

"Scared to death," the doctor agreed, then looked up sorry that he'd said that aloud. His friend's wife was already facing some realities he wished he could shield from her. He didn't need to knock her in the head with the probable truth of the matter. "But if he wrote this in a scary situation and somebody found it to mail it for him, then at least one of them survived." He hadn't thought that through but only grasped at the first thing that came to him that would give her hope.

She smiled that tolerant pleasantness that acknowledges the effort but doesn't believe the message. Ricartsen inwardly cussed the many night calls that had pulled him out of his bed these last few weeks. He needed sleep to be on top of any game with this educated woman.

"So," she said low, clasping her hands in her lap to compose herself, "what situations can you imagine that might lead my Willard into such a state of being?"

He shook his head. "In war, it could be..." Shrugging, he rocked forward the look at her, his elbows extended on his desk. "It's useless to speculate, don't you think? We need more information before we can make any reasonable guess, so why stew about what we cannot know?" Even as he said it, reasonable as it sounded, he knew it was useless to think that she would be able to simply put it out of her mind. Not to worry about her Will would be beyond even her self-discipline. Not when she was exhausted, sick with pregnancy and overwork, if not coming down with something else to pull her toward the grave. She needed straight answers. He doubted he could give her a single one that would matter, even if he'd just awakened from an uninterrupted ten hours of sleep.

"Nothing?" Grover Minnick turned from the stove to glare at his gray and shuddering wife at their kitchen table. "Mother, you gotta eat something. You're as skinny as Willard was as a kid. Only he was all sinew and runnin' around lookin' into everything. Is it my cookin'? You didn't used to mind it all that much before that woman went on to the Paislers." *Before that darky woman come to spoil everything. Cooking delicious and not eating either. You learned it from her.*

Grover knew that wasn't so. *Doris hadn't been much interested in food for a long time before Will sent his female and that pickaninny to us. Cute as a bug, but still half darky. And the woman worked hard. Cleaned and mended and learned to plow and feed and care for the livestock better'n Doris's been up to since who knows when.*

I'm losing my woman. Sweet Lord, she's slippin' away from me and there don't seem to be a thing I can do to stop her going.

Setting the wrought iron skillet to a cold corner of the stove, Grover shuffled to his seat at the head of the table and sat down. Even Bodie had chosen to go to his own shack for lunch rather than face what Grover could cook. Minnick looked over at the eggs and ham he'd left on the stove, but his appetite did not entice him to get up to fetch them to the table.

Leaning his chair back against the wall, he studied his wife. She sat with her head on her arms sprawled across the table. He started to look away when she snorted in her sleep. He grinned. "And you say you don't snore," he whispered. Fond as he was of this woman, her snoring was one thing he could have done without all these years, although she would never admit that he could be bothered by her doing a thing like that. His grin faded. So much they'd hoped for, indeed, planned on, never happened as they expected. And now they were saddled with a woman, her child, and another one expected—darkies. *How could Willard do that to us?*

The Tacker truck had a familiar sound. Beulah knew as soon as she heard it that her Dolph was coming. Oh, not that he was coming for her, she understood that. She was too plain, too heavy, too old-maidy for him to be interested. But she would see him, be able to drink him in with her eyes, maybe even talk with him—close enough to be able to smell the manliness of him. He might want something. Something she, and only she, could do for him. Then there would be that moment of gratitude when he looked directly in her. Almost saw something in her, even if it was just a little sister. Anything that made her part of him, however briefly.

"Grandfather," she whispered to the old preacher just rising from his chair to sermonize his small gathering. He looked over, irritated, but quickly acknowledged her right to speak. "Tacker," she mouthed, knowing he had not heard the truck.

The old man hesitated, hoping to see the muscular wild man at the flap door to the tent. But when there was no one, he shuffled to the front to address his faithful few. When Dolph finally did lift the flap and stand in respect where he was, the elder heard his granddaughter gasp but kept on with his message. *These young people gotta learn discipline. Gotta learn to submit to the Lord. And right now, I am the way to the Lord, Lord help me, so they gotta wait 'til I'm done.* He was determined to carry on, but, stealing a glance, the old man realized that Dolph Tacker was deeply troubled, even afraid. A chill whispered down his own spine.

Stepping forward, the aged preacher lifted trembling arms to call his flock forward to him. "We got trouble in among us, people. There's need for us to gather together to pray to the merciful lord."

Hearing Heinz Nickleberg slam the car-truck door, Gertrude shoved her sons to safety, not comprehending it was only the one, small boy. She turned, knowing she could not hide long enough for her husband to sober up enough to leave her alone. She had to face him. It was the only way, though she'd tried again and again to find any other.

Looking around for a weapon, she reached under the counter for her rolling pin. As she heard his feet shuffling into the hallway and the door slap closed behind him, she tucked her slaughter knife into the fold of her sling and hastily slipped her hurting arm into it. With a whispered prayer, Gertrude took her wide-footed stance to watch him appear at the kitchen doorway.

He stopped in the shadow of the hall. "Woman," he rasped. "You... you look like you been hurtin'. Better now?"

She blinked. This was a new tactic. Gertrude had never before heard him solicitous before the attack. She stepped back but held the rolling pin at the ready.

He shuffled into the dusty light of the workshop area of the huge kitchen. "Gert, it's me. Your Heinz. You don't have'ta be leery like that. It burns my middle that ya think ya do."

"Voice of experience…" she murmured.

"I'd never hurt ya. Never." He stamped one foot and shook his head.

"Maybe not my Heinz, but the bottle's man ain't so gentle."

He stepped toward her but stopped when she retreated behind the butchering table. "Gert, I ain't had a drink—not for days. Sheriff Yakes seen to that. How was I to know he hadn't locked my cell? Some joke. He knew I could'a left any time, but he made sure nobody let me know."

Gertrude swayed, considering how close she'd been to his visiting with heavy fist when she thought she was safe. When she thought at all. These past days were a blur. An aching blur she wasn't sure which parts she did remember were real and which parts only dreams—or nightmares. "Only my little son with me saved my sanity," she muttered.

"Whad'd you say about our son? The boys was with you?"

When Heinz stared at her, frowning, she cocked her head looking back at him, unsure. "Only the one," she faltered.

"Which one? Hiram?" His frown deepened as her head moved slowly left and then right. "Surely not Herman?"

Swerving to find her seat, Gertrude sat, looking at him. "Little," she murmured. Her hand trembling, she raised it, palm down, to shoulder height as she sat. Heinz guffawed.

"Neither of our boys's been that small since they were startin' grade school. What are you talkin' about, woman? Where's your brain?"

Cowering in her chair, Gertrude twisted away and saw little Garum peering around the corner from the pantry. He stepped forward, but she motioned with a quick hand for him to hide. As the child slipped back out of sight, Gertrude's mind cleared. It wasn't her fault. It wasn't her sons' fault. It was those damnable nightmares of his. Clenching her fists, she scooted back on her chair to face her husband.

"No'm," the boy whispered behind her. Twisting to admonish him, she met those huge, dark eyes pleading with her not to antagonize the man. Despite her own anger, she nodded.

"All right," she said aloud.

"What's 'all right'? Ain't nothin' been all right since who knows when," Heinz grumbled as he shuffled up to sit opposite her.

"Well, it might've been," she countered. She looked at this hulk of what had been a fine provider and man. A young man of promise. *What went wrong with you, Heinz Nickleberg?* Her fists unclenched themselves. Remembering her love for this man those many years ago, Gertrude leaned forward, reaching toward him. "Heinz, tell me about them dreams."

He sucked in air.

"They've gotten worse, haven't they? You remembering somethin' you seen? Somethin' you did?"

He slid rough hands clasped across the table. "Ah, Gert," he whined low.

Scraping her chair, she hitched closer. "Tell me, husband. Maybe if you talk about..."

"Women talk," he roared.

"So do men, if they're smart enough." She blinked again. She'd only ever contradicted her man in the heat of battle; and lived to regret it. But this time she'd spoken a truth gently. Looking up, she realized that he was as startled as she had been at the softness of her words. That rugged jawline seemed to give as though he'd stopped clenching his teeth. He was staring at her but not in rage and domination, the way it had been these past months. A little boy's eyes looked out of that weathered face. Pleading without words.

"Ah, Heinz, tell me, please."

Chapter 22

"I'm going to be brutally frank with you, Nandria Minnick. And I'm hoping you'll listen." Cynthia Paisler took Rose from her mother's arms as Nandria lay in what had been Todd's bed. "You cannot go on as you have been doing. That is a fact. It is also true that you are in danger of losing this second little one your Will has given you to nurture and protect. For these babies' sake if not for your own, you are to stay in that bed. Sleep. Do not whine about getting up. Too much to ask of me. I know what I can and cannot do, thank you. Sleep, young woman, and maybe it's not too late for you to heal. Do you understand?"

Nandria blinked, stared, swallowed, then closed her eyes and nodded.

"So, you just huddle down under that sheet, close your eyes, and sleep. Right now."

A single tear slid out from between long, dark lashes. Nandria's eyelids twitched but remained closed.

Cynthia waited a moment to be sure there would be no protest. "Good," she whispered finally. "Come, little Rose. We are going to set out dinner for our menfolk, and I think you are going to be a wonderful, good help—if only by keeping them happily distracted." Cynthia lifted the window as high as it would stay and left the upstairs bedroom with Rose on her hip, closing the door quietly behind them.

Nandria opened her eyes to turn her head to stare at the maple tree just outside the open window. Its brown bark caught bits of sunlight and of shade, appearing beautifully mottled among the delicate, fingered leaves. A chickadee landed on a branch close to the tree trunk. It cocked its head to look in and inquire, just as Will would have done if he were near. "I'm so sorry, my loved Willard," she whispered to it. "I never meant to harm this child you have given me. Please forgive my weakness. And bless this friend who respects you enough to be frank with me. I am sorry that she is correct. I have endangered... Be well, my love..." Tears flowed freely, though Nandria made no sound. And then she slept.

When the meal was ready, Todd took his turn to ring the dinner bell. His brothers and father hurried to wash up at the pump. Zeb was last, as usual, as he counted to be sure all sons were present. Except Greg, who still worked at the Minnick farm after the dispute with his brothers over planting cotton. Zeb missed his third-born. Greg had an idealism within him most people would not recognize off hand. It was so honestly held the lad seemed to have no need to advertise it. It rankled Zeb a bit to think that highly of one of his sons. He despised showing favoritism and hoped that his Cynthia would set him straight if he ever showed any.

He entered and stood at the head of his table. Sam took his cue and seated his mother. Then all the menfolk sat down and bowed their heads for their father's blessing. Rose, on Sam's lap now that his seating duty was carried out, had no mind to wait for prayer before reaching for food. The twins, peeking when they heard the sounds of flatware being scattered, giggled. Father frowned to hide his own chuckle, and all the sons went quiet. They, too, must have been squinting. With the back of his hand hiding his lips, Zeb grinned at Cynthia, said 'Amen' and resumed the patriarchal ceremony of filling each plate for his dependents. Even Rose settled into eating from Sam's plate.

The boys assumed their chores of stacking, rinsing, washing and putting away the mealtime dishes. Ma took care of the pots and pans at noon. Greg did them in the evenings as his contribution to the late meal.

With a half-hour break from farm work after dinner, the boys scattered to their own pursuits. Zeb took up his youngest and Cynthia held Rose. The couple settled on well-worn chairs on the back porch to chuck their littlest ones under the chin and marvel at their growth. They talked low. None of the sons came near unless there was an emergency they could not handle on their own or that parents needed to know about immediately. Respect went back and forth between generations in the Paisler family.

"How is the gal?" Zeb drawled as he supported his Levitt standing on his thigh. Rose lunged for Levitt. Laughing, Zeb and Cynthia set the little ones on the floor to play at their feet.

"Asleep. I think she was asleep before I closed her door. I hope Sam and Todd will get along bunking together in this heat."

"They're old enough to be able to adapt when there's need. And do it with a bit of grace, if I know those two."

"Yes, I believe they will. But I did hate to take away their privacy. Lord knows there's little enough of that around here."

Zeb chuckled. "Married folks don't get none at all."

"And I hope each and every one of them will find as happy a marriage as I have, Zeb Paisler. But still…"

"Is that part of Miz Nandria's problem, do you think?"

"Well," Cynthia sighed, "her sleeping on the closed-in porch is pretty much out in the open. I guess Will was beside himself with his father when he first came home and found his wife and daughter there. And then, when he was called away again, she was the one who wouldn't move on up to his bedroom. There's a stiff pride in that young woman. She's so smart and educated. College, Zeb. Can you imagine? And no one around here sees her for what she is because her skin happens to be darker than most of ours."

"You treat her well, Love," he murmured.

"As you do, Mr. Paisler, but you treat everybody with respect until they prove they don't deserve it. So, that's no help to Nandria. That Grover Minnick…"

"Now, my pet, we don't know what's going on with Grover Minnick. We know he has his own cross to carry with his Doris sinking like a ship torpedoed by one of those Nazi subs. Think how many doctors he's had her to see and still no answers. It's breakin' him. Unless Will's wife can work for her keep, he…"

"Work?" Cynthia humphed. "You know how he works her."

Zeb leaned toward her and stroked her calloused hand. "No more'n I do you."

"That's how things are on a farm, Zeb. And you give even more of yourself." Her eyes glistened with tears. "To this family. To me," she added in a whisper. "But that's what Nandria doesn't have. Will's gone. May never come back. And then what, for her? No one who truly cares. Did you know her whole family drowned in one of those Nazi torpedo attacks you were talking about?" Slipping her hand from under his, Cynthia lifted her apron to wipe her eyes.

"And now you're worried about the Nicklebergs, too," he chuckled. "Woman, you can't take on the troubles of the whole world."

"I can't even take on the troubles of Boonetown and the acres of pain around it."

"Nobody can."

They sat several minutes, simply together, again knowing reality, until Cynthia stirred.

"Have you heard anything more about Gertrude? Wasn't Gregor afraid the sheriff was gonna have to let the mister go free one day soon?"

"Now there's a troubled man." Zeb sighed. Her frown demanded explanation. "Word is, he don't sleep. Nightmares. Somethin' in his past, I guess."

"Something happened to him?"

Shaking his head, Zeb sighed again. "Or somethin' he saw. Or maybe done."

"You don't know what?"

He turned to face her. Sighing, he pointed up toward the bedroom where Nandria slept.

"Nickleberg hurt her?" she gasped.

"Not her necessarily. But word is he screeches stuff in his sleep before the nightmares wake him up."

"About Negroes? Oh, Zeb, not lynchings?" Her eyes widened.

"Now, Love, I don't know nothing for certain. But I want to warn you about undercurrents I think I'm hearin'. Stuff said. Remarks like, 'about due' and 'they're askin' for it.'"

"Who? What about? They aren't thinking of harming Miz Nandria, are they?"

He shook his head. "Not that I know of. More something about who beat up Mrs. Nickleberg."

"There's a question? I thought it was settled it was the mister."

"Well, he's been drinkin' a lot lately. That's for sure. But she won't admit it was him that did her so much harm."

"How could she dare? He'd only take that out on her, too."

Zeb clasped his hands together and dropped them between his knees as he leaned forward. "There's a boy been helpin' her out on the egg farm."

"A Negro child?"

"Dolph Tacker's boy. What's his name?"

"He's a friend of our Todd's. Gary? No, Garum, I think. Surely, no one believes that child could have hurt her that bad? He's not much bigger than our twins, if I remember rightly."

Zeb lifted his arms to rest his elbows on his thighs and his head in his hands.

"Nobody's thinkin'... Oh, Zeb, not Dolph himself! He couldn't. He wouldn't. He's harvested here for us. A good worker and honest; straight to what needs to be done and no slacking. You know that, Zeb. It couldn't have been Dolph Tacker." She leaned into her husband, and he took her in his arms.

"If only the woman would say for sure who done it," he murmured into her hair. "Elsewise..."

Chapter 23

"'Being of sound mind,'" Gertrude laughed. "That phrase always makes me chortle. Pa used it for his will, though he owed on everything they had so I guess he had to make it legal to be sure Ma would get what she needed." She laughed again, this time with bitterness. "Not that she got nothin' near what she needed. Ma didn't have any idea ahead of time how much they owed and thought she'd have somethin' from him for us. But damn creditors got it all. My parents were never in the Great Depression, but they never got out of their own little one. Pa'd borrowed just to keep us fed, evidently."

Hearing the plaintiveness in her voice, Heinz twisted his head on her lap to look up at his wife from where he had sprawled beside the sofa. He'd seldom seen her in tears that weren't birthed in anger. "Nobody had it easy, Gertie gal. You sunk or swum on your own."

"Or you took charity," she complained. "You should'a seen what that did to Ma. I wouldn't'a thought she'd have much pride left after losing him and the fields one by one, and then the farmhouse. But taking charity to feed us and then havin' to face the pity or whatever it was on the faces of neighbor ladies. It broke her, Heinz."

This time when he looked up the tears were flowing. Still, she cried silently. Heinz gave her credit for that. He'd never liked simpering ladies. But he couldn't make out why she was telling him all this now. He'd truly thought she'd go after him with her poultry knife. The sorrow that had overtaken him once he admitted to himself what he must have done to her—he might even have let her take a swipe or two at him in penance. Not that they could afford to let her really hurt him. Too much to do to catch up on things here at the farm. She'd been laid up and alone so often lately the place was going to wrack and ruin.

Holding her hand in both of his, Heinz only waited, saying nothing. He let her cry.

And when the shaking sobs ceased, she leaned over him, gathering his head and shoulders close. She kissed him. Smothered his eyes and cheeks with kisses. And then his lips. Such passion as he hadn't felt in years.

Garum waited where he'd hidden. Trapped, he couldn't leave without being seen. And if the mister knew what he'd seen and heard, he'd be skinned alive. Garum could picture his skin being stretched to make a drumhead. Though the pantry was stuffy and growing airless, the boy shivered.

Finally, there was little sound, and then none. Holding his breath, Garum rose to crack open the door enough to peek out. "Ahhh," he exhaled. They were both asleep. Both snored.

Creeping past them and up the hall, Garum slipped outside, heading for his bike. He'd leaned it just inside the gap-boarded barn, against the closed half door. He'd left it once in full sun and burned the inside of his thighs against the metal when he hopped on without paying attention. He wasn't about to do that again if he could help it. But as he passed the hen house and the new framework that he and the missus had erected the poultry 'porch' for, he stopped stark still. *What's Mr. Nickleberg gonna say when he sees this? He's gonna be mighty put out, ain't he? Maybe come after me for building without his permission. Oh, I wish I'd never come. I knew he wasn't gonna like nothin' I did, even if the missus did.*

Hands out to tear down what he had built, Garum stepped toward the porch, then stopped again. He couldn't do it. He and the missus had taken pride. He couldn't just tear it apart. They'd worked hard. She'd looked at him so proud of what he'd imagined and then was able to make happen, he couldn't—wouldn't—destroy it until the mister demanded that he did. Under threat of his life, he could do most anything. He'd learned that from Pa.

"Don't let fool pride get you killed, boy. Whatever it takes, you live. 'Cause when you're alive, you kin fight another day. We gotta do so much just to be human in their eyes, we all gotta fight with everything in us." Pa had said that more than once. He meant it. *Come to think, mebbe that's why Pa didn't kill that man that took Ma to Pittsburgh.*

Frowning in that new thought, Garum wheeled his bike out into the yard, mounted and took off down the Nickleberg's rutted lane.

It was well the boy was gone. When they awoke, Heinz Nickleberg inspected, frowned, gaped and then looked back at his wife gushing over what she'd managed to do while he was away. She didn't mention the boy. Heinz shook his head in wonderment at the ingenious design of the 'porch.' Smiled. Nodded, and still grinning, approached Gertrude with open arms. She blushed, forgetting the boy, even her own sons, and melted into her husband's warmth.

Greg drove home from working in the Minnick fields to the Paislers' farm with a bit of a detour to check on the Nicklebergs. He found the egg farmer smiling, shaved, legs outstretched, a glass of buttermilk in his hand as he sprawled in a wide chair on his front porch.

"Ev'nin', Paisler!" Heinz called as Greg's pickup stopped beside the sawed-off egg car-turned-truck.

Eyes wide in surprise, Greg leaned his elbow out his window, grinning. "Hi, Mr. Nickleberg. Just stopped by to see if you folks needed anything." He hadn't been invited to step in. He was deciding whether or not to open his pickup door when Gertrude came outside, a tall glass of buttermilk in her hand. She startled to see him.

"Oh, Greg Paisler, hello. I didn't hear you drive up."

"She was singin' so loud, I stopped hearin' the windmill tryin' to grind a few rotations in what little breeze we got," Heinz announced proudly. "Sounds just like that Kate Smith on Owens' radio. Say, you folks got a radio, don'tcha? Or is that Grover and his Doris?"

Gertrude had stepped toward Greg with the buttermilk in hand. But he knew she had poured it for herself and had been coming outside to sit beside her husband. He shook his head.

"No, thank you kindly, Mrs. N. Ma'll shoot me if I don't have a good appetite for supper—and it's almost time. Just stopped to see if you'd like me take your eggs into Owens' in the mornin'? Or your fryers, if they're ready?"

Gertrude retreated to stand at Heinz's shoulder. She looked down to wait for him to answer.

He glanced up at her. "Feel like a trip into town tomorrow, or you wanna wait another day or two?"

Greg felt his jaw drop at the civility of the question. Even the wonder that the man was asking his wife's opinion. He hadn't seen or heard that in a long time, the few occasions when he might have expected it in the past. At least, his father might have asked Ma. Mr. Nickleberg? He'd always seemed like the dominating type, though pleasant enough to friends with equally worthwhile farms.

"Maybe for a day or two?" Her smile was embarrassed in its suggestion of hoped for time alone together.

Nickleberg grinned as he turned again to face Greg. "If it wouldn't put you out," he drawled. "At least tomorrow. Give the missus a day to sleep in and finish getting well. Thank you for the offer, Paisler. I'll be ready by dawn."

Greg drew in his elbow and leaned to restart his truck. "If you need anything..."

It was Gertrude who answered. "Thanks, we got it all." Her cheeks reddened at the expression on her husband's face.

"Never saw him like that, Mrs. D." Greg shook his head in disbelief, even knowing Ella Mae could not see his action over the phone. "They were like, I don't know, like..." He blushed and was glad she couldn't see him. "...honeymooners."

The tiny seamstress giggled at her end of the phone in Doc Ricartsen's office. Greg could hear her muffled explanation to Doc, and the lanky physician's guffaw.

"Oh, Gregor, I'm so pleased. Gert deserves... but hold on, Doc wants to ask you."

"So, something come up good for a change, huh?" Ricartsen asked. "Good. How'd she look? Not beat up any worse? How are her bruises? Any new cuts or colors?"

"Nothing I could tell. She just looked happy."

"Happy? Well, I'll be..." Doc nodded to his unseeing friend and hung up the receiver without realizing that, at his end, Gregor blinked, laughed and hung up as well. He'd been ready to sit down to his mother's cooking anyway. He took no offense at being cut off.

"Wait'll I tell Piermont," Mrs. Drangler gushed. 'Imagine Gertrude safe and happy. There's no way any of us would'a predicted that when her man went on home."

"No," Doc agreed, tilting back his chair until it banged into the wall. "Nobody even thought of that possibility." He closed his eyes. In a moment, his breathing grew regular.

Ella Mae giggled. Covering her mouth with her small hand, she tiptoed out to hurry across the street to tell Sheriff Yakes the news.

"Oh, Piermont, you won't believe it..." She was right; he didn't believe it.

"Couldn't'a been."

"But young Paisler was there. Stopped to check, and he told me. And then he told the doctor. It's true. Ain't it wonderful? If only it'd stay that way."

"It never does," Yakes grumbled. "Just wait'll he has another of them nightmares."

Her round face drooped. "We gotta stop them dreams of his."

"How in this world could we do a thing like that?"

"Find out what they are. Prove to him they aren't true."

Did that work for your Raymond? He nearly asked aloud, but he couldn't hurt her like that. "What if they are true, Elm? What'll we do then?"

Dolph Tacker ate with a hearty appetite. Neither he nor his boy was much of a cook, but the preacher's flock had some women that could make beans'n'bacon and fresh ears of corn and cornbread so good they melted in your mouth. And dandelion-rhubarb pie that made his own efforts seem like cut-out cardboard. Most of the men poured the creamy top from the milk bottles over each piece, but Dolph went easy so as not to spoil that special tangy flavor. He laughed. "Acquired taste," he said, remembering something his missus had said as they chuckled together over the way her white folks talked.

Beulah looked up, startled. "Huh?" But she was distracted by Dolph's reaction to someone entering the Gospel tent.

"Where you been, boy?" Dolph demanded as his son approached. "What's eatin' you? You look like a mouse the cat's been playin' with for a while just before he chomps on it."

Shuddering, Garum looked up at his father with such sad eyes that the man reached to clamp him into his arms. "What, Gar? Somebody done ya harm, did they?"

"Uh, no. No. Nothin'."

"That egg lady you fuss with, that's who, ain't it? She remember...?" Dolph's voice strained. He lifted his shoulders. His grip went tighter until Garum flinched. He rose to stride away from the table, carrying the child along with him. "What's wrong?" he demanded as they slid out from under the tent flap. "Boy, how many times've I told you to have nothin' to do with white folks' problems? Why in...? Why don't you listen?"

Garum winced under his father's grip before Dolph thought to ease up, but he didn't let go. His expression demanded explanation.

"No, Pa! Nothin' like that. They... they was—they was makin'..." Garum yanked at his arm, but his father was far stronger than he was. There was no getting away.

"Makin' what?" Dolph demanded.

"Uh," the boy stammered, reddening. "Uh, you know..."

He looked so pitifully pained with embarrassment, that the man swallowed the tirade that had come to the back of his throat. He stared. Only one thing would embarrass the boy like that. His grip loosened, but still he didn't let go. "You seen 'em? You seen 'em doin' it?"

He nodded, head lowered. But a throaty sound made him lift his eyes to peer up. His father was laughing. Slapping his own leg with his free hand. Guffawing. Tears came to his eyes. Threatened to roll down those hollow cheeks. He let go of Garum's arm to bend over and hold his middle. At last Dolph caught his breath, stood up and subsided to a mere chuckle. He wiped his eyes with the back of his hand.

Garum stared.

"W...was she squealin'? Screechin'? You know, fightin' him?"

Garum's head moved side to side.

"Really?" Dolph scoffed. He studied the boy's expression. "You ain't tellin' me she was enjoyin' it? Huh." He sidled to the outdoor serving table to grab a mug of coffee but studied his son without drinking it. "Huh," he grunted again. He turned on the boy. "Where was you?"

"When the mister come, she shoved me into the pantry." She'd called him 'Hiram' although he'd told her any number of times it was Garum, not Hiram. But his father was concentrating too hard on something in his mind for Garum to bother him with that detail.

"You stayed in there the whole time?"

Shrugging, Garum said, "I couldn't get out. Not without him seein' me. And I knew he didn't want me nowhere near there right then."

"...didn't want you there right then," Dolph echoed the boy's explanation. He laughed out loud. "No, I don't reckon he would. Not then. You done good to stay hid." Dolph lifted to coffee to his lips, grinning to himself. "How'd you get away?"

"I waited 'til they was snorin'. Tiptoed."

Dolph nodded and laughed aloud.

Realizing Dolph was absorbed in his own thoughts, Garum eased out of his father's grip. He stood watching for a while as his father continued nodding and grinning and fingering the silver coins in his pocket. Something had changed for the man. Garum did not know exactly what that change was, but something about it frightened him. Frowning, Garum slipped away.

It was Beulah who came to sit quietly beside him on the streambank.

"You didn't get to tell him, did you?"

"Huh? I mean, tell him? What?"

"Whatever it is that has you so scared. For him, ain't it? What's happened, Garum? Is your father in danger? How? Who? You gotta tell him, boy!"

Chapter 24

The men who had gathered at the back of Owens' store after the reverend's afternoon sermon perched on crates and stacks of boxes. Doc Ricartsen, Ron Bean, Grover Minnick, Zeb Paisler and Isaac Owens waited, watching each other soberly, as Sheriff Yakes eased himself into the single chair Greg had set for him. With a nod of thanks, the sheriff indicated he wouldn't need Greg and told him to go on and enjoy himself with whatever a young man was allowed to do on a Sunday afternoon.

"That community picnic potluck is already looking and smelling mighty good," Greg grinned. With a nod to the circle of men, he hurried away. They smiled after him, pressed their own bellies and turned to get over with whatever the sheriff had in mind that would delay their own dinners.

"Sorry to bring you all here instead of out with your folks, men," the sheriff addressed them. "But I guess I need help figuring something out. Something important to us all."

They murmured. No distinct words, but their body language told Yakes he could continue.

"I had to let the egg man loose."

Mutterings of protest.

"Well, I had no grounds to hold him. But Doc wanted him to clear all the booze from his system." Yakes paused, grinning. "So, I just left his cell unlocked. Closed, mind you. But he was too drunk and then too miserable to notice I wasn't locking it after me. Had to," he protested at the increased volume of mutterings. "I didn't have one legal reason to hold him. His missus wouldn't say who worked her over like that. Wouldn't put the finger on him, no matter what I or nobody said to her."

Owens shook his head. "And I think my woman's loyal." He chuckled sheepishly, muttering, "But it never occurred to me to raise a hand to my Bernice. She was raised with five brothers. She'd probably whomp me across the store and sweep me down the steps."

They laughed, but knew it might well be true, just as it might be true of the women they were supposed to be masters over. That the store man could grin about it made it easier for all of them. Zeb wondered if the sheriff had set that up with Isaac Owens before they gathered here. If so, it was a master stroke of planning and cunning understanding of the men he would be talking to. But it didn't matter. The stage had been set. They were ready to listen.

"He's got nightmares," Yakes informed them, although most of them already knew. "I was wondering if anybody here knew what them nightmares was about." He studied each face; every man had known something, but it was evident no one knew it all. He frowned. He'd been right to bring them all here. Maybe with everybody, they'd be able to piece it together. "Something he seen? Maybe as a kid?"

Minnick looked down. All but Doc stared at him blankly.

"We've all seen stuff as kids that's probably twisted us some," Ricartsen muttered. "Sex stuff, for one." The men chuckled. "You'd be surprised how much I gotta explain to my patients, so they know the straight of it."

Several protested, but Doc merely lifted his eyebrows and wouldn't deny his allegation.

"Nickleberg's got two sons, so maybe he figured that one out on his own before you come, Doc," Ron Bean suggested. Smiling, Doc nodded that might be so.

"No, I'm thinkin' more nightmarish stuff," Yakes insisted. "Somethin' sets the man off to drink and go crazy. Really off his rocker to beat her like he does. You all seen what she looked like?"

They looked down, nodding. Each man had caught a glimpse of Gertrude's battered face, if not this time, then the time before, or the time before that. They knew how serious conditions had grown.

"Maybe somethin' he done?" Isaac Owens asked. "I know it's the fool things I do that worry me the most."

"Yeah, yeah, could be."

"But what'd he do?"

They looked at each other, but no one had a clue of any major brush with the law or horrendous misdeed Nickleberg might have committed. Rumors would have been fair game here, but there were few even outrageous lies that anyone had heard.

Minnick shook his head. "I don't think it's any of those things. He's not a bad man. But he's seen bad things."

They went quiet. "What bad things? Do you know?" Zeb ventured.

"We heard him once. Here, don't you remember?" Minnick glanced over at Isaac Owens, who frowned.

"I recollect his bein' here. After a KKK meeting, wasn't it?" Isaac concurred. "But what he said…" He shook his head and raised his hands, palms up.

"Doc?" Minnick prompted.

"Sorry, but if I remember the evening at all, I remember a sip from his jug and too many nights' without sleep. But what he said…" He shifted his hands and shrugged. "Sorry."

"Do you remember, Grover?" Zeb asked.

"Yeah, I remember, because I get them nightmares, too. Not often, but they tear a body up inside when they come. My Doris, bless her, says I shouldn't let them bother me because the coons deserve what they get. That a fine Southern man knows what he's got to do to protect his womenfolk." The multiple intakes of breath stopped him momentarily. But something inside was groaning to come out in the open. To see sunshine and be cleansed of the terrible guilt, or at least to have it shared. Grover Minnick could not face carrying it alone any longer. "Yeah," he whispered, "lynchings."

Zeb was the only clear-eyed man among them. He looked from face to face and held his wrenching gut as he took in the anguished pain among his friends. It was the sheriff who challenged him. "You was raised Southern, Zeb Paisler." It was an accusation.

Nodding, Zeb answered in a tone that was dragged from deep within him. "I was raised proud Southern, but not quite like you, Sheriff Yakes. My folks was Quaker. Heard of such things as lynchings, but only with horror. Never justification. Never a thought I should be doing such." Even more quietly, he added, "Can't imagine what you folks have been through being pushed like that."

Had his voice held pity, he'd have had five angry men reacting. But Zeb was soothing them with an understanding empathy that held them in their places, dealing with what had become of themselves.

The community potluck was well picked over before the six men shuffled from Owens' store and were handed plates. The womenfolk fussed but quickly knew to let be trying to feed them up. Something had happened between them. Something it was best to leave unquestioned. "I just ain't hungry" was taken as gospel, and the gathering broke up rather sooner than expected. A few pickups and carriages left as soon as their families could pack up. Others gathered in unusually quiet knots.

Doc waved away those who would talk with him, hoping for free advice without needing to bother about an appointment. Sadie and Ron Bean ran interference for him, citing his obvious fatigue.

The Beans' daughter Ronda begged to be allowed to go with Greg and Eli Paisler and that cute fellow from Fox Haven who drove the G.E.M. truck. Struan. *Stru, he calls himself. That smile. And those golden flecks in his eyes.* Ronda felt her ample bosom heave and her cheeks suddenly hot.

"Please, Ma," she begged. "All the gang is going down to the river. There'll be all the young people."

Sadie frowned and shook her head but looked to her husband. With a smile of hope she quickly suppressed, Ronda turned to her father with all the wheedling pleading she could muster.

"Please, Pa?"

Ron Bean considered. He'd seen Sadie's shake of the head, but, as always, he wanted to give his daughter everything he thought might make her happy.

Greg nudged his oldest brother in the ribs until, exhaling, Eli spoke up. "I'll be going with them, Mr. Bean. I promise to keep a close eye on your gal."

"Me, too," Greg chimed in.

Ron grinned at him, not sure Greg's promises were assuring. But he nodded to Ronda. "Go with them, then, Ronnie, but be sure they get you home by..." He glanced at Sadie.

"Seven," she mouthed.

"Seven," he said aloud.

"But, Pa, it won't even be part dark by then," Ronda protested.

Glad to have an excuse to appear stern, Ron thundered, "You heard me. Eight." He grinned. "Or so." But he glared at Greg and Eli. He was counting on them to keep her safe, even against her will if need be.

Greg blushed, but Eli nodded. It would be his charge; he would fulfill his duty as a Paisler was bound to do. He'd given his word.

"Get your stuff together and be off with you young people, now." Sadie slipped her hand into Ron's as they looked after the growing, excited crowd of youth. "Have fun," they both called after them.

Zeb Paisler walked up near. Seeing his expression, Sadie let go of her husband's hand. "If you men will excuse me, I'll go and help the ladies gather up. We women like to discuss what you men should be doing to save the world, you know."

Zeb chuckled. Nodding, he grinned at her and stepped aside, although there had been plenty of room. It was his token of respect and appreciation for a fine woman of good sense. He had no higher praise. Sadie's cheeks reddened, but she walked away tall and well pleased.

"Lucky man," Zeb commented low, squatting on his haunches to be shorter than Bean.

"Don't I know it!" Ron answered, squatting as well. "You weren't happy with our meeting at Owens."

"No, it's more that my boys are hearing things said." Zeb picked up a long straw of dead grass and settled it between his teeth. He lowered himself to sit sprawled on the grass of the empty field before the railroad's storage shack.

"Yeah, me too. On my milk route." Ron also sat. It was a far more comfortable position than squatting. "It scares me where this may be going. I say little things, hoping it might turn the tide a bit, but I don't think even bringing it all out in the open would do anything except make the ugliness louder."

Taking the straw from his mouth, Zeb looked at it. "Ugly. That's it. Real ugly. Why is it so hard for men to just say what truly is and deal with that? Seems like that would be a whole lot easier in the end."

"And save a lot of what we regret and try to deny later on."

"Is there no way we can stop this before...?" Zeb looked deep into the small milkman's eyes but saw only the same despair as haunted himself.

"Only if Mrs. Nickleberg would tell the truth," Ron muttered, "but the sheriff says she's happy with her man, despite everything. I don't think she's gonna tell on him and ruin this new good feeling between them."

"Despite what it's likely to cost the coloreds in our community."

Ron shook his head. "I doubt either one of them will even think that they might have prevented what's gonna happen. The way it always is."

"Lord, help us."

Sam watched little Rose inspect his 4H red ribbon. But when she lifted it to her mouth, he dangled one of his mother's biscuits where she could see it. Sure enough, the little girl dropped his precious prize ribbon and grabbed at the food. That treasure she knew would taste good. It went straight to her mouth. Smiling, Sam thanked his older brother Greg for teaching him that trick of exchange with the twins and again with Levitt.

Still holding the drooled-over, flaky biscuit, Rose twisted on Sam's lap. And then he heard it as well. Someone was coming down from upstairs. It had to be Miz Minnick. "You ain't well enough," Sam yelped. Gathering Rose against him, he hurried to the bottom of the stairs.

Nandria was pale and so awfully thin. She clung to the railing, but she smiled at the sight of the boy holding her baby daughter. Rose lunged toward her; Sam had to hold on tight to keep Rose in his arms.

"Oh, no, ma'am. Ma said you were to stay up there in bed."

Her smile widened. "I felt a degree of hunger. It was such a pleasant change from what I had been feeling these last weeks. Besides," she added, coming down another few steps on her own, "I could hear you two young people laughing together. It was such a welcome sound. Thank you," she murmured as Sam bounded up the few steps to take her arm to guide her to the ground floor.

He helped her into the kitchen and drew out a chair for her but held onto the baby. "You sure you're up to taking her? She's a lively one. And she don't always let you know when she's gonna change direction."

Chuckling, Nandria reached for Rose. "How well I know, Master Paisler. I cannot thank you enough for missing church and then this afternoon's service and potluck to stay to care for us."

At the stream's edge, Garum fussed with the flick of the wrist that would send his hook and bait into the shadows of the rocks. Pa had shown him how time and again, but he couldn't quite get the flip that would send his barbed invitation to the fish that rested there in the dark shade.

"Maybe you're just not big enough yet to have that kind of strength in those skinny wrists of yours," Dolph had told him before he moved away downstream. "Wanna try standing just about here?" He shifted his son so his shadow covered nearer rocks. "It'll take a while for the fish to find your shade, but they will if you're patient. Maybe."

Sometimes Garum wasn't quite sure whether his father was helping or teasing him. He'd stood there with the sun thrashing his neck, but if the fish had caught on that he was helping them move to where he could catch one, he saw no evidence of it. And no nibbles. Uncomfortably hot, Garum looked to his left to see if Pa was laughing at him. Hardly laughing, Dolph had gathered up his gear and was run-walking toward him. Pa lifted his hand to signal that they were to leave, and in a quiet hurry.

Garum ran back to scoop up his extra hooks and line and can of worms. He asked no questions; merely followed his father away from the edge of the water to the densest part of the stand of sycamore. Breathing hard, they stood listening.

Only then did Garum hear the unmuffled thunder of pickup engines and raucous calls and laughter of a dozen or more young voices. The boy knew without peering out or asking, that the gathering young people were white. His father's trembling told him to stay clear. This many fun-seekers would find a couple of darkies fair game for a bit of fun that neither Tacker would enjoy.

There was anger in Dolph. Garum could see it in the set of his jaw. Please, Pa, even if they spot us, please don't say nothin' to 'em. Afraid of more than one outcome to this unexpected invasion, Garum pulled at his father's rolled-up sleeve. "I know where we can fish. Away from here," Garum begged in a whisper. "Come on."

With a deep exhalation, Dolph allowed himself to be led through the trees toward the Paislers' spread.

"The Paislers got a pond on their creek. Todd showed me. We fish there after supper sometimes. At least we used to a lot before Miz Nandria started readin' to us of an ev'nin'."

They walked through the river birch; stopped at the willow that had comforted Garum more than once. The boy set down his pole and can of worms. Dolph stood at the edge of the pond that had been dug to enlarge the creek in the shade of a rounded hill of struggling cotton. Catfish tumbled over each other. Dolph watched them with his own shade of envy. He turned when his son drew up beside him, fitting a worm on his hook.

"We can't just put our bait in this pond."

Garum looked up, eyes wide in surprise. "But Miz Paisler said I could come whenever I want. Todd asked her for me."

"That didn't include you bringin' somebody else. We gotta aks. You know how finicky white folks can be. I don't want Mr. Paisler mad at me, no how. He's too good to work for to lose over something like our catchin' his fish."

Garum looked up at the sun. "They're prob'ly still at that picnic they was gonna have in town."

"No, them young folks prob'ly left from that. It's over. We gotta ask."

Father and son left their poles and gear under the willow and trudged over the hill toward the farmhouse. Inside the kitchen, Sam was just serving Miz Nandria and her little gal the French toast he'd made for them when they heard a strong but not loud rap at the back door. Sam brought the butter and syrup to the table and hurried to answer. "Hello, Gary, ain't it? You're a friend of my brother Todd."

"Garum," Dolph corrected. "And I'm his pa, Dolph Tacker."

"Oh, I remember you, Mr. Tacker. We're just sitting down to a bite to eat. Or Miz Nandria is. Won't'cha come in?"

Dolph stared. A white boy had just called him 'Mr.'

Garum took Sam's response in stride. The Paislers were always like that. "You got Miz Nandria here?" Garum asked. "I wondered why she wasn't readin' to us or showing us the music alphabet no more."

"She took sick, and Ma made her come here to sleep while we played with her little one. That Rose is some cute. We never had a girl crawlin' on our floors like that." Sam held the door for them to enter. Garum stepped forward, but Dolph held him back.

"We don't wanna disturb you folks none. Just wanted to know if it was okay for the two of us to fish in your creek pond. We'll pay you for any fish we catch."

Sam smiled. "Don't reckon Pa'd let you do that, sir. But I'm sure you're welcome to fish. Garum comes a lot with Todd."

"We need to aks your pa."

"My folks aren't home yet. But I'll sure ask Pa when they come in and run on out to tell you he said it was all right, if that'll help."

"You here alone with the lady?"

"We drew straws and I won." Sam grinned. "I didn't expect she'd be up to comin' downstairs, but she heard Rose laughin' and down she come. First time she's wanted to eat in a long while, I guess. Even my cookin'. I tried to make French toast."

Garum looked bewildered.

"Egg toast, but it got soggy," Sam explained. "So, I turned up the heat and burned most of it."

Garum wrinkled his nose. "My pa's a good cook, if Miz Nandria'd like somethin' more'n just burnt egg-toast."

Sam looked down, then laughed. "You know, Mr. Tacker, if you could? I mean, I wouldn't ask for me. But she's so frail lookin'. I hate to give her something that might make her tummy feel bad again." His round eyes looked up, pleading.

"Yeah, Pa, come on, please. Miz Nandria's special. She needs ya."

It was the first time Dolph had been inside the Paisler house, even as far as the kitchen. He took in a quick breath at the sight of Will Minnick's wife so skinny, pale and worn out. But he went right to work re-doing the French toast that had appealed to her. He watched her eat gratefully, although she stopped after only five or six bites. Her smile was reward enough. No wonder this son of his adored her.

"Thank you, Mr. Tacker. That was delicious. You can see for yourself that my daughter believes so, as well."

Garum and Sam looked over at little Rose devouring the toast and crisp bacon and laughed. Dolph merely nodded, uncomfortable to be seated at a white man's table and eating that white man's food in the presence of such a gracious lady.

Chapter 25

When the young men from Fox Haven proposed that everyone strip to dive into the river, Misses Freshstalk and Bean were decidedly among those who squealed and huddled in a panic of nay-sayers. But, the young men noticed, even as they crowded together, shaking their heads, each girl was hiding a wide-eyed smile of hope. So, they stripped. Stiff collars were ripped away or undone and carefully set in neat piles. Slender or muscular, tanned or pale above shirt sleeve lines, arms were raised to lift shirts above tousled, slicked-back, or curly heads of hair. Smooth, hairy, muscled, thin, wide-shouldered, drooped-shouldered male chests were revealed below grins or cheeks reddened with embarrassment. Youths strutted, edged, slunk and ran toward the water. A few farmers waded in; most had never had time to learn to swim. A very few galloped with large splashes until they tilted forward and dived with more or less grace and were hidden under the green-brown water. Heads broke the surface. Bare chests turned to be seen by those eight or nine giggling young women huddled in tittering knots on the riverbank.

Whoops of triumph and high spirits greeted their gasps. Horseplay among the boys. Laughter. Teasing.

After a while, a few of the girls, including Ronda, sat to slip off their shoes to wade.

Greg Paisler, soaked and dripping, shuffled toward her to steady her arm lest she fall in. But Ben Struan, who had not ventured out quite so far, got to her first. Blushing and clutching her skirt high and close, she let him help her wade in until the water was up to her knees.

"I can swim," she told him loud enough for the others to hear as well. "I wish I'd thought to bring my bathing suit."

Ben Struan laughed outright while the others hid their amusement with their hands at their mouths.

"Well, I am. Sorry." Ronda all but stomped her foot, as even banker Freshstalk's snooty girl was tittering. *She had no right, even if she was rich and the fiancée of the second Paisler son, Frank.*

Eli, seeing his brother Greg clench his fists as he watched Struan, sauntered over to stand beside the milkman's red-faced daughter. "Next time, we'll have to decide ahead of time to make it swim party, won't we?"

"Yeah!" Ronda agreed. She looked up at the tall farmer gratefully for giving her an out. Too embarrassed yet to smile, she blinked. It was the best she could do to thank him, handsome rescuer that he had turned out to be instead of the babysitter her parents had stuck her with. She startled when Eli blushed. "Hey, you guys, Ma sent me off with a heavy basket of goodies from the potluck," Ronda cried with the sudden insight that food was the answer to most if not all problems of relationships. "Anybody hungry after all that horseplay?"

It was Eli's turn to look at her with gratitude.

Nandria wanted to help clearing the table after what had become a happy meal among new friends.

"Oh, no, Miz Nandria," Sam protested. "You're the guest here. Besides, all we want is for you to get well again."

"We're good helpin'," Dolph proclaimed, eyeing again the skeletal figure. He wanted so much to protect her and see her well.

Sam nodded gratefully. He wasn't his happiest at women's work. Sharing it with other men made it seem closer to acceptable.

Garum reached but was outdone in gathering up dirty plates. Sam and Dolph were soon laughing at the sink, Tacker washing and Paisler drying and putting away. Not sorry to be excluded, Garum hauled his chair up near this teacher lady he longed to please. "We been missin' you."

Her smile only accented the hollow cheeks and deep-set eyes. Garum felt tears springing into his own dark eyes.

"We ain't complainin', you understand," he explained hurriedly. "Just you've come to mean a lot to a lot of us kids. Teachin' us about words. And now about music and such. I never knew singin' had a alphabet."

Her smile broadened, but she looked very tired. Rose had settled on her lap and rested her head against her mother's shoulder.

"I can help you go lie down," Garum offered, not sure where he would take her or whether he could manage both mother and child.

"We are well for the moment, Master Tacker, thank you. I was wondering how you were coming with learning to cope with your astounding news."

"My ma?" he whispered. "She don't hate me. That ain't why she left." Profound relief played across the child's face.

"And Pittsburgh is not located at the ends of the earth. You may yet go there to see her," Nandria encouraged. "Perhaps you and your father?"

He looked over at the sink where his father was having such an unexpectedly relaxed time. He looked down and shook his head, expecting her to comment. When he looked up at her, she was caressing her baby's back and rocking slowly in her chair. The sadness in her eyes made him turn away to blink to clear his vision. He felt and heard rather than saw Rose squirm. He twisted back, crying, "Oh, missus!"

Sam and Dolph spun around in time to see her grappling with her little one for an envelope that Rose had found in her mother's pocket.

"Oh, darling..." Nandria began, but the struggle even with her child was too much. She crumpled.

Garum snatched up the baby. Dolph leapt across the wide kitchen to scoop up the woman just as her body slid to the floor. His hand at the back of her head took the blow she would have suffered from the edge of the seat of the next chair. Sam stood, mouth open, staring, for a moment before rushing back to the sink for a damp cloth. Somehow, having a cloth for her face seemed important although he couldn't have told you why or how it would help.

"Wh-where..?" Dolph stood erect with the woman draped in his arms.

"Uh, the sofa," Sam decided. "In the living room." He pointed, and Dolph twisted sideways to ease her through the narrow doorway.

Rose puckered up and wailed. Her squirming made it hard for Garum to hang on to her. "Here, let me have her." Sam slapped the wet cloth onto his shoulder to have both hands free to take the baby. "She probably knows me better." Carrying Rose, he hurried after Dolph into the only formal area of the Paisler home. Together they settled Nandria on the sofa.

"Gar, there's a blanket on my bed. Second door to the left at the top of the stairs. Grab it for her, will ya?"

When Garum returned with the light flannel cover, Nandria looked like she was asleep. Her face was covered by the damp rag, but she was breathing slow and regular. Sam was on the floor beside her where the baby could see and touch her gently. He had a piece of Mr. Tacker's toast held up to entice her to pay attention to something other than her mother. Dolph took the flannel and spread it gently over her. He stood, frowning.

"What...?"

Sam shook his head. "I guess she really shouldn't have come downstairs at all. Always trying to do more than she really can, Ma says. We could carry her up to her bed, I guess."

Dolph shook his head to answer in hushed tones. "Leave her be. Least 'til she wakes up on her own. Your folks goin' to be home soon, you think?"

"I guess so. Ma'll know what to do."

"If they don't come soon, maybe we ought'a take her to see the doc." Dolph breathed out slowly. "But I hate to move her." He turned to his son. "What ya got there?"

Garum lifted the envelope the baby had taken from the pocket in her mother's blouse. He'd tried to make out the word on its face, but the only thing he could read for sure was the 'U.S. of A.' "That's our United States, ain't it, Sam?"

"To wife of Cap'n Willard Minnick, Boonetown, Missery, U.S. of A." Sam read aloud. "'Missery,' that's a funny way of saying Missouri."

Garum laughed, but Dolph said nothing.

"Hey, listen, that's Pa's truck. They're home," Sam cried, struggling to rise with the baby in his arms.

Frowning, Dolph lifted him by the shoulders to his feet. "Best we vamoose," he said, signaling to his son as Sam hurried out through the kitchen. He did not want to be caught in a white family's front room.

"We gonna just leave her?"

The man stood, swaying from one foot to the other, torn between wanting to escape and not wanting to abandon this dark woman who seemed white in everything she said and did.

Cynthia had her guest safely tucked back into her bed and sleeping while Zeb was still questioning Sam, Dolph and Garum. Cynthia entered her kitchen with Rose at her hip to hear her husband asking what had caused Miz Nandria to fall.

"She was tuggin' with her little one over that." Garum pointed to the crumpled envelope that had been smoothed nearly flat on the kitchen table.

"And then she simply slid down in her chair?" Cynthia asked as she set Rose on the floor to play with Levitt.

"Well, she sort'a went white. I mean," the boy stammered. "I mean, it was like the stuffin's just went outta her and the baby was fallin' and I grabbed for her."

"Good lad," Zeb praised.

"And I must'a squealed, or somethin' 'cause, all of a sudden, Pa was flyin' across the room." He pointed again, this time toward the sink where the last of the dishes still stood on the counter. "He hurt his hand so her head wouldn't bang on that chair."

Zeb stepped forward to look. Dolph merely shook his head that he was all right. But Cynthia took the hand between hers and motioned for Sam to bring her kit. Dolph tried to withdraw it, but she peered at him with the stern healer look that brooked no argument. Dolph settled back and let her work on his bashed and swelling knuckles.

While she worked, Zeb watched, finally turning to his son. He raised his eyebrows.

"It came so fast, Pa. I was still at the sink, so I grabbed a cloth and got it wet for her forehead. And we carried her into the living room to lie her on the sofa. I'd've called you but then we heard your truck comin'."

"Sounds like you three got things right in hand," Zeb said. "We thank you, Mr. Tacker. That could have been a nasty blow to her head if you hadn't gotten to our friend in such a hurry."

Dolph's chest lifted. He exhaled slowly before answering. "Thank you, sir. Glad we was quick enough to be able to help," he murmured, more grateful for the dignity of the address than he'd ever been to a white man. This day was changing a lot of long, hard-held truisms for him.

The two men nodded man-to-man agreement that nothing more needed to be said.

Turning to touch the envelope on the table, Zeb asked, "This here is the letter Miz Minnick was concerned over her little one wantin'?" He read the odd To wife of Cap'n Willard Minnick, Boonetown, Missery, U.S. of A.

"Yessir."

"Odd," Zeb muttered. For Zeb, nosing into someone else's business seemed like betrayal. But they were caring for the young mother-to-be. What if the contents made a difference in how they were to treat her? Or speak to her? He looked to Cynthia. Her raised eyebrows and nod told him she knew the contents, so, relieved, Zeb smoothed the envelope again on the table. "Sam, see if you can reach Doc on that phone. He should be told what just happened."

Chapter 26

Monday, August 19, 1940

Josiah Dover hauled his aching bones out of bed that morning. As he sat at the sagging edge of his mattress something warm suffused throughout his entire body. Something special would happen this day. It was sure as shootin'. "I ain't felt this in a blue moon, but it ain't never been wrong when I have."

With more youthful anticipation than had happened in a long while, Josiah pulled himself up to standing on his tall dresser and stood a moment until the spinning in his head settled and he could hurry to get dressed. Something good would come of delivering the mail this day. He couldn't wait to get down to Owens' store to sort through the bundles Isaac must have already stored in his screened-in far corner after the local train came through Boonetown while it was still dark.

Cynthia Paisler flipped the eggs and then quickly lifted them to her son's plate. Over real easy, the way Greg liked them.

He smiled his thanks that despite the large number of menfolk she cooked for, she always remembered what delighted each one. Waiting for the toast to pop up, Greg chuckled. "Remember, Ma? Remember when Pa first got you this toaster? Sam was a little one. Or was it Todd?"

Cynthia burst into a chuckling laugh just as she realized her Zeb was standing in the kitchen doorway, grinning. She gestured with the spatula for him to tell it, but Greg had continued without realizing the lines had been assigned to his father.

"The kid was telling Mrs. Owens a couple days later about how he had a tough time stuffing the bread slices into the slots, but he could flush them all by himself."

"'Flush them,'" Zeb chuckled aloud as he strode across the kitchen to buss his wife's cheek. "But it didn't take Eli and Frank long to figure out to cut the slices of your fresh-made bread thinner."

"And wasn't that toaster the best gift, dear father of this hungry crew?" She patted his arm as he went to sit at the head of his table. "And you, you young scamp. It was Sam, and I'm surprised you remember, Greg. You couldn't have been only so high yourself."

"Probably remembers the family telling of that story," Zeb commented.

Wiping the tear at the corner of her eye with the hem of her apron, Cynthia set her husband's full plate before him. "Remember, Greg," she said, turning to her son, "Doc said the sheriff wanted you to be observant when you pick up the Nicklebergs' eggs and chicken meat this morning. Any signs the two have slipped back into bad habits, he wants to know as soon as he can. And Doc'll remind you to tell the Minnicks when you get there how Miz Minnick is doing and she's not to go home to them until she's well."

Zeb looked up with a questioning expression.

"No, dear one, she's no burden here. And that wee bit of a Rose is a pleasure. Probably as close as I'll ever have to fussing with a little girl. It is a mite different, the way she reacts to things. People always told me little girls were different, but I wasn't sure I believed them until now."

"Thanks, Ma," Greg carried his dirty dishes to the sink, bussed his mother on the other cheek, nodded to his father and headed toward the door. "If that little Garum is with the Nicklebergs, I'll tell him again to thank his pa for saving our friend a nasty hurt to her head."

"No," Zeb interjected. "Best say nothing at all about the Tackers, son. And if the boy is there, unless you see him workin' well with Mr. Nickleberg, best tell him to go on home. Or to come here to work."

Both wife and son stared. Cynthia reacted first. "You're probably right, Zeb," she agreed. "Do that, Greg."

Greg frowned on his way out to his pickup. It wasn't until he was pulling up the egg farm lane that he understood and agreed. He knew his father didn't have any work right now that needed paying for on their family farm. But they couldn't pull the boy away from a paying job without giving him something as good, and, in this case, safer.

When Gertrude Nickleberg waved from her kitchen window that she was almost ready for him, Greg got out of his truck and moseyed up to the side of the chicken coop to where little Garum stood watching Heinz Nickleberg inspect the chicken wire 'porch' Garum and the missus had built. The man bent close, studying the construction details of the raised wire box attached to a hole in the coop wall. Several hens were walking carefully on the surface to the small feeder. Evidently, they had been doing that for a while. The ground under the box porch was beginning to be white and gray with their droppings.

"You done this, Garum?" Greg asked the boy quietly. "Where'd you get such a great idea?"

"Pa," Garum whispered proudly. "He studies the poultry magazine pictures real close. And I can read a bit to him. Mostly, though, he's got friends up along the river tell him what the words must say."

The egg farmer stood up, frowning. "Paisler. The sheriff send you to spy on us?"

"Well, no," Greg chuckled, realizing the man had forgotten it was only yesterday he'd asked him to come this morning. "Mrs. Owens reminded me as long as I was comin' into town of a morning before going to the Minnicks, I might as well offer to pick up your eggs and such to bring 'em to her. If that's okay with you? It was fine by Mrs. Nickleberg," he added and then regretted having let that slip. It would have been better to let the man assume the decision was his alone. Greg felt he was learning, but it wasn't a straightforward process. "Maybe I should go see if your missus has got things lined up for me to take now."

Nickleberg held up a palm. "Whaddaya think of this?" He pointed to the chicken's porch high off the ground. "Them foxes and coyotes are gonna think twice about tryin' to raid the coop with this up in the air like it is. I shouldn't lose near as many hens and them squawky ladies don't seem to mind stepping out on the wire none."

"And a bit less to clean out," Garum offered, then went quiet as Nickleberg growled that he was just going to point that out if the boy hadn't interrupted. No credit was given that it was child's idea and work to construct it. That porch was on his property and was, therefore, his own.

"Less to clean out and easier to shovel up for fertilizer." Nickleberg grinned.

"Smart! You certainly run a tight operation, Mr. Nickleberg," Greg praised, his hand on Garum's shoulder but nodding at the man. "I can't wait to let Pa know."

"Come on, then, Paisler. Let's see whether the woman's got everything ready for you."

Garum started to follow them, but the change in pressure of Greg's hand on his shoulder suggested it was best for him to stay where he was. The boy obeyed, knowing Greg would say a good word about the Tackers if the chance arose. He reached again for his shovel.

Bernice Owens' smile lit up when she saw Greg Paisler enter the back slaughter room of their store. "Ah, good. Looks like the feather farm is humming along again finally. How's Mrs. Nickleberg, Greg? Just leave them there on the mister's table for wrapping." She nearly turned toward the till to pay him for the delivery but caught herself. By rights, the Nicklebergs should be paying him, not her. He didn't seem to expect anything, so she made no offer this time. She'd need to talk with her mister about that.

"She seems so much better, Mrs. Owens. Bruises fading just fine. Good spirits. She was humming while she packed up the chicken parts. And the mister was quite taken with some of the new arrangements for the hens."

"New arrangements?"

Greg was about to explain when they heard Mr. Owens call his wife. She nodded and turned to hurry away. He grinned, slipping out the back to walk over to the seamstress's low-ceilinged home. The sheriff and Mrs. Dangler asked him the same questions; he repeated his answer.

"Humming, was she?" Mrs. D. wanted to know. "I'll be."

"Huh?" the sheriff demanded. "What's that tell you, woman?"

"That she's happy with her man, Sheriff Yakes. Looks to me like she won't be wanting you to press charges against him. Not right now, at any rate."

"If not now, when? So, you think we've got to wait until he turns on her again? And what'll he do to her next time? Kill her?"

All three went quiet.

Josiah Dover hummed through his huge grin as he loaded the leather bag with the mail he'd sorted to deliver along the rural route he'd run these thirty-odd years. He cared about his people. Loved watching what he carried to them change their lives. Hoped always that the change would be for the better, but, of course, that couldn't be so. He'd sat many hours with one of his people in great pain or loss over the news he'd brought them. His big heart would not leave them to grieve alone.

This time he knew it had to be good. It was Will Minnick's handwriting on the envelope, bold and strong the way it used to be. He couldn't wait to hurry up the Minnicks' long drive.

He stopped, considering. The letter was addressed to Mrs. Willard Minnick, and she wasn't with Grover and Doris any longer. Mrs. Paisler had seen to that and probably would continue until the darky lady was back sturdy on her feet again. But he knew Grover Minnick. If that man didn't get the news of his son first, there'd be the devil to pay.

"Oh, Lordy, Lordy." The humming succumbed to a plaintive whine. "I've never opened a letter to no one in all these years. How can I let someone it ain't addressed to open this one?"

He might pretend he hadn't known Miz Nandria was gone, but how could he do that? Everyone knew he was in on most secrets alive in the whole county. And her being with Mrs. Paisler was no secret.

"I gotta take it to her." But even as he posted two bills in the Minnicks' box, he felt the letter from Will burning in his leather bag. "Lordy, Lordy," he muttered and took the bills back out of the metal box to drive them up to the Minnick farmhouse. Minnick was just emerging from the barn smeared with the stock waste he'd been cleaning out.

"Josiah, that you?"

"Grover," the mailman acknowledged and walked toward him. "Got a couple bills for you folks. And I wanted to show you this since I was going by your place before I come to Paislers." It sounded almost believable. Minnick reached for the letter, but Josiah held it back, only letting him see the envelope without touching it.

"Why, that's Will's hand scribble."

"Just thought you might like to see it's good and strong like he's okay wherever he is. Postmark's hard to read, but looks like maybe he's somewheres in Wales?"

Again, Minnick wanted possession of the envelope, but Josiah kept it from him. "Gotta give it to her."

Grover's expression was every bit as unpleasant as Josiah had thought it would be.

"It's her name on the front. Gotta give it to her. Maybe she'll let you read it later on. I just wanted you to know your boy seemed good, if that'd be comfort to you and the missus. How is your Doris these days without all the help the darky was givin' her?"

"We do fine," Minnick snapped, taking the bills Josiah was handing to him. "These could've waited in the box by the road 'til they was molderin'."

"Yeah, they could that, for sure," the mailman chuckled and turned to go.

"Anyway, thanks for the news about Willard." The gratitude was well mixed with anger, but still his words were more gracious than Josiah had allowed himself to hope for.

"Anything I can do for a friend," the relieved man called back, hurrying on his way.

The twins carried the precious letter into the house between them, though it was a hassle getting them and it through the doorway since neither wanted to let the other go first. Feeding Levitt and Rose alternate spoonfuls of the junket she had prepared as a treat for Nandria, Cynthia looked up. "What you got there, boys?"

"Mr. Dover brung a..."

"Brought. Mr. Dover brought... so, what did he bring?"

"This here letter. He said it was for Miz Minnick. Said it ought'a make her chipper if he knowed anything about people."

"Oh, gracious," Cynthia whispered and reached to take it from both small hands. "Thank you, my sons. Do you think you two could finish feeding these babies their pudding?" She'd found her sons reacted badly to the treat being called 'junket.' Pudding, they gobbled up as quickly as she could make it. Only Zeb and Frank chuckled at the name 'junket.'

Travis hopped up on the chair she was vacating to take the spoon from her. "I get Rose," he cried. His twin was close behind him. He did not seem to mind feeding his littlest brother as long he got to slip himself an occasional spoonful. Soon all four children were happily eating.

Cynthia hurried upstairs. She paused at the doorway to Nandria's bedroom, hoping her guest was asleep, and hoping even more that she was awake and ready to receive the good news.

Nandria's dark eyes were closed, but the young woman stirred as though she'd heard her hostess enter. "Mrs. Paisler?"

"Nandria, my dear. Please, you are such a dear friend, I would be honored if you would call me by my Christian name. See here, what I have for you. The twins just brought it from a jubilant Mr. Dover."

"A letter? From Will? Oh!" Nandria scuttled up to sit upright in the bed. The hand she reached out was trembling.

Nandria had fallen into deep sleep with the letter clutched in one hand and the envelope in the other, Cynthia saw when she checked on her guest later. She did her best to read as much of the contents as she could without touching the young woman or the missive that had given her such peace.

"Lord be praised, he's coming home," she whispered, eyes tearing. "Her Will is coming home. Let's just hope it isn't to heal this time, but to take her and his children somewhere they can be respected."

Chapter 27

Wednesday, August 21, 1940

The Nicklebergs worked hard, and they used the dark boy just as hard. But he didn't mind; he was going to be paid, and that made it all worthwhile. Garum slipped into the house with a pile of household tools the mister had loaded on him to take to Gertrude to clean and put away.

"I'm gonna send you home early today, boy. Right now, as a matter of fact," Gertrude told him with a smile he couldn't quite make out.

"Uh, missus, it's been like a week now."

"Yes, it has, hasn't it, though I don't quite remember just when you first come. Oh, yes, that day." She went a pale gray that made him study her with worry. "Well, boy, I ain't talked to my man yet about what you're worth, but I don't want to send you away with nothing. So how about I give you some of this egg money?" She reached somewhere he couldn't see to bring out a frayed cloth bag. She spilled myriad coins onto the worktable. Carefully she separated a stack of seven quarters. "Will two dollars suit you for now?"

He eyed the stack again, knowing there was still a quarter missing. So that was how it was going to be. "Yessum, I guess a dollar and seventy-five cents is just fine for now."

"Two dollars," she started, then split the stack into two piles. They weren't the same height. "Ah, you're right, Hiram. Quick, you are." She added another quarter and set a dime atop that pile, smiling. "You're a smart one, and your pa and me'll see you grow to be a smart man." She slid the two unequal stacks toward him, laughing.

He grinned. "Thank you kindly, missus," he said, tucking all nine coins into a tiny cloth bag and stuffing it into the pocket of his faded trousers. "Shall I ask the mister if there's anything he still wants me to do?"

"Oh, no. You go on home. I'll let him know." She obviously had her own plans, but Garum had no way to know what they might be. Nodding his thanks again, he hurried away before the lady changed her mind. *Wait'll Pa sees these!*

Heinz stood at the back doorway staring down his lane at the boy peddling away fast. He stomped in through the hallway to the kitchen and spilled his own pile of tools onto the worktable with those the boy had brought to her. "Well, woman, I guess we got a lot of stuff been neglected for a while. It'd cost way too much to have to replace all this. What say we set ourselves to cleanin' and repairin' and see what we actually do need?"

She looked at him with an adoring smile and started to sort the tools in piles. Screwdrivers, files, various sizes and shapes of nails and fasteners. Gertrude hummed as she worked while Heinz poured himself coffee and pulled up his chair beside her.

"Where was that boy goin' in such a hurry?"

"Him? Oh, he had to go home for some reason. I told him it was okay. We didn't really need him the rest of today. I paid him a bit, too. Two dollars. And gave him a dime for being such a good help when I didn't feel so good."

Nickleberg winced, but she didn't stop her humming or dampen her smile when she looked up at him crooked.

"I'd never hurt you. You know that."

"Of course, you wouldn't."

"You ain't payin' no mind to what them gossipy folks in town say?"

"Talkin' against you? You're my husband, Heinz Nickleberg. I know who you are, and I'll never listen to anybody talkin' against you. Ever."

He harrumphed under his breath but said nothing aloud. When he looked over at her minutes later, she met his gaze with that smile that stirred him inside. Stirred him into ideas of how he'd missed her on the cot at the jail. How lonely he'd been turning over and not finding her there beside him. What difference did it make whether or not she snored? She was warmth. Warmth he'd counted on for how many years? Bad, good, bad again. But she was always there. His hand reached out to touch her arm.

She smiled, rising with him and following him to their bedroom.

When Nandria awoke, Cynthia was sitting in the straight chair beside her bed, weaving strands of thread to make a patch in a white, cotton sock that just fit over the wooden darning 'egg.' Seeing Nandria stir, her hostess smiled, lifted a handful of socks of various sizes to let them cascade onto her apron and laughed. "It's never-ending."

"Caring is never-ending," Nandria whispered.

"Good news?" Cynthia gestured toward Will's letter still clenched in one hand. "The way you slept so peaceful, I figured it might be." She gathered the holey socks and bent to stuff them into the darning basket near her left foot.

"He is coming home."

Cynthia sat up straight. "Coming home?"

"Willard writes that he is coming home." Her tears flowed, but her smile took her entire face. "Or, if he cannot, he will send for us."

"Send for you? Where is he?"

"England now. My England. He says he has found a place for us. A quiet place between Carlisle and Dumfries."

"Oh. Not in a big city, then. That's good."

"You have heard the information about the dogfights over the Channel?"

"Yes, on Zeb's radio. He checks every night. Says many expect Nazi bombers to be over English cities soon. I did not want to lose you."

"You have been such a fine neighbor. So much more than I deserve."

"Now, you listen here, young woman. I think I know better than you do what you deserve. I'm just not near enough to give it to you. It's your job from here on to regain your strength and be ready to travel and care for Willard's children. That's your job. Don't you let anything keep you from doing just that."

Shifting her precious letter to her other hand, Nandria reached to touch her friend's arm. Cynthia held her while, smiling, the two wept together until they giggled and laughed.

Gertrude awoke with her Heinz propped beside her on one elbow, peering at her. "Ach, Heinz, what is it? What's wrong?"

Without answering, he twisted away to sit up with his back to her. She heard a stifled sob and crawled behind him to hug his shoulders.

"Oh, my Heinz, what? That dream...?" Her voice cracked. The nightmare had cost them both so dearly. "No, no, please."

"It don't do no good to beg it go away. It don't go away. No matter what I do. It just never goes away, Gert. It never goes...away." He twisted to draw her around him to hold her, and to be held. He sobbed. She held him, and then gave way to sobs of her own.

"Ach, Heinz, tell me. Maybe if I know it, too...?"

"It was...so horrible. And all them adults around us little kids, laughin'. Like it was funny. I didn't know what to believe," he wailed.

Suddenly everything in her wanted him to stop. *Please, husband, this is yours. You keep it. It's been tearin' you apart and I don't wanna be tore apart—even with you.* But Gertrude hushed him, murmuring. Then humming. "This little light o' mine...," she hum-sang like a lullaby. *Just sleep, my angel. Just sleep. It's only a dream.*

"Jigaboos," he croaked, starting the story she dreaded to hear. "A spook done 'em wrong somehow. I never understood how, but that didn't make no difference. Nobody white was wanting facts or evidence. They'd heard rumors and they was out for blood."

"Ach, my love," she begged that he would stop, but he had started to open up. Her anguish never occurred to him in his rush for relief. Even the faint relief of sharing the images that had tortured him all these years.

"But that spook got away. So, they took up another one. Walkin' home from work, I think. Nice guy, the local kids told me long afterwards. Helped 'em with stuff when they'd ask. Pretty wife and kids they even let play with 'em when they was short for a team. But who knows? Maybe they was funnin' me, tellin' me that stuff 'cause they seen I was hurtin'. Kids can be cruel, too."

Gertrude clung, silently pleading, but he sat erect now. Using his hands to help describe, he rattled on as though what he was relating was a fairy story to be told at bedtime instead of what had been keeping him from sleeping.

But I can't heal you, Heinz. Much as I love you, much as you have been a part of me so long, if I'd lose you, I'd lose an arm and both legs. Please, no.

"Anyhoo," he said, and she collapsed against him, unable to stop her ears from hearing what she knew would haunt her now as well. "Anyhoo, they grabbed hold of this new guy even knowing he wasn't the guilty one. Started pummelin' him. Men with knives, chains. Right in front of his own house. Him screamin' finally, though he'd tried to hold in the hurt. He had to be hurtin' with what they was doin' and the folks around 'em—women, too, and us kids. Even little ones too small to stand on their own two feet. Everybody cheerin' and callin' names like it was some sort'a sportin' event. Laughin'. Suggestin' what else they could do.

"And then his woman come runnin' out'a his house, spittin' and fightin'. Tryin' to make 'em stop. Only them people laughed and cheered and egged them on to grab her up, too. The spitfire. So great with her own next child, she was waddlin' even when she first run outside. He was a goner by then, but she fought on. So, they held her and tied a roped around her ankles and threw the rope over a branch. Strung her up by her heels. They'd already done so much at her, but she was still cryin' some. She screamed. I'll... I ain't never gonna forget that scream. They was cuttin' open her big belly..."

At last, he was quiet.

Gertrude crawled to the end of their bed and buried her face in their covers. *No! No!*

Without looking at her, or seeming to remember she was there, Heinz continued. "It tumbled out. Took a breath and wailed. Once. Then, they was stompin' on it. A lot of 'em, like it was a frenzy dance. So many feet in patent leather shoes, boots, shoes with big wedge heels. Shoes all worn down and scuffed. Their faces..."

He went quiet again. After a long time, he wiped his face with his hands and got up to stagger to the kitchen. He had another bottle hidden deep in the back of the pantry.

Chapter 28

Zeb led his wife into the front room. "You have news, my love. Only for me, I take it?"

Cynthia smiled, delighted. "How like you to understand so many layers of what I want to tell you when all I can do in front of our sons is to look at you."

"Well," he grinned, " I gotta admit the twins were so anxious to tell me about a letter they carried in from Mr. Dover for our houseguest."

Nodding, she squeezed his arm. "Oh, Zeb, Willard is coming home. Or will send for them. He's found a quiet place where they can be together, at least some of the time. Somewhere far from London. And she knew about the Nazi bombers getting closer and closer to London. What she's had to cope with while working like a mule and so sick with this pregnancy and her first little one. If only we could keep her until Will can come for her."

Zeb frowned. "We gotta let all the Minnicks work out their own affairs."

"I know. I know, but…"

With raised eyebrows, he shook his head slowly side to side. She nodded agreement.

"All right, husband. But this is Nandria's news. We mustn't say anything until she is ready to announce it."

This time he nodded in agreement, then smiled and took her shoulders to draw her close against his none-too-clean shirt. She made no objection.

Ella Mae Drangler looked up from her hemming. The old clock on her mantle was too worn to chime the hours any longer. But it kept good time, and her sheriff had stayed in his office far longer than she'd hoped. That is, if he stayed at the jailhouse all this time. What if he'd taken off to do sheriffing duties? *Stubborn man, why don't you learn you have to let yourself finish healing? It only sets you back when you take on more than you're ready for. Stubborn. Men are so stubborn.*

Setting aside her handwork, she wrapped three scones and filled her glass-lined thermos with sweetened tea to carry to the jail. She found him, snoring, mouth open, sprawled across his desk. Smiling, she fetched the cushion from the corner seat where she often sat to be near him. Gently she slid it under his head. *How good it feels, doing kindly for a kind man. Oh, my Raymond, I thought when we lost you, I'd never feel this way again. But I do, God bless me. Please forgive. Please understand and forgive me. It isn't that I've stopped loving you or the children. It's just that it's been so very long.*

Tears streamed down her cheeks. She hurried to the back to open the door to the cells. Fortunately, no one was there. She needed the privacy. Weeping, she sat down on the cot in the farthest of the three cells. She never heard him until he was bending above her.

"Ah, little lady Elm, ah, don't cry. Whatever it is, we can work it out."

"We?" she sniffed. "Piermont, you don't want to work anything out with me. I...I'm such a fool. Such a silly, stupid fool."

"That you aren't, lady," he remonstrated, sitting down beside her. "I've seldom met so good a thoughtful, caring person. In my whole life."

"Your wife?"

"Oh, she was a blessing. Far more than I deserved, but you're you. So different, but with all the qualities that made her wonderful. Just a different way of combinin' 'em. She was warm and smooth and delicate. Like – like satin. But you're Elm. Homespun, sturdy. And just as warm. My Elm. Marry me, woman. If you'll have me. I want you close for the rest of my life."

He looked around at the stark bars of the cages for the worst of mankind.

"I guess this ain't the place to be asking such a thing."

"Romantic?" Ella Mae laughed through her tears. "Anywhere is romantic with you beside me, stubborn man. And, if you're sure, the answer to your question is a joyful, joyful 'YES'!"

"Bodie, won't you stay for a bite?" Grover Minnick had never pleaded with his hired hand. But as the faithful helper and friend continued on toward the west field, Minnick looked so pathetic Bodie nearly gave in and agreed to stay and help him make the evening meal.

"Uh, sorry, Mr. M., but I gotta..." No excuse came to his mind. He stood there, head hung, mouth open but sure he couldn't watch another supper between his boss and the missus. She was going downhill so fast these days without Miz Nandria to prop her up and take care of her. If only those doctors Mr. Minnick took her to could find out what was wrong and do something to make her better. He looked up at Grover, pleading to be let loose to go home.

"Yeah, yeah," Minnick told him, defeated. "You go on. See you in the morning. With that tractor actin' up again, no use comin' until near full light."

"Or I could come early and hoe the vegetables by hand. At least that'd get us somewheres."

"Yeah, maybe." Shoulders rounded, Minnick turned and started toward his farmhouse.

"Mornin' then," Bodie called after him. There was more to say, but he had no words. He trudged on into the west field, hoping that Will's lady would be well soon. He hadn't realized just how much they all were depending on her until she wasn't up to helping them any longer.

"Oh, Bodie!" Minnick called. "I forgot to let you know. Josiah Dover showed me a letter from Will. Didn't get to read it. But his handwriting this time was his own hefty scrawl."

"He's well then? Ah, ain't that good news to hear. Thanks, Mr. M. I'll sleep better tonight." Bodie's slouched stride picked up a bit as he lifted his eyes to the gathering hints of sunset colors, more content than he had been in days.

"That you, Mr. Minnick?" Doris called from the kitchen.

"Yeah, Mother, it's me." He slumped onto the brass bed to yank off his boots and set them by the back door of the enclosed porch. He shuffled into the kitchen in his stocking feet, watching his right big toe lead the way through the widening hole in his sock. "I think I'll wash up good before I tackle the meal."

"Oh, I got it all ready for you. Ain't I a wonder?"

Fondly, he reached to touch her shoulder as he looked with dismay at the chaos she'd created in the kitchen. Eggs, brown-black and toast even blacker huddled on his plate as though they were ashamed to be seen. Eating them would be hard, but he would do it, praising her efforts. Later, when she was asleep, he'd find a way to gather something edible.

"And speaking of wonders, Mother, I seen a letter this day. From your Willard."

"Will's home?" Her wrinkled face lit up the way their sons' had on so many Christmas mornings.

"Well, no. Not home," he hurried to correct her. "But fine. He's well and strong and doin' fine. Says he misses you and your cookin'. Remember how his buddies used to happen to come by the farm around mealtime? Couldn't keep 'em away, pests that they come to be. But you never turned 'em away. Always found a plate for 'em even when it got to be too many to all set around our table. You did fine, Mother. Real fine."

"Will liked my cookin', didn't he, Mr. Minnick?" She smiled as he helped her sit at her place at the table.

From their bathroom with the door open, he could hear her singing. "I'm gonna let it shine, let it shine..."

"Lord, if only you could," he cried to the wall between them.

Since Miz Nandria wasn't yet up to read to them or to teach them about music, many of the neighborhood boys went back to their baseballs games played with old plates set upside down as bases that moved under sliding feet. Garum was too small for his age to be chosen early. Or, sometimes, even late. Watching the teams fill up without choosing him, he stayed a while with his hands in his pockets, fingering the bag in which he'd carried his treasure of quarters. Remembering his father's face. The surprise. The obvious wanting them all. The pride when his son set all the coins into his palms. The sudden sadness Dolph expressed with those dark eyes as he took and kept them. All except the dime which he solemnly returned, nodding his thanks.

Garum stood away from the few adults and very small kids who'd gathered to watch the ragged game. He frowned, wondering what that feather farm lady was up to. Or, rather, what her husband might be doing. Was he drinking again? If he was, would he turn his fists on Mrs. Nickleberg again?

Suddenly, even while Todd was stealing from second to third, Garum had to go out to that farm and see for himself that his lady was all right. He peddled in the ruts for a while, but they were too crisscross to be fun in the deceiving shadows of coming twilight. And he was kicking up a lot of dust that rose up around him and refused to blow away behind him. "Ach!" he cried aloud, startled at how much it sounded like Mrs.

Nickleberg venting frustration. Chuckling, he swerved to the edge of the dirt road just beside where the pebbles and rocks gathered and concentrated on getting to her as fast as he could.

His shirttail clung to the sweat on his back by the time Garum reached the Nicklebergs' turnoff. Exhaling, he dismounted and started climbing their lane, walking his bike. The farmhouse was just within sight when he saw the old hound that gave the fox pause about going after the hens. The dog's only reward was occasional treats of chicken offal, but evidently that sufficed. The hound was scratching half-heartedly at the back door. It was crying, the way an old man howls when he's too tired to give full utterance to his grief. It looked up at Garum approaching with infinitely sad eyes.

"No, Lord, You can't let it happen to her again!" the boy cried, dropping his bike and running forward though his churning gut commanded that he curl up in a ball in the dust. "Don't look!" his being told him. But he had to.

Chapter 29

Todd saw him first. The young Paisler stood with his fishing pole at his shoulder and his mouth open, watching his friend peddling hard up their lane. Something was wrong. Awful wrong. The kid looked frantic. Or scared by something so evil, Todd swallowed hard to keep himself from a panicked run toward home. *Hang on, Todd Paisler. Ma and Pa'll wanna know what's scared ya, and you don't even know. Yet.* But Garum was about to tell him, and he knew already he didn't want to hear it. It took all his courage to make himself call out. "Gar! Garum Tacker!"

The boy nearly fell off his bike. Startled, he twisted hard on the handlebars to keep himself from going down. And then he was down. In a heap that went so still, Todd found himself calling, "Help!" back over his shoulder and racing toward Garum. He'd just gotten to him when Eli, with his long legs, thundered up behind them.

"He fell," Todd said, but Eli could already see that. "He—he was peddling so hard and when I called out to him, he just..." Todd lifted both hands empty of explanation.

Between the brothers, they lifted and turned the boy so they could see his face.

"Breathing, that's good," the oldest Paisler son commented so reasonably that Todd took hope. Those big hands were checking over the boy's body. "I don't feel nothing broke and there's no blood." He lifted his hands to inspect them to be sure. "Head's not scraped or banged up, that I can see. Ah, good, he's coming around. Garum, isn't it?"

"Yeah. Garum Tacker, and he was coming up our lane like somethin' awful was right on his tail. His face..."

"Hey, Garum, we've got you now. Nothin' to be scared of here. You're safe," Eli soothed as he helped the boy sit up. "You okay? Not hurt anywhere, are you? Did you hit your head when you fell?"

"The missus! She's dead, I think," Garum whimpered.

Zeb shook his head when Todd wanted to get into the Paisler truck to drive to Nicklebergs' farm. "The boy seems to like you, son. It'll help him to have you close until we can get his father to him."

Todd knew his pa did not want him to see whatever it was that had happened at the Nicklebergs', but his excuse made sense. Garum would feel safer with his friend there beside him. "Yessir," Todd said and headed inside, feeling more relieved than he wanted to admit.

Eli and Frank waited until their father climbed up on the passenger side. Greg had already taken off for Nicklebergs'. The sheriff had wanted him to keep away anybody else who might have listened in on the party line and decided to gawk. They'd mess up whatever evidence might still be there.

Inside the farmhouse, Cynthia had settled Garum at the kitchen table sipping warmed apple juice with a cinnamon stick to stir it with. Knowing how much the child liked his teacher, she sent Sam and Todd upstairs to help Miz Nandria to the kitchen to comfort him. The twins sat wide-eyed at the far end of the table, sipping their own juice. They were obviously too frightened to say much, but they wouldn't let themselves be excluded from whatever was going on. Thank goodness, little Levitt was sleeping through the whole thing.

Garum looked up when his teacher entered. Tears sprang to his eyes, but he struggled to keep them from spilling onto his cheeks. Without a word, Nandria seated herself beside him. He curled up against her. She held him, crooning, "This little light of mine..."

Sheriff Yakes huddled in the front seat of the doctor's car, holding his belly. The roads—if you could call them that—down to Tacker's place were pot-holed. The jouncing had not done his recovery any good.

"I'll fetch him," Ricartsen said, but he hadn't needed to get out of his car. Dolph Tacker bounded out of his house before Doc opened his door.

"Doc?"

"He's okay, Dolph. Your boy is okay, just frightened, they tell me."

Dolph's eyes widened; his fists clenched at his sides. "What happened? That drunken wife-beater shoot him?"

"No, no shooting," Ricartsen assured him, and then thought better of it. "At least, not that I know of. Paislers called. The boy went to them. He evidently found Mrs. Nickleberg. That's where we're going now, if you want to ride along. But we've got to hurry as she may still be alive. You can hike up for your boy from there." He was already restarting the car motor.

Tacker lunged into the back seat as Doc pulled away.

Greg knelt on the kitchen floor, applying pressure to pumping gashes in Mrs. Nickleberg's breast and side. He barely looked up when his father and brothers arrived. Zeb issued orders as he knelt with Eli at the woman's side to take over her care.

"Frank, you go with Greg and find the mister."

Despite his pallor, Frank nodded and hustled behind Greg in a quick search of the house and outbuildings. It was frantic hens' panicked cacophony that guided them to the man.

"Oh, sweet savior!" Frank gasped before turning away to heave his evening meal. They found Heinz Nickleberg in the white muck under the fowl porch Gertrude and Garum had erected. The chicken wire was ripped away in one corner. The outermost post had knuckled under the assault. It was splintered and bent askew but had not broken off. The man's hands, tangled in the wire above him, were bleeding from multiple cuts. His face hung twisted into his upper shoulder but appeared also to be slashed. Red oozed from beneath his shirt and at several levels at the waist of his baggy pants. He moaned when the Paisler brothers detached his fingers from the wire and dragged him to level, relatively clean ground away from the coop.

"He's alive?"

"Sounds like it," Greg answered between pursed lips. "Only wish I was sure she was."

Frank exhaled something like, "Yeah."

Greg tried to open the man's shirt buttons, gave up and grabbed the lapels in both hands to yank them apart. The buttons remained where they had been sewn, but the shirt tore away in pieces. Clearing thick, curly, graying hairs with the edge of his palm, Greg inspected Nickleberg's chest.

"Lots'a slashes, but none look too deep. Help me haul down his pants, Frank."

His next older brother paled. "We...we can't do that."

"Gotta see if anything's pumping blood. Or he'll bleed out. Come on, give me a hand."

Gingerly, Frank helped work the pants over the man's broad hips. Frank looked away as Greg lifted boxers to inspect private parts. Grunting satisfaction there was no immediate danger there, Greg scooted to the man's feet to haul down the pantlegs. "Nothin' Doc or Mrs. Bean can't sew up later. Or me, probably. They'll be busy with the missus." Looking down with disgust written on every feature of his frown, Greg took a sharp breath and let it out slowly.

"That how you keep from up-chucking?"

"It helps," Greg muttered. "Listen, take a look around for anything he could use for a weapon and then come on back to the house. I'm gonna check on Pa and Mrs. Nickleberg."

"You gonna just leave him lying here?"

"Without a weapon, he's as good here as anywhere until the sheriff tells me what he wants done with him."

Frank was just about to enter the farmhouse back door when he saw dust rising from the lower lane. "It's gotta be Doc coming," he called, then added under his breath, "I hope." Even Frank, who always seemed to see only the good in people, knew this situation could get confused, if not outright dangerous. So many people listened in on party lines. And some would be eager to spread the gossip. Who knew who might get word of the Paislers' call to Doc in town? So many overheated men had never believed it wasn't a colored who had harmed Gertrude Nickleberg in the first place. Frank exhaled in relief when he saw that it was Doc's car approaching.

Frank could see finally that is was Doc driving. And it looked like the sheriff himself in the front seat. But who was that in the back? A colored man? Had Sheriff Yakes found a suspect already?

Frank loped to open Yakes' door and help him out. Closer, he could see that the guy in back was a colored who came to their farm to help with harvests. Father of, oh, yeah, the kid who'd found Mrs. Nickleberg. The boy had been working for her, hadn't he? Had the father been working for Heinz as well?

"Where is she?" Doc wanted to know.

"In their kitchen," Frank twisted to point. "Bad off."

"Where's he?" Yakes demanded.

"Passed out up by the chicken coop, all cut up," Frank told him, feeling squeamish again. "I checked; there's nothing anywhere near he could use as a weapon, so Greg said it was okay to leave him there."

Ricartsen, clutching his silvered bag, was disappearing into the house. The worn black leather shone in the slanted rays of a sun thinking about calling it a day. Frank slowed, then stopped, still holding onto the sheriff, bent now to rest.

"Damn this middle of mine," Yakes muttered, grimacing.

"Yes, sir," Frank assured him there was no hurry. "Doc'll be a while with her, I'm afraid. And Mr. Nickleberg's probably gonna be out cold a long while. Mostly drunk, I gather. He sure smelled like it."

"Okay," the sheriff exhaled when he could straighten up. "Let's us take a look at him." Yakes turned to dismiss their passenger. "Tacker, you know the way from here to Zeb Paisler's place? Go on, then. Come on," he directed Frank to go with him toward the outbuildings. Neither looked back to watch Dolph leave.

"I see—and smell—what you mean," Yakes muttered when they approached Nickleberg. The sheriff bent to lay a hand on the man's chest. "You think he's the one hurt the missus? Or was it someone come from outside and hurt them both?"

Frank gulped. It wasn't in his nature to enjoy accusing anyone. But, being a Paisler, he had been asked a question, and he was duty bound to answer to the best of his ability. "Well," he hedged, "I didn't see any sign of somebody else. No hat or weapon except the knives on the floor in their kitchen and hallway. And they both looked like fowl slaughter cutters." Only after he'd said it did he realize that he was accusing the Nicklebergs of having hurt each other. "Uh."

Yakes looked up at him. He took young Paisler's arm to haul himself upright. "Yeah. Especially since it's happened before."

"But it could've been an intruder who was careful what he left, I guess, Sheriff."

"Could'a. But was it? How're we gonna prove it, one way or the other?"

Frank shook his head as he turned to help the sheriff toward the farmhouse. That was something he wanted no part of. He liked good and bad, guilt and innocence to be clear and agreed upon.

The grunt and growl behind them made them spin. In opposite directions at first, until Frank twisted back to accommodate the sheriff.

"You awake, Nickleberg?"

"Wha'? Who?"

"Yakes. We come to help your missus again, but it looks like you got a fair share of whatever happened yourself this time."

"My Gert?"

"Cut up bad. Doc's with her. Who done that, Nickle?"

Nickleberg struggled to sit up, but the sheriff kept Frank from helping him.

"Who sliced her with your slaughter knife?"

"My?"

"Looks like it. Two of 'em, right there. Both yours, man."

Frank paled again, knowing that wasn't strictly true. Or at least had not been proven yet. He gasped, but, at a look from the sheriff, swallowed hard and shut his mouth.

"What'd you do to her? Why? It's been you all along, hasn't it?"

"Me? No! That kid. The little darky kid hanging around with her. Days now."

Yakes shook his head, disbelieving. "Won't make it, Nickleberg. Kid's too small. He could never inflict as much damage as we got in front of us."

"Not the kid," the farmer yowled. "Him!" Lifting a trembling arm, he pointed.

Frank twisted with the sheriff this time. They looked back at Dolph Tacker standing, feet apart, mouth open, behind them. He looked to be about to take off running and then changed. His mouth closed. His jaw tightened. He stood still, angry and defiant.

Chapter 30

Dolph stood handcuffed to the wing window frame on the passenger side of Doc's car. Silent, he followed with furious eyes the whites maneuvering to bring Mrs. Nickleberg out to lay her on the mattress they'd spread in the bed of the Paisler pickup truck. No one spoke to him until Zeb himself approached.

"We're gonna put you up in the corner beyond the missus, if that's okay."

"You'll do it whether it's okay with me or not."

"Well, yes, I guess we will, Mr. Tacker. But the sheriff'd like you to duck down when we get toward town. So nobody sees you, you understand?"

Dolph almost spat at him, but this man had been decent and fair. He nodded.

"Maybe it'll help. He's gotta bring you in once you've been accused. But we're bringing Mr. Nickleberg in, too. He thinks to Doc's."

Dolph cocked his head, peering at the farmer with all those sons, trying to understand what was being said. It was beyond hope. "You believe me?"

"Innocent until proved."

"That don't apply to folks who look like me."

"Someday, I hope."

"If we live long enough," Dolph exhaled.

Nodding sadly, Zeb undid the handcuffs to free him from the car frame. "Hands behind you, please," he directed. Tacker complied. At least he was still being treated with dignity. Imagine a white man saying 'please' as though what he says is a request instead of a command.

"Mr. Paisler?" Dolph said low. Zeb continued fastening the cuffs around the man's wrists, but he was listening. "My boy's ma is in Pittsburgh. I got a friend to write out her address for me. It's at my place. In the tea tin. Neither the boy ner me likes tea, so it was empty."

"You would like me to get in touch with your wife?"

"Yeah. Please. Maybe she kin find a way to get Garum so he can stay with her. Or at least have somebody take him in so he's got somebody to protect him."

"Of course. But when we get to the bottom of this..."

"You know as good as I do, there ain't nothin' for me at the bottom of this as soon as them crackers hear that feather farmer open his mouth about me."

Zeb's lips pursed. He nodded. "Wait here," he said and turned to walk over to the sheriff. They conferred heatedly for some time. Finally, Yakes stared over at the prisoner. Thought a while, and finally nodded. But he was shaking his head as Zeb walked back.

"I'm gonna put you in my son Greg's truck. He's gonna take you to my place to be with little Garum for a while. Maybe we can straighten this out before anybody knows you've been accused."

"Oh, Lord. Sweet Lord," Dolph exhaled. Hanging his head, he worked to breathe. Until he heard Sheriff Yakes call Greg to him.

"You, Paisler, when I call, you're on your honor to bring that—that fella to me in town. On your honor, you hear me?"

Greg stared at his father, but there was no help for it. He nodded, and the sheriff let him lead Dolph to his pickup.

"Hey, Sheriff!" Nickleberg screeched. "Where's he goin' with the jigger? Didn't you hear what I said about him?"

"I heard, Nickleberg. It didn't seem fittin' to have him in the same vehicle with your wife."

Sam was the first to hear Greg's truck coming up their lane. Surprised that it was Greg, he hustled out to the edge of the lane from where he'd been sitting in the scant shade of the scrawny apple orchard plantings. Sticking his thumb out for a ride, he pulled it in. His grin faded. That was little Garum's dad in the truck with his brother. Belatedly, he stuck out his thumb again. Greg slowed and stopped. The dark, broad-shouldered man slid as best he could to the middle to allow Sam in beside him.

"Uh, hello, sir," Sam stammered.

Dolph's eyes widened, then closed. His face contorted. He couldn't answer. To cover for the man's embarrassment, Greg asked about Dolph's boy.

"Garum's pretty much okay by now. Mom's apple juice and cinnamon stick and then Miz Nandria taking the boy in her arms. He was crying, but who wouldn't be, seeing somethin' like he seen? Did you get to Mrs. Nickleberg in time? She gonna be all right? Who hurt her?"

Dolph gritted his teeth, but Greg answered over him. "Nobody knows yet. The sheriff was there. He'll figure it out. Give him time."

"Mrs. Nickleberg's okay?"

Greg shook his head. "Knifed. Bad. But Doc is with her."

"Knifed? Gosh," Sam gasped, grabbing his door handle as Greg was coming to a stop. "I'll run in and tell Ma we got company." In that moment, he was out and on his way.

Dolph's shoulders eased, but he did not move over.

"You okay, Mr. Tacker?"

"Mr. Tacker. I ain't heard that a lot." When Greg shook his head, Dolph turned on him. "Listen, you tell your pa to take care of my boy. Never mind about me. I'm a dead man and I know it. But the boy. He deserves livin'. You hear, Paisler? Tell your pa to get hold of my woman. Pittsburgh, tell him."

"W-where in Pittsburgh?"

"Don' know. Working for white folks."

"Who? What's their name? How would we find them?"

Dolph shook his head, tears flowing down his cheeks.

"Did your wife ever write to you? Maybe there's a return address on her envelope."

"Uh, yeah. Twict. At my place. In the tea tin." He stopped to wipe his face with the back of his hand. "Your ma's comin'."

"Don't worry. She'll understand. Here," Greg said, offering him a rumpled but clean cotton handkerchief from his hip pocket. "Let's get out and you can kind'a stand behind me."

Nodding in exhaustion, Dolph clambered under the steering wheel to get out of the truck after Greg. He was sliding over the running board when Greg turned on him.

"Or I could give you my keys. We've got extra gas in the shed. Garum could be ready in no time and you two could take off. When they ask me, I'll tell them I sold you the truck and you took off. If we don't know where you're going, there's no way we can tell 'em."

Dolph staggered back, banging his left elbow into the pickup's doorframe. Cynthia came to them on the run. Greg turned and helped him sit on the running board.

"I got nothin'. How kin I buy your truck?"

"A handshake's a good downpayment. You'll make good. Sometime. Pa'll help me get another one for now. Go on, Dolph. Get clear. You save that boy of yours."

Cynthia was with them now, brushing her son aside to check on the man collapsed on the running board. "What happened, Mr. Tacker? Are you all right?"

"Just tired, missus," he breathed, struggling to rise to his feet before her. "Don'tchu worry none about me. I'm thankin' you for takin' in my boy."

"Garum? He's a fine child. We are proud to have him. And we'll be happy to keep him if you are thinking of leaving?" She glanced at Greg, somehow knowing what her son had proposed.

"I'll be takin' the boy with me," Dolph decided. "I guess it's best we was quick about it."

"Yes, quick about it," mother and son chimed together. Greg unlocked the handcuffs and took off for the extra gas in the shed. Cynthia hurried Dolph to the farmhouse.

Nandria held Garum in her arms, humming "This little light...gonna let it shine," as though 'gonna' were a word for her, which it was not. But her quiet lullaby had lulled him to sleep. Dolph stopped in the doorway, staring at woman and child. How could such a frail woman be so strong against all he fought without hope? He staggered; Cynthia set a supporting hand at his elbow.

"They're leaving right away," Cynthia hurried them.

"You are taking your son with you, Mr. Tacker?" Nandria asked. Her voice seemed to rouse him.

"Yes'm. Right away. But thanks..."

"Please, there is no need." She shook the boy gently. As he stirred, she whispered, "Garum, your father is here for you."

"Wha'? Pa? Pa!"

Cynthia sent Ned and Travis upstairs to gather clothes from their drawers for the Tackers to take with them. "Does your brother have blankets in his vehicle, Sam?" At his shake of the head, she pointed toward the winter storage area down in the basement. "And get boots," she called after them. Cynthia was already at the refrigerator collecting food. "Todd, find the hamper for me... Todd?"

"He's still outside, Ma," Ned told her. He was the first to carry his pile of shirts and socks downstairs. "Greg told him to be watching for anybody coming."

"Good! Ned," she beckoned, "fetch the hamper from the pantry."

"There ain't no time, missus," Dolph cried, "but I thank you for the thought—and the human..."

The Paislers hustled out behind him as Dolph carried his son to Greg's truck. Dolph piled his boy onto the bench seat. He turned to Greg finishing pouring gas in to fill the tank. "I'll tell 'em I stoled this." He shook his head at Greg's protest. "It won't make no difference to what they do to me, and it'll be easier on your ma."

Reluctantly acknowledging reality, Greg nodded thanks. He lifted his hand. The handshake between them made them lifelong friends—however long the black man's life might prove to be.

Sam just had time to stuff blankets and clothes behind Garum's seat before the truck motor roared to life. Garum scrambled to the window to wave. They were gone.

Young Paislers stood open-mouthed, staring at each other. Cynthia took Greg's arm in both hands. "So like your father," she murmured. Then she realized Nandria was at the back door. "Now, Mrs. Minnick, you best go back in to lie down. It's been a dither, all right." She hurried toward the house. As she mounted the steps to go inside, she turned to her young men. "Chores all done?"

So familiar was the question that the boys turned automatically to tasks before remembering their assigned work had been done long before. But at least they were functioning again. And chuckling at their own reaction. Until Sam spotted Todd racing toward them.

"Ma!"

Everyone turned.

"They're comin'! Up our lane. A bunch of 'em!"

Chapter 31

Cynthia was about to turn away when she saw something in her third son's expression that stopped her. "What, Gregor? Something terrible? Do you know who is coming?"

Shuddering, he made himself smile. "No, no, nothing like that. But I don't think we can count on this bein' a friendly visit for now. We'd better get the little ones tucked away. Fast."

"Yes." Cynthia froze, thinking. "Yes, all right." In a moment, she was geared for quiet commands to her family. "Greg, meet them. Talk to them. You're the oldest son here, so you will need to stand in for your father. Mrs. Minnick, the twins will help you back upstairs to your room. Lock your door and do not come out no matter what. Ned and Travis, take Mrs. Minnick back upstairs and then stuff all those extra clothes back into wherever you got them and close the drawers. We don't want whoever this is to know that you were getting them out. And you stay up there. Don't you come down; do you hear me? Sam and Todd, carry the babies upstairs with Mrs. Minnick. Go!"

The children scattered instantly. Cynthia could hear the clatter of small feet on the stairs and Mrs. Minnick urging the children to go ahead in front of her. Todd refusing her help with the babies.

"Oh, Lord, help me. These are our neighbors. They've been our friends," Cynthia whispered. "Please keep them civil. Please keep all of us from harm."

"Ma?" Sam hurried back to her to touch her arm in concern.

"No, I am all right, my son. I'll start the coffee. I think there are cookies and a fruit pie in the pantry. You go with your brother." She gestured toward Greg's back as he walked through the porch with a quiet confidence that showed them that he had himself in control, at least for now. Sam watched Greg take up a hoe left leaning at the back door. Sam hurried after him, lifting the broom from beside the lead-lined sink. It felt ridiculous in his hands, but it was the only thing close enough to grab. He felt his knees shaking as though they would spill him on the ground as he stepped out the door, but he managed to keep upright and walk as slowly as Greg had to the middle of the yard to greet the visitors.

"Hello, neighbors. Welcome," his brother called. Beside him, Sam nodded; he couldn't have spoken if he'd had to.

Peering intently, Sam saw no sign of Greg's pickup. There were two other pickups, dusty and dented, and a rusty car following on bald tires. Sam could not remember ever having seen any of them before. In the confusion of all the men and boys—it seemed like a dozen of them—jumping down and milling around, rifles in their hands and chains wrapped around their arms, it wasn't easy to be sure he knew any of these people.

"Where ya got 'im, Paisler?" a drawling man demanded. A chain dangled from his left shoulder along a limp and withered arm.

Greg frowned. He glanced at Sam, who shook his head. "Don't know him," the boy mouthed. "None of 'em."

"If you mean my father, sir, he is busy helping a neighbor."

The man spat. "Yeah, we know the neighbor, don't we, boys?"

Inside the kitchen, Cynthia banged down the heavy tray of cups and glasses onto the kitchen counter and spun to face someone behind her. "What? What are you doing here?"

"I'm sorry, Mrs., er, Cynthia," Nandria apologized but made no move to retreat. "The children are locked in their rooms." She slid the round-ended keys into the potato bin and turned to face her hostess. "I am here to do whatever is asked of me. This is your home to defend. I am behind you in whatever you decide. Have you telephoned for help?"

Something like, "What good is a wisp of wind like you in your condition?" came to the farmwife's lips but she only leaned forward over the heavy tray. Her closed eyes betrayed her fear for only that moment. "Oh, Lord, no. I forgot the first thing I should have done." She glanced at her friend, grateful for her coolness under pressure. Grateful to share the terror with someone who was still thinking clearly, the way Zeb would have been. Methodically, she began to remove some of the cups so the pitcher of lemonade would fit on the tray. "I'm going out there with my boys. Please try to reach someone on our party line. Anyone." Gesturing to the crank wall phone, she struggled to again lift the tray. "At least, since they're here, they didn't come across our guests in Greg's truck."

Nandria nodded in relieved agreement. "Is there a weapon in this house?"

"Back of the tallboy in the front room. If you need to, my friend, shoot us all."

Nandria nodded, knowing it was Cynthia's way of telling her to protect the littlest ones at all costs. But Cynthia never turned back to see her. Her head was high as she reached the outer door. Nandria could hear her gracious cry to the men outside.

"Gentlemen, welcome to the Paisler farm. You must be hot and thirsty. Why don't we have a seat there at the picnic tables and refresh with some cold lemonade? Hot coffee is brewing, and I'll bring it out as soon as it's ready."

Not waiting to find out how the intruders reacted, Nandria bustled to the phone. She tried listening first, but there was no gossiping voice on the line or answer to her call. She tried clicking for the operator but got no immediate response. She stood, frowning in concentration, trying to remember Doc's number, or Mrs. Owens'.

"Sorry," the operator's voice sounded breathless as she finally came on the line. "I had to step outside for a moment... What? Oh, dear Lord, I'll roust everyone in reach. Of course, right now. You be safe, now, you hear. Help'll be comin'."

The click was loud in Nandria's ear. "Please give swiftness to that aid," she whispered. "Yes, now, the weapon. Behind the tallboy. What is a tallboy?"

Chapter 32

Garum huddled against his father's shoulder, his fist in his mouth to keep from screeching in terror. Dolph was sweating, and shivering, but he risked twisting to bring the boy into his arms to stroke his cheek. "Easy now, son, easy," he whispered. "They're goin' on by. They didn't see us up here between the trees like we got."

When the two pickups and rusted sedan had gone up the rural road and disappeared over the hill, the Tackers exhaled. Garum reached up to hug his father's neck until Dolph needed to pry him loose a bit. "Hey, big fella, we're okay. See, they're gone. Plumb outta sight. All we gotta do is sneak back to the road and off we go."

For once, Dolph waited, holding him, until Garum settled. At last, he could coax the boy into sitting on his own, close at his father's side.

"Okay?" *Of course, he ain't. Seeing the old lady he thought was kilt. And now white folks after us. How could he be okay? But we got no choice. We gotta get movin'. Get outta here.*

There's gotta be someplace safe. Someplace far away from here.

"Y-yeah. Yeah, Pa."

Patting Garum's leg in reassurance, Dolph bent to restart the truck. It purred into lusty life the way no vehicle of Dolph's had ever done. What a difference it makes to have the money to take care of a truck's needs as they came up instead of beating it up trying to juggle when all the coins in his pockets needed to go somewhere else.

As he backed out from between the trees, the back panel scraped a tall stump he hadn't seen. He cussed low. Garum cowered. "Mebbe we can smooth it before Mr. Greg sees it, Pa."

"He ain't gonna see it."

"Huh?"

"The truck's ours, boy. I bought...stoled it from him."

"Stoled it? Pa! Paislers was our friends." It was a statement of betrayal.

Dolph winced, but clamped his mouth tight and drove off, saying nothing more.

Hanging up the receiver, Nandria turned so quickly to get to the front room that she found herself staggering and dizzy. She lunged for the table to prop herself until her spinning head gradually settled. Whatever a tallboy was, she could only hope she would know it when she saw it. And there it was. A highboy chest of drawers. That had to be it. But there was no room in the drawers for a rifle, she realized. Instead, she peered behind it at a slender closet wedged closed by the piece of furniture. It took all her strength to nudge it out to reach for the door handle. Locked.

"Ah," she breathed, then willed herself calm enough to think. *I need a key. Where? In the highboy?*

She started with the top drawer. That would be convenient for the adults but not for small children. There it was in the far, back corner. She needed to scoot the highboy forward a bit more to be able to reach in to insert the key. The closet door opened. No rifle in sight. It must be disguised under the winter clothes. Fighting through layers, Nandria finally came across an ancient rifle. Unloaded, of course, with all the inquisitive small children running and crawling through this house.

Where were the bullets? Rising panic threatened to overwhelm her as she fumbled through the top three drawers. Nothing.

Steady, Nandria Brown Minnick, she chided herself. *Where would the Paisler adults be standing when they realized there was danger that needed to be met with a firearm? Outside, probably. Or in the kitchen.*

Leaving the rumpled coats and sweaters where they'd landed, she hurried back to the kitchen. And stifled a scream.

"Todd! I locked you in with the little ones."

"The twins got 'em. I went out through the window—done that a hundred times. Don't worry, them fellas never saw me. How can I help? You called town already?"

Nandria sagged into the nearest chair at the table. "Yes, the operator was most concerned and will do her best to summon aid."

"Mrs. Johnston? She'll do great." He gestured toward the rifle in her hands. "You know how to use that?"

"Yes. My father taught both my younger brother and myself the skill required to utilize a number of different weapons. However..."

"Not loaded, is it? I know where the ammo is." He scampered to the pantry where she heard the scuffling of his climbing and a grunt as he reached. Todd appeared grinning as he untied a bag marked 'zucchini' carefully wrapped around a cardboard box of shells.

"Are you proficient with that weapon, Master Paisler?"

"I can shoot a quail at twenty yards if it sits long enough."

"Then take the rifle and the shells to the top of the stairs. Remain quiet and please keep the children still. You will protect them as need be."

"Oh," he muttered. He hadn't thought of being the last stand for the littlest ones. "Ma'am, you're still weak from being sick. That's a job for you, don't you think? I'm a whole lot stronger than you are right now. I can sneak..."

"Master Paisler, I am leaving my beloved daughter to your strength and courage."

He had no answer to that. Solemnly he took the weapon from her hands, tucked the box of shells under his arm and headed back toward the stairway. That he didn't promise to stay there, he never mentioned. He didn't know himself how things would turn out.

Nandria slipped quietly from the kitchen to the basement. She peered around and beneath the clotheslines strung for drying. Nothing. Moving quietly, she stood a moment beside the round tub of the washing machine, touching its built-in wringer and wishing her father-in-law had such an apparatus at the Minnick farm. But the wish soon gave way to her current need for a weapon. A broken shovel leaned into a far corner. She was hurrying toward it when she spied a crowbar among tools to one side.

"Leverage," she murmured. "To multiply my pitiful strength. It will accomplish something, perhaps."

There was nothing more suitable in sight. Turning, she hurried back up to the kitchen. The phone jangled. She hesitated. If she lifted the receiver, the men outside would know there was someone inside the house. But whoever was calling was a contact that might help them.

"H-hello," she said. "P-paislers' residence."

"Thank the Lord. Somebody's left alive at least." It was Sadie Bean's voice. "Miz Nandria, that you?"

"There are about ten or twelve of them," Nandria explained without bothering about greetings. "Two pickups and a rusted sedan. Men and a few boys. None I recognize. They are checking everywhere in the outbuildings. None have come into the house as yet. Mrs. Paisler has slowed them down with cookies and lemonade and supposed welcome. Our earlier guests had left before they came. The visitors have weapons."

Sadie had not interrupted her until now. "We know what those weapons would be. So, no one's hurt yet?"

Nandria nodded, unable to speak. She cleared her throat.

"Who's there with you?"

"Gregor and Samuel. Mrs. Paisler. They are in the picnic area serving the visitors. Young Todd is at the stairwell guarding the smallest children locked in their rooms on the second floor. Todd has the only weapon I know of within the house," Nandria explained. "Oh, I do have a crowbar."

"Here's hoping you'll never have to use it," Sadie breathed. "Listen, my Ron and a passel of men he rounded up in town are on their way out there. They'll probably meet up with Doc and the sheriff and Zeb and bring them to you, too. But Ron says to tell you to try to get them to go to Nicklebergs'. To their egg farm. Get 'em away from you, however you can."

"Oh, they are coming in."

"Hang up! Play 'em nice as long as you can but try to get 'em to go to Nickles' place. Bless you," Sadie breathed and hung up.

Hands shaking, Nandria set the receiver back into its nesting hook. Scurrying to the pantry, she hid the crowbar. As she reentered the kitchen, she heard the coffee maker gurgle its boast of being ready. She hurried to gather mugs to set them out on the table. She was pouring cream into a small pitcher at the refrigerator when the man with the withered arm stomped in.

"Who's here?"

Nandria pantomimed to show that a little one was asleep upstairs.

Behind him, two whiskered men settled their rifles and chains into their non-dominant hands to reach for a mug. The man with the withered arm gestured. Without a word, they moved on inside to check the house. A youth with many days growth of scraggle for his first beard shoved his shotgun to his buddy and offered to pick up the tray.

"Right kindly of your mistress, girl," he said. "I kin carry this out to the picnic table for the fellas. Did you know she's got oil cloth on them tables? She's right smart to have a cloth you kin just wipe off with water for the spills. I gotta get one for Ma."

"How thoughtful you is," Nandria murmured in a whining voice.

Rolling his eyes, the would-be ringleader came to stand beside the table, feet apart and chain clanking from his deformed hand so the young man could hear his displeasure. His terror onslaught had dissolved into a Sunday school outing. He was beginning to realize why most raids were done in robes and at night.

"Uh, sorry, Joe Bob. She can take it out, I reckon. What'll we do about the little one asleep upstairs?"

With a final, vicious clang of the chain, Joe Bob stalked outside.

The scraggly youth shook his head. "I guess I better at least check if that coon what sliced up Mr. Niggleberg ain't up there."

"If you'll carry this out, I kin take you up. Just you alone, so they ain't too scared. Cry an' carry on somethin' fierce," Nandria fussed. "Your ma wouldn't like that no-how, would she? You makin' 'em cry."

Oddly, the boy did as she asked and carried the coffee outside. Nandria pawed through the potato bin for the keys and was ready to lead him upstairs. Todd was nowhere in sight. Only Levitt and Rose lay asleep on the double bed in Nandria's room. The other rooms were tidy—and empty. Nandria swallowed hard as she again locked the doors.

When the young man frowned to see her with the keys again, she said the first thing that came to her. "Keeps 'em safe 'til I kin get up to them. Them stairs is steep."

Nodding solemnly, he followed her down to the kitchen and helped carry more cookies outside. But Joe Bob swept the plates from their hands. "We ain't here for no lemonade and cookies," he bawled. "We come to teach some zigaboo to go messin' with our women!" He started as though just then realizing how dark Nandria was. "You his woman?"

Realizing her danger, Nandria cowered as the sniveling, terrified maid she'd been trying to portray. Greg's jaw dropped at seeing Miz Nandria servile, but a quick shake of his mother's head instructed him to join the cast of whatever act the woman was determined to play. He reached for Sam's shoulder to hold him back and let mother and guest lead the way.

"I ain't nobody's woman. I's jus' a poh workin' gal. I heerd all the comin's and a'goin's, an' the missus there said to feed you folks. I done like you tol' me, ma'am. I didn't mean no harm." Nandria's explanation was pitiful. Only the Paislers knew they'd never heard the British woman speak that way before.

"Now, now, Nannie, it's okay. Come on here and help Sam pour out the coffee," Cynthia ordered. "No need to be scared of these gentlemen. They wouldn't hurt my best hired gal."

Swearing low, Joe Bob took a step toward Cynthia but was stopped by the murmuring of his troops. This was a Southern woman they were bound to protect, even from him. "Fool, lily-livered, mama's boys..." he snarled under his breath, then turned on the youth who had been helping carry cookies, of all things. "You checked inside? You checked good?"

"E-ev'ry room, Joe Bob. I swear. She was with me," he waved toward cowering Nandria, who nodded vigorously in agreement. "He ain't in there."

"Then...?"

The boy wavered. Behind him, Nandria hissed a single low word, "Nicklebergs," so the irate leader would not hear.

"Nicklebergs'?" the youth said aloud over his scruff of beard. His eyes opened wide with surprise that he'd dared to say anything at all. He stared at Joe Bob, terrified of the man's reaction until Joe Bob developed a slow smile.

"Yeah. Could be. Come on," Joe Bob hollered. "We gotta make sure he ain't still hangin' around the man's place somewheres, afraid to move. We'll teach 'im to be afraid." His laugh promised nothing amusing for whoever was there.

With renewed excitement about finding their quarry, the men and boys wrapped up their chains, scooped up handfuls of treats and, whooping, scattered to the vehicles.

"You comin'?" a couple of them hollered to Greg. "And how about the kid?" They were beckoning to Sam. Cynthia stayed him with a hand on his shoulder.

Greg stood motionless, trying to figure how he could turn down their summons. Until he saw Joe Bob grab Nandria at the waist and haul her to his truck. "I ain't sure you ain't that jigger's woman so I'm takin' you along to coax him in."

With a desperate look at his mother, Greg stepped up to join them. "Sure! Got an extra rifle?"

"We'll find ya somethin'!"

"Me, too!" Sam cried, wriggling free of his mother's hand.

Chapter 33

Greg managed to snag his middle brother's collar and drag him up with him as the caravan pulled away. "Why the devil couldn't you have stayed to take care of Ma and the little ones?"

Chagrinned, Sam stammered, "I – I don't know. I thought maybe I could help you."

Greg bit his lip. Tousling Sam's hair, he crouched in the bed of the truck and pulled him down beside him. "When we get there, try to scoot away out of sight and keep an eye out for Miz Nandria. It ain't going to be... Pretty!" he bellowed the last word.

The young buck with the hint of a scraggly beard was pointing a pistol at them. "It's really something, ain't it?" the boy whistled, squinting down its barrel. "It's a Luger. It was my uncle's." He turned to Sam, one of the few in the group he was older than. "You ever seen one of these before?"

Sam swallowed. He knew rifles, but not handguns. Pa wouldn't allow them on the farm.

"Sure, he's seen one, but never got to touch one before," Greg interrupted, chuckling. "Our pa was in the Great War.

Said he'd had enough of handguns to last him a lifetime—and ours, too." The Paislers, relieved, watched the boy aim at a scrawny hare leaping across the ditch. "Is it a nine? Or a seven-six?"

The kid stared at him. Slowly he reached into his pocket to show them the extra bullets he had.

"Are those nine-millimeter or Luger nine-millimeter?"

"They work."

Greg nodded. That was what mattered. He reached as though to ask to hold it, but the boy grabbed it back to himself.

Finding his voice, Sam asked, "It's your uncle's?"

"Yeah." Again, the boy lifted it, aiming this time at Sam's midsection, making Sam gasp. "What's it to ya?"

"J-just wonderin' why he ain't here usin' it hisself," Sam managed. "He m-must like you a whole l-lot to let you have it."

The boy chortled. "Oh, he'd be here, and he'd be the one holdin' it if he wasn't up to Misery State doin' a couple years. The sheriff caught him stealin' turkeys, but my uncle didn't know them was the sheriff's gobblers." His squinty eye closed completely as he laughed. The pistol lowered to point toward Sam's leg, then was lifted to aim again at the field and another small, tawny, four-footed animal streaking away.

All of them in the truck bed jostled and needed to hang on as the pickup turned sharply into a rutted lane. They passed the broken-down coop that Sam and Greg recognized as the signpost for Nicklebergs' place. The pickup jolted in dust up the lane.

Out on the county road, Eli pointed at Ron's car coming toward them. The men inside were waving. But Doc barely acknowledged whatever the new problem was. "Go on," he urged Eli. "We gotta get Mrs. Nickleberg to my surgery."

The others slowed and stopped. Leaving Heinz Nickleberg in the back seat, Zeb Paisler and the sheriff got out to talk with Ron Bean. Three farmers in Ron's car leaned out to listen.

"Somebody must'a been listenin' in on your party line, Zeb," Ron told them.

Yakes sucked air and scowled. "Damn it all. Wouldn't ya know?" He spat on the dirt road.

"Who? Where were they going?"

"Miz Nandria got hold of Raelynn Johnston. Said there was near a dozen of 'em. Nobody she recognized. Men and boys with weapons. Probably guns and chains."

The three men in Ron's car looked at each other. The one in the far back seat shook his head as Ron continued.

"Nobody hurt yet. Your Cynthia and a couple of the boys were servin' 'em lemonade and cake, evidently."

"My place?" Zeb's broad shoulders sagged. "Sweet Lord," he breathed and turned to race to his family, but his truck was carrying Mrs. Nickleberg into town. He swayed, unsure how to get to his wife and littlest ones.

Ron shoved open his car door. Looking up at the farmer twice his size, he set his hand on Paisler's arm. "Easy, Zeb. Miz Nandria said Dolph and the boy got away just before they come. So, they won't find nothin' to set 'em off."

"We told Sadie to tell 'em to get them guys to go to Nicklebergs' place," the man in the front of Ron's car told them.

"Smart," Yakes commented. "Knowing your missus, I wouldn't be a bit surprised that she got 'em to go there. Her cake can get a man to do just about anything she might ask."

Zeb nodded; the others chuckled but it sounded like the rattling of dry paper.

"So, where now?" Ron asked.

Clearly not wanting to, Yakes made the decision. "Zeb, take my car and one of you men in Ron's car, go with Paisler, will you? Ron, I'll go with you to check out Nickleberg's place."

The switches were soon made. "Next stop, Nicklebergs' place. Hang on, then," Ron called as he watched Zeb's fishtail start up the washboard dirt road.

"What'cha doin', Pa?" Garum sat up when Dolph slowed the truck. They had been heading east on the county road toward Boonetown. Probably to get to where they could get to the road north toward Fox Haven and from there to Kansas. The boy knew that much. Heading for Kansas. Out of Missouri where a troop of vigilantes might think twice about following them across a state line. Todd and Frog had taught him the fundamentals of reading a map. Dolph had vast knowledge garnered in his own untutored way, but no way to pass it onto his son until the boy, too, was the victim of experience. The pickup stopped.

"Get out, boy," Dolph ordered, reaching across the seat to open the passenger door. "It ain't that far from here to our place or to the Bible river camp. Hide somewheres. Stay there 'til all this blows over. Stay there, you hear me?"

"Pa? What're you doin'?" The child clung to his father's arm and neck until Dolph peeled away his hands.

"Get out, boy. If they catch me, I don't want you nowhere near me."

"I don' wanna be nowhere else, Pa."

"Go to your mother."

"Ma? I don't know her. I don't even know where Pittsburgh is."

"Just over the line into Kansas there's a Pittsburg."

Garum shook his head. "No, and even if there was, that ain't where my ma is. If she was that close you'd've got her back by now."

"All right, so it's the other Pittsburgh. Up north, but that's something people can tell you when it's safe for you to go. Get out, will ya, boy?" He was beginning to shake with frustration as well as fear. The child clung to him, then sat up, exhaling slowly.

"No." As Miz Nandria had taught them, Garum's answer was quiet, firm and final.

Dolph stared. Letting out his own long breath through his nose, he twisted away to restart the engine and pull Greg's truck back onto the country road.

The caravan of battered pickups and rusted car scattered fluttering chickens as it jostled up to the Nickleberg farm. Heeding Greg's instructions, Sam managed to melt out of sight soon after jumping out the back of the pickup. He hid a while on the far side of the house to watch where that Joe Bob was hauling Miz Nandria. He winced that the man with one good arm was being so rough with her. No man should treat a woman that way. Ever.

Greg stepped to the edge of the crew spreading out to search all the buildings. He saw Joe Bob manhandle Miz Nandria into the house, but he went first to be sure no one else had come to the 'party'. As he passed each vehicle, he stole a glance to check whether he could grab the keys without being seen.

The outbuildings had been visited. Someone else must have been listening in or heard what had happened on the Nicklebergs' feather farm. Most of the tools that had always hung on the barn walls had been stripped from their hooks and nails and were gone. Bales of hay were ripped apart and scattered like tinder. One had obviously been set afire, but it had been doused by someone kinder to the Nicklebergs. A fire like that could have taken the barn and other outbuildings in quick order, to say nothing of burning down the farmhouse itself. All the damage would undoubtedly be blamed on the coon who had harmed the farmer and his wife in the first place. Greg pressed his lips tight to keep from howling protest at the insatiable cruelty of mobs.

Not entirely satisfied that no one other than the few he'd ridden here with were on the farm now—they might well have hidden their vehicles—Greg looked around for the boy with the Luger. It would be a handy weapon to have if he could wrest it from him. Remembering he'd seen out of the corner of his eye that the lad had headed toward the farmhouse, Greg made his way to the back where he'd seen Sam.

His middle brother startled at his unheard approach. "Oh!" Sam gulped.

"Yeah," Greg whispered, pretending not to notice his brother's fear. "Listen, that Joe Bob took Miz Nandria into the house. Did you see him? Did he come out? Where is she now?"

Swallowing before he could speak, Sam lifted his shoulder to gesture toward the house. "I can get a glimpse of them sometimes. She's still in there, but he ain't paid her much attention except to get her to make coffee on the stove. But I don't think anybody's gonna drink a lot of coffee. There was a couple other fellows in there first. Drunk."

"Guys not with them we came with? How many?"

"Hard to tell, three, maybe four?" Sam shrugged.

Frowning, Greg nodded. "Where's Miz Nandria?"

"On a chair in the corner farthest from the hallway to the door. I think Joe Bad boxed her in deliberate. She'd hafta climb over all those guys to get out. They found some bottles Mr. Nickleberg must've had hid. They're all over the table where the Nicklebergs clean their chickens. And all over the floor."

Sam felt sick to his stomach at his brother's low swearing.

"How far is it to Pittsburg, Mr. Hyke?"

The stove-up, dark man in the dusty Chevy coupe raised an arm too thin to fill his faded russet shirt sleeve. He pointed back the way he had come: the way Garum's pa had gone when he'd seen the jalopy ahead and stopped to force Garum out of the Paisler pickup. Dolph had sped away. The old man, creeping along, had stopped for the boy.

"Eight, ten miles, boy. Mebbe more. A bit of a walk." Milky dark eyes let it be known he would have liked nothing more than to give the boy a ride there. But, Garum knew, the old man probably had only a whiff of gas left and aching bones crying for rest.

"Oh, I don't mind walkin'," Garum assured him. "Do it all the time."

"Well, then, you prob'ly won't mind the extra bit from the preacher's place. Come with me, boy. Our Beulah'll give ya a bit of somethin' cool to drink and a cookie or two to keep ya goin' on the road. Good woman, the preacher's granddaughter." His bony shoulders sagged as though to hide under the straps of his overalls. "You ever been in a 1928 Chevy AB before?" the old man asked but didn't look over or wait for an answer. "Man who owned the factory I was workin' in'd just bought it brand new the year before everything went caplooey. Shot hisself, he did. His widow put it up for sale, but in the early thirties nobody had nothing to buy it with, 'cept me and the missus. We offered her what we'd saved under our mattress. I thought I could take it to Saint Louey and sell it and make some real money. But nobody even in the city had nothing more'n we'd paid." He heaved a sigh that brought on a fit of coughing.

Garum twisted to look back. The thought of walking eight or ten miles in the afternoon sun made his dry mouth ache for a cool drink. And a cookie. His growling midsection voiced a vote even the old man could hear.

"Just wish I could take ya to your Pittsburg, but Beulah'll be watchin' for me. Don't like to worry 'er none."

When Garum had climbed in over the unopenable door, the ancient roadster hesitated and then decided to obey the command of the gas pedal, kicking up dust as it lurched forward. Beulah was indeed watching for the old man to chug up to the meeting tent.

"Mr. Hyke, you're so late. You won't have time for a proper nap before meetin'. Oh!" The wide-hipped, wide-smiling dark woman stopped, flustered at realizing who the small boy beside him was. "Uh, Garum, hullo. You come to dinner?"

Garum's eyes widened.

She laughed. "Oh, you aren't the only scamp to come just before a meal. Mr. Hyke's always bringin' me one or two bedraggled boys in need of food and a good dose of the preacher's tellin' it like it's s'posed to be. Come in, come in." As suddenly as she'd laughed, she looked fearful and twisted to look down their lane from the shack she'd only now invited him to enter.

A pickup was climbing their slope to the high bank of the river.

"That's a white's truck," Mr. Hyke cautioned. "Somebody after you, boy?"

"No, no, that's Pa. Greg Paisler done loaned it us. Pa!" Garum cried and took off running down the incline. "Pa, you come back for me!"

Beulah bent to help her grandfather's stove-up parishioner out of his coupe. "Lordy, lordy," she whispered.

"Amen," the old man's lips formed but there was no sound except a grunt of pain as he got himself to his feet. Letting go of her hand, he turned to face the pickup coming on slowly with the boy clinging to the driver's neck as he rode the running board. "Go on in the house, gal," he said.

Beulah wrung her hands but shook her head. "It Dolph, Mr. Hyke. I'm afraid… Why don't you go on in and make yourself to home? I'm afraid Dolph's come to ask for something, and he'll probably not want witnesses." She faltered, but he grinned and took her hint. She knew he'd be watching. Probably come running out with the mop or broom in his hands if she were under threat. The image in her mind made her smile.

Both Mr. Hyke's and Dolph's faces relaxed at the sight of her smile. The old man shuffled toward the shack of a house. Dolph picked up Garum in his arms as he got out of the truck. "Beu," he called.

"Got away from ya, did he? Kids are so fast."

Dolph nodded, tightening his hold on his son. "Hey, now," he whispered, setting Garum on his feet and wiping wet tears from his neck. His own expression stretched oddly between laughing and crying.

The preacher appeared at his doorway. "Come in, son. Beulah's probably got hot coffee," he called. For all his advanced age, the church man's very presence was commanding.

Dolph stiffened. He felt naked in front of this man. Naked but not ashamed. For the first time he wanted to explain rather than to justify but knew he would probably not get that chance. There was so little time. He looked at Greg's truck rather than the minister, ashamed only that he might be bringing danger to these people who had only been good to him. But what other choice was there? Taking Beulah's hand as he approached the house, Dolph set Garum in front of the old man of God.

"I need to leave the boy with you, sir."

"Come in, then. We'll talk," the old preacher intoned while his granddaughter gasped and bent to put her arms around the child.

"No, I'm sorry, but they're after me. There's no time but I couldn't just dump him. I know what I'm aksing, but..." He stopped, spreading his hands palms up. He started to explain, but the old one shook his head.

"No, son. Don't tell us nothin'. If somebody aks us, we can tell 'em the truth. We know nothin' about you. Have no idea where you might be. The boy here just come to share a meal with us like he's done a time or two before."

"The truth is important to you," Dolph breathed.

"Come right down to it, truth and love's the only things that matter."

Dolph thrust his son from clinging to him again. Beulah held him the best she could.

"Stay here, Gar. I need to know you're safe. For me. Stay here." He looked down toward the trees by the river, silent, even with the boy staring up at his father's face. Garum's tears streamed, but he, too, had gone silent.

"Will you keep my boy? Until I can send somebody for him? The man who loaned, no, the man I stole that truck from. White. Mebbe you know the Paislers? I told 'em how to get in touch with the boy's ma."

"Pa, no!" Garum cried as Beulah drew him closer against herself.

The preacher reached toward Garum. "You come in with us, son. We'll mind ya until somebody comes like your pa says."

"They're riled, Preacher. They'll do to somebody else," Dolph said.

"Ah," the old man sighed. "And you don't want the boy to see."

"What're you thinkin', Pa?" Garum slid his hand out from under the woman's and half-stood, staring at his father. "You ain't goin' back? You can't!"

Dolph staggered backward against the white pickup. "They'll find somebody. Anybody. How can I run and leave that?"

"But we ain't runnin'. We're goin' to Pittsburg to see my ma. Mr. Hyke said Pittsburg was that way." The boy lifted his arm to point one way and then another, openly weeping with each turn in his confusion.

"There is a Pittsburg in Kansas, Garum," the preacher explained. "But it seems your ma is in the other one. The big one. In Pennsylvania, way up north."

"There's two Pittsburgs, boy," Beulah whispered, but Garum heard next to nothing of the words as he fought too many fearful wars. Finally, he ran to cling to his father's waist. "I done this, Pa. I aksed you to help with my white lady, and now everybody wants to kill you." His words held all the sense of betrayal and abandonment his small frame could hold.

"I should've knowed better, Pa. You told me again and again to let white folks be. No way I can help 'em 'n' they'll only get me in trouble." Garum stared up. "I done this to you, Pa. It's me they ought'a hang."

Tears flowed unheeded now, Beulah's as well as the boy's.

Dolph turned away, stopping only to open the pickup's door.

"Go on, son," the old man whispered to Dolph's back.

But Garum tackled his father. "Pa," he wailed.

Dolph bent to draw his son close against his shoulder, but he looked at the old man. "How can I?" His voice was half-swallowed as he continued, "I know every black man for miles hereabouts. Near every woman and kid, and most of their dogs. How can I go off and leave one of 'em to be stretched up and hung?"

The preacher clasped his hands and looked up with a single question. "Was you the one who done the deed?"

"No!" man and boy exclaimed.

"It was her mister," Garum protested.

"White? You sure, boy?"

"I come up early. He said be there early if I wanted the job with his chickens, so I was there before the sun. Onliest thing pa did was help me get her in to Doc's place in town to patch 'er up. Only the sheriff aksed and she wouldn't say who done it. And then, this last time, I seen her on the floor. So bad, I just knew she was dead. I run to Paislers."

"White?"

Dolph nodded. "Quakers, or somethin.' Dif'rent."

"Theirs?" the old man asked, pointing to Greg's pickup.

"Greg told Pa to take it. Pay him back sometime."

"That is different," Beulah breathed.

"I stole it."

"No, Pa, you didn't steal nothin'."

"He says that to protect your Paisler friend, Garum," Beulah explained. "A white mob would take it out on him if they knew he'd give his truck to you to escape in."

"Oh."

Dolph, still holding Garum against himself, turned to the old man. "So, I did do it. I helped move her. She needed Doc. Her man was dead drunk. Didn't even remember next day or after." He shook his head. "What all I been tellin' the boy, and I done it myself." With a last hug, he peeled Garum away from him and shoved the boy toward Beulah, who again took him in her arms. "Will you keep my boy, sir?"

All who had gathered to watch knew he wouldn't be coming back as Dolph spun and climbed into Greg's truck.

Beulah, still holding the child, cried out, "Why?" She hauled the boy to her grandfather and ran after Dolph. She caught his door before he could close it. "Why? I'll take care of your boy, but you gotta tell me why you're doin' this, damn you."

Wide-eyed, Dolph stared. He'd thought this woman was one of the Jesus-Savior-Christians who knew in their bones the depths of the cross and the lynching tree and the killing of the innocent. This first time he'd heard her swear dumbfounded him. He couldn't answer.

"Why're you play-acting some hero?" she demanded. "That boy needs you, not some totterin' old man and his old maid granddaughter. He needs you." She hauled on Dolph, toppling him from the truck. He spent a moment on all fours before rising to stand up to face her anger.

"You asked me to mother your boy. I will. But you owe me. Why? Why are you playing this wicked game?"

"Game?" He wiped the dirt from his hands onto his overalls, staring at her. "This ain't no game. It's dead serious," he told her. Then grinned. Chuckled. Moaned and laughed aloud. "*Dead* serious. Don't you see?" His eyes begged her to understand and laugh with him.

After moments of incredulity, she did. Understand. Grin, chuckle, laugh until she had to sit on the pickup's running board or risk falling to the ground.

Garum darted forward, but the old man—spryer than he seemed—caught him and held him there to watch. "Let 'em be a bit, boy. Let 'em work it out together."

"But what...? Don't make sense."

"Sense is only a wee part of what's goin' on inside your pa right now."

Garum wanted his father. Wanted to be hugged, reassured. Told this really was a laughing matter, not a nightmare. Wanted the warmth and security his mother might have given him. Tears in his eyes, he leaned to watch and listen but allowed the old man to restrain him. He frowned as his father sat down beside Beulah on the running board.

Lowering her head and wiping her eyes, she leaned against him. Dolph stiffened a moment, then drew her close so her head rested on his shoulder.

"You know I hafta."

"It's phronema. Like in Grandpa's Bible study book. Will, mind, resolution, courage. Pride."

He sighed, nodding. "I guess mebbe it is. The pride part anyway."

A long silence took them. Finally, Beulah lifted her head to look into his eyes. "I'll love the boy. Make him proud of you."

He studied her face, homely as it had seemed at first. But there was beauty there, the kind that comes from goodness deep inside. "Why didn't I meet you a long time since, woman?" Again, he drew her close and rocked her against him. "Tell him not to be a fool like his pa."

"No, I'll never tell him that." She sat erect, defying this man she had given up hope of ever having.

He smiled. "No," he whispered, brushing back her hair from her face. "I didn't ever think you would. Fierce. Strong. You'll be good to him. And for him." He drew her to him once more, then set her aside and stood.

She rose, lifted his hand and kissed it. "Tell him."

"No. You'll do a better job. Good-bye, dear Beulah. Married woman."

"That's only what Beulah means in the Bible," she said, shaking her head. "You got a wife."

"Ain't seen her in years. I loved her. Couldn't keep her agin the whites. Mebbe that's why I can't let 'em take what's left of me."

"Proud."

"I guess I am. Too proud."

"No, I'm proud you are. I only wish..." She hugged him once, reached up to kiss him, gave him up and hurried to the shack of a house to take his son in her arms. But her grandfather pointed on down among the trees.

"Couldn't hold him. Let's give the boy time to try and work this out on his own," the preacher told her, setting his arthritic hand on her shoulder in a rare gesture of sympathy. Together they watched Dolph climb into the borrowed truck to drive away without his son.

Chapter 34

Owens had closed up his store, insisting that Bernice and all the women-folk go either home or over to Doc's place for safety. He'd leave their protection, if not to Doc himself, then to Sadie Bean.

Isaac had heard the protest of a few of the women. He knew some of them wanted to be in on the action, if only as spectators. He tried to placate them. "I got word the coon's left the county already. Stole a truck and hightailed it, so we're only going up to Nicklebergs' to be sure their farm doesn't get tore apart by outsiders."

That news had changed the looks on the faces of some of the ladies. It wouldn't be nearly as exciting as they'd hoped. Most of those went on home. Bernice protested. They could hardly bear another day of no sales. But her husband's expression of concern moved her to sigh with relief at the thought of time to simply sit and chat with friends. She blinked, and acquiesced. (And found herself helping Sadie Bean at the clinic, but at least it was doing something different from her own day-to-day.)

The men who had piled into Owens' truck were not at all sure what they were getting into. Or how they would react. They tried to hide their churning fear.

The rutted farm lane up to Nicklebergs' hadn't hosted this much traffic since their two sons had grown up and moved away. And only a few times before while they were popular youths. That was before their father had restarted his drinking bouts and cussedness. His confused, sometimes violent, insistence on superstitious charms and curses. His fear. His bald terror that lost him his sons' respect and, gradually, their love.

Ron Bean's car moved up the slope with the sheriff in the passenger seat holding his belly at the jolting climb. His gut was already twisted hoping the other men in Ron's car were mostly law-and-order farmers Ron trusted. If he ever did find that Dolph Tacker, the sheriff wasn't at all sure who would end up on which side, especially the cousin who'd been visiting Richard Fox, a descendant of the original Foxes of Fox Haven. But Yakes had not dared to ask further than his first few, probing questions. The sheriff knew he could have brought himself a ready mob. A lot of sheriffs had co-operated, joined or even led lynchings in the past, but Yakes also knew—if only from his own nightmares and Heinz Nickleberg's—how such a few hours of ghastly glee could haunt those who were part of it.

"This here is the twentieth century," he told himself. "Not the Dark Ages, like before." He could only hope.

Hearing their coming, Sam and Greg froze. The few of the guzzling crew inside the house who could still mentally connect the sound of an approaching vehicle with possible consequences sat up, eyes widening.

"Get out there into the field and lie down, Sam," Greg ordered. "I might need you – bad," he softened the command so Sam would understand he was needed in reserve. "If I signal, hightail it on back to our place. Hear me? Just go!"

The middle brother slunk away. Greg took a huge breath, wiping his palms on his denim thighs. He eased to the back corner of Nicklebergs' house to peer down the lane to see who was coming. Exhaling in relief, he nearly stepped out to be seen, but caught himself. He had no proof yet that Ron Bean, Mr. Owens and Sheriff Yakes were coming of their own accord. That he wasn't sure he could trust the others not to be vigilantes only barely pierced his consciousness, but he stepped back out of sight and whipped around to be sure Sam was staying hidden.

He wasn't. Grinning, Sam was getting up when Greg motioned him down again. The skinny middle brother frowned at Greg's frantic signaling, but he did drop back out of sight.

The two pickups and three dusty sedans hauled in and stopped at various angles. Ron Bean swung around in the yard to park facing back down the lane. Looking around, the new-comers got out clutching whatever weapons they must have snatched up in town. The sheriff was last. Pale, he stood leaning into the car with one hand on his belly. He startled at a catcall from the farmhouse.

"Hallooo," Joe Bob hailed as he leaned into the frame of the Nicklebergs' door. "Looks like we missed the main event, but we foun' some comfor' drink the old man'd stuffed here and there."

He stopped short on wobbly legs as the youth with the Luger whispered in his ear. "Looks like Yakes, the sheriff here in Boonetown."

"Booneytown-Looneytown," Joe Bob muttered.

"Who might you be?" Yakes called, his expression fierce and decidedly take-no-prisoners.

"Uh, oh, it is the sheriff," the boy warned again.

"I know. I know. So, shuddup and lemme do the talkin', will ya?" Joe Bob hissed.

"Who are you men? Where'd'ya come from?" Yakes demanded as he approached, pistol in hand. Owens and about half the others lifted their own weapons.

Joe Bob gulped and raised a shaky hand. Grinning, he waved them all to join him inside. The sheriff and three of the others stepped in to look around. At Yakes' gesture, Isaac Owens and several stalwart farmers remained outside to check the rest of the property. "Zeb ought'a be here any minute," Yakes whispered to Owens before they separated.

Isaac nodded but knew Zeb might have a calamity on his hands that would keep him on his own farm. He sent the others toward the outbuildings but stepped cautiously around the corner of the farmhouse. He thought he'd seen something or someone moving into the back field. So, it was Isaac who met Greg at the back of the house. "They've got Miz Nandria in a corner in the kitchen," Greg told him.

"Will Minnick's, er, woman?"

"Yeah."

"Why?"

"Their leader, Bobby Joe? Joe Bob? He seemed to think she was Dolph Tacker's girlfriend, so he brought her along."

"Or for other reasons," Owens muttered as Greg pressed his lips tight and nodded. "The sheriff'll find her. Anybody else around? Much damage?"

"Nobody who's not drunk as the skunks they are. Yeah, the whole place's been damaged, but nothin' we can't help him fix when all this is settled. Or help the missus, if Mr. Nickleberg gets sent up."

"You think he's the one who busted her up?"

Greg nodded again, this time definitively.

They both looked up when they heard sheriff bellow at the intruders as he herded them outside. "You don't belong in this county. Get along home before I run the lot of you in for stealing the man's booze and tearin' up his place!"

Greg turned to wave his brother in, then followed the store owner and the rest of his crew to the dooryard. They watched sodden men and boys stagger to their vehicles, obviously glad to get away with only a yelling-at.

"So," Yakes turned on Greg when the dust began to settle behind the out-of-the-township intruders. "You let Tacker steal your truck, did you?"

Greg stopped, feet apart, eyes down.

"You gave me your solemn word."

He had given his word, and he'd broken it. Greg had nothing to say. He didn't look up as Sam came to stand behind him.

The other men stared and then looked away. They didn't need to hear what was said to know Greg Paisler's shame from his rounded shoulders. A few, like Owens, were glad Zeb wasn't here to witness this. The store owner thought of sidling over to draw Sam apart but decided against interfering.

"Where's he goin' with your truck?" Yakes demanded.

Greg shook his head. "I don't know, Sheriff."

"Your word of honor you don't know? What's that supposed to be worth to me now?"

Greg lifted his eyes to meet the sheriff's. "He has his boy with him. It meant his life and little Garum's. It was a choice. That doesn't make it right, but I'd probably make the same choice again, sir. Sorry," he added low.

Yakes stared. Lifting his shoulders and barely realizing he could do that again without tearing a burning void in his gut, Piermont Yakes nodded, finally. "Me, too, probably," he muttered. Yakes straightened and looked around before asking aloud, "Should we leave a guard here?"

"To guard what?" Owens answered when no one else did. "About the only thing more they could do to this place is to burn it down. And one or two guards wouldn't be able to stop that, most likely, if it was a determined mob."

"So, it seems like we're missing our prisoner. And," he looked up at Greg, "and Zeb. Just hope that don't mean it's something worse at your place, Paisler. Lawd almighty, if only that woman'd say out loud what's really been happening to her." Shaking his head, he shuffled toward Ron Bean's car. Without telling the others what he expected of them, Yakes began the slow process of stuffing himself into the passenger seat. He never looked over when Greg and Sam helped Miz Nandria into the passenger seat of Mr. Owens' pickup, then climbed into the bed of the truck.

No one volunteered to stay on as guard.

Ron Bean and Isaac Owens turned up the dirt road from the feather farm lane. All the others turned toward Boonetown. The sheriff, exhausted, didn't seem to care who did what.

Chapter 35

Travis leaped up with his hands on his twin's shoulders. Pointing, he cried, "C-comin'!"

Ned, ducking out from under, staggered back. "Comin'? Who? Is it Pa? Greg?" He blanched. "Somebodies else?"

"L-looks like M-Mr. Owens' truck." Travis used to stutter a lot when he was a little kid. Ned understood the degree of his fear now by the number of letters he doubled. His own round eyes widened. His twin was no coward. What if it really wasn't the store man in that truck?

Both boys stuffed their shaking hands into their pockets. Both started breathy whistling, then stared at each other and giggled. Together they scurried toward the farm lane to hide in tall grass to watch. It was a vantage point they'd used many times before. From there, if they needed to, they could sneak to the barn and the farmhouse without being seen by whoever was approaching.

But there was no need for strategic retreat. It was Mr. Bean's car with what looked like the sheriff beside him. And behind him, the store man was driving his pickup with Miz Nandria beside him. Greg and Sam waved from the bed. The twins rose up, waving back, their arms high above their heads. They turned away from each other to get a head start racing to the house to tell Ma. Ned yelled first, but Travis joined in the news by his brother's third syllable.

Cynthia hurried out the back door, wiping her hands in her apron. Her face was radiant as she took in who was in the bed of the pickup. But quickly her eyes were trained back down the lane for Zeb. Greg looked around as well. His eyes met his mother's in mute questions. Neither had an answer for the other; both hearts sank.

Todd struggled out the door with little Rose in his arms. Greg had scarcely set Miz Nandria on her feet beside the pickup truck before she was running to her daughter. Todd handed her Rose and ducked back into the house for Levitt. The Paislers hugged and talked over each other until Greg's, "Where's Pa?"

Silence clamped down on the gathering.

"We thought he was with you. Sadie Bean called. Eli and Frank are helping Doc..." Cynthia's voice trailed off.

Zeb sat up as he could, bound to the steering wheel of the sheriff's car, sickened behind his gag. The driver—Mert, was it?—and one of the hooded men who'd been in Mert's back seat were dragging Kane Oswine's unconscious body up close.

"Back of this one," their leader, Barclay, they'd called him, ordered. The two men were careful not to disturb the gorilla-like Barclay as they stuffed Kane onto the bench seat behind Zeb.

Barclay bent at the driver's open window. His teeth were brown-gray and breath fetid from long years of tobacco chewing. Barely hitching back from the sill, Barclay lifted his hood enough to half-drool, half-spit a wad onto the dirt road beside the patrol car. He grinned as Zeb swallowed to keep his nausea behind the gag.

"Stubborn damn fool," Barclay commented in slow, melodic drawl. He jerked his wet chin toward Kane. "Kept tellin' us he didn't know the son of a black witch. You gonna tell us that, too, Paisler?"

He flicked his wrist toward the only man Zeb thought he might know. Zeb had almost spoken to him, but, realizing Stewart would not like being identified, he had clamped his mouth tight and said nothing. Stewart scurried around Yakes' car to climb in to loosen Zeb's gag.

"Sorry, Mr. P.," the man whispered low. It was Stewart. A rancher with a small herd of beef cattle just north of Fox Haven, Stewart's big-knuckled hands had helped restrain unruly, 4-H project livestock for a number of the Paisler boys and other kids at county fairs. He'd held no chains or shotgun and only watched the beating of Oswine now, but he seemed to be voluntarily with this group of vengeance-seeking men. He could or would be of no help to Zeb against whatever was coming.

A Quaker by birth and deep conviction after the Great War, Zeb knew his only defense now was a calm, reasonable, non-judgmental tone as the driver fumbled to remove the gag that muzzled him. The brutality of Barclay's words was so incongruent against the man's sweet, slow tone. But after being forced to watch what these men had done to the reluctant and unknowing farmer who had been with him, it was all Zeb could do to keep from crying out in anger—and, if he was honest, in fear.

These were not the young fools that Isaac Owens had described to the sheriff on the road. These were grown men in stained white sheet robes and hoods. What showed beneath the cloth was mostly worn denim. Neighbors. Probably from only a few miles from the Paislers' farm. Most could have been friends. It was the hate in the eyes peering out from holes in the cloth that made Zeb swallow.

"Well, Paisler?" Barclay's drawl held a sharp note of worn patience.

"You're right, I'm Zebedee Paisler," Zeb began to answer each question he could remember. "Our place is just up the road a piece. And the good wife has given me eight fine sons, thank you. Yeah, we got one of them talkin' gadgets. Phone. It's mostly the older boys who call and get calls. And the good wife. You know the man of the family's only real privilege is to get to pay the bill." He chuckled and screwed up his face in what he hoped looked like a grin.

But if there was any amused reaction in the gang surrounding him, Zeb could not see it under the hoods. Even the quiet talk he'd learned to practice was not reaching these irate men, and the leader's next words made him arch his back to press it deep into the seat.

"You know 'im, don'tcha? You've had him workin' for you more'n once." Knife in powerful hand, the man reached in to grab the steering wheel. "Take us to him."

Zeb exhaled slowly, pursing his lips as though considering. "Well, now, I don't rightly know where this man you're talking about might be about now."

"Tacker, Dolph Tacker. You know where his place is?"

"Only the area..."

"We only need to get close."

"We got long arms," someone piped up, chuckling. It was Stewart.

Barclay swore at the cattleman.

Zeb met Stewart's now terrified eyes where only the moment before he had seen, not malice, but the matter-of-fact assumption that this was something expected of him. Something a white man simply must do in his role as protector. There would be no questioning in him, and not near enough hours in this day to make him change his mind.

Zeb studied the others quickly. The driver Mert and the one who'd helped drag Oswine seemed eager. The stance of the other, on the far side of Stewart, also looked as if he would remain an on-looker by choice.

Barclay had let go of the steering wheel, He twisted and snatched his hood aside to glare at Stewart. Zeb could see deep creases in skin exposed to summer after summer's punishing sun and winter after winter's soul-icing frost. The eyes appeared to squint as much from hostile elements as from emotion or commanding purpose. But their gray was fierce. Intent. They closed in a long blink as he decided. He yanked on Zeb's door.

"You're goin' with us, Paisler. Stew, take this car he's drivin' and the guy there on his back seat and ditch them out by the Bog."

"But how'll I get back?"

"Walk." That would teach him this was a lynching, not some county fair picnic.

Sheriff Yakes laid his arm across the Paislers' table and rested his head on it. He'd obviously done as much as he could for now. Ron Bean peered around at those seated and realized everyone was looking to him to tell them what to do next.

"Doc's got Mrs. Nickleberg at his place by now, I guess," Ron declared, glancing around again, hoping someone else would take the lead, but no one stepped up. He squared his narrow shoulders. "With my Sadie's help, he'll do all that can be done for her. And Eli and Frank probably have the egg man in jail again. But word's out. Probably the whole county thinks they know something that they really don't."

"Probably out farther than just this county by now," Greg sighed. "It doesn't take much to get some folks het up for a lynchin'." Counting the number of rings on the party line without thinking, he patted his mother's arm in reassurance when the phone jangled on the wall behind them.

Sam jumped to answer.

"No, it surely doesn't," Cynthia said, her voice thick and hands busy moving flatware and condiments here and there around the table. But her attention was on Sam's part of the conversation behind her. "All we wanted was to maybe keep them from finding the poor man. He's got his boy with him." Her voice broke; Greg settled closer.

Ron's own breath came hard as he realized what she must be feeling after long hours of dealing with impossible odds. He wanted to comfort her, but there were no words that would ease the worry and still ring true.

"Uh, sir?" Sam held the telephone receiver out. "It's your Mrs. Bean. At Doc's."

Ron got up to hurry over. He nodded and grunted agreement with whatever it was Sadie was telling him, then replied, "Yes, Miz Nandria is lying down. Asleep, I think, but at least resting with the baby right beside her. Sam and Greg are fine. Sheriff Yakes is sleeping for now, but there was one thing he wanted Doc to know. We, uh, we'd sent Zeb Paisler on up to his farm before we looked in on the Nicklebergs' place. He, uh, never got here, it seems." Ron went back to listening and nodding. He looked over at the table, extending the receiver in his turn. "Miz Paisler, uh, here's my Sadie. She'd like to talk to you." She wouldn't want to, he knew, but she would do it and be far more help than he was at this point. "Sadie says it's quiet in town for now though every once in a while, a car or a couple of strange pickups drive through slow, lookin' around," Ron told the group as Greg helped his mother to the phone.

Ron lowered himself onto the straight chair beside the crumpled sheriff. He knew as Yakes lifted his head, that the sheriff had been awake, listening.

"So," Yakes rasped but his throat was dry. He reached to swallow some of the lukewarm coffee in the mug in front of him. "So, nothin' much goin' on in town, you say?"

Ron nodded and reached for his own mug.

"So, nobody knows yet that Nickleberg is in jail again," the sheriff mumbled, looking around the table. "But that won't mean nothin' even when they do find out, except maybe they'll try to get him out. Mrs. D'd call that irony. Them rushin' the jail to get him out but not to lynch, even though he's the one caused all this mess with his fists. No, they'd ply the brute with liquor to celebrate what they all knew they was gonna do to some poor slob with a black face.

"What's gonna happen is a couple of hotheads aren't gonna be cheated out of seein' blood. Any darky bleeding red blood and screamin' in pain, guilty or not." Yakes closed his eyes as cold sweat trickled down his back. With a suddenness that startled everyone, he pounded on the table. "We gotta get to town. All of us. If your Zeb was here and the oldest boys, I'd say you might could fend for yourself, Cynthia Paisler. But the way it is, pack up quick. We're all goin'. Now!"

"So, you won," Ella Mae Drangler clucked as she fussed to get the sheriff to settle into his easy chair in her low-ceilinged home.

"Not hardly," he grumbled. "Not a bit hardly."

She stood up, though that didn't make her much taller. "Why in blazes not?"

He stared over at her. "What's changed? Nothin's got better."

"But you run off them lynchers with a flick of your wrist."

"Them? Lynchers?" he guffawed. "Not hardly. Just a straggled gang of punks out for a joyride that come on somethin' they thought they could mess with. We ain't got a real mob yet. But if we don't get that woman to tell on her crazed husband, that's what we're gonna have. And, if they can't find Tacker, they're gonna settle for any Negro and try their darndest to skin that darkness off'a him before they hang him. Elm, they're gonna whip themselves into a fury like you could never believe if you ain't seen it."

She'd sunk to kneeling on the floor in front of him. She raised both her hands to cover her mouth. "Ah, Piermont, you have seen."

He didn't answer except to close his eyes.

Chapter 36

Going around Boonetown was easy enough. Dolph Tacker had been avoiding the center of his nearest metropolis all his life. He knew the back roads and lanes that weren't roads even by Boonetown reckoning. The way north was less familiar. But getting around Fox Haven was going to be trickier. Dolph had seldom had a trustworthy-enough vehicle to go sightseeing that far from home. Any work he'd done on farms up that way, he'd ridden to in the back of high-walled trucks filled with field hands like himself.

The farmers were going to pay for work, and work was what they demanded. Most paid up at the end of the day, reluctant but prompt. A few paid the first couple in line and then threw up their hands. "No more money. They got it all." Trying sometimes to shift the disappointed toilers' anger to those who had lined up first. As though it was their fault for taking all that they had earned. Dolph never fell for that lie. The fault was not his fellow workers'. He'd said so. Out loud. He'd had the aching bruises later to prove that he'd protested. What did that ever gain him?

What did anything ever gain him?

He clutched the steering wheel of Greg Paisler's pickup, balled his left fist and pounded the dash.

In the bed of the pickup, Garum startled awake at the pounding. He scampered up in the bed of the truck.

"Arrgh!" Terrified at seeing a sudden figure behind him in the rearview mirror, Dolph twisted the steering wheel. He had to swerve on the washboard ruts to keep from going into the ditch.

When he had stopped, still on the road, thankfully, Dolph leapt out of the truck, knife in hand to confront whoever was there.

"Sweet Yahzu, Gar! You scared me out of five years livin'." He bent, then sat so heavily that dust rose in a cloud that settled lazily. He chuckled. Then laughed, rolling on the roadway until he lay on his back, guffaw-sobbing.

Garum climbed down to stand gawping at his father. "P-pa?"

Dolph rolled onto his side and reached for the boy to lie down next to him. "Easy, boy, it's all right. Just your pa cussin' hisself out for a damn fool."

But Garum only stared. "B-but you was laughin'..."

"'member I told ya that ya scared me out of five years' livin'?"

Nodding, Garum crouched in the dust beside him. "Y-yeah."

"Way things is now, I ain't got five years. That's funny. Don'tcha see? Ah, come on, son, see how funny that is. Else, what is there?" He drew the boy into himself. They laughed and cried together right there in the dirt road until Dolph could sit up with Garum still in his arms. "Well, I guess we better pull ourselves..."

He laughed that terrible sound again. "Remember the one about the guy walking the railroad tracks and seein' an arm and then a leg and then a hand? And then he hears a train whistle?"

"Y-yeah, Pa. An' the guy says…" Garum tried, but there was no laughter left in him. He turned to bury his face in his father's chest.

"Yeah, yeah, I know. And the guy stops and looks around and says, 'You better pull yourself together, 'cause here comes another one." He rocked the boy and then set him on his feet. "I know. It weren't much of a joke, but…" He shrugged and climbed to a stand to brush off his denim overalls. "Well, so, you're with me, I guess. The preacher know? Or Miz Beulah?"

Garum shook his head. "They didn't see me. W-what're we gonna do now?"

"Ain't sure now that you're along." Dolph leaned into the tailgate of Greg Paisler's pickup and looked at his boy. He had planned to hide somewhere just south of Fox Haven to see whether the killer mob would actually grab up some poor dark man. He knew what he should do then, but even contemplating turning himself in brought his breathing to a gasping halt. But with the boy with him… "I don' know a sneaky back way to get out to the highway for crossin' the border."

"For Kansas?"

"Of course, for Kansas! Think we can stay in Missouri all the way north or south? What're ya thinkin', boy?"

"I dunno, Pa. Jus'…"

"Jus' what?"

"I ain't thinkin' real good. The only thing I knows around up here is that old lady that got her furniture stoled. Remember?"

Dolph unclenched his fist and slapped the dash. "Remember? Sure, I remember. 'Two of the biggest horses' asses…'" He laughed again, but this time there were no tears in his voice. "Wasn't it the sheriff followin' a white livestock trailer that was supposed to be hauling out people's furniture while they were away? Only the guys they stopped was hauling draft horses from a state fair. Yakes got feisty when they told him he could look in the trailer, but all he'd see was two of the biggest horse's asses he ever seen. An' that's what he seen. Not furniture. Who was that? Zern," he cried. "That was her name. She lived up this'a way, didn't she?"

"Zorn," Garum stated, then clamped his mouth. There he was again, correcting people he shouldn't just because they were wrong. He'd never learn. He'd never live to learn, doing that. How many times had his father warned him? Like he'd warned him not to help white folks. Only that Miz Nickle. She was so hurt. And now she was hurt even worse. He looked up at his father, sorrier that he'd gotten them into this mess than he'd ever been about anything. At his father's wave of the hand, Garum stumbled getting up into the truck cab.

His pa climbed in after him. "Her place is up here, ain't it? You remember her road, do you?"

Garum looked out the window again, studying the land now. "Over that way, I think," he said, pointing.

Paisler's pickup made good time, even on the rutted dirt lanes. "If only...," Dolph murmured. If only he'd had a decent truck like this one, he could have made something of himself. Like delivering produce from the fields instead of breaking his back to pick it. Something steady, not beholding to stingy, cheating farmers. But even now he had to admit most of the white men he had worked for were honest enough. They just didn't have enough money themselves to pay much or regular. They were almost as hurting as he was. And the boy.

He glanced over at Garum, who was busy studying the land, trying to figure out the way to Mrs. Zorn's. *Such a good little guy. Imagine a kid of his age finding work. Actually bringing home two dollars. And I took it all. Except that dime. Lord knows we needed it. Food. Materials to fix the hole in the roof. It went a long way toward that. Come winter we'll both be glad of it – if we remember. Funny, how quick we remember the hurts and forget the blessings. This boy's mama kept remembering me, but I couldn't keep it in my head. And now she's gone. And our Garum is on the run with me. How'd all that happen? What've I done?*

"There, Pa!" Garum pointed, excited to have found what he was pretty sure was the end of the widow Zorn's lane. "She lives up there."

"Alone? You sure, boy?"

"Well, I..." Garum drew into himself. *What if the woman had found someone to help her with the farm? Mrs. Zorn had always been kind and more than the normal Christian help. But could they count on a strange man who saw his duty as taking care of her? What would he think of a coon and darky boy driving up?* He looked up at his anxious father, his eyes pleading for him to understand that he just didn't know. Not for sure.

"We'll jus' aks directions. That's all. Ain't nobody mean-spirited 'nuff to keep directions to hisself."

"Yeah, Pa, that's right," Garum agreed, hoping it was true.

The place had run down a lot in the years since Mr. Zorn's passing. The question was whether it would hold up long enough to outlast the missus, or would it force her out of where she'd spent nearly her whole life, working herself to death alongside him.

Dolph parked near the barn. He sat, brow furrowed.

"Mebbe it should be a little boy goin' up to aks, Pa."

Dolph's face brightened. "Yeah, maybe. Hardly a woman alive is scared of a little boy." *But a dark little boy is scared of just about any woman—or man—if they're white.* Dolph cussed himself again for a coward and a fool.

At Garum's timid knock, Mrs. Zorn, in a man's plaid robe and flowered, pink, satiny blouse over a cotton housedress of printed red roses, opened the door at once.

Garum sucked breath and then giggled. "You must'a seen us comin'."

"That I done, boy, that I done. What you want? I ain't got 'nuff to be givin' no handouts. Is that your pa in the truck? With a pickup like that, you should be givin' me handouts."

"Oh, we would if we could, missus. I tell you that. But it's only dee-rections we're wantin'."

"Directions? To where? And from where?"

"From here," Garum explained. "We wanna go to Kansas, ya see, and we got lost on these back roads."

She studied him. "Wantin' to go to Kansas. But you ain't from around here or you'd know how to get there. But you need to be outta this state, so you've got something or somebody after ya."

"Oh, no, missus..."

"Don't lie to me, boy. I'm too old not to know what you're up to."

Lowering his head, Garum said nothing.

"But you come way up here off any through road for somethin'. What?"

"To...to see a friend," he murmured.

"A friend? Who?"

"You, Mrs. Zorn."

"Me? I don't know you." Lifting her hand to shield her eyes, she peered out trying to place Dolph Tacker as someone she'd had dealings with before.

Seeing her gesture, Dolph stepped out of the truck and stood full before her. He faced her stock still, so he wouldn't be a threat, but tall and too proud to cower.

"Who are you?" she called.

"Dolph Tacker, ma'am." He doffed the straw hat he'd found behind the seat and stood erect again without explanation.

"And I'm Garum Tacker, ma'am," the boy hurried to tell her. "You wouldn't remember us none, but once when I was just' little. In Boonetown. You come across a white lady hittin' Pa with her umber-ella for lettin' his shadow touch her skirt. She was comin' from around a corner, and Pa didn't see her before his shadow done. But she was sure mad. You grabbed her umber-ella and said somethin' to her, and she stopped hittin' him. I hugged your leg. I could'a kissed ya, but Pa pulled me away."

"She did twaddle away in one big huff, didn't she?" Mrs. Zorn laughed, remembering. "And you was that little boy?

Well, I'll be." She took his shoulder to turn him so she could look him up and down. "I wouldn't have recognized you; you sure are growing big and strong."

Even knowing she was puffing him up, Garum swelled with pride at her words. But his father's repeated warnings kept him from verbally agreeing with her.

She smiled. "And now you're here with him to ask a favor."

"Y-yes'm. We're lost. I hardly knew how to get here, after all the times I's worked in your strawberries. I should'a knowed easy."

"And to think I didn't see you as that boy." Mrs. Zorn clucked her tongue against the roof of her mouth the way Mrs. Nickleberg did sometimes when she found herself less than she'd hoped. "Well, no matter, I guess, as long you're here now. Where is it you're tryin' to get?"

"Well, ma'am, I gots a cousin in Kan-sass that me and Pa promised to visit." He knew he was spinning a yarn. He knew, too, that she could see that he was, but she didn't question him except to ask, "Where? What town?"

He stiffened, too startled to think. "Uh, Pittsburgh," he blurted.

Her eyebrows lifted and then settled in a frown. "Pittsburgh? That's in Pennsylvania. Oh, wait, there is a Pittsburg just over the Missouri line, ain't there? Just where it is I can't tell you, but you want to head west from here."

"Yes'm, we figured that. But what's the road from here?"

"Oh, it'll be more'n one road from here. Can you read a map?" She moved to a small round table to snatch what looked like a recipe from a pile of papers. Tearing off the blank bottom half, she scribbled intersecting lines and labelled them. "Here, give this to your pa. That should get him into Kansas, anyhow. And I don't think Pittsburg is too far from where you'll cross the state line."

"Yes'm, thank you," Garum said, taking the treasured paper. On impulse, he ran the few steps toward her and hugged her legs as substitute for the kiss he would have given her in gratitude long ago. Turning, he ran outside and scampered up into the pickup. Dolph sat a moment before pulling ahead and making a wide half circle in leaving.

Mrs. Zorn stood a long time watching the dust cloud they raised before closing her door and walking to the phone on her kitchen wall. She was a long time cranking. For once, there was no one on the party line.

"Doc Ricartsen's office," Sadie Bean answered. Her voice sounded so weary that Mrs. Zorn hesitated to speak.

"Sadie, gal, could it be that the sheriff's there? Or could you get a message to him? This is Lizzy Zorn up near Fox Haven." Mrs. Zorn waited in the silence, wondering if Doc's nurse had fallen asleep leaning against the wall. But in just over a minute, she heard shuffling and fussing and then Sheriff Yakes was on the line. His breath was coming in huffs. He sounded even more exhausted than Sadie had.

"Yeah? Yakes here."

"Sheriff, this is Lizzy Zorn. I just had a couple visitors in a white pickup like I've seen before when that young helper of yours come out to answer a call I'd made to you."

"Yeah?" Yakes' voice had perked up some. He was listening carefully and seemed to appreciate that she was talking in circles. "You been chatting on the party line, have you?"

"It's all true, then?"

"Knowing how folks gossip, prob'ly not all," he all but chuckled, "but enough."

"I give 'em a map I drew for 'em. It'll take 'em a while to get to Pittsburgh. Pennsylvania's a long ways north." She could hear the sheriff shifting the receiver to call to someone near, probably Sadie Bean. His voice was sharp with command when he again spoke to Lizzy.

"Just big and little?"

"Ah, huh."

"First visitors you seen up your way?"

"So far. "

"Mound City's pretty this time of year. Hope you sent 'em up through Columbia." Yakes' voice sounded almost playful. Knowing he was dead serious, Mrs. Zorn went on with the game he was playing to fool—hopefully—anyone on the party line.

"They got the best Burma Shave signs coming into Columbia from the south. Did I tell you the one about the man, the miss…?"

"The car, the kiss/ He kissed the miss…"

"And missed the curve," she chuckled. "I'll mention that on the line if anybody calls."

"Good one, dear lady. You take good care of yourself. Bye."

The 'thank you' didn't get said, but Mrs. Zorn could hear it in his tone. She nodded, though he couldn't see her. *Men have a funny way of saying things without words*. She'd learned a lot from her Julian, gone though he was now. In many ways, the sheriff was a lot like him. Sighing, she hung up and stared out her window at the little clump of beech trees she'd chosen to shade her husband's grave.

Chapter 37

"You need to sleep," Sadie told the sheriff when he'd seen Cynthia Paisler and the little ones off with the Owens. And sent Greg and what was left of those who had come with him to various strategic places throughout the town. And heard Eli and Frank's report on Nickleberg drunk in jail.

Mrs. Drangler tried to jockey him into the cushioned chair in the lobby that Mr. House usually claimed, but Yakes set a stiff arm at the back of that chair, resisting. "I got a lot more to do this day," he growled.

"Yes, yes, Piermont, and we will help you with all of that, but you simply must at least sit down and rest while we have a lull in the storm."

"Makes sense," Sadie agreed. "I even got the doc up in his bed for a few minutes anyway. How about we put you on the table in one of his exam rooms?"

"Too much I gotta stay on top of. If you're gonna make me curl up somewhere, at least put me by that phone of his." He rubbed his eyes but let Ella Mae lead him into Doc's office. Sadie dragged in the cushioned chair and set it where the sheriff could reach across the desk for the phone. Plopping down, he closed his eyes. He felt rather than heard Mrs. D. bustle up beside him.

"You want a footstool, Piermont? Or are you better off with your legs outstretched like they are?"

He opened his eyes to this butterball angel he'd come to love. She was frowning with concern and held a glass of lemonade with ice. He grinned as best he could and lifted the welcome cold drink.

The phone rang. Sadie beat him to the receiver. When she turned, Ella Mae frowned to see her worried expression.

"That was Mrs. Owen. She and Mrs. Johnston have been canvassing their friends. Nobody she's felt safe asking has heard or seen anything of Zeb Paisler."

Ella Mae just had time to snatch the glass from Yakes' hand when he heaved up and reached to engulf her in a hug that took her breath away. He looked at Sadie over Drangler's shoulder. "Can you drive me out to a couple places? I've got men to talk to."

Ella Mae shook free. "Doc needs her for Mrs. Nickleberg. I'll drive you."

His fear of losing this woman he'd just found played on every wrinkle of his face. But she wasn't to be commanded or dissuaded.

"Can you get yourself out to that sidewalk? I'll hustle for my Studebaker."

"No, no," Yakes protested. "Call Owens back, will you, Miz Bean? Tell him to bring over those Paisler boys. Maybe we can scare up a full posse around town here to scour out crazy groups as they're comin' in. Bust this thing up before it starts so we can search for Zeb."

"In this county, Piermont? Against lynchers?" Ella Mae questioned.

He swore under his breath but nodded. "Okay, you're right, Elm. But run get that purple Studie of yours, will you? And, Miz Bean, lemme talk with Isaac again."

Sadie Bean watched the sheriff turn, knowing he would need help even getting to the door. She also knew his deep pride and independence and offered nothing. Until his knees buckled. She was there to support him, not to the lobby, but to the second examination room along the hallway. There, she ordered him to lie on the table. He stammered, fidgeted and fussed, but Sadie had heard it all before. Lying down, finally, Yakes looked up, snarled, grinned and closed his eyes.

Sadie covered him with a worn, clean blanket and tiptoed away, closing the door behind her. She set her forefinger against her lips to warn Ella Mae as she hustled back inside the clinic.

"Asleep before I got him on his back. I think he'll be good when he wakes up."

"He'll need to be, won't he?"

Sadie exhaled slowly. She didn't need to nod for Mrs. Drangler to understand. "Come on with me to talk with Raelynn Johnston." Out of habit, she knocked on the door to Doc's office, then laughed at herself as she sat to bend over the phone. "Raelynn, it's me, Sadie," she said when Mrs. Johnston finally responded. "You've been busy."

The harried woman at the exchange sighed. "It's like I know there's a firestorm comin' but I can't for the life of me gather more'n a cupful of water at a time to throw at it."

Sadie looked up, startled, when Doc's door was flung open. "Who?" Doc stumbled in looking disheveled and in need of more sleep than he'd gotten. He'd evidently heard the voices and had come downstairs thinking he was needed.

Ella Mae hurried to him as he fell heavily into his chair. He waved her away and peered at Sadie, who gestured to tell him to just listen to her conversation.

"Yeah," Sadie breathed into the phone when she caught a break in Raelynn's end of the conversation, "but at least you know pretty much who to call and who not to."

"I hope."

"Well, this one'll be easier, at least. Can you get through up at the Paislers'? See if Zeb is there?"

"Can't promise any time soon, Sadie. Unless I break in, which..."

"Which you aren't supposed to do. But will you, please? Just see if the mister answers. We got the missus and most of the boys here in town, but nobody seems to know where Zeb's at. It's a worry."

Sadie could tell by the operator's long sigh that she wished she could just hang up and walk away for a week or two. *Come to think of it, I don't know for sure which side of the fence Raelynn Johnston is on. Her late husband...* "Stop it, Sadie Bean," she scolded herself low.

"What's that, Sadie? I didn't hear you."

"Never mind, Raelynn. Just trying to keep this on an even keel here at Doc's. I find I'm chasing my own tail half the time."

"Yeah. Well, my best to the Nicklebergs. And thank Dr. Ricartsen for his helping the poor woman. I gotta go."

"Take care," Sadie whispered, meaning that on more levels than she'd realized when she first rang up. *If that firestorm did blaze up and Sadie found out Raelynn had fanned the flames...*

"Okay, so what did that tell me?" Ricartsen demanded as Sadie hung up the receiver but was slow to face him. His tirade was swallowed before it had fairly begun. Her expression of uncharacteristic uncertainty sent a cold dowsing up and down his spine.

"I don't know," she breathed, plopping into the chair across from him at his desk.

"What?" he started, but Mrs. Drangler gestured to them.

"I'm ready for some tea," the little woman announced. "You two just unwind a bit here. I know where everything is. I'll be right back." Ella Mae hustled from the room after setting her reassuring little hand briefly on Sadie's arm.

Tipping his chair again back against the battered wall, Doc kept his eyes on his nurse. Finally, he spoke quietly, even tenderly. "What's tangled you, gal?" His tone, for once, acknowledged that she might be vulnerable. "Why don't you pack up and go home? Lie down. Let Ron steep you some chamomile or mint or whatever kind of tea it is you fix to fool your body into thinking it has a moment to relax. I'll send for you if I need you. You can bet your mortgage that I'll call when I need you." He lowered his chin, stared up at her under his eyebrows and grinned. "Don't I always?"

"Why're we slowin', Pa?"

Cussing, Dolph swiped hard at the dashboard. "Look at where the sun is."

"Huh?"

"We should be goin' toward it by now. West. It was on our left for a while an' that's north, but we should be headin' toward it by now. That map ain't doin' us no good."

"But she said..."

"She's white, boy. And you said she's got a phone, so she prob'ly knows them lynchers is after me. Prob'ly sendin' us right to 'em. Drown me for a damn fool. Again." He slammed on the brakes and slapped his open palm down on the horn and let the cacophony howl.

Garum tumbled from the bench seat onto the floor on the passenger side. For a moment he lay there, crumpled in a whimpering ball, before he could gather himself enough to crawl around to look up.

Dolph wanted to kick himself for scaring the boy the way he'd done, but he was too angry at the supposed friendly woman's betrayal to do anything but snarl. "Damn all white people anyway!"

Wide-eyed, Garum stammered, "Not all of 'em, Pa. Some is real good."

"Like that Mrs. Zorn?"

The boy was near tears. "Why'd she do a thing like that?" Garum was in no hurry to climb back up beside his father. He'd seen his rages before, but he'd learned that sometimes if he could get the man considering something else, it helped the anger settle. "We wanted west, didn't we?"

"Yeah, we wanted west. Kansas. What did ya tell her we wanted?"

"Kan-sass. I told her Kan-sass. To see a cousin." He straightened some to hoist himself up. "An' she aksed where in Kansas. What town. An' I told her, Pittsburgh, so, she drew this here map." Twisting the paper in his hands to try to make sense of the sketched lines, the boy stuck out his tongue and captured its end with teeth and pink lips. Grinning, he stabbed the map. "She wants us to find 160 an' go west." He turned the paper again. "Or get near Joe Pin. No, Joe P Lin. Jopy Lin."

"Joplin? Hell, that's big. Too many folks will see us. It's a city. We don' wanna go there."

"Welllll," Garum drew out the 'luh' sounds, concentrating again. "Maybe not that far. Looks like Pittsburg is just above it. That'd be north. Road H'd go west for us. Rough, but it'd get us 'cross to Kan-sass. Looks like she's tellin' us to find Road H."

"H?"

"That's the one like goalposts."

"In football? Two poles 'n' a bar across 'tween 'em?"

Garum grinned. "Yeah. That's a H, Miz Nandria says. It says 'huuuh,'" the boy huffed and grinned again.

"You look funny, doin' that."

"We all did, trying. But when we learnt what each letter said, and strung 'em together, all of a sudden, they said words."

"That's all there is to readin'?" Dolph was incredulous.

"So far." Garum cocked his head to one side. "I could teach you what I know, Pa. If you want."

"Yeah, well, mebbe if there's time. But first we gotta get out'a this mess we're in."

The boy went quiet. He'd almost forgotten.

Dolph found the battered sign, 'Road H.' His boy's chest swelled. His proud smile was so wide it threatened to displace his ears. Dolph saw it, marveled, and spent the next minutes studying the road. But he couldn't help looking over. They exchanged a look that went deep into both of them.

About three miles along the rough track of a road, they saw a towering line of trees and then a field bright with swaying, yellow welcome. Sunflowers nodded their oversized heads to a rhythm the breezes expounded. Beyond them, a willow and a small stand of birch.

"Must be a stream over there, boy. Tell me how I know that."

Garum looked, frowned, peered again to his right and suddenly realized that his father was teaching him. Deliberately teaching. Not just 'if you watch me close enough, you'll learn.' He was pointing out a clue and wanting Garum to be able to figure it out for himself. Suffused with a warmth he'd seldom known from his father, Garum set himself to study… that line of green. Dusty tan green, but green, nonetheless. "Trees! They wouldn't grow that big without there bein' water right close."

Dolph grinned. "And where's there's shade and water…?

"Folks," Garum breathed.

"Might be a white man's farm. But along a road this raw…"

"More likely some of our people," the boy murmured. The warmth drained. He turned to stare at his father.

"Watch good for a lane in," Dolph said, pointing. Catching Garum's worried, wide eyes, he slowed Greg's pickup to a stop in the middle of the rutted dirt road. "It's best, boy. Get out here, will ya? Just walk on until you find a lane. If they're our people, somebody'll take ya in or know who to send ya to. There's gotta be a little church some'eres. They'll feed ya. See to ya." When the boy did not move or answer, Dolph reached across him to yank on the door handle. "Go to 'em, son. Get yourself back to Beulah. Don't ya see, it'll keep me from worryin' about ya. Make it easier…"

"No, Pa. Don't make me. Please."

Closing his mouth and eyes, Dolph waited.

"We was goin' to Pittsburg," Garum pleaded.

Dolph inhaled as though his lungs were starving for air. Sighed. "You find her, Gar. You grow up strong and big and smart with you bein' able to read. And knowing what white folks truly are. You find her. Help her, if ya can. Tell her..." He couldn't say more. Reaching across, he opened the boy's door and shoved him out.

Garum landed on both feet, raising a ring of dust like a slipped, foot-entrapping halo. The pickup shifted into gear and jerked forward, raising more dust in angry cloud. The boy stared at his feet, watching them being coated as the grime settled, and then stood a long time rooted to the dirt road, seeing nothing. No truck passed. No rusted sedan. No tractor. The rutted roadway was his alone.

And then it wasn't. What looked like a grasshopper, then more like a praying mantis, leaped noisily passed his ear, landing on the edge of the ditch with that curious itchy-dry click. Startled, Garum jumped to one side. Frowning, he watched the insect quiver, then leap again. All but backward and to the side.

"Mama!" Garum cried. "My mama's in Pittsburgh." He pointed after the skittering insect. Stumbled forward. Ran. "Mama!" he cried until his running took all his breath and his tears washed both cheeks and the snot from his upper lip.

"Your pa's the one done it? Brought all this grief..." The slender woman with unlikely chestnut-colored hair kept poking her crooked pointer finger into Garum's breastbone.

The boy had walked toward those trees his pa had pointed out, and, sure enough, there were coloreds there.

"No!" Garum stomped both feet in front of the gathered folks. "The onliest thing Pa did was help me. I'm the one who was workin' for her. Pa just helped me get her to Doc Ricartsen."

Murmurs erupted: 'Good man, that Ricartsen.' 'He seen me in the back room when I was coughin' so bad I couldn't breathe none. And ahead of white folks, too.' 'I's still givin' him a half-dollar when I has one for fixin' my Lida Lu's broke leg, but he don't fuss about it none.'

Garum was beginning to think these people would believe him when an old man with wrinkles crossing wrinkles like maps of some crowded cities shuffled forward, raising his hand for silence. "Boy, you say you was workin' for 'em? That feather-farmer?"

"Well, sir, he hired me, but then forgot and was...was away..."

"In jail, wasn't he?"

"Yessir, that's where. But the missus, she had me stay an' help her so I..." Garum's voice trailed away as he thought of how much he had seen but did not want to tell.

"So, you seen him hit her?" the old man demanded.

Garum stared. He hadn't actually seen that, he knew. He'd seen what had been done when it was fresh and bloody, but he hadn't seen the act. How could he answer? How could he say more than he actually knew?

"Don'tcha see, boy?" the old man went on more kindly. "Nobody white's gonna believe ya since ya didn't actual see her man beatin' her. Even if ya had see'd it with your own two eyes, they wouldn't wanna believe, so they wouldn't. All your pa can do is run."

"Fast 'n' far," more than one other voice told him.

Garum slid to a sitting position, tears flowing. He knew they were right. He lifted his face, eyes begging someone to give him hope. There was none. "An' P-pa said he knew just about every Negro in this county, their k-kids an' wives, even their d-dogs. That's why he can't run and let somebody else get l-lyn..." He stopped, unable to say the word, though every person silently filled it in for him.

The muttering stopped for long moments. Women turned away, hands to their faces. Men looked down. Finally, the old man spoke. "Where is he, Garum? Where's your pa?"

"We was goin' to Pittsburg, but he shoved me out'a the truck. He's prob'ly goin' back to Boonetown."

"Merciful Jesus!"

The explosion of burbled sound twisted Garum's insides until he could no longer hold his breath. The boy's exhalation threatened to deplete his core until that crooked index finger moved up from his chest to his shoulder for the woman's hand to draw him to her.

"Come, child. Come now, we'll do what we can for ya. It's just...it's just..."

"We need to know what's best for ya, boy," the wrinkle-faced old man muttered. "We need to know whether your pa really is in Boonetown, but with white folks riled up they way they is..." He looked around at the gathered people, now silently backing away. He sighed.

"I'll go look see," a young buck murmured, holding his ground.

"Rails, no! If they catch you..." The woman lifted her crooked finger from the boy's shoulder to point at the youth and then to cover her mouth. "Ah, Rails!"

"It's all right, Ma. I've worked for Mr. Owens now and again. He knows me. I'll sneak in the back of his store. He'll tell me the way it is." Rails turned toward his battered pickup, but the old man stayed him with a wave of his gnarled hand.

"I'm gonna take this boy back to the Preacher's river Bible camp. You're from there, ain't you, boy? Miss Beulah and her grandfather. There the ones ought'a know what's best for ya."

Rails nodded and hurried to open his truck's door and clamber in before his mother could stop him. Her long, black eyelashes were glistening with tears, but that crooked forefinger had again drawn in Garum.

Chapter 38

Gertrude Nickleberg moaned and stirred. In the corner of the exam room, Ella Mae Drangler set aside her hemming and rose to go to the woman on the narrow cot.

"Awake, are you, dear Mrs. Nickleberg?"

The battered woman opened her eye, but not long enough to register who was with her before losing consciousness again. Still, coming awake at all was definite progress. Ella Mae hurried to the hall to find Sadie Bean; Heinz heard her.

"My woman awake?" he moaned low in his tiny exam room before remembering where he was. It took a dizzying moment to realize he'd clawed at his wounds and made them bleed. Vaguely he recalled two tall, young farmers half-carrying him to Doc's place from… the jail? Again? Why had he been in jail? What was going on? And why was his Gertie here at Doc's?

Flinging aside the light flannel sheet, he swung over to sit up and leap to his feet to get to her. But his head spun so that, sick and dizzy, he fell back. Swearing under his breath, he clasped his head in his hands and waited for the nausea to sweep over him and away. It took long minutes before he could rise again, this time more slowly. Finally, he could stagger the few steps to brace himself against the wall.

Where is she? I gotta get to her before all them others. Gotta talk to her. Make her un'erstand.

Shuffling to keep himself upright, Heinz cracked his door open to peer up and down the hallway. The next room to his left was open. It had been closed when the men had brought him from the jail into Doc's clinic. All of them had been. Pretty sure his wife must be in there, he slipped into the hall and entered. A pale, purple-bruised body lay unmoving on the thin mattress.

"Poor chap," Heinz muttered. "Somebody done you dirt, sure enough." He looked around and then back again at the bloody body. That couldn't be his Gertrude. So, where had they put her? He couldn't just wander around the old house looking for her. Doc or that Sadie Bean or the sheriff or somebody would be sure to see him. They'd start in again asking him fool questions. All but accusing him of hurting his woman. *But I wouldn't. I'd never do that. Never. Not Gert, even when she grated on my nerves, which she sure could do with her fussin' and worryin' and doin' so much to bring the devil down on us. Shoes on the table, for glory's sake. I've told her often enough. Why don't she learn?*

Low whispering from the hallway brought him up short. Panicked, he looked around for a place to hide. The room was so small. Even under the poor guy's cot, boxes were stored. No place for him. *Where? Oh, for the love of St. Pete!*

Sadie Bean opened the door. She stopped, staring. Mrs. Drangler ducked to peer around her waist.

"Mr. Nickleberg," Sadie growled.

"Ah, settin' with the good missus," Mrs. Drangler chirped. "Ain't that nice?"

Sadie frowned at both cowering man and grinning lady as she stepped up to check her patient.

"'Th-the good missus'?" Nickleberg stammered. Turning to look, he trod heavily on one foot to keep his balance. "Th-that's Gertrude?"

"Well, of course it is. She's pretty bloody still," Mrs. Drangler explained, "but once Doc got her chest wounds to stop bleeding, he said she needed sleep more'n she needed cleaning up. We can sponge bath her when she wakes up."

"If she does," Sadie snarled.

Nickleberg's jaw dropped low as he stared at the huge, angry nurse. She couldn't have just said what he heard her say. "Ch-chest wounds?" he tempered, afraid to ask what he really wanted to know.

Sadie looked straight at him. "Chest wounds. Through ample breast tissue, thank the Lord. That took some of depth of the stabbing, so Doc says the knife didn't reach the heart itself."

Nickleberg moaned and stumbled back against the wall. Seeing him about to fall, Mrs. Drangler slid the doctor's stool under him. It nearly worked but only directed his fall into the far corner.

"Don't fret about him, Mrs. D.," Sadie snapped.

"But he's bleeding."

"Oozing. It'll stop. Come over here and show me just what made you think Mrs. Nickleberg might've come awake. Doc'll want to know."

Zeb Paisler startled at seeing the pickup truck pass them going the other way. It was a quick turn of his head that he tried to cover with an elaborate cough. But the man beside him had recognized his reaction.

"You know that pickup, do you, Paisler?"

"With the dust all over them, they all look alike. Except Nicklebergs'," Zeb chuckled. "That sawed-off roof of what used to be a car. Nothing around here looks like it. Everybody knows it soon as they see it."

But no one else laughed, and Barclay turned to stare at Zeb from the front seat. "Who was that? In the pickup that just passed."

Zeb shrugged. "Ain't sure. A neighbor, maybe?" He closed his eyes, confused. *Why would the man this mob was looking to lynch be driving Greg's truck back into Boonetown?*

The broad-shouldered man in the front was not buying it. "Who?" he demanded.

Zeb pondered. It wasn't in him to lie. But how could he admit that the truck was his son's? "Um," he compromised, "I'm thinking it belongs to a fella that works for a neighbor."

"You know the fella?"

"Yeah. Some."

"Have him over for dinner, do you?" the driver wanted to know.

"You mean, the owner?" Zeb questioned.

"Why you want to know, Mert?" Barclay demanded.

The driver looked over with a smirk. "Be-cause the guy drivin' was a zigaboo."

"Oh?" Zeb asked.

"You didn't see him?" Shifting again to stare at Zeb, Barclay squinted over his frown. Merciful compassion had no place in that facial expression. "A bootlip monkey drivin' a truck like that? Who was it?"

"If I didn't see him, how would I know who it was?" Zeb shook his head. "The worker I was thinking of—he's helped with our harvest before."

"It was our guy, wasn't it?" Barclay lifted a clenched fist. "It was, wasn't it? The spade that busted up Nickleberg and his wife." When Zeb went quiet, Barclay swiped with that fist, but the angle did not allow for much of a blow.

"Lemme pull over, Boss," Mert laughed. "I know how to knock some sense into him."

Greg's pickup rolled to a stop just below the entrance to the jail. Dolph sat erect, head back, eyes closed, arms extended, forearms resting atop the steering wheel. It was a long time before he could open the driver's door and step out. He walked upright into the sheriff's office.

"Sheriff Yakes? Sheriff?" he called, but there was no answer except a groan from the jail cell area in the back.

Exhaling, Dolph made himself walk back there. Mr. House, obviously drunk and evidently feeling sorry for himself, started up, moaning.

"Can't nobody get some sleep even here?" House griped from the cot in the last open cell. "Whaddya want, yellin' your fool head off..."

"Where's the sheriff?"

"How'd I know? Doc's been too busy to take care of me, and the sheriff shoos me away like I was dirt. So, I come here for a snooze. Say, you're a spade. Can't get a whole lot more colored than you be, boy. Whatcha want with the sheriff? Come to turn yourself in, did ya?"

For a moment, Dolph feared that the man recognized him, but from the way he was grinning and swaying at the edge of the cot, Dolph was sure Mr. House was making a joke that would fit any and all colored men. "Where...?"

"Still insistin' on seein' the sheriff? Whyn't ya try over at the little lady's that makes all the clothes for the banker's gal? He's been there most of the time since he split his gut. Jus' go away an' lemme sleep."

"Makes clothes?" Dolph had no idea who made clothes for anybody's gal.

"Yeah, that dressmaker. You know, the short one. Funny place she's got. Real low ceiling, so she's about the onliest one can stand up inside.

"Oh, Miz Drangler."

House rolled his eyes and nodded. "Go, will ya? Get outta here, boy, 'n' leave me in quiet."

Dolph paused at the door to look out to see if anyone would be watching him cross the street toward Mrs. Drangler's place. He took two deep breaths and stepped out onto the road. If anyone saw him, he heard nothing that sounded like a challenge. Bending, he knocked at the seamstress's low door. At the sheriff's call, he crouched to enter.

"Tacker!" Yakes bellowed from his easy chair. "What in Hades are you doin' here?"

Chapter 39

"Shut the door, man! Do you want the whole town to see you?"

Dolph stood as erect as the low ceiling would allow him. "Why not, Sheriff? I ain't done nothin'."

"That ain't what most folks around here think. You saw Nickleberg pointing at you."

"He's a liar and a drunk. The only reason folks believe him is that he's white."

"Shee-ooot, Tacker, are you dead set on getting yourself strung up and burnt?"

"'Dead set'?" Dolph's slow smile set Yakes back in his chair. "I ain't got no dee-sire to get strung up or burnt. But I guess I can't live neither with what MISTER Nickleberg called me. Go ahead and call that prideful. I guess maybe it is. But I got me a son I want to look up at me with respect in his eyes. And him grow up standin' tall and knowin' he's a man, no matter what white folks nor nobody calls him."

"What's to say he'll grow up at all if he follows like his pa?"

"Look, sheriff, I know there's lots of police and sheriffs all over this U-nited States that gets into the spirit of a lynchin' party. And I know you ain't one of them. And I know it's hard on you to buck all of what's going on around here. So, I'll tell you now thanks for what you've been trying to do. But I'm sick to death of living like a slave when there ain't been none for more'n seventy years, even here. I'm a man, damn it, and I aim to stand up like one whether you nor nobody else likes it." He stood there, feet wide apart, hands on hips, chin jutted forward.

"Uh," the sheriff grunted, looked up, took careful aim and rose suddenly striking the top of his head hard against the point of that chin.

Dolph collapsed like a pricked balloon. Yakes fell back into his chair with both hands to his head. He moaned. That had hurt more than he'd expected. His stomach churned. He swallowed and took in breath after breath to keep from bringing up Mrs. Drangler's delicious scones and strawberry jam. He was still working on his consequences when Mrs. Drangler herself knocked once and hustled in without ducking at the low door.

"Dear Piermont, I seen Greg Paisler's truck in front of your... Oh, Lord, what..." She hurried to step over the dark body on the floor to get to the sheriff. "You hurt?"

"He come."

"To hurt you?"

"No. The damn fool come to confront Nickleberg. Accuse him of lying and the whole damn town of behaving like slaveholders. Get his fool carcass strung up and burnt even blacker'n he already is."

For once, Ella Mae made no fuss about his swearing. She stepped back carefully to kneel at Dolph Tacker's side. "Out cold. What did you hit him with?"

Yakes rubbed the top of his head. "The real question is, what are we gonna do with him?"

"Get some help carrying him over to Doc's to confront Nickleberg."

"Are you crazy, woman?"

"It's what he wants. Why not give the man what he wants for once in his life?"

"Not in my town, I ain't gonna contribute to no lynching. I thought we'd gotten him far away from here. Maybe even on his way North where he's got a chance anyway. Even folks who don't like lynching are sick of his making like he's as good as whites."

"Maybe he is," she breathed, but too low for Yakes to hear her. She stood to face him, eye to eye as he sat. "Here he is, Piermont Yakes. What are you going to do, hide him? Where? For how long? And then what? He has a gripe against a lying drunk. We both know it's true. Half the town knows it. It's Nickleberg that beat up his wife again and again."

"I know, goldarn it. I know. But unless and until that wife tells on him, there ain't a thing I can do about it."

She sank to sit on the floor at the sheriff's feet and leaned over Dolph Tacker's legs to tug at Piermont's pant leg. "I've been thinking about that. What if we trick him? Make him think she done just that? Told on him. Accused him of hurting her. Knifing her now. He's seen how God-awful he left her."

"What?" frowning, he studied the pleasant wrinkles around her eyes. He liked it better when they were deep with laughter, but her thought was intriguing. Could they really trick Nickleberg into confessing? "How? Nickleberg's no fool except when he's drunk and Doc ain't going to give him no booze and neither am I. Unless..."

She shook her head and struggled to get up. He reached to help lift her to his lap where she fit as though it had been made for her. That there was room for her on the arm of the chair never occurred to either one of them. Snuggling together, they conspired to make plans.

"We discussed this a long while before we brought the boy here to you, Preacher," the old man with the wrinkled map face explained. "One of our young men took it on hisself to go to

Boonetown to check if, like the boy told us, his pa must's went there on his own."

"That young man's my son. An' if anything happens to him..." The skinny woman waggled her crooked index finger at Beulah's grandfather before letting Garum squirm free to scurry to Beulah.

The others from near Pittsburg watched the old preacher look over at his granddaughter. They wondered what this man of God would do with the boy, and what homely Beulah was saying as they argued low between them.

"We ain't heard from Rails yet," the old man interrupted their dispute. "But from what we been hearin', I's sorry to say we think the fool man did go into that lion's den. So, what can we do best for this here boy? He keeps trying to run away to go to his pa."

"Foolish? Prideful, you mean." The preacher shook his head in anger, but he had heard something in his granddaughter's voice that he had never expected to hear. "His father entrusted him to us. I hate to put this boy in danger." He shook his head again as he looked at Beulah pleading with him with those soulful eyes.

"We gotta go after him, Grandpap. For the boy." *For the man*, she realized and blushed, startled at the depth of her feelings.

The preacher looked at her, eyes widening as he recognized the feminine in this girl he hadn't thought of as a sexual being. Only a tool to be used and depended upon. The woman's raw awakening. Accomplished so quickly. He sighed. Humans get so mixed up and complicated. He wanted her at Meeting. She did so much behind the scenes that made the gatherings productive for the Lord. *I don't think I've ever even thanked the girl.* He swallowed and sighed again. Without her, he was not at all sure he could lead their gathering in prayer and praise. *Then where were they? Any of them. Worse, where would they be even on the fringes of a lynch mob?*

"Alright, find him a jacket to make him presentable." He looked over at the visiting folks who had brought him the boy. "You people don't need to come. There's going to be a lynching, and we all know it. If it ain't Dolph, then it could be any one of us."

"I'll take him, Grandpap," Beulah cried. "A woman and a child shouldn't be no threat."

It made sense and it relieved them of the danger they didn't want to face. But it made them cowards in their own eyes. The preacher leaned thin arms along the table and turned away to look at the trees beginning their evening dance as breezes stirred along the stream.

Beulah took that as permission. The preacher led the others in prayer as Beulah took Garum by the hand and hurried to her grandfather's ancient car.

"Why're you..." Garum started, but Beulah gave him a look that made him hunker back into the worn upholstery and go quiet. Anything that pleased her enough to have her take him to Pa.

The headlamps of the ancient car were every bit all the years of the old man. One was almost as bright as he still seemed to be. The other had about given up. For all her skill with crossing the wires to get the car started, it was evident that she wasn't an experienced driver. She probably used the car to drive for groceries or to collect parishioners for church and that's about all. Beyond the dirt road in front of their shack, Beulah was skittish about directions, road surfaces and any other traffic. Garum nearly offered to do the driving, but knew he wasn't any better than she was. It would only spook her more to be criticized. He confined himself to being sure they stayed on familiar roads.

"Gee, Barclay, the guy's bleedin' again. You think we should get him to the doc's in Boomtown?"

Shaking his head in frustration, Barclay twisted to look into the back seat. *Such a stupid crew beating up on a white and still no sign of the golliwog we come for.* "Paisler?"

Zeb lifted his eyelids to half-mast to stare at the gorilla of a man. He lifted his left hand to wipe the bloody snot from his upper lip.

"Why don't we take you to the doc? What's his name? The sawbones in Boonetown. Richards?"

"Ricartsen, Boss," the driver informed him. Mert glanced over, surprised to recognize his leader's anger was toward Mert himself. "What?" he started, then swallowed and focused on the road ahead of him. "You wanna go back into Boonetown, Barclay?"

"We ain't having a lot of luck finding no jiggers out here to get a lead on that Tacker fella."

Mert hawked and spit from his window but said nothing aloud about what had just happened. He knew from Barclay's rigid quiet that all hell would break loose if they squabbled. But he really wanted to know about that pickup that Zeb had recognized and then refused to acknowledge. They'd looked forward to a high old time like they hadn't seen around here in a coons age. *'A coon's age,' yeah!* Mert grinned, then frowned. Something was all wrong here, but Mert knew, finally, when to keep his mouth shut.

Chapter 40

Ronda giggled, and Sadie giggled, too. Ella Mae Drangler wiped her pricked and calloused fingertips on her skirt and smiled. The large nurse making such a little girl sound sent Mrs. Drangler into paroxysms of twittering, but she needed to be serious. Lives were at stake. "Alrighty-dighty, then," she addressed Doc, the Beans and Eli, Frank and Greg Paisler, Grover and Nandria Minnick and the Owens. "We've got Ronda slipping a black cat in front of him to cross his path. And Mr. Owens is gonna set a ladder, so he has to go under it to get out of his room to see the sheriff."

"Where are you gonna hold this here meeting Mrs. Drangler?" Bernice Owens wanted to know. "Did the sheriff say?"

The store owner took up his wife's concern. "Not at your place, I hope. We all have to bend double and, if we're gonna need to fight Nickleberg, we'd be falling all over each other. How about the jail? A bunch of us men could be waiting in the back where he wouldn't see us, ready to gang up on him if he needed it."

Bernice nodded to approve her husband's suggestion.

"Nickleberg will wonder why we're taking him there," Ron Bean pointed out. "He might even refuse to go there, especially with the ladder to walk under."

Sadie agreed, raising her eyebrows.

"Well, I can't be away from Mrs. Nickleberg," Doc said. "So, if you want me to be a part of this charade, you'll have to have it here." That settled that.

"I'll bring a ladder over from the store," Owens promised.

"Unless you've got one that would suit, Sadie Bean?" Mrs. Owens suggested.

"I think I do," the huge nurse nodded. "It'll be a lot easier for me to find it and drag it out than having you carry one all the way from your store, Mr. Owens. I'll go look."

Sadie started out of Doc's office, but Greg stepped in front of her. "I'll get it."

Doc lifted a hand palm up, and Greg and Sadie waited to hear what he would say. "Okay, so, what other tricks have you got up your sleeve to set his teeth on edge? I've got the eerie feeling that this has got to go down as soon as we can get it going."

"The town seems like it's a target and we're in the bullseye." Frank's forehead was shiny with sweat despite the fair breeze meandering in the hallway. The others stirred, as concerned as the Paislers' second son but unwilling to voice it.

"Well," Ella Mae said, consulting a short list she'd made with the sheriff. "We were hoping that a couple of you would be eating so you could spill salt without throwing it over your shoulder."

Doc grinned. "Maybe somebody could complain about tight shoes and lean over to take one off and set it on the table."

"Oh, man, that'll set him off," Owens chuckled.

"Was there not a fear of the ace of spades?" Nandria asked quietly from her seat in the corner where little Rose slept on her lap.

"Yeah," Greg chimed in. "You gotta stop the game as soon as that dark ace gets knocked to the floor."

"So, we could be playing a game of cards. A rigged game," Owens grinned.

Ella Mae danced in her chair. "So then, when he's thoroughly spooked, Piermont can wrangle what we need to hear out of him, and we'll have lots of witnesses so there won't be any mistake."

"Praise the Lord, let it be so," Bernice breathed to a chorus of murmured Amens.

"They not only agreed with what you suggested, Piermont, they had good ideas of their own," Ella Mae giggled as she squatted to help him with his socks. "Do you feel up to going over to Doc's? He says he can't leave Mrs. Nickleberg to confront the mister anywhere else. "

"We'll need to take him along." Yakes thrust out his chin to indicate the still stunned and now bound and gagged Dolph Tacker. "You did tell them he was here in town?"

Ella Mae stared at the sheriff's boots.

"You didn't tell them?"

She squinted up at him. "I clean forgot. Sorry."

"Oh, boy. Well, he's gotta come wherever I go. I ain't leaving him in the jail to be scoured out and strung up."

"I'm sure it'll be alright," she said, but she wasn't sure at all; in fact, she doubted it. She bent to tie the laces of Piermont's boots and caught a glimpse of the Paisler sons crossing the street toward them. "Oh, good. Those boys can help you with him while I get some food and cards rounded up. I was gonna leave one of your boot laces loose for you, but probably it'll be easier for one of the other men to bend down to take off his shoe and set it on Doc's desk.

He smiled, shaking his head, and reached to caress her cheek. "Remind me not to make an enemy of you. You have a way of fighting that would be tough to get the better of you. Not that I'd ever want to." He helped her stand.

She greeted Frank and Greg and hurried to the kitchen, leaving the sheriff to explain what Dolph Tacker was doing on the floor.

"He come back to town on his own. I had to head him one to keep him from marching himself in broad daylight over to Doc's. So, how are we going to get him over there with us without the whole world knowing where he is and inviting a mob?"

After sharp discussions—which Dolph, tied and gagged but awake and furious, fumed to hear—they settled on a wheelbarrow. Frank and Greg wrestled him into one and covered him with bolts of cloth that would hide him as long as he stayed quiet. Greg asked him the favor of cooperating. There was no guarantee of how long the favor would be granted. Greg took up the handles and wrestled the wheelbarrow out the door. Frank, carrying a box of goodies in one hand, supported the sheriff's elbow with the other. Mrs. Drangler, carrying yet more food, toddled along behind.

Ron Bean helped Greg up the low steps at Doc's door. He lifted the cloth. "Tacker? What the...?" he muttered as he helped Dolph to his feet. The others gasped but said nothing as Yakes told Ron to help Greg take Dolph upstairs to Doc's guest room turned storage room.

"He come into town on his own," was all the explanation the sheriff gave. Instead, he looked down the hallway to the eight-foot ladder propped against the far exam room door. "That's Nickleberg's room ain't it? He ain't gonna like coming out under that ladder."

"The more unsettled he is when he gets here to talk with you, the better. That's how we figure it," Ron Bean told him.

"And we plan to make sure he's out of his gourd by the time he gets to you," Eli muttered as he helped Yakes to a chair at the far side of Doc's desk.

Ella Mae bustled by to the kitchen and returned in a minute with scones. Bernice was right behind her with sliced apples, wedges of pear and wild berries on a blue plate. She set a tall saltshaker in front of Dr. Ricartsen. His stare under raised eyebrows brought her quick explanation. "Ronda is cutting up tomatoes almost too ripe to be sliced for somebody to put salt on."

Sadie Bean took the cards from Mrs. D. and peered around the room. "Ready, I guess. Wish us luck."

The sheriff joined her in the survey. He nodded to Greg, who nudged Frank to follow him. "You do this kind of thing for Yakes all the time?" Frank demanded in the hallway.

"It gets interesting," Greg chuckled.

"I bet."

They stopped at the door blocked by the step ladder. Greg looked at his brother, lifted his shoulders with a deep breath, blew it out, crouched to fit under the ladder, and knocked. They heard an angry, unintelligible remark and ducked to enter.

"You're drunk," Frank snapped. "Where did you get anything here at Doc's?"

"You thin' the good doctor only sipz on tea? 'sides, I got friends. Not everybody's goody-goody like you damn Paislers."

Sensing Frank's tense reaction, Greg moved in front of him to help the chicken farmer sit up. "Doc wants to see you. Here, button up your pants, and I'll help you with your shirt."

"Don' need no hep," Nickleberg slurred. But he did need help, even to shuffle to the door. When he saw the ladder arching the doorway, he needed both of them to hold him upright. "I ain' going through there!"

Greg, supporting Nickleberg's right shoulder, ducked through first and pulled the man toward him. Nickleberg balked. "No!" the egg man bellowed, but Frank shoved him from behind. The trio tumbled through under the ladder. Both brothers were quick to scramble out of Nickleberg's kicking range.

In the hallway, Ron Bean saw that the Paislers had the man in hand. He hurried into Doc's office. "Drunk." He shook his head at the sheriff's questioning expression. Doc raised his hands, palm up. Who knew where the man had gotten the liquor?

Ella Mae looked over at Yakes as they heard Nickleberg approach, grunting and swearing. She realized again that taking care of her lawman wasn't going to be easy as she acknowledged his signal not to fuss.

They waited, tense but quiet until the scream of utter terror.

"Sounds like our Ronda let loose the black cat in front of him," Ron explained to Mrs. Drangler, who had gone quite pale. "Better get the cards set up like we've been playing them. Got the ace of spades set aside so you can get to it?"

Sadie laid out the cards. Doc splayed his hand on the desk surface, tipping Owens' cup, which he rescued without mishap with a skill that proved much prior practice. Sadie bent to slide the ace of spades two down in the sheriff's pile. He nodded that he had seen it. The door opened, and Ronda slipped through, leaving it ajar. The girl handed her plate of mangled overripe tomatoes to her mother and settled in a chair near her. Sadie set the tomatoes in front of her husband and perched on the arm of Ronda's chair. The men spread their cards in their hands and looked over them at the doorway.

"Come on, Mr. Nickleberg," Frank panted. "Here's Doc's office. We're almost there. You can make it."

The Paisler brothers entered with their moaning burden. Owens half rose to shove the chair so Frank and Greg could lower the chicken man into it. They hauled it around to face the desk and a bit toward the sheriff, then stood up, breathing hard.

Owens lifted one of his cards in front of his face as though to study it. "Let's play out this hand. I just may win this time." He set a card out with a triumphant grin. "Beat that, if you can."

Nickleberg's eyes fluttered open. He moaned. "Basserds. All'a'ya."

"Now, now, my man. There's ladies present," the sheriff drawled as he selected a card to follow the others in playing.

Owens chuckled as he gathered the trick he'd won.

"There's a ladder at the door to my room. These... these..." Nickleberg sputtered, trying to think of a sufficiently nasty name to call the Paislers with ladies present. "They drug me unner it. Unner a ladder, sheriff! Wha's the devil gonna do with an openin' like tha'?"

When Yakes merely shrugged and looked again at the cards in his hand, Nickleberg growled and shifted to sit up on his own. With a glance at Yakes, Owens led another card. "There, beat that one, if you think you can."

The chicken farmer glared at him, but Owens never looked over. Angry, Nickleberg turned to the nurse. "And you, Mrs. Sadie almighty Bean," he grunted. "You got a cat in this here horsespiddle. A black cat!"

Sadie shook her head but would not turn her attention from the card game. "Not here. We don't let animals in here. It's a health clinic. Here, Ron, have a tomato instead of them sweets. Your gal cut them up special because she knows you like them." She slid the plate toward her husband. "With salt," she added and shoved the shaker to him as well. Ron smiled at Ronda with a nod of thanks and lifted a drooling red treat. Adding plenty of salt, he spilled some but left it on the table as he opened his mouth for the tomato.

Nickleberg rocked forward. "Pick up tha' salt you spilled," he ordered. "Throw it over your left shoulder. Now!"

But Bean only looked at him with lifted eyebrows as he wiped his fingers on his large, cotton handkerchief.

"Toss that salt," Nickleberg demanded. "You're gonna let the devil in!"

Bean shrugged. "Seems like the devil's here already." The small man leaned forward. The move was surprisingly intimidating. "We know, Nickleberg. The whole town knows."

Heinz rocked back. "Wha'?" He stared at one man after the other, but each pretended interest only in the cards. Frustrated, he turned on the women, first Ronda, who squirmed but said nothing. Then Sadie, and then Bernice. They met his gaze without comment. Nickleberg twisted to stare at

Nandria in the corner, but Mrs. Drangler suddenly moaned as though in pain.

"Oh, these new shoes are just killing me. I just gotta take them off." She bent and, after a minute, lifted a pair of tiny lace shoes and set them on the corner of the desk.

"Woman, don' do tha'!" the egg man cried and swept them onto the floor. His hands reached to grasp the tiny woman by the throat, but Greg, Frank and Ron were on him faster than he could focus and direct his drunken movements.

"Tie him to the chair," Yakes ordered.

"No, don't," Nickleberg whimpered. "I didn't mean to hurt her, just shut her up. Fool woman. Nobody can't leave a pair of shoes on a table. Lord knows what'll happen."

Yakes lifted his hand to tell the men to let him go. "Behave yourself, then. We'll finish this hand and then you and me can talk. There's a lot I want to know."

"'bout what?" Nickleberg was saying some of his 't's' again. His fear seemed to be wedging itself into his drunkenness.

"We ain't talked much about your Gertrude, Heinz."

"Yeah, we did. At my place, remember? I told you who done it. Pointed straight at the dirty spook."

With everyone looking at him, the poultry man turned to glare again at the youngest and most vulnerable. Ronda crouched against her mother. He looked at Mrs. Drangler, but instead of being intimidated, she rose to her bare feet. "I think I'll fetch some fresh bread I brought over. I know we didn't finish but half of yesterday's loaf, but what could it hurt to slice into a new loaf since it's been made new this morning?"

"No!" Heinz yelped, but no one paid him any heed.

"Let's get this game over with while I'm still winning," Owens said. He picked up the trick on the table and led another card. Each man played. The sheriff played his ace of spades. Doc slapped his card beside it, brushing the dark ace to the floor.

Nickleberg threw himself across the desk, scattering the rest of the cards, the plates of goodies and everything off the doctor's desk. "No!" he shrieked in terror.

A haunting scream echoed from the hallway.

Chapter 41

Sadie and Ron, being closest to the door, reacted first—Ron to renew his hold on the prisoner's arms to bind them, Sadie to check the hallway.

"It's Gertrude!" the nurse hollered.

Ricartsen dropped his hold on Nickleberg and barreled past everyone to get to his patient. He bent over her as Sadie lowered her to the floor. "Mrs. Nickleberg, how did you get out here?" Not that he expected an answer. But he got one.

"Heinz," she gasped. "My Heinz screamed."

"He's fine, Gertrude," Sadie assured her, lifting the woman's head to her own lap and caressing the violet-bruised cheek to calm her. Ricartsen checked her stab wounds to be sure she had not opened any of them. He rocked back on his haunches, cheeks puffing out in relief. He had never expected the woman to be able to get up on her own, let alone stagger out of her room. He looked up at the others spilling out of his office and gestured to them that she was all right. They disappeared again into the office at Nickleberg's roar.

"Gert? What've they done to you, Gert? What's going on?" And, after an impatient pause, "Lemme outta here, you blamed Yankee-bred coon lovers. You got no right!"

"Heinie?" Gertrude struggled in Sadie's arms.

"You hush now, Gertrude Nickleberg," the nurse ordered. "Your man's just fussing in his own drunkenness. He's all right. It's you he... Ah! Sheets of flannel!"

Ricartsen glanced up at her sudden cry. "Oh!" One hand on the wall, he got to his feet to face the armed and hooded men at his front door. "Get those women outta here," he hissed at Sadie, then turned to stride toward the intruders. "I'm Dr. Ricartsen. You bringing someone hurt for me to see, are you? Or sick?"

Barclay grinned at that. "Not as sick-hurt as he's gonna be, Doc," he drawled.

Ricartsen felt his eyes lifting to look upstairs where he knew Dolph Tacker lay bound and gagged. Deliberately, he rolled those eyes as though in disdain to keep his reflex from giving away the hiding place. Behind him, Sadie scurried into the office.

"I've had a full day, Gentlemen," Ricartsen was saying as he pressed forward, hoping to block his front door. "And two or three nights before that. If you need me, you're going to have to speak without riddles because I'm too tired to even try to figure out what you mean."

Barclay smirked. "You know who I'm talking about. I got half the men in town looking for him around here someplace. We'll find him." He lifted his hand as though to direct his men to start searching the clinic house. But he hesitated when Sadie Bean reappeared in the hallway. He hadn't realized how large a woman she was. Or that when she meant business, it might be smarter to be somewhere else.

Behind Sadie, Greg motioned for Ella Mae Drangler and Bernice Owens, with Rose in her arms, to rush out of the office and down the corridor to the kitchen and back door. Ronda followed, but hesitated when Barclay lifted his shotgun and pointed it at her, despite Doc.

"Hold it, right there, little lady," he barked.

With everyone—except the two women who had already escaped—focusing their attention on him, Barclay dropped his hand and assumed a social smile that made his teeth look sharp. "So, who you got spread out on the floor there? No other room at the inn?"

Sadie rose to full height. She was even bigger than he'd surmised. "A patient of the doctor's here," she said, tight-lipped. "She was a bit premature trying to come from her bed. Maybe you know her? Mrs. Nickleberg."

"Hey, yeah," Mert exclaimed. "Boss, she's the one the jig..." He grunted at Barclay's quick elbow against his ribs.

"Looks like he hurt her bad." Barclay's expression was so practiced, even Sadie might have believed he spoke from compassion. But she knew why he had come to Boonetown, and she frowned.

Doc snorted as he knelt again beside Mrs. Nickleberg. "He did, though I doubt we are referring to the same 'he.' It wasn't a Negro who battered this lady."

"Huh?"

"What are you talking about?" Barclay demanded.

But Sadie Bean had seen her doctor's concern for Gertrude. "Move your plug-up of this hallway," she snapped. "Or bend down and give us a hand moving Mrs. Nickleberg back to her bed."

"No, not them," Doc countermanded. "We need skill and caring to not hurt her any more than she is. Get your Ron or Greg."

"No," Gertrude groaned. "Heinz. I gotta see Heinz."

"She won't rest quiet 'til we do," Sadie said.

"Okay, bring him out," Doc conceded. Even the hooded men seemed to hold their breath until Nickleberg stumbled from the office. But no one was quick enough to keep the drunken man from bumping into his wife as he got to the floor beside her.

Gertrude screamed. She couldn't help it. Mert lifted his hood to gape at her. Her neighbors cringed at the doorway from Doc's office. Heinz howled. "I'll kill whoever done this to you, Gertie gal," he swore.

She stared at him. "You..."

The sheriff shuffled out. "Heinz," he began with a sternness in his tone that brought their attention to himself. "We gotta get this right. You can see for yourselves it's spread way outside of Boonetown to folks who don't know us and want a vengeance that ain't called for."

Barclay and Mert stared at the sheriff and then at the egg man they'd come to seek that vengeance for.

"That up there's Boonetown ," Garum chirped and sat erect to point. "And that there's Greg Paisler's pickup. The one Pa borrowed. See, over there by the jail."

Beulah glanced over at the boy, then followed the path his pointing finger showed her. "Ah," she sighed with something that sounded like relief.

"Looks like a bunch'a people's at Doc's. Over there, see?"

She slowed and stopped only partly off the unpaved cross street. She stared around her, unsure.

"Maybe we better park over behind Owens store. Somebody'll get snoopy, this being a strange car in town and all," Garum coaxed. But the homely woman only stared with pale lips forming words he couldn't hear. "Hey, Miz Beulah, come on and move over here and let me park for you. Sister?" he added when he got no response. That at least got her to look at him. Smiling encouragement, he gestured for her to slide across the bench seat. He crawled around her to get behind the wheel. His experience with the Nicklebergs' car-truck helped, but he was awkward at best. Finally, they made it to an out-of-the-way area near the back of the town store.

"Miz Beulah, why don't ya stay here while I look around to see where my pa might be? You'll be okay here, won't ya?"

When the woman made no answer, Garum simply slipped away. He ducked first into the alcove behind Owens' store where he'd first been hired by the drunken Mr. Nickleberg. How he wished now he'd just run away from the man. A memory nagged at him. Something about a strange car and being afraid. "Oh, boy!" he whispered, realizing the truth at last. That time he'd been kicking the worm can down the road when he needed to jump out of the way to save himself from being hit, the vehicle that had nearly gotten him had been the sawed-off egg truck. It had been the feather farmer behind the wheel. Oh, if he'd only realized that instead of being so happy about earning some money. Like Pa, the man had warned him. He just hadn't listened.

Shaking his head, Garum peeked into the back of the store. There was a woman sitting darning socks by the cash register. She was an older woman with a double chin, stringy gray hair and black, tie shoes with worn-down wedge heels it must have taken many years of treading about on their farm to get to that angle. The woman seemed oblivious and content. No one was shopping, so she could sit with an easy conscience even without labor. Neither Mr. nor Mrs. Owens seemed to be anywhere in the store. The boy nearly stepped in to ask her where the owners might be when he recognized that she had a shotgun leaning on the counter beside her. Shuddering, Garum backed away.

He ran back to check on Miz Beulah. She sat unmoving except for the rhythmic wringing of her hands. Without trying to speak to her, Garum continued his search.

Nothing. No one was at the jail. With Greg Paisler's pickup parked nearby, Garum had half-hoped he'd find his father, even behind bars.

From what he could see through the front window, there was no one at home in Mrs. Drangler's, either. No one, even that Ronda gal, was at Mr. Bean's. *Where? Where else could anybody his pa might turn to be? Doc's! The sheriff still wasn't real well. And Doc would still be taking care of Mrs. Nickleberg if she, praise the Lord, was still living.*

But as Garum hurried between houses toward Dr. Ricartsen's big, old place, he saw a sedan he didn't know. It was parked around the corner, mostly hidden by sheds in the alleyway. There was somebody in it.

As he got closer, Garum could see through the dust that there were more shotguns. One was leaning against the passenger window in the back. A skinny man lay with his head back, mouth open under the felt hat that mostly covered his face. The other shotgun was being played on by the large hands of a broad-shouldered man in the passenger seat in the front who looked like a farmer. He was strumming at the weapon's stock as though it were a banjo. The man's shoulders and head were dancing to a beat Garum couldn't hear.

And then, in the far back seat, Garum saw another man, droop-shouldered, head down. He didn't recognize him at first, but there was something familiar. *Mr. Paisler! That's Todd Paisler's pa!*

Garum ducked behind the nearest shed. *Holy cow! Mr. Paisler looks like he's hurt. What's he doing all slumped over in there? Why wasn't he going to see Doc? Why ain't those men helping him?* Men with shotguns.

Chapter 42

"I seen him, I tell you," Bybee sniped from the back seat of the sedan.

"Hell, you were sound asleep. Must'a been a dream," Monroe dismissed the Fox Haven plumber's assistant's claim.

"Listen, farm boy," Bybee insisted, "when I dream of somebody peering in a window at me, that somebody's got a lot lighter skin and a whole lot more curves. You get me? I tell you there was a colored kid here, standing on tip toes, nose pressed all but flat against this window. We was eyeball to eyeball when I woke up." The gangly youth shifted long legs, bumping Zeb Paisler, who grunted in pain. "Oh, sorry. But do you have to take up the whole back seat? Say, you take care of him, Monroe. I can't just sit here all day." Bybee shifted again and hauled at the door lever.

"Barclay ain't gonna like you leaving when he told you to stay put."

"There's action somewhere in this one-horse town and I'm gonna find it."

Zeb grunted again as Bybee leaned hard against him to fold himself enough to get out and stride away.

"You all right, Mr. Paisler?" Monroe asked.

Lifting his shoulder to move into the vacated corner, Zeb nodded. "I'm okay, I guess. Sure is good to spread out some."

"You were awake. Did you see a kid?"

"I wasn't looking."

"Like you wasn't looking at that pickup Mert was all heated up about? Your boy Sam told me years back that you don't lie. But you don't always tell everything you know, do you? Seems to me that was your pickup a while back. I've seen it often enough at county fairs. But you said it wasn't. So, it was one of your boy's then, wasn't it? What was a darky doing driving it? Who is the kid? The guy we're after, he's got a boy, don't he? So, if the boy's here, Tacker prob'ly is, too. What are you doing sheltering the one who beat up and hurt a neighbor of yours? And a woman."

"What made you decide Dolph Tacker is the one who did the hurting?"

"Everybody knows that."

"Seems like 'everybody' can be wrong."

"Well," Monroe said, stretching out to scratch his belly through his coveralls, "I guess. Maybe. But, if it wasn't a coon, then who? Nobody but a spook would use his fist, let alone a knife on a woman."

"I wish with everything in me that that was true."

Monroe stopped scratching his midsection and stared. He scratched his head. He closed his open mouth and shook his head again. "What? You can't be sayin' a thing like that, Paisler. Not without knowing something you ain't telling."

Zeb patted the puffed bruise under his left eye and wiped under his nose with the back of his hand. "Whatever I would say now would be my guess only. No proof. And a man ought to have proof before saying such a thing one way or the other. But that includes you, Mr. Monroe. And Barclay. And Mert. We shouldn't be going after anyone without seeing proof and then giving that guy his right to a trial. But what proof have you seen to be so sure you know who hurt Mrs. Nickleberg?" Zeb nodded in emphasis, though it made his battered nose run again.

"So, you don't think it was that Tacker fella?"

"Everything I know about the man says he's not the one who hurt her."

Monroe eased back against the car door and looked out at the window to consider. He respected Zeb Paisler. But it had never crossed his mind that anyone other than the darky could be guilty. No one had offered any evidence. He hadn't even asked for any proof. *I'd'a wanted some notion of what went wrong if a white man had been accused.* "Hey, where do you think you're going? Barclay said you was to stay here."

"I'm going to see if maybe Mrs. Sadie Bean can stuff something up my nose, so this blood and snot doesn't keep oozing down into my mouth."

It had been said reasonably but with an edge that told Monroe that there would be no stopping him. With a quick look around to be sure no one was there to see them, Monroe climbed out to follow him up the alley.

"Ps-s-s-s-t," the boy hissed from behind a trashcan.

Paisler slowed, then stopped to wipe his nose without looking over. "That you, Garum?" he whispered.

"Yeah. Oh, Mr. P., them men with hoods—I seen through Doc's windows. They got most folks tied up and their mouths stuffed with stuff."

"Folks? Who, son?"

"Most ev'rybody. The sheriff. And your Greg and... Miz Bean, she's on the floor. Doc's madder'n a hornet, but they got guns on Miz Nandria and that pretty gal of the Beans'..."

"Hush, son. A man's coming up behind me, isn't he? Don't let him catch you."

Monroe stopped beside Zeb. "They trundled ya up pretty good, didn't they? Didn't make sense to me to take it out on you that they couldn't find the coon. Sorry." The last was almost too quiet to be heard.

"It's not the first time I've been trundled, as you put it. I was in the Great War. But it would be good to have Doc Ricartsen take a look at me, I guess. You comin' along to his place?"

Monroe shook his head, uncertain. "Not rightly sure what I better do now. Don't look like nothin's happenin' here in Boonetown. And Barclay, he's gonna be pissed with me when he sees you walkin' around."

"Go home, Monroe."

"Yeah, mebbe. It sure ain't been a fun day, this one."

"No," Zeb sighed, "it hasn't. For a lot of people. Go home. Stay out of this nightmare." He offered his hand to say there were no hard feelings.

Startled, Monroe took that strong hand, pulled away and hurried back toward Mert's car. When he was clear, little Garum peered out from behind the garbage container. "What're you gonna do, Mr. Paisler?"

"I'm not sure, son. But if those brutes have women... What did you say about Mrs. Bean?"

"All I seen was that she was on the floor beside Doc's desk."

"Do you know where my sons Eli and Frank are?"

The boy shook his head.

"Do you think you could find them? Tell them what you've seen and tell them to gather men to come to Doc's clinic, armed?"

Garum nodded. "But my pa?"

"Maybe they know where he is. From what I can gather, I think he came to town on his own. Did you know that? You should be proud of a man as brave as that."

"Yeah," Garum agreed. "But they'll kill him when they find him."

"We'll try to see that that doesn't happen, son. We'll try."

"Bybee, what the hell're you doin' here?" Barclay was mad; his honey-drawl had given way to a sharp, high tone.

The plumber's assistant grinned. "It's just the place to be. They got the jigaboo here."

"What? Here? You sure?"

Bybee shrugged. "Folks in town seen him come in in that white pickup and park near the jail. The pickup's still there."

"I told ya that driver was a jigger," Mert wheedled, but, ignoring him, Bybee continued.

"A couple guys in town told me they seen the sheriff getting a wheelbarrow rolled over here. And took out the back, empty."

"So what?" Mert snapped, but Barclay stood thinking, a smile growing on his face.

"Finish tying up those people in the office," he ordered. "But bring me that little gal. And that doctor."

"The gal with...?" With both hands, Mert lifted out an imaginary chest.

When Barclay grinned, nodding, Ronda was soon brought to him. Barclay could hear the muffled protests of several of the Boonetown men. "Doc?" he demanded.

"He won't leave the big nurse on the floor, Boss."

"I'll maim this one if he don't!"

Ricartsen hauled himself up on his office doorframe. "You bloody..."

"Listen, Doc, you got that coon Tacker here, and I want his hide." He held a knife against Ronda's cheek. "Tell me," the leader drawled slow and easy, smiling.

At the window, tears roiled on Garum's cheeks as Doc led the men down the hall.

"Go find help, son," Zeb Paisler whispered behind the boy, sending him scurrying away from Doc's clinic window. "I'll see what I can do to slow them down, so they don't do more harm," the man promised. What would come next, he had no taste for. It would be a fight, but he squared his shoulders. A fight it would have to be. *Sorry, Lord.*

He hurried around to climb the back stairs. His bursting in at the back door startled the men at the bottom of the inside steps. Barclay was the first to react, forestalling Doc Ricartsen's belated attempt to swing down at him from the stair above.

"Hold it!" Barclay warned, his knife against the corner of Ronda's eye.

"Jesus!" Doc exhaled and cowered back. "Leave the child alone!"

"She sure looks big enough to me," Mert taunted. He had his gun aimed at Zeb's chest. He was enjoying this, finally.

Zeb raised empty hands. "Sorry to bust in like this, Dr. Ricartsen. I stumbled... What're you doing?"

"Takin' this girl upstairs," Mert sneered. "What'd ya think?"

"What're you doin' outta the Chevy, Paisler?" Barclay demanded. "Where's Monroe?"

"He was still in the car when I got out," Zeb told him, straight-faced. "Just wanted Doc or Mrs. Bean to stop this blood and snot from running into my mouth."

"Well, Doc's busy right this minute. And I don't think his nurse is gonna be much help to ya, for a while, anyway." Mert laughed out loud.

"Oh? Why not?"

"They're all tied up," Bybee quipped, and Mert doubled over, laughing.

"Yeah, all tied up," Mert echoed.

"Put him with the others," Barclay ordered, turning to continue upstairs. He felt more than heard the pantomimed argument between Bybee and Mert about who would have to tend to Paisler and who would get to help find and take care of that Tacker. "Mert, you do it. And stay there with them to make sure nobody's working his way loose. We'll bring the darky down—there's lots of other people wantin' to be in on the action, too."

Furious, Mert watched Bybee and Barclay push Doc and the girl to the second floor. "Come on, then," Mert snapped. "How come you hadda bust in when you did?"

Zeb let himself be propelled up the hallway toward the lobby. "Oh, Lord," he breathed when he saw Nickleberg huddled beside his wife on the floor. But Mert shoved Zeb into the office, where he stumbled over the nurse's thick-heeled shoe. "Dear lord," Zeb cried aloud, seeing Sadie Bean sprawled on the floor between the bookcases and the doctor's desk. The bodice of her dress lay ripped open. Both of her hands gripped its edges, which is probably why she'd been able to be felled. She moaned now.

Ron and Greg, crumpled in the far right corner, grunted through their gags as they struggled to get up. The sheriff, doubled over at Miz Nandria's bound feet on the other side of Doc's desk, did not move.

Nickleberg spat, "You, Paisler! You and your busybody sons. Always interfering. Making friends out of jiggers."

"I am a Friend," Zeb said low. "Or at least I try to be."

"So you say. But you and that female," the egg man sputtered, pointing angrily at Nandria. "You're teaching them they ain't the scum of the earth. And it was prob'ly you two that got the sheriff here to think he could keep honest white men from doing their duty toward their womenfolk."

"Yeah, our duty," Mert spat.

"Is what you've done to Mrs. Bean part of your duty protecting white women?" Zeb asked. If the question made the Mert pause, Zeb couldn't see it. He turned to face Nickleberg. "Or what you've done to Gertrude part of your duty toward your own wife, Heinz Nickleberg?"

Nickleberg, at least, blanched before again turning defiant and angry. But whatever the poultry farmer might have answered was lost in yelling from above them. Pounding. A child's scream. A resounding curse and thud.

Chapter 43

"Hey, Barclay!" Mert shouted. "What's goin' on up there?"

"Got him-uh!" The answering call went from triumphant to pained.

Mert scurried toward the hallway to see what was happening upstairs when Zeb, for all his shuffling and bloody nose, dove into the man. Mert's revolver skittered across the office floor. Above his gag, Greg's eyes grew wide as he watched his Quaker father fight. Noises from above didn't quell the Mert versus Zebedee battle until clattering on the stairs brought Bybee hurrying along the hallway with his shotgun pressed into Ronda Bean's back. "Leave be, Paisler!"

Looking up, seeing the danger to the girl, Zeb let go and lay back to take a final, unprotected punch to the face. "Uh," he grunted and then made himself go still.

Doc, coming up behind Mert, knelt beside him to check. "Sorry, Zeb."

But the Quaker farmer only brought up both hands to his face, grunting in surrender. "I can see how they got everybody to do what they say," he muttered, coughing and reaching for a towel on Doc's shelf to wipe his nose. "'Duty to white womanhood' be..."

In the hallway, Dolph Tacker stumbled from a kick from behind but caught himself with his shoulder against the doorframe. As he regained his balance, he stood feet wide apart, twisting to look back at Barclay. That gorilla of a man held his knife at Garum's throat. "Inside, monkey. On your knees."

"No, Pa," Garum cried, "don't do it."

Eyes flashing anger, lips compressed, Dolph knelt.

Nickleberg stumbled to the corner. "Where's that revolver? I seen it skid over here someplace."

"Nickleberg, we got him," Bybee boasted. "Fought like a dirty cornered rat, but we got him. Wanna fry him first or go right on to hanging?" he laughed.

"Gotta keep your thumb right on 'im," Barclay warned. "Give 'em an inch and they take the whole town with their thievin' and their women-beatin'."

"Pa didn't hurt the missus," Garum screeched.

"That right?" Bybee bent level with the dark boy. "Well, Mr. Nickleberg here says he did. So, who's more like to really know? The man? Or you?" Poking the boy in the chest harder with each question, Bybee laughed so he sprayed spit onto Garum's cheeks.

The boy stiffened but did not wipe his face. "Me!"

Lifting to almost stand upright, Bybee stared down in surprise at the vehemence of the answer.

Garum wasn't finished. "He was drunk. But the mister does know because he's the one who done it."

Bybee stood erect, jaw dropped, ready to scoff or to rage. He cuffed the boy. Garum squirmed out of his hold and turned to glare up at him, defiant. Dolph lurched to his feet, stumbling head down at the man. Mert grabbed the newly retrieved revolver from Nickleberg's hand and wacked Dolph in his exposed ribs. Bybee grabbed his arms. Barclay set his knife blade along Dolph's throat as Bybee held him.

"Go ahead, cracker," Dolph hissed. "Quicker this way. In the end you're gonna kill me anyhow."

"Stop!" The sound was low, guttural and weak, but commanding.

"Gertie?" Nickleberg stumbled forward to look past the two furious whites holding Dolph. "You awake, woman?"

"Hiram?" she wheezed.

"What? Hiram ain't here, Gertie. Both our boys moved far off. Never here when we need them."

"No. Little boy." She reached for her husband.

"They ain't little boys no more. Grown and gone."

"So little. But good ideas. That wire porch for the hen house." She sank back.

"We saw the wire, Mrs. Nickleberg, but it was all torn apart," Dr. Ricartsen told her gently. "A porch you say for the chickens? Why?"

"So coyotes can't..."

"A lot easier to clean," Garum took up the explanation. "Ya just shovel the poop away and spread it in the garden. 'Course you still gotta clean the inside of their house." He stopped when he saw the way his father was staring at him.

"You built it? For them whites?"

"Well, I told her about your ideas with the chickens, and she liked them a lot. So, we tried."

"Neighbors can be friends," Zeb mumbled, then lifted the towel away from his face. "Even black and white neighbors. We learn from each other."

Bybee sputtered. "Ain't nothin' a darky can do better'n a white. Nothin'."

"So, there's nothing to learn from coons," Mert insisted.

"If not, we continue to act like animals." Zeb turned toward Nickleberg with an expression of compassionate sadness that made the chicken farmer look away. "Tell them about your nightmares, Heinz. Tell them what your actions against your dark neighbors has brought you to do to your own family."

With everyone staring at him, Heinz buried his face against Gertrude's torso, but her cry of pain made him fall away. "Nightmares. Godawful nightmares. Don't lemme sleep. So tired," he whimpered.

"Is that when you started drinking?" Doc's voice was neutral as though he were simply asking the man to clarify a point in his medical history.

"Uh, drinkin'. Yeah. For a while it helped. It did, Gertie. Let me snore. Made the pictures in my head blur some so I could sleep. You never knew."

"Never knew what?" Mert demanded. "What're ya talking about, Nickleberg? What nightmares?"

"Tell him, Heinz," the sheriff prompted. "Tell them about the lynchings and what they've done to you. Tell them about your dreams, Heinz. Tell them what you did to Negroes and what it's made you do to your wife."

"Nothing! Lynchin's don't do nothing to white people," Heinz protested.

"They keep darkies down where they belong," Barclay sneered, "because every black one of 'em knows it could happen to them."

"Yeah," Mert and Bybee agreed.

"Does it look like no whites get hurt in a lynching, Mr. Barclay? What about this young girl you've terrorized? And Mrs. Bean here," Zeb asked, looking at Sadie still sprawled on the floor. "They're both white."

Even Bybee looked stricken as they stared at the large, unconscious woman.

"She tried to stop us."

"From what? Hurting her daughter? Isn't every mother supposed to try to stop somebody from hurting her child? And every father?"

"Shut up, Paisler," Mert snapped. "You're getting me all mixed up."

Zeb raised his shoulders and let them ease down, deliberately controlling himself. What he said next mattered.

"An interesting point has been raised: That lynchings do no harm to whites," he said quietly. "I wonder if that's true. In a way, I believe it's lynchings that got Gertrude Nickleberg knifed in the chest like she is."

Even Barclay gaped at that. "You're off your rocker, Paisler."

"Is it fear of what will be done to a man that keeps—or doesn't keep—him from beating a woman?" Zeb asked.

"W-what're you asking me for?" the chicken farmer stammered.

"Or is it just that in that moment is what is happening more than he can handle?" Zeb continued. "No sleep in so long. Years of crushing debts even when he works himself to aching deep in his bones. Nobody cares. Even his own sons."

"Stop it! Leave me alone! I never harmed Gertie. I wouldn't." Unable to stand, Nickleberg flung himself onto all fours.

"What're you saying, Paisler?" Barclay gaped between the father of eight to the man on his hands and knees that Paisler seemed to be accusing. "That's the man's wife, for cripes sake."

Zeb ignored him. Nickleberg was so close to confessing what he'd done. Zeb pressed on in ways he hated. It was like having stabbed the man in the belly; now he must twist the knife.

"How many wives would take a beating—many beatings—like your Gertrude has and yet refuse to name the man who hurt her? Is it love, Heinz, that makes her do that? Or just fear of not being able to keep up the farm on her own if the law sent her man away?"

"It ain't love," Nickleberg panted. "She keeps pushing. Keeps asking for it. Even shoes on the table. Telling the kids to keep playing the game even when the black ace got knocked off the table. Invitin' the devil hisself to come in and ride my back."

"What's all this?" Bybee started, but Barclay elbowed in.

"Whaddya say, Nickleberg? Is any of what this guy is saying true? You the one cut up your wife like this?"

"Stop! I didn't hurt her! I swear!" Heinz wailed.

"You did, too!" Garum yelped. "It weren't my pa. It was you and you know it!"

Tears streaming, Nickleberg crawled back to hunker down beside his woman. "Gert, tell 'em. Gertie, tell them I never."

But Garum had scrambled to kneel at her other side. "Tell them, missus, please," he begged. "Else they'll string up my pa. And he's the one helped you when you was so hurt. Don't you remember?"

Gertrude struggled to focus on the pleading child.

"We took you to the Doc's here in your funny car you made into a truck. Please, missus, remember how we tried to help you." He reached to press the woman's white hand.

"Hiram? Of course, I remember, boy," she whispered. "He... so gentle, lifting me. He tried to be... So gennel..." Her voice faded

"Me!" Nickleberg insisted. "I always tried to be gentle with you, didn't I, Gert? I done everything I could to give you a good home. Everything you wanted, I tried to get ya."

She stirred. Opening her eyes with difficulty, she peered at her husband. "You tried, Heinz. Lord knows, we both did. Them dreams. Nightmares. That baby you seen. Her mama hung upside down. Belly sliced open and that baby dropping out. You screamin' in your sleep. All them folks stompin' on that infant... That trampled baby—that's what killed me."

"Nooooo!" Heinz Nickleberg's cry was muffled against his wife. This time Gertrude moaned and went deadly still. Heinz lifted his face and saw pity in the eyes of Dolph Tacker. "You! You ought'a be hanged," Nickleberg snarled, rising up. "How dare you, nig..."

"No, he is not!" Pulling herself up on Doc's desk, Nandria rose to her feet, holding its edge with her bound hands to steady herself. But her voice was strong and authoritative. All in the room went quiet to look at this Negro woman contradicting a white man.

"Uh?" The feather-farmer's mouth gaped, but he could only stare.

"You are completely wrong, sir. Mr. Dolph Tacker is not that offensive epithet I just prevented you from using. Mr. Tacker is a man of uncommon honor and courage. He is raising his son to cherish integrity, even to the point of putting his own life in jeopardy. He has come to face you, his accuser, though he knows you have every means of harming him. He fears what you and others will do to someone else without regard to proof of innocence—which you know you would and will if not prevented. He fears loss of his knowledge of his own worth as a man and his son's respect more than he fears what you will do to him. He has come on his own volition to face the man who accuses him despite that man knowing full well that he himself has perpetuated the heinous beatings of his own wife."

"You, you spade witch!" Fists clenching, Nickleberg struggled up to go after her.

The sheriff tried to rise; Ron Bean, Isaac Owens and the Paisler sons fought their ropes to protect Nandria, but it was little Garum who ran between the man and his beloved teacher.

"Yes, you did! I don't know why your missus won't tell on you, but I was there after you left her bloody. I'm the one who aksed my pa to help her. It was Pa and me that took care of her. You was drunk."

Gertrude groaned. "Our boy's right, Heinz. For once, admit it. You was so drunk."

He broke. Howling, Nickleberg slumped against the chair, thudding his head against the desk.

In the general exhaling of breath from those who had witnessed, Barclay grunted his disgust and stomped around Gertrude in the lobby. Mert and Bybee stared open-mouthed as they heard the front door slam. After a long moment, Mert hustled out to follow Barclay.

"Wait," Bybee cried. "Mert, ain't we gonna do nothin'? Where's all the fun?" Left with his mouth open and his weapon ignored, Bybee hurried out after his buddies.

"Sweet mercy, 'fun' he calls it," Ricartsen murmured, grabbing a scalpel out of the bleach in the enamel tray on the high shelf of his bookcase. He sliced through Greg's bonds. Greg in turn ripped open Ron Bean's bonds as Doc knelt beside Sadie Bean to check her. Greg barreled after the trio as Doc, satisfied to leave Sadie for now to go to another patient, rushed to Mrs. Nickleberg.

Ron gave Zeb the scalpel to free the others. He dropped to the floor and drew his Sadie's head and shoulders onto his lap. She stirred at his touch and moaned. He'd never seen her this vulnerable, even while giving birth. It filled him with something he could neither name nor face.

Zeb cut loose Dolph Tacker and the others and went to help Nandria back to her seat. "There is a spirit in you, Mrs. Minnick. Your husband will be proud when we tell him of your courage and wisdom. I know we Paislers are proud simply to have you as a neighbor."

Nandria looked at the man with her deep, dark eyes, then closed them and pressed both hands into the desk to try to control her trembling. Zeb looked helplessly at Ronda as the only other female.

"Go to her, Ronnie, please," Ron whispered from the floor. "She needs you as much as you've needed her."

"Oh, Daddy, I..."

But Nandria pounded the desk with both fists as she stared around her. "All this, and your country is not even yet at war."

Chapter 44

Monday, August 26, 1940

Nandria rocked forward, clutching the letter, weeping and laughing.

Cynthia Paisler twisted with little Levitt on her hip to stare at their houseguest. "Oh, dear Lord," she murmured and hurried to the end of the kitchen table to rest her free hand on Nandria's shaking shoulder. "Mrs. Minnick, please, what is it? Bad news?"

When she found she could not speak, Nandria lifted the envelope and note for Cynthia to read.

Levitt puckered up, ready to cry, until he heard his mother's sigh and saw her smiling through tears.

"'I cannot come, my darling, but I have secured a passage for you to bring my loved family to me...'" Cynthia read aloud. "Oh, Nandria, dear, you'll be going to him. Thank the Lord. You'll be going to Will. When? And from where? Does he say?"

"Three weeks and four days. Out of New York City, if I can understand his excited cursive and have calculated correctly from the date this missive was sent," Nandria answered.

"So soon," Cynthia exclaimed, then chuckled. "But it can't be soon enough for you, can it, dear Nandria? Oh, so much to do to get you ready to go."

Nandria reached to draw her friend into a hug. "Rose and I have been half-packed for weeks," she confessed.

"So soon?" Mrs. Drangler exclaimed. "Oh."

"'Oh'?" Sadie Bean asked, confused by her short friend's crestfallen response to Miz Nandria's good news.

The sheriff stirred in his easy chair in Mrs. Drangler's low-ceilinged living room. "Now, Elm, we can just move up our plans, if you like. I won't deny the sooner the better for me."

"Sooner get it over with?" Ella Mae laughed.

"The wedding part, anyway."

"Wedding?" Sadie Bean went from bent nearly double to sitting suddenly on the sofa when she had meant to stay only long enough to tell Nandria's news. She nearly asked, 'Whose wedding,' but the look of love between them made that an absurd question to put into words. Instead, she nodded, smiling. "Congratulations, Sheriff Yakes. You are getting a treasure; I hope you know."

Yakes nodded, his expression clearly communicating his awareness of the value of the gift he was about to receive.

"Oh," Ella Mae breathed, "I'm the one reaping treasure. But, Sadie, I was hoping to ask Will Minnick's wonderful wife to stand up with us. I wanted to make her a special dress to wear that would give her some idea how much we are indebted to her courage and her smarts. She's done so much to make us grow even where we really hadn't wanted to. The whole of Boonetown. All of us. How different we look at things now. You know, Sadie."

"Indeed, I do. If only for what she's done for our Ronda. And for those children she's taught to read and to think on their own."

"How long does it take you to sew a dress, Elm? Maybe we can still get her to agree before she leaves."

"Well," Ella Mae studied the pile of cloth pieces in the stack in the corner. "I guess I could use something I already have for the banker's girl and replace that later so I wouldn't have to order and wait for the fixings. I guess I should ask, but it ain't like they paid for everything yet. I wouldn't have time to hassle the Freshstalks for very long." Her frown looked almost comical on such a round face.

The sheriff chuckled fondly. "I reckon if they ain't paid for it, it ain't theirs yet. You go ahead and do like you want, little lady."

"But maybe it'd be a good thing to check first with the bridesmaid?" Sadie laughed.

"Or maybe not," Ella Mae said with the sparkle in her navy-blue eyes that the sheriff was beginning to realize was sign that his bride-to-be was beginning to hatch an impish plot.

"I don't understand," Doris whimpered. "Where's the girl goin'? How're we gonna get the harvestin' done if she won't help, Mr. Minnick, dear?"

"I don't know, Mother, but we've managed on our own for a good number of years, so I guess we'll make it this time, too. No use in frettin' about it."

Doris sat with her elbows on the oak kitchen table with her head cocked in her hands to look up as though she could see through the ceiling to the floor above. "What's she doing up there? That's gotta be Willard's room, don't it? What's she doin' prowlin' around up there in our son's room?"

Bodie turned enough at the stove to study his boss's wife from the corner of his eye. "That's her husband's room," he wanted to say. "She's gathering a few things her husband must'a asked her to bring with her to him in England. That's what's doin' up there, though you never let his room be hers all these months she's been with us, helpin'." But he pressed his lips together until he could taste his scraggly beard rather than say anything aloud. He knew as well as Mr. Minnick did that if Willard's name were even mentioned, it would be hours—perhaps even days—before the poor woman would regain anything even close to her right mind. Nandria did not need to deal with that. She had enough to do to prepare to go to her Will. He turned at a knock at the door to the back porch.

"I'll get it," Bodie told the Minnicks, gesturing for them to stay seated at their kitchen table. The old handyman tweaked little Rose under the chin as he shuffled past her highchair, but she only glanced up and went right back to picking big, yellow kernels out of her corn pudding.

Bodie smiled as he hurried across the enclosed back porch to open the door to a Negro woman. He realized as he greeted her that she was much younger than she had looked from a distance when he'd driven the Tackers out to the river Bible camp. It was her housedress and tied-back hair that had made her appear matronly.

"Hello," he said, holding the door but not yet inviting her in. He knew how the Minnicks' whole life and upbringing had taught them to feel about darkies.

She had made no demands, and Bodie realized she would not. This old-young woman had been taught her place, probably through many unpleasant experiences.

"This here is the Minnicks', is it?"

"It is."

"Ah, good," she said, looking relieved. "I got a message."

"For Miz Nandria?"

"The teacher woman."

Bodie nodded, reaching out a hand to take whatever note or envelope she would have, but she shook her head. It wasn't on paper. She leaned closer to tell him something quietly. "They're safe. On their way to Pencil-vain-ya," she whispered. "Will ya tell her that?" Beulah read his eyes a long time before she was satisfied that this old man wouldn't betray her trust.

He nodded. His relief showed in his expression so she could step back, gratified.

"Both man and boy?" Bodie asked.

She nodded. "T'was the boy insisted I come tell her. I was so scared at them Paislers' when they said she weren't there no more."

"She'll be taking a boat to go to her husband soon. Tell them, will you, how happy is she is to be seeing her Willard again. Beulah, isn't it?"

Fear crossed her face as she realized he knew her name.

"Miz Nandria spoke so highly of you, Miz Beulah. To me. Just to me. We are grateful that the egg man made it clear to all around here it was him caused all the grief. Hoping with everything in us that things stay quiet now."

So many feelings flashed through the young woman's expression that Bodie stood looking after her a long while as she scurried away. If there was a vehicle waiting for her, it was parked out of sight somewhere down the Minnick lane. Bodie lifted an arm to wish the visitor well, but she did not turn to see.

"Who was that?" Mrs. Minnick wanted to know as Bodie returned to the kitchen.

"Just somebody wanting directions. I think everything'll be okay now."

Saturday, September 7, 1940

Reverend Dean Kylie stood feet wide apart in the narthex of his church and slid a forefinger under his high, starched collar. The Minnicks greeted Ella Mae and the pastor and strode on in to take their usual pew. Bodie carried Rose toward the stairs to the loft.

"Mrs. Yakes-to-be so very soon, you look beautiful," Nandria exclaimed as she entered.

"And you, Mrs. Minnick," Ella Mae giggled in her delight, "you look a dream, you do."

"It is this lovely dress you made for me," Nandria murmured, pirouetting to show off the flowing lines of the emerald green skirt. "Thank you. Willard will find it lovely when he meets us at the dock."

"You know full well that your Will won't see anything of a dress, only you. And little Rose. Nothing else will matter to him. But I did make it to show you off. I was just telling the reverend here that Piermont and me want you to stand with us for this wedding ceremony." Unable to contain herself, Ella Mae giggled again. "Don't we, Piermont? Want Miz Nandria to stand with us."

The sheriff sidled near. "We do."

Kylie gagged and coughed.

Yakes turned to pound the preacher's back without pausing in his explanation. "Greg Paisler has agreed to be my best man, though he wasn't too excited about getting dressed up until he saw young Ronda Bean's reaction when she saw him." Yakes laughed, more pleased with himself and the world than he had been in a decade. "You all right, Pastor Kylie?"

The minister sputtered something. Yakes, grinning so hard his face hurt, led the man to the entrance to the center aisle. "Here's Greg," he declared, "and it looks like the church is fuller even than on a good Sunday, so how about we get this shindig over with before the food gets cold."

With one more firm stroke at his back, Kylie had no choice but to start down the aisle. At the sheriff's nod, Greg bowed low, handed Nandria a bouquet of multi-colored asters and offered her his arm. With a grin back to Ella Mae and Piermont Yakes, he escorted his favorite teacher proudly before the entire community, so much more open to the world now than it had been when she'd arrived to slurs and glares only nine months before.

Recipes

CORN AND SQUASH SOUP

INGREDIENTS:
1 Yukon gold potato, diced (about a cup)
2 yellow squash, diced (about 1 lb)
1 small onion, diced (about a cup)
2 large cloves garlic, minced
¾ tsp salt
¼ tsp white pepper
¼ tsp ground cumin
3 cups low-sodium vegetable broth
3 cups, cut off cob, frozen, or 2 cans fire-roasted (15 oz each)
4 oz can fire-roasted green chiles

Red Pepper Relish
½ red bell pepper, finely diced
¼ cups Italian parsley (*or cilantro*), loosely packed
1 Tbs fresh lemon (*or lime*) juice
1 tsp maple syrup
¼ tsp salt

INSTRUCTIONS:

1. Add diced potato, squash and onion to Instant Pot
2. Add vegetable broth and season with salt, pepper and cumin
3. Cook on MANUAL for 7 minutes with a 10-minute natural pressure release
4. Carefully vent any remaining steam and remove the lid
5. Add 1 cup corn and puree in batches in your blender or use an immersion blender to
    blend until smooth

6. Return to Instant Pot and stir in remaining corn and green chiles
7. Heat through on WARM setting for 30 minutes
8. For the relish, mix all ingredients and refrigerate until needed
9. Ladle soup into bowl and top with a heaping tsp of relish

thanks to Chuck Underwood, brandnewvegan.com

ALISA'S CORN PUDDING

2 cans of Corn
2 cans of Creamed Corn
2 boxes of corn bread mix (Jiffy?)
1/2 cup margarine
4 eggs
2 cups sour cream

Preheat oven to 350.   Place 1/2 cup margarine in a 13X9 inch baking pan and melt in the oven while it preheats.

Remove baking pan from oven and add corn, creamed corn, and corn bread mix - and mix well directly in the baking pan. Add eggs and mix thoroughly.
When mixture in pan is well blended, add in sour cream and mix in the baking pan until there are no sour cream streaks visible.

Bake at 350 degrees for 30-40 minutes. It is done when the top is golden brown, and the middle does not "jiggle" (you can bake another 5-10 minutes if the middle is still jiggly)

Enjoy!!
Thanks to Alisa J. Hampton, Cornelius Oregon

POACHED PEARS

INGREDIENTS: 1 lemon
    ¾ cup sugar
    3 cups water
    1 vanilla bean, split lengthwise
    1½ lb pears
    2 cups raspberries
    ¼ cup powdered sugar

DIRECTIONS:

Cut lemon in half. Juice one of the halves.

Combine lemon juice with sugar, water and vanilla bean in big, heavy saucepan

Stir over low heat until sugar is dissolved, bring to boil, then remove from heat.

Peel pears and rub with other half of lemon (to prevent browning), slice pears in half and remove core.

Return syrup to boil, add pears so fully immersed (do small batches if necessary) and simmer until pears are tender to knife (about 10 to 12 minutes).

Remove from heat and let cool completely while still immersed.

Remove vanilla bean and place pears and syrup in bowl. Cover and chill, up to 2 days

Puree raspberries, strain to remove seeds. Whisk in powdered sugar. Cover and chill, up to 2 days.

Serve on dish with syrup and raspberry sauce spooned over.

Remaining raspberry sauce may be served separately.

NOTES: Anjou, Comice and Bosc take best to poaching. Bartletts tend to be somewhat more fragile.

Fruit juice (white grape, apple or pear) may substitute for water, but sugar should be reduced by about half.

DANDELION- RHUBARB PIE

INGREDIENTS: 1 unbaked, 9" pie crust
   Filling: 3 cups rhubarb chopped into bite-sized pieces
                ½ cup dandelion flowers
                2 eggs
                1½ cups unrefined or cane sugar
                1½ tsp vanilla
                3 Tbs flour

   Crumb topping: ¾ cup flour
                ½ cup brown sugar
                1/3 cup butter softened to room temperature

DIRECTIONS:
 Heat oven to 400^0
 Put chopped rhubarb in mixing bowl
 Harvest ½ cup fresh dandelion flowers, rinse clean,
  cut flower petals from green base (the green will make it bitter)
 Mix dandelion flowers with rhubarb pieces
 Beat the two eggs and stir in vanilla, sugar and flour
 Pour liquid mixture of rhubarb and dandelion petals
 Stir and pour into unbaked pie crust
 With a fork, stir topping flour, brown sugar and butter
 Sprinkle crumbly topping on top of pie filling
 Bake for 10 minutes at 400^0, then reduce heat to 350^0
 Bake another 35 to 40 minutes until crust is golden and rhubarb
      soft when stuck with a fork
 Remove from oven and allow to cool a few minutes
 Slice and serve plain or with a scoop of vanilla ice cream
 Recipe thanks to The Montana Homesteader, by Annie Bernauer

APPALACHIAN DANDELION BEVERAGES

Green Tonic:
   Cook Chickweed and Dandelion separately. Sieve and add cider
      vinegar.

Coffee Substitute:
   Gather dandelion roots. Peel. Roast until dark brown; grind.
      Percolate as though real coffee.

Dandelion Wine:
   Gather one gallon of dandelion flowers. Pour over flowers one
gallon of boiling water. Let stand until blossoms rise (about 24 to 48
hours). Strain into a stone jar. Add juices of four lemons and four
oranges and four pounds of sugar, plus one yeast cake. Stir four or
five times a day until it stops fermenting. Keep well covered. In two
weeks, strain, bottle and cork tightly.

FOXFIRE 2, Eliot Wigginton, editor (page 90)